THE HOT MESS EXPRESS

FLIGHT OR FIGHT SERIES - BOOK 1

STACEY O'LEARY

Dedication

To the women and girls who have lost their mother and parts of themselves. Grief is a thief. It shatters, reshapes and lingers. But it's also a quiet reminder that love never truly leaves us and that joy and sorrow can coexist in the same breath. Wherever your mum is now, know this; she's proud of you. So damn proud

To my mum, I miss you every day. My heart aches for you. Thank you for creating me, allowing me to be who I am and teaching me to be strong. I'll love you forever.

Trigger Warnings

This novel contains themes of grief and parental loss, anxiety, a false paternity scandal, medical emergencies, public/media scrutiny, and emotionally intense situations. It also includes sexually explicit content and strong language. Reader discretion is advised. Please note - all sex in the book is always consensual, however, it is unprotected. While writing, it didn't feel right to stop the heat of the moment to discuss protection lol. However, it's a silent understanding between Sage and Maverick and is still consensual.

Playlist

Sell it All, Run Away – Hilltop Hoods

Australian Girls – The Viper Creek Band

All right Here – Morgan Evans

Coffee With Her – Brett Kissel

Drinkin' Problem – Midland

Tequila Makes Her Clothes Fall Off – Joe Nichols

Aussie Girl (Parody) – Hype Duo

Day Drunk – Morgan Evans

Hornbag – Playlunch

Island In the Stream – Dolly Parton

My Girl – Hoodoo Gurus

Please, Please, Please – Sabrina Carpenter

Swear Jar – Illy

Are You Gonna Be My Girl – Jet

Thinking bout that – Tigirily Gold

Margarita – Luke Bryan.

Bad Infulence - Pink

Sage Davidson rule book

For maintaining total control and zero emotional damage

1. Leave before sunrise. Always. No exceptions.

2. If you call it "making love," you're already disqualified.

3.Sleepovers are for relationships and rom coms. I do neither.

4. No pre-planned anything. If you need a calendar invite to see me, we're done.

5. Kiss wherever you want—just not on the mouth. I'm not here to catch feelings.

6. No men in my bed. No men in my house. Temporary pleasures stay temporary.

7. Pillow talk is banned. Silence or sass—those are your options.

8. Cuddling? That's how soul ties happen. Hard pass.

9. No names, no numbers. If I can't ghost you easily, you're already a liability.

10. No glove, no love. I don't do surprise babies or collect baby daddies. You supply, or there's no ride.

ONE

SAGE

Have you ever woken up and just known the universe has it out for you? Like the second your eyes flutter open, the day slaps you in the face with a steaming pile of fuckery? No? Then congratulations on your charmed existence. For the rest of us, welcome to my Thursday morning. My phone is dead, perfect, because my alarm lives there. My hair dryer blew up mid-blast, sending a puff of hot air and a few sparks into the abyss. So now, instead of sleek and composed, my hair is a feral halo of chaos. Add in bumper-to-bumper traffic (thanks, Grand Prix), and the world's most unnecessary 9 a.m. meeting, and you have my personal hell wrapped in cheap lipstick and regret.

But really, the cherry on top? I was out last night. Not just out, I was tangled in sheets, pressed against sweaty skin, doing things that would get me fired twice over if HR ever got hold of my little black book. Wednesday nights have become my thing, my outlet. Fast and anonymous. The kind of sex that leaves marks and no expectations. Last night was no exception.

Jesse? James? Jonathan? One of those J-names. Doesn't matter. He was forgettable the moment his rhythm fell flat, which was about two minutes in. That's why reverse cowgirl is my go-to. It gives me control, hides my face, and lets me finish the job myself if need be. Which lately is always.

I park my car like a getaway driver and sprint to my desk. I barely make it into the meeting room without flashing someone. I drop into my seat with a breathless apology and a silent prayer that no one will comment on the frizz, the lateness, or the faint scent of last night still clinging to my skin. *I really need to stop these hard and fast fucks,* I think to myself as I try to focus, nodding at charts I haven't read and pretending like my mind isn't still replaying the feeling of hands on my hips and the sound of a stranger's voice in my ear.

"Sage?" My boss's voice slices through the fog of my fantasy.

"Any thoughts about the project?" I blink, offer a polite smile and say smoothly.

"It all sounds great to me," hoping no one could hear the echo of moans still lingering in the corners of my brain.

Twenty more minutes of corporate torture later, the meeting ends, and I gather my things, ready to salvage what's left of the morning. But deep down, I have a feeling this day is just getting started. If the devil really is in the details... then I'm already halfway to hell in these damn heels.

It's 10 a.m., and I have committed the ultimate crime against myself: going this long without coffee. My hands are jittery, my brain foggy, and my soul is utterly parched. Nothing could go wrong while I get coffee, right? I mean, it's just coffee. Easy. Simple. Sacred.

I shove away from my desk, mumbling something incoherent about 'self-care' to Josie, my best friend and co-worker, who gives me a knowing smirk. She knows better than anyone: caffeine isn't optional for me. It's vital.

The moment I walk into Bitter & Sweet, my one and only coffee haven, the familiar hiss of steaming milk and the rich scent of roasted beans wrap around me like a warm hug. Home. My barista—yes, my barista—flashes a grin as I approach. I've been coming here so often that they had my order memorised. Some days, I swear the cup is waiting for me before I even step inside.

"Morning, babe," calls Luca, the tattooed barista who flirts with everyone but still makes you feel like you are the only one. "Latte extra hot?"

"You know me too well," I said, sliding a ten over the counter.

He winks, "You're predictable, and sexy."

My laugh is still bubbling out of me as I grab the drink and turn to leave, taking that first, godly sip. Heaven. Warm, smooth, creamy perfection.

And then bang.

It feels like I've just run into a brick wall. Though it's not a wall at all— it's warmth and muscle. There is the unmistakable press of my breasts against something solid, something human, something that makes my pulse stumble. Coffee explodes down my front, seeping into the delicate threads of my white silk blouse, and I freeze, empty coffee cup still in hand, shirt clinging to my nipples, and completely unwilling to look up.

"Fuck! Are you okay?" a voice says — deep, smooth, and British, with just enough gravel to stir something low in my belly.

I blink, still processing the fact that I was dripping with caffeine and embarrassment.

"Ugh… yeah, I'm okay. That was probably my fault." I finally lift my gaze, and holy hell. The man standing before me is… not real. Couldn't be. Unless someone carved him out of marble and dropped him into my weekday routine just to ruin it in the best way, no one looks like that. All sharp-jawed and tousled brown hair. A fitted charcoal suit that clings to his body like a second skin. And those eyes, piercing ocean blue and slightly amused, like he's already undressed me with them and finds it cute that I'm trying to recover from my coffee baptism.

"No, entirely mine," he states, smiling. That smile? Lethal.

"My shirt is ruined," I mutter, mostly to myself, trying not to look at the way his gaze lingers just a second too long on the clingy, now-translucent fabric that clings to my chest.

"And your coffee's gone," he adds. "Will you at least let me buy you another?"

"Another coffee, or another shirt?"

He laughs. Actually laughs. It's a laugh that hints at sin. A laugh I feel between my legs.

"Coffee," he utters, voice dipping lower, "but I'd be happy to pay for the shirt too," and a giggle slips out of me completely uninvited.

"Coffee would be nice... and very much needed." Luca, bless him, has already made me a new one and hands it over with a smug grin that says, "*You owe me a story later.*

I take the cup and turn back to the man, who's gesturing to an empty table by the window. A part of me wants to sit. Desperately. To lean forward and let his eyes crawl over me while I 'accidentally' sip too slow, but I check my phone and sigh. Ten minutes until my next meeting.

"I'm really sorry," I say, stepping away. "I have to get back before my meeting and try to clean up a bit."

He nods, disappointment flickering behind his smile. "Understandable. But for what it's worth, you wear coffee very well."

I roll my eyes, smiling despite myself. "Thanks for the coffee. And again, sorry for bumping into you."

"Anytime. And hey, maybe I'll get lucky and bump into you again."

That laugh, that goddamn laugh that slips out of me again. I spin on my heel and practically ran back to the office, adrenaline and lust swirling in my veins.

"Fuck," I muttered, breathless. "I didn't even get his name."

I burst through the office doors like a woman on fire, racing toward Josie's desk.

"Swap shirts with me. Please. Before my meeting. I'll explain later."

She blinks once, then nods. She knows better than to argue. Five seconds later, I'm shimmying out of my soaked blouse behind her cubicle while she hands me her extra tee and a knowing look.

"From your face, I'm guessing this isn't just about coffee," she said.

"Oh, babe," I whispered. "It's never just about coffee."

I'm sitting in this never-ending meeting wearing Josie's t-shirt, which is slightly too tight in the chest and definitely not what I walked into the office in. And yes, they've noticed. I can see the looks. The questions. I'm sure they're dying to know why I'm suddenly dressed way too casually for a Thursday. I'm not going to admit that my morning went from barely functional to full-blown chaos when some six-foot-five brick wall spilled my latte all over me. Nope. Not giving them that satisfaction. They don't respect me as it is, always talking about me behind my back, probably bad-mouthing me, saying I don't deserve this position… I work my sweet ass off for this position, I deserve it, and I'm damn good at it. I earned this role

— every long hour, every briefing pulled out of thin air at midnight, every problem fixed before it even hit someone else's inbox. Josie says they don't deserve me. And honestly? She's not wrong.

Phil — corporate mansplainer-in-chief—is still droning on about strategy alignment and quarterly budget, every "synergy" scraping across my nerves. My pen pauses mid- scribble, my attention shot. Not because of the meeting, but because of him. Unfortunately, I'm not zoning in on productivity. No, I'm zeroing in on him, coffee guy. Tall, stupidly hand-some, probably has a six-pack you could do laundry on. That damn accent — British, obviously, the good kind. He looked at me as if I were some-thing worth devouring. Like he had plans. I can't stop imagining how his mouth would feel dragging across my skin. Heat coils low in my stomach, my pulse tapping out a rhythm I can't ignore, and I just walked away, as though I wouldn't be thinking about him hours later in a meeting that feels like death via Phil.

Sage, get it together. He's probably a tourist or here for the Grand Prix. Definitely not local—no one around here wears tailored pants like that unless they're a wannabe influencer. Jesus. I need to focus.

"Right, questions?" Phil's voice finally breaks through my internal thirst trap spiral.

"Sage, do you understand your part?" I blink, smile and try to make it convincing.

"Yep. Crystal clear. If I hit any roadblocks, I'll reach out directly." Professional. Polished. Totally not imagining what that accent would sound like, moaning my name—or what my nails would look like dragging down his back. I glance down at my notes…. Nothing but dicks. Great. Really mature, Sage.

TWO

MAVERICK

It's 10 am, and I need caffeine like I need oxygen. Four hours of sleep isn't cutting it, not when my body still thinks it's midnight, and the sun here is already glaring down like it has a personal grudge. Jet lag always hits like a freight train, and this UK-to-Australia haul is the worst of them. My head is foggy, my temper thin, and every fresh headline about my so-called "career-ending move" only pours salt in the wound. So, no—I'm not about to paste on a smile and play nice. Not today. Not when I can barely keep my eyes open, let alone my patience.

I duck into the coffee shop around the corner from the hotel, Bitter & Sweet. It's quiet, unassuming, and usually ignored by the tabloid crowd. I've been coming here every year since I started racing in Formula One. No one here gives a shit who I am. I like that. Luca, the barista, spots me and gives a chin nod. He says nothing, never asks for autographs or a selfie for his sister. Just makes my usual, Americano, black, no bullshit.

I'm checking my phone, half-scrolling through a headline calling me the "washed-up champion of the world," when the universe slams into me. Literally. Hot liquid. A startled breath and a soft, feminine gasp, and the sound of coffee spilling onto the ground.

Shit. "Fuck! Are you okay?" I ask, stepping back, already shrugging off my jacket to offer it to whoever I'd just turned into a human latte. Then she looks up, and my entire day — no, my entire world tilts.

She's got a dazed, flushed look on her face, and she wears it exceptionally well. Wide hazel eyes and pink lips. A silk blouse that's wet and clingy and leaves absolutely nothing to the imagination. And those curves… tight waist, perfect tits and long legs. She's soft in all the places my hands itch to touch. She looks like a distraction I don't need and a mistake I want to make.

"Ugh… yeah, I'm okay. That was probably my fault," she mumbles, eyes flicking down to her ruined shirt. It wasn't her fault. I was the one not looking.

"No, entirely mine," I state, voice low, trying not to stare and failing because this woman, even all coffee-stained, is sex on legs.

"My shirt is ruined"

"And your coffee's gone," I add. "Let me buy you another."

She blinks at me, "Another coffee, or another shirt?" and a laugh breaks out of me—an honest one. That hadn't happened in weeks.

"Coffee, but I'm happy to pay for the shirt too." She giggles, and it's dangerous; the kind of sound that makes you want to lean in and hear what she sounds like, moaning your name.

"Coffee would be nice… and very much needed."

By some miracle, or, more likely, good barista gossip, Luca hands her a fresh one right on cue. I gesture to a nearby table. I want ten minutes. Hell, I want ten hours. I want to peel that wet blouse off her, wrap her in my jacket, and take her somewhere far less public. But she checks her phone and curses under her breath.

"I'm so sorry, I've got to get back before my meeting and try to clean myself up a bit."

"Understandable," I say, trying not to sound too disappointed. "But for what it's worth, you wear coffee very well," and her smile short-circuits my already fried brain.

"Thanks for the coffee. And again, sorry for bumping into you."

"You're welcome. And hey, maybe I'll get lucky and bump into you again." She laughs. Goddamn, that sound again. I watch her walk away, tight ass swaying in those high-waisted trousers that should be illegal—before she disappears through the door.

And just like that, she was gone. No name. No number. No clue who the hell she is. Just coffee, silk, curves and a laugh that has no business haunting me like this. As she darts across the road, I can't take my eyes off her. Her body is pure fucking sin, legs—long, toned and smooth—like they were made to lock around my waist, the sway of her hips drives me insane, that perfect curve begging for my hands and my mouth. Her ass is tight and round, the kind of view that makes me hard just watching her walk away. Coffee in one hand and her blouse clinging to skin, skin that I want to touch, taste and mark. She scrambled up the steps and disappeared into a slick glass office building like she hadn't just walked straight into my bloodstream.

I stand there, gripping my lukewarm Americano, kicking myself, *her name Maverick, you didn't even get her goddamn name*. But I know where she works now. Is that creepy? Probably. Do I care? Nope. I stare up at the office building, burning it into my brain like it's turn three in Monaco. If I can memorise a new track layout in 90 seconds, I can damn well remember her office building. My phone buzzes in my pocket, snapping me out of it.

Media day. Reality crashing over me like cold water. My me time: over. I shove the chair back under the table, eyes flicking back to the door one last time. I let the image of her wet shirt, flushed cheeks and that giggle burn behind my eyelids. Then I turn and start walking back toward the hotel, coffee abandoned in a bin. I need something stronger or her. Either would do. Both preferably.

Media day, the circle of hell reserved for drivers between practice and lights out. I'd rather take Eau Rouge blindfolded at 300 kph than answer another recycled question.

"Maverick, was it a tough decision to leave Havoc Racing after a decade of dominance?" *No shit.*

"Maverick, how's the transition going with Apex Motorsports? Rumours say your team dynamics are already hard." *Hard like my hard compound dick after seeing coffee girl.*

"Maverick, what would it mean to win your ninth championship with a new team?" *It'd mean shutting all of you the fuck up.*

I give them the polished answers, the half-smile accompanied by the shrug that says I'm chill, when really all I want is to be anywhere else. Preferably with that woman's lips around something other than a coffee cup. Twelve years in this sport. Eight titles. Millions in endorsements, and somehow, the only thing I can think about today is her.

There was something in the way she looked at me, like she didn't know who I was. Certainly not 'Maverick Carter, the GOAT.' 'Maverick Carter, the F1 Legend and International Playboy'. God, that's hot. I need her legs wrapped around me in the backseat of my car. I need to feel her nails running down my back while whispering how good she looks in nothing but my team hoodie. I want her bent over her desk, coffee still steaming, while I make her moan loud enough for the boardroom to hear. Yeah. I have a problem, a very hard problem with no name and legs that won't quit and no clue how to find her again. But I had one advantage: I know where her office is, and I have time. She doesn't belong behind a desk; she belongs under me, while I bury myself deep inside her.

I'm staying in Melbourne until Tuesday. My schedule is tight, but I can always make time for a coffee, especially if it's at Bitter & Sweet. This wasn't just a meet-cute; it was a collision course. She's ruined me in under five minutes, and I need to return the favour.

THREE

SAGE

Yesterday was a full-body fuckery. If I could claim emotional compensation, I'd need a month-long spa retreat, a therapist, and maybe a priest. But today? Today I wake up feeling human. The stars had aligned. My hairdryer, bought impulsively over a stress-fuelled lunch, was worth every damn cent. My blowout is bouncy, I have eyeliner on both eyes, and I walked into the office looking like I have my shit together. Which is a lie. While my lips sip the lukewarm coffee I made, my brain is still obsessing over *Mysterious Brick Wall Man*. British accent. Ridiculously tall. Absurdly hot. And that smirk that says he could ruin me in the best possible way.

I should've skipped that meeting. Josie had a field day when I told her about it. Over lunch, she nearly choked on her salad, laughing.

"You mean to tell me you walked away from a walking orgasm with an accent... for a meeting? Girl. He could've been your permanent one-night stand."

She's wrong; I don't do permanent.

Now it's Friday, technically the weekend, and I'm manifesting a chill day — one where I didn't embarrass myself, spill anything, or make eye contact with hot strangers that haunt my dreams.

I stroll to my desk, pretending to be a functioning adult. Laptop open.

Lip gloss poppin' and making small talk with the team. Most of them are heading to the Grand Prix this weekend. It's a big deal. Huge party. International-grade man candy and an excuse to wear something short, tight, and probably wake with regret in the morning. Honestly? My kind of scene.

I'm in the middle of a daydream about pit crews and sweaty drivers when Josie messages me.

> Josie: Coffee?

> Me: Not at Bitter & Sweet, though. Still embarrassed after yesterday.

> Josie: Sure thing. Let's try Drops.

I met her downstairs, pretending not to care.

"You're an idiot," Josie declares as we walk. "Luca probably doesn't even remember what happened."

"It's not Luca I'm worried about," I mutter.

Josie stops mid-step and narrows her eyes. "You mean the British brick wall?" I avoid eye contact.

"I just think it's good to support new local businesses... sometimes," and she gives me a smirk that screams bullshit.

Drops is cute. The coffee? Not even close to the dark roast heaven I'm betraying. I mis Luca. I miss the vibe. I miss the stupid hot man who ruined my shirt and possibly my standards forever.

"This coffee tastes like wet cardboard," I say with a grimace.

Josie snorts. "It's what you get for running from your destiny." She's not wrong. "What are you doing this weekend?" she asks, sipping her over-priced sadness-in-a-cup. "I've got tickets to The Kim's playing at the GP after party tonight," she states. "Wanna come get loose?"

Does she not know me?

"Yes. Did you even need to ask?" She grins like she's just handed me an invitation to my sexual awakening.

"Let's get ready at my place."

"Oh, we're getting ready," I smirk. "I'm wearing something illegal." Josie cackles. "Oh, you're manifesting a collision course tonight."

Josie wasn't kidding when she said, " Let's get ready.' She hands me a tiny black dress that looks like it was sprayed on and declared it race-weekend energy. It's scandalous. High hem. Lower neckline. Dangerous enough to get arrested, or laid, maybe both.

My golden hair curled. Eyes Smokey. Heels strapped. I look in the mirror and almost don't recognise the woman staring back. Tonight isn't about work. Or meetings. Or coffee disasters. Tonight was about reclaiming the chaos.

The afterparty was already electric by the time we arrived. Red lights, chrome accents, and loud music had transformed the club. Drivers, celebrities, paddock crew, and the kind of beautiful people who always look like they're doing something illegal.

VIP balconies loom above us like royal boxes as we head straight to the bar. I need something strong and fast. Tequila, obviously. Josie and I down our second shot, and I feel it. That stare. It lands on me before I can turn around. That slow, deliberate burn of someone watching like they own the fucking room and maybe, just maybe, wants to own me too. I turn, and there he is. Brick Wall. British Accent. Tall as sin. A vision in a black shirt, tailored to perfection, sleeves rolled just enough to show ink and veins. A drink in hand, a smug little smile that says, Yeah, I remember you, and I've thought about ruining that dress since the moment you walked in. Our eyes lock. My pulse drops into my panties. He doesn't wave. Doesn't smile wider. He just tilts his head slightly, inviting me up with nothing but a look.

Josie leans over. "Is that… is that him?" I don't answer. I just down my third tequila shot, smooth my dress out, and walk towards the stairs like I have every intention of doing something reckless. Brick wall is about to be another name in my little black book.

MAVERICK

I spotted her the second she walked in. Hair golden like the sun. Legs for miles. A dress that made my mouth dry and my cock twitch. Fuck me. It's her. Coffee girl. Silk blouse. Giggles in her throat and espresso in her veins. Except tonight, she doesn't look like a woman who spilled coffee; she looks like a goddamn sin I want to confess to. She saw me. Didn't blink. Didn't shy away. Just walked like temptation in heels. She hits the top of the stairs and stops in front of me, hands on her hips and a smile on her lips that screams danger.

"Didn't expect to see you here," she declares, voice all confident and warm. I step closer.

"I was hoping to bump into you again." I fire back.

"This time, maybe you can wear the coffee."

"No need," I say, my eyes dragging down her body. "You already look good enough to drink."

She raises an eyebrow. "Is that your line?"

"No," I grunt, voice dropping low. "That's me trying not to bend you over the balcony railing."

Her breath catches as she steps forward. "Then don't try."

That was all I need and I pull her into me. The girl I can't get out of my head is about to be in my bed.

"Buckle up, babe," I say with a devilish grin.

FOUR

SAGE

The elevator ride is silent, not an awkward silence, but a loaded one.

With his hand on the small of my back, guiding me into the lift like I'm something expensive he intends to ruin slowly. His touch burns, possessive, like his holding back the flood. I can feel it — his restraint, and the way his body vibrates with heat.

We hit the top floor. We don't speak. The hallway blurred. I barely see the suite door swing open before he has me pressed up against it, the click of it shutting behind us barely audible over my gasp.

His mouth finds mine like it were starving for me. The kiss is hard, hot and impatient. Hands gripping my ass and pulling me against him. He's solid everywhere. And I mean everywhere. That bulge grinding against my stomach is promising things I'm not sure my legs are ready for.

He works his way down my throat, kissing as he goes and slides my dress down enough so my boobs pop out, and he closes his mouth around my nipple, tongue swirling with slow, deliberate strokes that make my toes curl. Then he pauses, pulling back just enough to glance down, eyes gleaming with something between surprise and mischief. His fingers pull at my nipple, thumb brushing over the delicate metal.

"Well, well… what do we have here?" he murmurs, pinching gently as he lifts his gaze to mine.

"You've been holding out on me." Before I can answer, he leans in, taking the other nipple into his mouth, sucking deep and slow. A moan slips from my throat as he teases the piercing with his tongue, then pulls back with a grin so wicked it makes my stomach flip.

"Both of them?" he growls, voice low and hungry. "You naughty girl."

"You've been in my fucking head for two days," he growls against my chest, nibbling.

"I've already imagined a dozen ways to fuck you."

"Pick one," I whisper, "And don't be gentle." He groans, lifting me in one smooth motion. My thighs wrap around his waist instinctively as he carries me to the bed, lips never leaving mine. When my back hits the mattress, he stands over me, breathing hard.

"You want slow?" he asks, already undoing his shirt. I bit my lip.

"I want real."

His shirt drops. Holy. Fuck. Someone carved him from stone—someone designed every muscle and every inch of him for strength, and sin. Tattoos wrap around his biceps and slide down his ribs, and I'm going to trace everyone with my tongue. I reach for him, but he is faster, sliding my dress over my hips, yanking it off in one clean movement. I'm not wearing much underneath, and his eyes darkened as he takes in the sight of the soaked-through centre of my panties.

"Goddamn," he murmurs, dropping to his knees. "This all for me?"

"No," I smirk.

"It's for your replacement if you keep wasting time talking." He growls and bites my inner thigh, dragging my panties down with his teeth. I gasp, legs falling open automatically. And then, his mouth is on me. Hot, wet and perfect. He licks slowly and teasingly, then fast and filthy. Fingers sliding inside me, curling just right as he sucks my clit with purpose. I'm grinding into his face, moaning like I don't care who hears. Like I want the whole hotel to know.

He doesn't stop until I shatter and soak his face. Doesn't even come up for air. Just keeps going until I'm shaking, breathless, wrecked and begging for him. He stands, pulling off his belt, then his pants, and his boxers. Holy. Shit.

"You, okay?" he asks, cock heavy in his hand, tip glistening, veins veining. I laugh breathlessly.

"If you don't fuck me right now, I'm walking out naked." He doesn't need more. He climbs over me, slips the tip of his cock through my slick folds once, twice—then pushes in deep. We both gasp. He is thick, long and perfectly brutal.

He starts slow, deep thrusts filling me until I'm gasping. But the rhythm doesn't last. The second I moan, he snaps, his thrusts turning hard, fast and relentless. My nails are digging into his back as his hand fists my hair.

"Fuck, you feel so good," he groans, lips on my throat. "Tight and wet like you were made for me."

"Don't stop," I beg between thrusts.

"Not planning to. You take me so well, such a good girl". Hearing those words coming from his mouth does something feral to me.

"Fuck", I scream, as he pulls out, and before I can protest, he flips me over, ass in the air, face in the pillows and spanks me once, hard enough to sting and make me whimper. Then he slides back in and fucks me like it was a race he has to win. We come together, it's loud, raw and messy. Then he collapses beside me, pulling me against his chest, all sweaty and breathless and completely undone.

"Still embarrassed about the coffee?" he murmurs, voice rough with satisfaction. I smile, kiss his jaw, and whisper,

"Not if this is what it gets me. "

Snuggled in the arm of this god of a man, I feel myself drift off. I don't normally snuggle after a hookup, but for these abs, I'll make an exception until I hear my phone ring. I look to my left and notice the British brick wall fast asleep, so I scurry to search for my ringing phone. Finally, finding my discarded handbag near the door, I take out my phone and see that it's Josie calling.

"Where the fuck are you?" Josie yells down the line.

"With the coffee guy. I'm in what I'm assuming is his hotel room," I whisper-shout. "I'm getting dressed and coming back downstairs. Are you ready to go?"

"If you are, I can make my way home if you are sleeping over, though," Josie replies cheekily.

"Come on, Jo, you know that's not my style, be down in ten," I say as I gather my stuff, pull my dress back on, sneak one last look and slink out the door, down the hallway to what I'm hoping is the main elevator.

I tiptoe through the hallway like a thief in heels that weren't made for stealth. The hotel carpet cushions my steps, but my heart's thudding like a goddamn bass drum. I glance back toward his suite door, half-tempted to go back in. Crawl into that bed and let him pull me under his arm and let his hands wander just one more time. But no, that's not my style. I don't sleep over. I don't do morning-after breakfasts. I don't do post-orgasmic small talk while wrapped in hotel sheets.

…Except, apparently, I do now. Because I snuggled, I'm disgusted with myself. (Okay, fine, mildly turned on too.)

I find the elevator, press the button, and pray to whatever gods handle hangover-free mornings that no one else is waiting in the lobby when I get there. My hair's wild, my dress creased, and I'm not wearing underwear. They can be a nice little thank-you gift for him. Ding. The elevator doors open, and I walk in like I've got my shit together.

Josie is already waiting outside, leaning against a marble column, phone in hand, with a smirk that could slice through steel on her lips.

"Well, well, well," she says, handing me a bottle of water like the angel she is. "Walk of shame looks hot on you."

"Shut up," I mutter through a smile, taking the water like it's a lifeline. "It's a strut of power, thank you very much." She gives me the once-over.

"How's the coffee guy's... espresso?"

"Josie," I hiss.

"Oh, come on, I need details. Was he a tall latte with a shot of sin?"

I take a long sip and smirk.

"Double shot. All cream." She cackles, looping her arm through mine.

"I knew it. Now tell me everything while we figure out where you parked your dignity."

I glance back one more time, up toward the hotel, and my chest does that annoying flutter again, soft and unfamiliar. Then I shake it off because this was a night. Just a very good night, and now we go back to normal.

Right?

FIVE

MAVERICK

I wake up slowly, which is rare for me. Usually, I'm out of bed by six, running laps in my head before I've even had a coffee, but this morning? Something feels different.

I roll over, expecting to find her curled up, tangled in the sheets, maybe using my arm as a pillow, but she's gone. The bed's cold beside me. No note. No number. Just a dent in the pillow and a faint trace of her perfume in the air.

It hits harder than it should. I sit up, scrub a hand over my face, and glance around the room, hoping she's just in the bathroom, but it's quiet. Too quiet. Fuck. I get up, pull on a pair of sweats, and walk to the window. The city is already awake, cars honking and people rushing to start their day. And somewhere down there, she's walking away from me like last night never happened. Like I didn't have her writhing under me. Like she didn't fall asleep on my chest with her fingers curled into my side like she belonged there.

Yeah, I've had one-night stands before. Hell, I've had more than I can count, but this wasn't that. She was… different. From the second she crashed into me outside the coffee shop, she'd had me all twisted. That wide-eyed look when she spilled her drink. The way she laughed when I offered to buy her another. The way she made me feel like I was the one being chased, even though she walked away, and now she's gone again. No name. No number. Just… gone.

I should let it go. Focus on the race. Focus on qualifying, the same script I've played for years, but I can't stop thinking about her. Her taste. The way she moaned. The way she curled into me afterwards, like she'd done it a thousand times before. I grab my phone and shoot off a half-assed text to my race engineer Ricciardo, telling him I'll be at the paddock in an hour. Then I scroll, just to make sure. Nothing. No number. No contact. Not even a goddamn clue.

Except… her office. I remember it. Burned it into my brain like a fucking lunatic. Might be time to do a walk-by. Casual. No big deal. Just in case she walks out that door again, and if she does? I'm not letting her leave without getting her name.

My plan was solid. Show up at her office. Wait casually for her morning coffee run. Pretend I was just in the neighbourhood on my morning run. Easy. Except… It's fucking Saturday. So, here I am standing like a total idiot outside a locked office building, sunglasses on, hoodie pulled low like I'm casing the joint, not trying to track down the girl I slept with last night who ghosted me and now I can't stop thinking about her.

Brilliant.

I glance at my phone. 10:40 AM. No missed calls. No mysterious texts from an unknown number. No flirty photos. Just Ricci's latest meme in the group chat and a reminder I've got a sponsor thing at 1.

Great. Tail between my legs, I jog back toward the track. Fast enough to call it cardio but slow enough to preserve some dignity. If anyone asks, I'm 'clearing my head', but if Ricci asks, it's 'a warm-up run.' I slow to a walk, grab my phone, and hit Drew's name. If anyone can talk some sense into me or at least laugh at my misery, it's him. Drew has been my best mate since school. Between my constant travel and his life as a rugby superstar, we don't catch up as often as we'd like, but we always pick up each other's calls.

"Playboy!" he answers, voice far too cheery for the situation. "What's going on? Out running from another broken heart?"

"Yeah, mine," I mutter. "On my warm-up run, trying to clear my head before the afternoon session. But tell me something, Drew— "

"What's that?"

"Have you ever been ghosted before?" I ask casually, like it's no big deal. Like I'm not secretly spiralling a little.

There's a pause, then: "Like actually ghosted?"

"Like... radio silence. Left after sex. No name, no number. Just poof." I wipe a hand over my face. "I got pulled. She pulled a me on me."

And I hear it — the slow, growing cackle of my best friend being absolutely no help at all.

"Damn, Carter. She played your ass," he says, full grin in his voice. "Sounds like you've met your match."

"Yeah," I say quietly, chest tightening as I slow to a walk, "Something like that."

He goes quiet for a second, which is rare for Drew. "You, okay?"

"I will be." And I mean it. I just don't know when.

We chat for a bit longer, mostly about the race tomorrow, the headlines, and a ridiculous memory from school that ends with both of us howling. I hang up as I reach the edge of the track, shaking my head. Helpful as always, Drew. But as I pocket my phone, one thing sticks in my head. She pulled a me on me, and somehow, that just makes me want her more. This girl, coffee shop chaos and all, has me wrapped up, and I don't even know her fucking name.

QUALIFYING Day

Normally, I'd be laser-focused. Run my timed laps in my head, debrief with the engineers, block out the media noise. I've done this a thousand times. Ten years, eight World Championships — this should be routine by now. But today? Today my head's not in the fucking game. It's with her.

I'm strapped into the car in the garage, helmet on, visor down, pretending to focus while my race engineer walks me through the plan for Q1. I nod in acknowledgment, but I'm barely there because all I can think about is her lips, her laugh and the way I woke up in an empty bed that smelt like her. I should be angry. I'm used to being the one who leaves. The one who forgets names, who never looks back. But now? I'm checking office buildings like a psycho and scanning the paddock crowd hoping for a glimpse of her.

"Get it together," I growl to myself.

The lights flash green, and I roll out of the garage. The car hums beneath me like a living, breathing thing. This is where I'm meant to be — on the edge, with nothing but rubber, metal, and my instincts, but yet, even at 300kmh, I can't get her out of my head.

The first few laps are clean. I set a decent banker, enough to make it into Q2. But I'm not dialled in like I should be. I feel the car shifting beneath me, trying to communicate, but I'm only half-listening.

When I get back into the garage, Ricciardo is already smirking from the other side of the pit wall. "You're driving like someone who didn't get enough sleep last night," he teases over the comms.

I shoot back, "It wasn't sleep I was short on." The team laughs. I hear it through the radio. But I don't correct myself. I'm not short on sleep. I'm short on answers, and now I'm here, chasing lap times and phantom thoughts of a girl I only had for one night. The visor's down again, Q2's about to start. Focus. Drive. Win. And maybe, just maybe, she'll be watching.

SIX

SAGE

A quiet Saturday at home is exactly what I need. After last night's… activities, my body is grateful for a break. My dignity? Still hanging by a thread.

Sometimes I wonder if I should stop living like this — corporate by day, slutty chaos after dark. I've lost most of my childhood friends because of it. You know, the ones who swore we'd be each other's bridesmaids? Gone. Judged me too hard when I started choosing one-night stands over long-term relationships. They couldn't handle the way grief and heartbreak changed me. But thankfully, I've still got Josie. Work bestie. Wine whisperer. Partner in crime. And Margot - my person. Uni ride-or-die. No judgment, just tequila and therapy when needed or whenever she's in the same country.

I'm deep in Saturday reset mode, the floors mopped, sheets changed, and the laundry rolling when I finally settle onto the lounge with a coffee that isn't dripping down my shirt. I flick my eyes to the TV. It's on for background noise at this point, with the Grand Prix qualifying being on the opening channel. Well, at least it's something mildly entertaining.

That's when I see it. Him. Helmet half off, sliding into the car with that arrogant grace I remember. Eyes as blue as the ocean, that sharp jaw and those broad shoulders. The same ones I fell asleep on not even 12 hours ago. Mystery coffee god. The brick wall I bounced off. My one-night stand.

Maverick fucking Carter. Not just an F1 driver. Not just a hot guy with a good dick. The driver. Global superstar. F1's golden boy. Multiple world champion. Cover of GQ. Literal billionaire. *Oh, my fucking god.* In a blur, I fumble for my phone, typing his name into Google like a woman possessed. The search results? A minefield of information I should've known before climbing on top of him.

MAVERICK CARTER

8x World Champion. British.

Recently transferred to Team X from Team Y in the most controversial move in F1 history.

Net worth: Don't even ask. WHAT. HAVE. I. DONE.

No words. No thoughts. Just pure panic. I copy the link and send it to Josie.

Me: [link]

Josie: FUCK. FUCK. FUCKKKKKY.

Me: I've really done it now.

Josie: I'm on the way over. We need to drink about this.

Yes, we do because apparently, I didn't just sleep with the random guy who spilled my coffee and ruined my shirt. I slept with Maverick Carter, and now he is on my TV, tearing up the track like he didn't just blow my mind and then get ghosted in return.

Josie lives twenty minutes away. Tops. But I swear she materialised at my front door in five. Either she broke every road rule known to man… or she teleported via sheer gossip adrenaline. She burst through the front door like a hurricane — no knock, no warning. I forgot I had given her a spare key. Rookie move.

"MAVERICK FUCKING CARTER? Are you kidding me?" she shrieks, not even pretending to contain the volume.

From the lounge, I blink at her, holding an empty margarita glass that's waiting to be filled.

"I didn't know, okay? I don't exactly keep up with celebs. If it had been an NRL player, maybe, but a Formula One driver? Not really my wheelhouse."

She paces, hands in her hair, like she's the one who slept with him.

"Sage, he's not just any driver. He is the driver. Maverick Carter is like… if David Beckham and Lewis Hamilton had a baby and that baby grew up to be Maverick Carter, and now he can fuck." I groan, throwing my head back on the lounge.

"I've only ever heard his name mentioned, never any photos, and let me tell you, those photos wouldn't prepare you for him in real life. He bumped into me. I did not know who he was. Then we… You know, and then I left."

Josie stops mid-pace and points at me. "Girl, you ghosted Maverick Carter after a one-night stand."

"I didn't ghost him. I left before I made it weird." She cackles.

"Babe, you are the weird."

I glare at her "Okay, fine. But what the hell am I supposed to do now? What if someone saw us? What if this gets out? I don't want to be plastered all over the media as some… random slut who shagged a racing god." Josie softens.

"It was a private party. I didn't see any media there. No one was taking photos. I think you're safe."

She grabs the blender, clearly on a mission to margarita the panic out of me. I intercept her mid-step, snatch the bottle of tequila from her hands, and take a swig straight. Instant. Fucking. Regret. I gag. She laughs like the menace she is and reclaims the bottle, pouring measured shots like a responsible alcoholic.

"If I were you," she says, "I'd be proud. You bagged the literal hottest man alive. We celebrate that kind of slut behaviour in this house."

Four margaritas in, and we've officially descended into hysterics. We haven't even started unpacking what this means emotionally, spiritually and vaginally, but suddenly, it hits me.

"We need to call Margot"

Josie nearly chokes on her lime wedge. "Yes. YES. We do"

I FaceTime her. She answers on the first ring, impressive, considering she's in a completely different time zone, somewhere in Asia, I think? The background looks like a rooftop bar. She's glowing, already drunk, holding a cocktail the size of her face.

"SAGE!" she slurs. "Why do you look like you've seen God?"

"I did," I mumble. "And then I fucked him." Cue explanation. Cue her nearly falling out of frame from laughing so hard.

"Of course, this happened to you," Margot says between giggles. "Only you could accidentally bang the world's most eligible man and then ghost him. Honestly? Icon behaviour."

I sigh. "Margot, this isn't funny. What if he thinks I'm a psycho? What if—"

"No, no," she cuts me off. "You're mysterious. He's probably obsessed with you now. You'd better get back in that bed, Sage. For the people. For me. I want details and pictures." I hang up. I can't deal with Margot's brand of chaotic encouragement right now.

I turn to Josie, who's giggling at her phone. "What did you do?" I ask instantly, suspicious. She holds up her screen, smug as sin.

A text thread.

Her dad is a Grand Prix sponsor. Pit passes.

"YOU GOT US TICKETS TO THE RACE TOMORROW?"

Josie grins. "Not just tickets, babe. Access. We're going to the pits. Think you can handle seeing your mystery man again?"

I sigh as drops of margarita slosh down my arm. Tomorrow just got a hell of a lot more interesting. What happens if I run into him again? Worse —what if he's looking for me? Though I highly doubt that.

SEVEN

SAGE

I wake up with a dry mouth, a slight headache, and the lingering scent of tequila and citrus as my phone buzzes obnoxiously next to my head.

God help me.

I drag myself out of bed, the events of last night crashing back like a poorly edited flashback montage — discovering who I slept with, Josie's margarita rampage, Margot's FaceTime meltdown, and the pit pass bombshell. I shower like I'm trying to wash off evidence. As if water can erase the fact that I accidentally fucked an eight-time world champion and then ghosted him.

Josie arrives twenty minutes later, armed with caffeine, croissants, and her full glam squad energy. She's wearing cut-off shorts, a vintage tee knotted above her belly button, and more highlighter than anyone should legally allow before noon.

"Do I look casual-hot or slutty-desperate?" she asks, holding two other outfit options: one has sleeves, one does not.

"You look like you're about to blow an entire team of mechanics", I deadpan.

"But make it fashion, " she winks.

"That's the goal"

We turn my bedroom into a war zone of denim, eyeliner, and strategic nipple tape. I hold up outfit after outfit, trying to find the exact right level of effortlessly sexy. I finally settle on black jeans that fit my ass like a promise, a cropped racer-style tank that hints at my cleavage without fully committing, and boots that scream I'm not here to flirt... but I might ruin your life anyway.

Josie whistles. "If he doesn't lose control of the car when he sees you, I'll eat my pass," I smirk, twisting my hair up and spritzing perfume like I'm preparing for battle.

"Just remember, we're there to watch."

"Sure," she says. "Watch him fall in love with you." I roll my eyes, but wonder... *What if he remembers me? What if he's pissed? What if he doesn't recognise me? Or what if he's already moved on to the next girl?* Before I can spiral, Josie grabs my arm.

"Come on, mystery girl. Let's go remind the fastest man in the world that you're the one who left him naked and alone."

We arrive at the track fashionably late, which is to say... right on time to look like we meant to be casually cool, not two girls fighting hangovers with dry shampoo and iced lattes. The air is thick with engine oil, testosterone, and overpriced cologne. It's like walking into a colosseum built for men who live off adrenaline and adoration, and right in the middle of it is him—Maverick Carter. My vagina clenches at the thought of him.

We walk through the pit lane like we've done it a million times; this is a thrill like no other. I spot him before Josie does. Helmet off, race suit peeled halfway down and hanging from his waist, and a black fireproof under shirt clinging to every carved inch of his chest. His jawline could cut glass. His mouth is set in a half-scowl; he looks focused, dangerous and ridiculously hot. My stomach flips, and I nearly drop my lanyard. Josie notices my reaction before she notices him.

"Oh, my God. You've seen him, haven't you?" I nod, I can't move, can't breathe—frozen in place, words locked somewhere in my throat. Maverick is talking to his engineer. He looks unbothered. Like he didn't spend a night inside me in sex-soaked sheets. Like he didn't wake up alone in a hotel bed.

"We should go say hi," Josie whispers with a devilish grin.

"We should leave the country," I hiss back.

She snorts. "You're being dramatic."

But before I can pull the pretend you're a ghost act, he turns. Slowly. Like he sensed me. His eyes lock on mine, and the noise of the track disappears. I see a flicker of surprise on his face. Then curiosity. Then something I can't quite place — something between recognition and remembering what my moans sounded like in his ear. He says something to his team, hands off his water bottle, and starts walking toward us.

Josie grabs my arm. "Incoming. Hot. British. Trouble."

I panic. Do I Smile? Act cool? Run? Vomit? I settle on doing absolutely nothing because my legs have stopped functioning.

"Mornin'," Maverick says, that accent as smooth as silk and as sharp as sin. Oh God, his voice.

"Hey," I manage. Brilliant.

"You two enjoying the pit lane?" he asks, glancing at Josie for the briefest of seconds before his eyes land right back on me.

Josie jumps in. "We're loving it. Thanks to my dad, we scored passes."

He quirks an eyebrow. "Small world, huh?"

"I'd say tiny," I reply, giving him a wry smile.

"I didn't expect to see you again," he exclaimed. There's no anger. No bitterness. Just that cocky, undeniable confidence.

"Didn't expect to see you on my TV yesterday, Playboy," I shoot back. His smile widens slightly.

"Hope I looked good."

"Too good," I admit, before I can stop myself. There's a flicker of something in his eyes — heat, maybe? Or satisfaction? But before anyone can say more, someone calls his name from the garage.

"I've gotta run, but" he says, turning slightly ", you should stick around for the race. Might be a good show." He walks away, then throws one final line over his shoulder: "Don't ghost me again."

Then he's gone, helmet back on, crowd roaring, cameras flashing, and

I'm standing in the middle of the pit lane, thighs clenching, and my heartbeat is chaotic, trying to pretend I'm totally in control.

Josie leans in, "Babe. You're screwed."

I nod. "Yeah. And I think I like it."

EIGHT

MAVERICK

There's a rhythm to a race day. It's like slipping into a second skin. I know the drill; I know the questions the media will ask before they even speak. I know the braking zones better than I know some of my family. And yet, the moment I step into the garage to meet my engineer, I feel it. Her.

It's not logical. There are hundreds of people in the paddock. Media, Influencers and VIPs. But something in the air shifts, a tension that snaps tight in my chest like a pulled safety harness. I glance towards the pit lane, and there she is. Coffee Girl.

She looks different in the light of day. Not sated and freshly fucked like she did in my bed, but sharp and alive. Tight jeans and sunglasses perched on her head with a confidence in her shoulders, even as she freezes the second our eyes lock. It hits me harder than it should. Fuck. I didn't imagine her, and I haven't forgotten her.

She looks like she's trying not to run — or maybe trying not to melt into the concrete. I can't get the dress she wore Friday night out of my head, but this version of her is even more dangerous. The same girl from the party is beside her. Her best friend, probably. The ride-or-die type who'd stab me with a stiletto if I so much as made the girl cry.

I should turn back and focus. I've got twenty minutes until the formation lap. I've got strategies to review. I've got a fucking race to win. But I don't; instead, I walk straight to her. The closer I get, the more nervous she looks, and I hate that. I hate the distance that's suddenly grown between us since Friday night; she just up and left. But now she's here, and this is my shot.

"Mornin'," I say, keeping my tone low and casual like I'm not already mentally replaying the way she moaned against my throat less than 42 hours ago.

She stumbles out a "Hey," and I catch the way her eyes trail down my chest before snapping back up. Good. She remembers. Her friend fills the space with words, giving me just enough to work out how they ended up here. Sponsor passes. Her dad. Inside connection, my way to find out her name.

"Small world," I say. My eyes are still on her.

She fires back. "I'd say tiny." Fuck, I love the sass. God help me, I want to taste that mouth again.

"I didn't expect to see you again," I say, honest and pointed. She doesn't flinch.

"Didn't expect to see you on my TV yesterday, Playboy," she fires back. I smile, great, she googled

"Hope I looked good." She gives me the once-over and rolls her bottom lip through her teeth.

"Too good."

I feel a bolt of heat straight through me. My blood sings with it as someone calls my name; they need me back in the garage. It's time. I want more of her, though. More words. More time.

"I've gotta run," I say, backing up, "but you should stick around for the race. Might be a good show." Then, I pause just long enough to let the words burn. "Don't ghost me again," I say as I walk away, trying like hell to switch gears back to the race, but she's in my head now. Coffee girl. My race-day distraction. The one-night stand I suddenly want two nights with… maybe more. As I slide my helmet on and strap into the car, I'm thinking to myself, 'Fuck the race win' She's here, and I've already lost control.

The grid is full. Engines rumble like thunder trapped under carbon fibre. I sit strapped in, heart thumping in sync with the machine beneath me. Helmet on. Visor down. Radio check clear. I should be calm. I've done this a hundred times. Pole position is mine. The strategy is sharp. My team is sharper. I've won races half-asleep, but today, I'm not half-asleep. I'm wired, alive because she's here. I felt her eyes on me as I stepped into the car earlier. She didn't say much. But her stare — that flicker of something between regret and want — lodged itself in my chest like a goddamn missile.

Five red lights line up. All I can hear is my breath. All I can see is her. Lights out. I launch, and my tyres scream. I nail the start, just like always. But this time it feels different. Every turn is sharper, like I've got something to prove. Like I'm chasing more than a podium. Lap 5. Radio crackles in my ear.

"Gap to P2 is one point three. Keep pushing."

"Copy", I snap back, but my mind flashes to her laugh and the way she took my breath away. Those god damn nipple piercings. The way she snuck out before I could ask her to stay.

Lap 12. DRS open. I defend like hell. Don't lose P1 now. She's probably watching from the paddock club. Maybe with her fingers curled around the railing, maybe she's biting her lip, wondering if that night was a mistake or maybe something more. Maybe she feels this pull, too.

Lap 25. Pit stops, two-point-three seconds. Perfect. Back on track. *Focus, Carter.* But every time I hit the straight, I see her eyes. Wide and curious. Like she sees through the image I'm paid to portray— the world champion, the playboy, the face on every billboard. She didn't want any of that. She didn't even recognise me. And fuck… that felt so good. Lap 42.

Radio: "Purple sector one. Keep going. You've got clean air."

I'm in the zone now, even though my head is still full of her. The taste of her mouth. The way she screamed as I slammed into her. The softness I didn't expect to crave again so soon. Last lap. I hit the apex perfectly. The rear sticks like it's made of glue. I cross the finish line, and the team explodes in my ears.

"P1, Maverick! That's a win, baby!" cheers, and my name is echoing across the track. But all I care about is if she stayed to see the win. Helmet off, I climb out of the car and raise my arms in the air. Cameras flash. Reporters shove mics in my face, but my eyes scan the crowd, the paddock, the stands. Where is she?

Winning feels fucking incredible…but if she's not waiting for me at the bottom of the podium, it won't be enough.

NINE

SAGE

I shouldn't have come. I really shouldn't have come, but here I am, standing just meters from pit lane, the roar of engines vibrating through the soles of my shoes, travelling through every inch of my skin. Josie is beside me, jumping and yelling like she was born for the paddock life, but I can barely breathe.

He's out there. Maverick Carter. Eight-time World Champion. My accidental one-night stand. I knew he was something the second I looked into his eyes. The way he moved, the way he touched me, it was like he was used to being in control but still knew how to let go. But this? This is another level.

I watch the screen above the garage — P1. He's leading. I catch a glimpse of his eyes through the helmet cam, and for a moment, I pretend he's looking for me. God, this is insane. What am I doing here?

Josie grabs my hand and yells over the noise, "This is so much better than I thought it'd be!"

She's not wrong. The tension, the noise, the smell of burning rubber and champagne just waiting to be uncorked, it's addictive. But even that's not enough to distract me from the one thing making my mind race faster than those damn cars: Him.

The man who made me coffee-stained and breathless in under sixty seconds. The man who wrecked me in a hotel room without even asking my name. The man who is out there, slicing through the air at 300 kilometres an hour like it's nothing. I should hate him and his cockiness. Or at least not… want him. But the way he touched me— The way he held me. It didn't feel like just another night. It felt like a secret. One I shouldn't want to keep.

The crowd explodes, and I'm pulled back to the screen — final lap. He's still in the lead. Still unstoppable. The car crosses the finish line, and the entire pit wall erupts. Mechanics cheer, and the crowd eurpts. Josie throws her arms around me, but my eyes are locked on one thing only. Maverick. Helmet off, he climbs from the car like a god, all swagger and sweat and adrenaline. The smile that spreads across his face is the same one that was pressed into my neck on Friday night, and my stomach knots. This isn't just what anymore, it's danger, because I didn't just fuck the world champion, I think I might want to break all my rules for him, and I have no idea what the hell I'm going to do next. I'm frozen. Every part of me is screaming to bolt, to vanish into the crowd and never look back. I don't do this — feelings like this; I don't do flings. I do fumbling hands in dark hotel rooms. Names I barely remember, and numbers I never save.

But then there's him. Maverick Carter. A walking fantasy with a world championship smile and the ability to unravel me with a single look. And now he's on the top step of the podium, drenched in champagne, a laurel around his neck like a Roman god, and his eyes — his eyes scanning the crowd. Searching. I don't move. I can't move. Josie notices. Of course she does. She always does, and she grabs my arm and pulls me toward the front like it's her personal mission to shove me straight into my destiny.

"Don't even think about it," she mouths, giving me a look that dares me to disappear. A look that says If you run now, you'll regret it forever. But my heart is a thunderstorm, and my skin feels too tight. And Maverick? God help me, he's looking at me.

"Girl," Josie whispers, her grip tightening, "The way that boy is looking at you? This isn't just one night. This is the beginning of your fucking future."

I want to laugh. Or cry. Or vomit. Instead, I stare up at him, still on the podium, gold sparkling against his chest, champagne clinging to his jawline like it belongs there, and when his eyes finally land on mine…The world stops. It feels like it's just him and me. And suddenly, I'm not thinking about escaping. I'm thinking about that night. The way he touched me like he was trying to remember every inch of me with his fingertips, like he didn't want the moment to end. Like maybe, for once, I didn't feel like a placeholder in someone else's life.

Maybe… He wants more, too. I shake my head, trying to snap myself out of it. I've built walls so high no one's ever gotten through them. Not even me. I've never let anyone get close enough to ruin me. He is a notorious playboy. To him, I'm probably just a new girl in a new city who's running from heartbreak. And yet, here I am, halfway ruined by someone who didn't even ask my name before he fucked me into oblivion. What the fuck is happening to me? He lifts the trophy above his head, the crowd roaring for him… but his eyes don't leave mine. It's obvious that this isn't over. And for the first time in a long time… I don't know whether that scares me or excites me.

After the chaos dies down, Josie's deep in conversation with her dad and a few of the bigwigs from his company. I'm lingering nearby like the awkward plus-one at a fancy wedding, smiling when someone looks my way, nodding like I understand car telemetry when really, I'm just counting the seconds until I can disappear.

I've met Josie's dad once. He's nice, polite, very… formal. The kind of guy who probably has a favourite pair of cufflinks and opinions about port wine. I'm not quite ready to dive into a deep philosophical chat about tyre degradation and legacy. So, I stay quiet, politely adjacent, trying to look interested in the pack down happening around me. Riveting stuff. And then I feel it. A hand. His hand, strong, deliberate and slipping around my waist like it owns the space there (because, let's be honest, I kind of want it to). His mouth finds my ear, voice low and needy.

"Come with me," he murmurs.

God, that voice — it does things to me. Dangerous, wicked things. Before I can even process what's happening, he's spinning me with one hand on my hip and pulling me away with the other, fingers laced with mine like a promise he has every intention of keeping. I don't resist. Like hell I would.I shoot Josie a glance, but she doesn't even notice. Good, because I'm about to be very, very distracted. He leads me through the crowd with purpose, like a man with a mission, and when we slip into his driver's room, and the door shuts behind us, I know exactly what that mission is, and I'm very, very happy to help him complete it.

The noise outside fades the second the door clicks shut. Gone are the fans, the crew, the podium chaos now; it's just me… and him. Maverick Carter. Still glowing with sweat from victory, still half-dressed in red and temptation. His fireproof undershirt clings to his frame in all the right ways, outlining every cut of muscle, every inch of heat beneath the surface. He turns toward me, his chest rising and falling like the adrenaline hasn't left his system yet, like maybe I'm the next finish line he's chasing.

"I was expecting you to run away again," he says.

"I thought about it," I answer honestly. "But Josie is fast. She would've tackled me without hesitation." He chuckles, and that sound alone nearly buckles my knees.

"Dominant race, by the way," I add quickly, anything to ground myself, to keep from combusting under his stare. "Congrats on the win."

"I haven't won anything yet." His reply lands heavy between us, the weight of it pressing into my chest as he steps forward, closing the gap. My breath catches. His hand finds my waist again, the same confident grip from moments ago, and he pulls me in until there's nothing between us but the thrum of shared electricity.

"I don't understand you," I whisper, trying to keep my voice steady and trying to avoid completely unravelling at the edges. "You're—this. You're you. And I'm—"

"I don't care what you think you are," he cuts in gently, fingertips brushing up my side. "I only care that you're here. That you stayed."

That's when his hand slides up, fingers tracing the line of my jaw, thumb brushing my bottom lip like he's trying to memorise it. Like he's claiming it.

"Maverick…"

"Tell me you don't feel it."

I don't answer. Because I do. God, I do. It's pulsing in the air between us — this tension, this need, this impossible pull that feels more dangerous than any high-speed turn he's ever taken on track.

"You make it hard to breathe, make it hard to think," I admit softly.

"Then stop thinking." His voice is pure gravel now. "And just feel." And then he kisses me. No hesitation. No warm-up. Just lips crashing into mine with all the intensity of a man who's been holding back for days. Hands in my hair, body flush to mine, and I let go — of fear, of logic, of the voice in my head screaming, don't. Because right now, I'm already doing it. The rest of the world doesn't exist. Just this heat. This man and this moment that feels like it was always meant to happen. Maybe, just maybe… Maybe I don't want Maverick Carter to be just another name in my little black book. Maybe I want him to be the last one I ever write.

Haha, who am I kidding?

TEN

MAVERICK

She tastes like adrenaline and temptation. The second my mouth finds hers, I know there's no turning back. I've kissed women before. Plenty of them. But this? This is different. Her hands grip the front of my fireproof undershirt like she needs it to anchor herself, like she's trying not to float away. But it's me who's drowning, in her scent, in the warmth of her mouth, in the indistinct sound she makes in her throat when I press her back against the door.

I reach down, undoing the race suit hanging at my waist, peeling it back until I'm in nothing but my fireproofs. Her eyes drop, just for a second, and that hunger, that raw, open want, flickers across her face. Fuck. That look is going to ruin me.

I lift her easily, her thighs wrapping around my waist like it's second nature. Her lips are back on mine instantly, frantic and needy. I press her back harder against the wall, my hips grinding into hers, and she moans into my mouth — a sound so wrecked it makes me lose whatever sliver of control I had left.

"Tell me you want this," I whisper against her jaw, dragging my lips down her neck.

She nods, breathless, but that's not enough.

"Say it," I growl, biting gently at her collarbone, dragging the strap of her top off her shoulder.

"I want you," she whispers, and it's the softest goddamn thing I've ever heard — and the sexiest.

I move fast, I don't just want her body; I want to burn every inch of her skin into my mouth, my hands, my memory because I haven't been able to stop thinking about her since I bumped into her outside that coffee shop like a fucking amateur. Her jeans come off in one slow pull, like I'm unwrapping something sacred. She's laid bare in front of me, and it knocks the air out of my lungs. Her pussy bare, so pink and perfect and so ready for me.

"Jesus, Sage…" I don't even realise I said her name aloud until I see her eyes widen. The name I had to know. The name I tracked down Josie's dad for, the name I had to beg for. She should be angry. Ask how I found out, but she just smirks, breathless, eyes dark with need.

"It's about time you knew it."

And then she's kissing me again, dragging her nails down my back, as we both tumble onto the small leather lounge behind us. Limbs tangled and breath ragged. My fireproof undershirt is next, and her fingers are there, tugging it off, desperate and damn, so am I. There's no teasing. No slow build. This is combustion. The moment the red lights go out, everything explodes into chaos. When I finally push into her, the world shatters around us.

She's heat, tightness and fucking perfection. I can't stop the groan that tears out of me as she wraps around me like she was built for this, built for me. Her nails dig into my shoulders. Her mouth finds my neck, and my rhythm turns rougher, faster, chasing that edge neither of us can hold back anymore.

"Sage…"

"Maverick—oh—"

Hearing my name on her lips? It undoes me. We fall together. Hard. Breathless. Shaking.

"Maverick," She gasps, the head of my cock tapping against her clit as I slide it teasingly through her folds before pushing it against her entrance.

I shudder, pressing forward just enough and then stilled, my forehead falling against hers. My breathing is ragged and desperate.

"Fuck, you're unreal." I push deeper, inch by inch, stretching her cunt until she's arching off the lounge, her groan vibrating through my chest as I bottom out, burying myself to the hilt.

"Jesus Christ," I breathe, eyes screwing shut, jaw clenching. "So, fucking tight, baby."

She whimpers, nails digging into my shoulders. I pull out slowly, the drag of my cock making her gasp, before thrusting back in with a deep, shattering stroke. The sound of our bodies meeting echoes its wet and obscene, I drop my head with a groan, eyes focused on where our bodies meet.

"Listen to you," I rasp, hips setting into a rougher pace. "So, fucking wet for me. You're perfect, you know. This pussy-" I slam into her, the wall jolting behind her, "-was made for me, baby." My voice cracks with something raw, almost reverent. I lean down, lips brushing her ear, whispering filth that has her walls clenching around me. And when it's over, I don't pull away. I stay there, wrapped in her, heart racing like I'm still out on track, but this time, I've already won. And maybe… Maybe this is a finish line I didn't know I needed to cross.

We're still tangled together on the narrow lounge, the heat of us lingering in the air like a secret. Her head is resting on my chest, her fingers tracing lazy circles along my ribs, and for a moment, the chaos of the paddock doesn't exist. It's just her and me, the silence between us soft and full. Then there's a sharp knock at the door. She jumps, startled, and I curse under my breath. I sit up quickly, grabbing my running shorts from the floor and sliding them on. I help Sage gather her clothes, pulling her top over her shoulders while pressing a kiss to the top of her head. She's flustered, her cheeks pink, but God, she's still so damn beautiful it hurts.

"Stay there," I whisper, smoothing my hair back and striding over to the door.

I crack it open and, of course, it's Ricci.

"Ricci," I greet, keeping the door mostly closed, trying and failing to hide the stupid grin on my face. "What's going on, mate?"

"We need you for the team debrief, Carter. Ten minutes," he says, giving me a look that's a mix of professional urgency and… amusement?

"Yeah, no worries," I reply, nodding. "I'll throw on a shirt and be right there." He raises an eyebrow but says nothing. Just smirks and turns on his heel, walking off down the corridor. I close the door with a sigh and turn back to Sage. She's standing up now, trying to smooth herself out and tame her hair. She looks at me with that half-defiant, half-exposed expression she wears so well — like she wants to pretend this didn't happen, but it did.

"I'm sorry," I say, reaching for her waist. "The team needs me."

She nods, clearly trying to play it cool. "I figured. You did just win a race."

I pull my phone from my pocket and hand it to her. "Put your number in. I'm calling you the second I'm done here." She hesitates for the briefest moment, then takes it, tapping in her details. I watch her fingers, memorising the way she types and the way she bites her lip as she does it. I stand, tugging a shirt over my head and stepping back toward her.

"I'm in Australia for two more days," I say, voice softer now. "And I want to spend them with you… If you'll let me." Her eyes lift to mine, wide and unsure.

"I've got work. But… I'll figure something out."

I don't push. I can see the war going on behind her eyes, but I also see that flicker of want — the same one that's been pulling us toward each other since day one.

"Do you have a ride home?" I ask, brushing her hair behind her ear.

"Yeah. Josie's still around; her dad's giving us a lift," she replies, her voice barely above a whisper.

"Okay. Good." I take her hand and pull her closer, steadying her as she wobbles slightly. She's still glowing, still wrecked from us. Still covered in me.

I lift her chin gently, forcing her to look at me.

"I'm calling you," I say, firm and low, and then I kiss her. Slow and deep like I want her to remember it. Like, I want to leave a mark. Because if I know Sage like I think I do, she could disappear again just like that, and if this is my last kiss with her…I'm going to make damn sure it's one she never forgets.

SAGE

The door closes behind him, and I just… stand there. My lips still tingle from his kiss-soft, slow, like a promise. I stare at the door, willing myself not to go chasing after him like some lovesick teenager. But my body is buzzing, my head spinning, and my heart? It's acting like it doesn't know the rules I clearly laid down years ago.

I'm not this girl. I don't do attachments. I don't get tangled up in 'what ifs' and 'could be's.' I live in the moment, keep it casual and move the hell on. That's the deal. That's the armour I built after everything love once put me through, but Maverick Carter is a wrecking ball in a race suit. And I'm the fool who seems to want to keep stepping into his path.

I sigh and take a seat, slipping my heels back on. I glance around the small driver's room, his scent still clinging to the space — smoky, rich and masculine. I try not to breathe it in too deeply, but I'm failing miserably. My phone buzzes as I put it back in my pocket

> Josie: You alive in there or what? Dad's about to leave.

I quickly type back:

> Me: On my way. Be out in 2.

I smooth my jeans, take one last look in the mirror — cheeks flushed, hair slightly wild, lips swollen from him, and grab my bag. I make it to the car just as Josie and her dad are climbing in. She raises an eyebrow but says nothing in front of him. Thank God. The ride is quiet, just small talk between Josie and her dad while I stare out the window, letting my head rest against the glass. I should feel satisfied. Hell, if this were any other guy, I'd be making jokes by now, replaying the dirty bits with Jo, then erasing him from my mental file by Monday morning, but this feels different. He's different.

The moment we pull up outside my place, Josie turns to her dad.

"Thanks, can I just pop upstairs with Sage for a bit?" He nods, distracted by a work call. The second we step inside, she shuts the door behind us and pounces.

"Well?"

I flop down on the lounge. "I'm screwed." "Details, now." Josie screeched.

"I didn't even make it two hours before I was in a supply closet masquerading as a driver's room."

"YES!" she squeals, high-fiving me. "Was it good?"

"Jo, it was more than good. It was… dangerous. Like I forgot who I was for a second." Josie plops beside me.

"That's not dangerous. That's called human connection." I groan, "That's what I'm afraid of."

She snorts, "Please. You're scared of letting someone in again, but newsflash, babe — you already did; you let me in and guess what? You didn't die." I throw a pillow at her face, and she catches it with a laugh.

"He wants to see me before he leaves. He asked for my number. Said he'd call tonight."

Josie stares at me. "And?"

"I don't know if I'll answer." "You will."

I say nothing. Because maybe she's right. I already know I will.

ELEVEN

SAGE

I'm home. Finally, Josie left 30 minutes ago, and I'm fresh out of the longest shower of my life, skin pruned, hair up in a towel and already wrapped in my holy grail of comfort, baggy sweats, fluffy socks and a hoodie two sizes too big. I pour myself a glass of red (because I'm an adult, legally anyway) and yank my questionably reheated pizza from the air fryer. It's not gourmet, but it's cheese and carbs and that's all that matters.

I collapse onto the lounge like I've just completed a marathon and queue up my comfort show Kath & Kim, because chaos in a thick Aussie accent is my serotonin. I'm about halfway through an episode when my phone buzzes.

Unknown number. Oh, no. No. Surely not.

I freeze mid-bite. Heart racing. Pizza hovering in the air like I'm in a dramatic slow-mo moment from a telenovela. I pick up my phone and decide to text the group chat.

Group Chat - Sassy, Snark and Secrets

> Me: SOS. He's calling me. Like actually calling me.

> Unknown number. I'm sweating. What should I do?

Josie: Uhhh… YOU ANSWER, YOU CHAOTIC WOMAN.

Margot: WHAT. You gave the superstar your number?!

WOOHOO. Go get it, girl!

Josie: Put us on mute and speaker. We need to hear this.

Margot: No wait. Don't. That's weird. But also… Do it.

> Sage: I haven't even brushed my hair yet. I'm in sweats. There's pizza sauce on my boob.

Josie: And yet you're still hotter than 97% of the population. ANSWER. THE. PHONE.

Margot: Do it before I fly over there and answer it for you.

> Sage: Ugh. Fine. If this ends with my vagina accidentally professing its love while I'm mid-ride on his monster of a cock, I'm blaming both of you.

Josie: Please do. And record it.

Margot: Tell him your boobs say hi.

So naturally, bullied by my hype squad I swipe to answer using my best, I'm totally calm and not spiralling voice.

"Hello, this is Sage."

Maverick's voice slides down the line like velvet, and my thighs clench. "Sage. You gave me your real number; I'm impressed."

I smirk. "You actually used it. I'm shocked."

He chuckles, deep, British and completely illegal. "Of course I did. I can't get you out of my head. I'd give anything to hear your voice again."

Okay, wow. That one-liner just turned my wine into holy water.

I laugh nervously because I don't do this. I don't give out my number. I don't take late-night calls from men who look like gods in race suits.

"You busy?" he asks.

"If watching reruns and drinking wine counts as busy, then yes—I'm wildly unavailable."

He laughs again. Rude. But fair.

"I want to see you," he says, voice low and a little rough. "Can I pick you up? Spend the night with you?"

Heart. Doing. Cartwheels.

"Can I wear sweats?" I ask tragically.

"I don't care if you wear a garbage bag. Just pack an overnight bag. I'm not letting you sneak out again." Oh God. He remembered. That shouldn't make me melt… But here we are.

Should I tell him I don't do sleepovers? That this breaks rule #3 of the Sage Davidson Dating Constitution? This is dangerous territory because he's leaving on Tuesday and probably won't even remember my name after he leaves.

Apparently not, instead, I say, "Okay."

I pack my essentials, comfy undies, mascara, toothpaste, lip balm, and a t-shirt that says, 'hot mess, but make it fashion, some clothes for work and rattle off my address, and hang up before I can chicken out. Twenty minutes later, the low purr of an SUV pulls into my driveway, and just like that, I'm not watching Kath & Kim anymore. I'm starring in a whole new kind of rom-com.

The headlights wash over the front of my house, and for a second, I hesitate, standing in my doorway with my overnight bag slung over my shoulder and a thousand butterflies going ballistic in my stomach. What the hell am I doing?

I never do this. Ever. I haven't spent more than one night with a man for 6 years. But here I am already locking my door behind me and heading toward the sleek, matte black SUV parked in the driveway. The passenger door swings open before I can even reach for the handle. Maverick's wearing a hoodie and a backwards cap, joggers riding low on his hips. He's out of uniform, but still every bit the fantasy, except now, he feels dangerously real.

"Hey," he says, a soft smile tugging at the corner of his lips.

"Hey," I answer, sliding into the car, trying not to overthink the way my breath catches. He says nothing else for the rest of the drive, just rests his hand on my thigh and drives, like this is the most normal thing in the world, like we've done it a dozen times. Like we're something more than sex. The city glows around us as we drive through the quiet streets. It's late enough that the world's winding down. But inside me? Everything's wide awake. We pull into an underground parking garage at the hotel, and before I can even touch the door handle, he's around to my side, helping me out like a goddamn gentleman. His hand lingers on my lower back as we ride the elevator up, and when the doors open to his floor, he looks at me — really looks at me — and murmurs,

"You okay?" I nod. But I'm not okay. I'm floating, feeling like I'm outside of my body.

He unlocks the door to his suite and lets me step inside first. The room feels bigger than my entire house. It's sleek, modern and impossibly clean. It doesn't look like the same suite I was in on Friday, but things tend to look a little blurry through tequila eyes. He tosses his keys on the table and kicks his shoes off, and I don't know what to do with myself.

"Make yourself at home," he says, "And you look good in those sweats."

I glance down at my oversized hoodie and drawstring pants and roll my eyes.

"You clearly have a head injury."

He laughs, then walks over and pulls me into him like it's the easiest thing in the world. "Maybe. Or maybe I just like seeing you without all the armour on." That comment lodges somewhere deep inside my chest.

Before I can deflect with a joke, his lips are on mine, soft at first, then firmer, like he's been waiting all day. I melt into him, let myself fall just a little and allow my bag to fall to the floor. I should fear this, fear him. But at this moment, all I feel is... Peace. And fire.

We don't rush it this time. He takes his time, guiding me backward until we hit the window. Fingers tracing skin, lips trailing warmth. There's no teasing, no games, just pure want. The kind that's heavy and real and impossible to fake.

He's holding me up like I weigh nothing, my back pressed to the cool glass of the floor-to-ceiling window, city lights glittering behind me like we're putting on a show. He slides my pants and panties down in one swift motion, and my legs wrap tightly around his shoulders, anchoring me as he buries his face between my thighs like a starved man. And fuck, he's devouring me like this is his last chance.

The wet, obscene sounds of his tongue working me over echo in the otherwise silent room. I'm soaked, shameless, my body rocking with every flick of his tongue. He groans low; the vibration pulsing through me as his mouth seals over my clit and sucks hard.

"Fuck, baby," he growls, voice rough and muffled. "Your pussy is divine."

Him calling me baby does something undesirable to me. My head thuds lightly against the glass as I cry out, clenching around nothing, needing everything. I grip his hair like it's the only thing tethering me to this earth while he feasts on me, relentless and worshipful like this is all he's ever wanted.

MAVERICK

I'm drinking in every second of Sage like this — completely wrecked, completely mine. That mouthy, confident woman who can bring a boardroom to its knees? Yeah, she's the one with her legs locked tight around my head, screaming my name like a prayer gone filthy. And I'm not even close to done.

I shift us to the bed, tossing her onto the mattress with a thud. She sprawls out, flushed and glistening, her chest heaving. Fuck, she's a vision with messy hair, swollen lips, eyes half-lidded and begging for more. I could spend hours just staring, but I've got other plans. I crawl over her, grinning as she moans my name again, breathless and aching. My fingers trail over her nipples, teasing and toying, pinching until her hips arch off the bed. Every reaction is addictive. The way she gasps, the soft whimper in her throat — it's all for me.

"God, you're perfect," I murmur, dragging my hand down to grip her ass, spreading her open to watch her melt around me. When I slide into her, it's slow, deliberate. I want her to feel every inch, every stretch, every damn heartbeat of this moment.

"So, fucking tight," I growl, sinking in deeper, inch by inch. "Always so fucking tight for me."

Sage moans, desperate and raw, her mouth brushing my jaw as she whispers, "Just for you."

That does something to me, something primal. Her nails rake down my back, her thighs clenching around my waist, hips rising to meet every thrust like she's chasing the edge and dragging me with her. I can feel her getting close. I can feel her pussy tighten and shake, her breath catching every time I slam back inside. She's holding on like she'll fall apart without me. And then I give her one last, brutal thrust.

She breaks, and it's loud and wild and fucking perfect, calling out my name as she unravels beneath me. Her body quakes, clenching so hard I almost lose it right there. I pull out, grip my cock, give it three long, firm strokes, and I'm spilling over her tits with a groan that rips from deep in my chest.

Marking her. Claiming her. Mine.

Exhausted, we lay in silence, limbs twisted together, my hand splayed protectively over her stomach. Her face rests against my chest, my heartbeat steady beneath her ear. I should say something. A joke. A snarky comment. Anything to cut the tension before it gets too heavy.

But I whisper, "Stay."

And she whispers, "Okay."

TWELVE

MAVERICK

The hotel room is dim, early morning light seeping through the heavy curtains, casting a soft glow. Sage is still asleep, curled on the side of the bed, mouth slightly open, one hand tucked under her cheek, the other draped across my side. Right where she has been since Sunday night, on Monday she got up and went to work, just like she will today - except the only difference is tonight she'll go home, and I'll be in Japan.

I've been lying here, wide awake, for the past hour just watching her. That sounds creepy, I know. But after everything I've seen— every win, loss, contract, headline — this feels like the rarest thing in my world: calm. No pit walls. No team radio in my ear. No endless media headlines or pressure to perform. Just her. Sage. And I'm fucking dreading what comes next.

I leave in a few hours. The car will come, I'll board the plane with the rest of the team, and by dinner, I'll be in Tokyo. New country. New pressure. New race. New distractions. But I know with absolute certainty that she won't be one of them. You can block out a distraction, but how do you block out a woman who looked you dead in the eye and ran, only to come back, let you in, then kiss you like her whole soul was in it?

She doesn't do this. I know that now; she told me as much on Sunday night. I don't know how or why, but I've seen it in the way she stiffens when I get too close, the way she checks herself every time her smile gets too wide. She's terrified of feeling something real. And yet, here she is in my bed.

If I were a smarter man, I'd have left already. Avoided a messy good-bye, kept her locked in that memory of a perfect night and perfect sex and left it as a story she'd tell over too many margaritas, but I can't because the idea of walking out without saying something feels wrong. She stirs a little beside me, eyelashes fluttering as her body shifts closer. Her leg tangles with mine like it belongs there. And I feel it again — the irrational, thunderous pull of her. I don't even know what this is. I don't know whether she feels it too, but I know I'm not ready to let it go.

I reach for my phone on the nightstand, thumb hovering over the camera icon. I want to remember her like this — messy hair, sleep-swollen lips, curled into my body like it's hers. But I stop myself. She's not a souvenir. I lean over and kiss her temple, slowly and softly. She doesn't wake, but she murmurs something in her sleep and burrows closer. I close my eyes for a moment, breathing her in. She smells like vanilla and coffee, and I think this is what peace smells like.

My alarm goes off minutes later — brutal, mechanical, insistent. I silence it and slip out of bed, careful not to wake her. I scribble a note on hotel stationery and slide it under her phone before heading into the bathroom to shower and get ready. By the time I'm dressed and grabbing my bag, she's still asleep. I linger at the door. Then, I force myself to leave.

SAGE

I wake up to the stillness of a room that doesn't belong to me. For a split second, I don't know where I am. Then the soft weight of the duvet, the faint lingering scent of him — it all comes flooding back, and every-thing clicks into place. Maverick. The race. The phone call. The sleepover I swore I'd never agree to. Rule # 3 broken. I roll over, stretching into the space beside me, already expecting him to be there, but it's cool. Untouched for at least an hour, maybe more. It shouldn't bother me. It shouldn't. But I hate how hollow the room suddenly feels. Like the gravity left with him.

I sit up slowly, brushing the tangles out of my hair with my fingers and adjusting the oversized t-shirt I fell asleep in. It's his, of course — soft and worn and too big in the best way. I breathe him in from the collar. God, this is bad. I'm spiralling. Then I see it. A small, folded square of paper propped up against my phone. Thick hotel stationery, sharp pen strokes, slightly rushed. My heart is already racing as I reach for it.

SAGE —

I DIDN'T WANT TO WAKE YOU. YOU LOOKED PEACEFUL — SOMETHING ABOUT SEEING YOU LIKE THAT MADE IT ALMOST IMPOSSIBLE TO LEAVE, BUT I HAVE TO. DUTY CALLS. ANOTHER COUNTRY, ANOTHER RACE, SAME CHAOS. THIS TIME, I'M LEAVING A PIECE OF ME BEHIND. YOU.

I'LL BE THINKING ABOUT YOU, PROBABLY MORE THAN I SHOULD. PROBABLY MORE THAN IS WISE. BUT I CAN'T HELP IT — YOU'VE LODGED YOURSELF IN MY HEAD, AND FUCK IF I KNOW HOW TO SHAKE YOU LOOSE.

CALL ME. TEXT ME. YELL AT ME IF YOU NEED TO. JUST... DON'T DISAPPEAR.

- MAV

P.S. I'M GLAD YOU WORE THE SWEATS.

I stare at the letter, heart pounding, a swirl of things I don't know how to name crashing inside my chest. He doesn't want me to disappear. I should run. I always run. But something about this letter — the honesty, the softness — pins me in place. Like he saw past every wall I didn't even realise I'd put up and reached for me, anyway. The buzz of my phone breaks the moment.

> Josie: Is he gone? Are you spiralling? Want a flex day with brunch and bad decisions?

I smile, wiping a tear I didn't know had escaped. Then I type back:

> Me: Gone. Spiralling. Bring mimosas. And maybe... hope.

I fold the note carefully, tuck it into my bag, and let myself believe just for today that this might be more than a one-night story after all.

The city air is warm with the promise of a day wasted in the best way, and I need that more than I care to admit. I'm dressed in his shirt and some worn-in jeans, sleeves rolled up just enough to pretend I'm not emotionally spiralling underneath it. Comfy. Familiar. Safe.

I spot Jo before she spots me — already at our regular table at Dolly's, sipping something orange and bubbly like she's a Real Housewife in training. Her chestnut waves are flowing over her shoulder; her oversized sunglasses and smug grin tell me she's ready for war… or brunch. Probably both.

"Skipping work with me and drinking mimosas before noon? Who even are you?" she teases as I slide into the chair beside her.

I shrug. "Work was optional today. Mental health day. Medical emergency."

Jo smirks. "A Maverick Carter emergency?"

I groan. "You're hilarious."

The first mimosa disappears fast. The second one, I drink slower, like it might ease the ache creeping up behind my ribs. This is why I don't do feelings, why I keep things casual. One-night stands don't come with vulnerability hangovers. I may act confident, but I'm built out of splintered glass and scotch tape. Grief turned me bitter. Trauma made me flaky. And loneliness? Loneliness turned me into someone who wears borrowed shirts like a security blanket. Josie knows this. Margot does too. They're the ones who've seen me crying on the bathroom floor at 3 a.m. They're my chosen family, the ones I didn't need to impress or seduce or explain myself to.

"Sooo," Josie drawls, already grinning as she sips. "Do you want to talk about it?"

I shoot her a look over the rim of my glass — the kind of look that says I'm hanging on by a thread, please tread carefully.

"Right. ... drink about it instead," she says, topping up my glass without waiting for an answer.

"You and Margot both encouraged this, remember?" I say, waving my hand like I'm blaming the universe and not just myself. "'He's hot. What could happen?' you said. 'Live a little,' you said." I pause. I skull. Josie watches, knowing what's coming.

"Well, this could happen. The Hot Mess Express could happen. Congratulations, we've arrived."

She laughs, warm and loud and exactly what I needed to hear.

"Babe, at least your hot mess comes with abs and a black card." I crack a smile, but it doesn't quite reach my eyes. Not yet. Somewhere deep down, I know this isn't over. Maverick Carter isn't just another name in my little black book. I wore his shirt today because a part of me didn't want to let go, and that scares the shit out of me.

THIRTEEN

MAVERICK

That was the longest fucking race week of my life.

Japan is usually a place I thrive. I love the people, the energy, the precision of it all. But this week? I was off. Not terrible, still managed a podium but not where I should've been. Not where the team needed me to be. It's early days still, adjusting to a new team, a new car, a new rhythm with Ricci. But if I'm honest with myself? My head wasn't in the race. It was back in Melbourne. With her. Sage.

Her name feels like fire and silk all at once. She's wrapped herself around every damn thought I've had for the past week. I can still taste her lips, still feel her body pressed against mine. I hear her laugh in the back of my mind when I close my eyes. I've had dreams of her curled up in my arms, of waking up next to her again. Of her fingers tracing the line of my jaw like she's memorising it.

I haven't heard from her since I left. I wrote the note; I poured out more honesty on that one scribbled page than I have in years. And still… silence. I wanted her to call. To say anything. Hell, even a 'you left your toothbrush' would've been enough. But the only proof she's still breathing came in the form of an Instagram story — her and Josie, half-drunk on mimosas at some brunch spot. She looked happy, beautiful, and completely untethered from me. She was wearing my shirt, though, surely that means something, right? Because I've never felt more hooked.

The second I'm released from the post-race debrief, still smelling like fuel and sweat, I head straight to the airport. No team jet. Just me, my headphones and an absurd amount of overthinking for a man who's usually cool under pressure.

I'm thirty-three, and sometimes it hits me that I've built an empire, but it still feels like I'm chasing something I can't name. Yeah, I've got more money than I know what to do with. Properties in cities I barely visit. Fans who scream my name like it means something. On paper, I've won. I'm the F1 golden boy, the headline, the legacy in motion. But off paper? It's quiet. Being me sounds glamorous until you're sitting in another five-star hotel suite at 2 a.m., jet-lagged and alone. Another city, another bed, another one-night stand who doesn't know the first thing about me. Hell, half the time, I barely know their names.

It's not that I regret the ride; I've worked too damn hard for this life. My parents worked too damn hard for me to have this life, but I'd be lying if I said it doesn't wear thin sometimes. My parents took out a second mortgage and worked multiple jobs for me to be able to achieve my dream. I worked my way through the ranks of Formula 3 and Formula 2 and signed my Formula One contract at Twenty-One and never looked back. I know I've made my parents proud; both my sister Eden and I have. While I turned my parents' sacrifices into being at the very top of my sport, Eden became a leading fertility specialist in Britain. She's married, with two kids, and I see the love Lachlan and Eden have for each other, and lately I've been wondering what it'd be like to have that. I wonder what it'd be like to win a race and have someone waiting for me in the garage who isn't my race engineer. Someone who looks at me and sees more than the trophies. Someone who makes it all mean something. Because the truth is, fast cars and fast nights are great, but they don't hold you at 2 a.m. And lately… I've been feeling that gap in my life more than ever.

I haven't booked a hotel. I don't have a plan. I'm banking on something I can't quite name. Hope? Madness? Maybe both. I could text her, let her know I'm coming. Give her time to come up with a reason not to see me.

Or... I could just show up at her door. Uninvited, vulnerable, probably a little pathetic.

I haven't decided which option makes me look like less of an idiot. I just know I need to see her again, to look her in the eyes and find out if this thing is real, or if it was just another story she'll file under One-Night Stands: Hall of Fame Edition. So, I call her, and she doesn't answer…fuck. The plane starts to taxi, and I buckle my belt, my jaw clenched and heart racing. For a man who lives life at 300 kmh… this might be the scariest thing I've ever done.

SAGE

I should feel better by now. Lighter. Clearer. It's been days since he left and still… I feel like I'm holding my breath.

I've been trying to distract myself with work, wine, and terrible reality TV. Anything to stop me from re- reading the note he left or, worse, opening his Instagram for the hundredth time like some lovesick teenager. I can't even bring myself to throw out the shirt I borrowed — his shirt. I told myself it was comfy; that's why I keep sleeping in it.

God, I hate that I'm like this now. I told myself I didn't want anything serious. That I couldn't handle anything serious. That one night was enough. Then why did I feel like the oxygen left the room the second he walked out of it? Josie and Margot keep checking in, like I'm some fragile doll that might break if they poke too hard. I keep telling them I'm fine. And I mean it — mostly. I'm not heartbroken, just… unsettled. Like I've opened a door I can't close.

I haven't texted him. Not because I don't want to, I do, but because I don't know what I'd say. "Hey, thanks for making me feel things I've spent years avoiding. Hope you're well! Yeah, no. Hard pass.

So here I am. Curled up on the lounge, with candles lit, pretending my house feels cozy instead of lonely. It's shark week. Aka the monthly hell cycle where my uterus tries to kill me from the inside out. My period's here, and with it, a full-blown endometriosis flare. I'm bloated, cramping, nauseous, and radiating 'please don't speak to me unless you have snacks or morphine' energy. My wine glass is half-empty — or half-full, depending on how optimistic you are about red wine and period pain. My heat pack's spinning lazily in the microwave. I parked my spew bucket next to the lounge like an emotional support accessory, perched on a towel because I'm not taking any chances.

I'm wearing a ratty hoodie — the one that smells like sweat and safety and my favourite pair of stretched-out sweats that have a red wine stain from last month's meltdown. My hairs in a bun. I gave up halfway through tying, and there's a rogue chocolate wrapper stuck to my thigh. Glamorous, really. Kath and Kim are on as background noise for my brain while I scroll through Instagram. Specifically, his Instagram.

Maverick Carter. Formula One's golden boy. And a thirst trap enthusiast, apparently. Jesus, no wonder he's been called the Playboy of the paddock. Every second photo is a shirtless pic, or a smoulder that should be illegal, or one of him in that damn race suit with the zip halfway down. Abs. Jawlines. Biceps. Cocky grins and captions that should come with a warning label.

Knock. Knock. I freeze. It's after 9 p.m. I'm not expecting anyone. Josie would've called. Margot is in Bali. No one just... shows up. I peek through the peephole, heart in my throat. It's him. Maverick.

My breath catches. He's standing there with a duffel bag slung over one shoulder, cap pulled low. That ridiculous GQ jawline is impossible to miss even in the dim light. I'm not ready for this. My hair's a mess, I'm wearing clothes that probably smell like vomit and death, and I don't even have a bra on. I should let him knock again. Let him sweat a little, but instead... I open the door. Did he fly from Japan for me?

His eyes lock with mine. And for a second, neither of us speaks. Then he smiles. A real one. The kind that crinkles the corners of his eyes.

"I know you didn't answer my call, but" he says. "I just... had to see you." I stare at him — confused, and suddenly very aware of the way my pulse is doing somersaults.

"So, you casually flew back from Japan to see me?" I whisper. He shrugs like it's nothing, even though I know it's everything.

"Yeah," he replies, stepping inside, "and I'm not leaving unless you tell me to."

FOURTEEN

SAGE

I step back, just enough to let him through, then close the door behind him. My fingers fumble for the lock — I need something to do, anything that delays me from turning around and facing this... whatever this is. He walks in like he's been here before — comfortable, familiar, and that unnerves me more than anything.

He drops his bag by the door and looks around. "You lit candles," he says with a soft smile.

"It's Sunday night," I say flatly. "I always do."

He nods slowly, the smile fading as he picks up the shift in my tone.

"Right. Sunday candles. Rituals." I watch as he scans the lounge room, watch as his eyes pick up on the bomb site, the bucket on the floor, the wine glass, the empty food wrappers.

"Are you okay, Sage?" he asks. I cross my arms, more to anchor myself than anything.

"Why are you here, Maverick?"

He blinks at me. "You… I mean, I told you I'd call. I told you I wanted to see you."

"Yeah, and I never answered. That should've been your sign."

He steps toward me. "You did answer. You opened the door."

"I opened the door because I'm confused," I snap, the tension bubbling over. "Not because I know what the hell to say to you. You don't get to just drop in like this, with that face and that voice and think it fixes—"

"Fixes what, Sage?" he cuts in, voice sharper now. "What exactly is broken?"

I blink. Hard. There it is. The crack. The part I've been holding back starts to unravel and slip through.

"Me," I say finally, voice cracking. "I'm the thing that's broken."

He stares at me as if I've just punched him in the gut.

"I told myself this was just a night. A thing. A blip," I go on, unable to stop now. "But you… You make me feel things, and that's not part of the deal. You were supposed to be one more story. Not someone I…" I trail off. I can't say it. I won't.

He steps closer again, softer this time, voice gentler. "I didn't ask you to fall for me, Sage."

"I didn't!" I snap a little too quickly. I glance away, heat rising to my cheeks. "Not really. Not fully. But I think I'm close enough that it scares the shit out of me. We've known each other for what—two weeks? It's way too fast for anything real."

He's silent for a second.

"You think I'm not scared, too?" I look at him. And for the first time, I see it. I see past the cocky charm and confidence, past the calm media-trained cool. There's fear behind his eyes. Raw and real.

"This wasn't in my plan either," he says. "You're the chaos to my routine. Fire to my Ice. But, Sage, for the first time in years, I feel like something matters outside the track. You matter."

It's too much. I fold my arms tighter, holding myself together. "I don't know how to let someone in without breaking more."

He takes another step. Close enough now to touch, but he doesn't. He waits. "Then let me break with you," he says softly. "Let's figure it out. Together."

I close my eyes. God, it'd be so easy to let him in. Let him fix it. Fix me. But I've never needed a saviour. What I need…is someone who'll stand beside me while I rebuild myself. I open my eyes and meet his gaze.

"One night," I say, almost a whisper. "We start there. No promises. No pressure."

He nods, solemn. "One night," he echoes. And as he reaches for my hand, I take it — knowing full well this isn't going to stop at one night.

Not now. Not with him.

FIFTEEN

SAGE

Monday mornings are usually chaotic, full of messy buns, last-minute coffee spills and mismatched socks, but today, there's something eerily calm about it all except for the fact that my uterus is still trying to kill me. My alarm went off and, for once, I didn't hit snooze five times. Maybe it's because I slept more than two hours. Maybe it's because Maverick is still asleep in my bed. Correction: Maverick Carter F1's golden boy, international sex symbol, and the last man I ever expected to see again is snoring softly into my pillow like he's lived here his whole life. I tiptoe through the room, pulling on my favourite high-waisted trousers and a white button-up I normally save for important meetings. I swipe on some lip gloss, then frown at myself in the mirror. I look too polished. Too in control for someone who's anything but. Last night was... more than I meant it to be. We didn't talk about the future or what this was. We didn't need to. Maverick rubbed my back through the cramps, like he'd been doing forever. The silence between us wasn't awkward — it was warm. Heavy, in a good way. But now the sun's up, and so are all the walls I worked so hard to build.

I peek back at him, sprawled out, blanket barely covering him, hair tousled, and lips parted like some sort of goddamn Calvin Klein ad. His phone is buzzing faintly on my nightstand. Probably the team, or his manager, or the PR people want a run sheet for his next move. He's got a jet- setting life. A schedule. Sponsors. Cameras. And I've got a desk job and a boss who counts the minutes I'm late. I scribble a quick note on a sticky from the fridge:

I had to run to work. Lock the door when you leave. Coffee pods are in the third cupboard. - S

I stare at it for a solid thirty seconds. Too casual? Too cold? I add a smiley face. Then, immediately cross it out. God, I'm losing it. I grab my tote, shove my heels into it, and slide on white sneakers. My chest is tight, and it has nothing to do with the underwire bra I regret putting on. It's the feeling you get when something is just starting, but your brain's already preparing for the end.

As I open the door, I hear a sleepy rustle behind me.

"Sage?" I freeze. He sounds like gravel and honey, like temptation wrapped in sunlight.

"Yeah?" I glance back halfway out the door.

He props himself up on one elbow, squinting. His hair's a mess, and he looks devastatingly good like it's some kind of joke.

"You're not disappearing again, are you?" There's a teasing edge to his voice — but his eyes? They're asking for something deeper.

"No," I whisper. "Just work. I'll be back."

He nods slowly, satisfied, and lets himself fall back onto the pillows. And just like that, I'm walking away again. But something's different. This time, I want to come back. I park the car and just sit there for a second, the engine ticking softly as the world starts another Monday. My hands grip the steering wheel like it's the only thing keeping me tethered to reality. What am I doing? Scratch that — who am I right now? Because this version of me, the one who wakes up after a night with a man like Maverick Carter and doesn't immediately spiral? Yeah, I don't know her. I should probably book an appointment with a doctor; something must be medically wrong. Maybe a fever. A tumour. A personality transplant.

I let out a low groan and lean my forehead against the wheel. God, Sage, pull yourself together. And yet... the thought of him — the British accent, the ridiculous bed hair, that he knows exactly how to make me come, every damn time— it all makes me smile like an idiot. No. Stop that. Un-smile. Be cool.

I catch a glimpse of myself in the rearview mirror and force the goofy grin off my face. The last thing I need is for my pain- in-the-ass boss to catch wind of anything remotely resembling personal happiness. He'd have an HR meltdown just for sport. Trying to make a name for myself as a woman in IT is hard enough, but most days it feels like I'm climbing uphill with a target painted on my back. No matter what I achieve, there's always someone ready to cut me down, to second-guess me, to make me prove myself twice over just to earn half the credit. It's exhausting—always bracing for the next comment, the next side-eye, the next reminder that I don't quite belong in a room full of men who assume they know better. Some days I wonder if I'll ever be enough for this industry… or if the only way to survive it is to keep fighting like I've got a target strapped to my back.

I grab my laptop bag, smooth my shirt, and walk into the office like a woman with her life together — even though my insides feel like a shaken soda bottle ready to blow.

I've just sat down and fired up my laptop when my phone buzzes.

> Josie: COFFEE. NOW.

I smirk, typing back instantly.

> Me: K. Meet you downstairs in 5.

I slam the laptop shut before I can get roped into an email spiral and grab my bag again. Honestly, Josie's timing is freakishly perfect; it's like she can sense when I'm one awkward inner monologue away from spontaneous combustion. As I head for the elevator, my heart's still racing, but at least now I've got caffeine and Josie to look forward to and maybe… maybe I'm ready to talk about the British boy who's turning my rules into rubble.

We walk into Bitter & Sweet, and it's like Luca had a sixth sense —

two perfect lattes already sitting at the counter, the foam hearts as symmetrical as my anxiety right now.

"Thanks, Lu," I mumble, grabbing mine like it's a lifeline. That first sip? Heaven. Absolute, creamy, caffeinated heaven. It's a rare, quiet Monday morning. The usual rush hasn't kicked in yet, so Josie and I slide into our favourite window seat, and Josie wastes no time.

"Wanna tell me why a British sex-god is posting an Instagram story from your backyard?"

My head snaps toward her, and my fingers fumble over my phone as I open the app. Sure enough, there it is. A short boomerang: Maverick's bare feet kicked up on my deck chair, espresso in hand, with the caption recharging. Damn it, it's too early for this kind of confrontation.

"I plead the fifth," I say with a sheepish smile, trying to hide behind my coffee cup. Josie glares.

"Nope. Not happening. You are not getting away that easily."

"I agree with Jo," Luca chimes in with a too-smug grin, wiping down the espresso machine like he isn't casually inserting himself into the drama. "Don't act so surprised, Sage. He's in here every year. I've seen your backyard, and his coffee is in your favourite mug." I sigh. I'm absolutely done for.

"He showed up at my door last night," I confess, eyes flicking between Josie's smug face and Luca's curious stare. "I let him in. I felt bad — he flew all the way from Japan. We talked… I drank wine, died from an endo attack, and we ordered in."

"And?" they say in perfect unison, leaning forward like we're in some low-budget courtroom drama.

"And… we shared my bed," I admit, raising a brow before they can interrupt. "Because he's too tall to sleep on my lounge and be comfortable. That's it. End of." Josie gives me a look that says liar, while Luca raises an eyebrow so high I'm pretty sure it touches his hairline.

"Do I look like I believe that?" Josie says, crossing her arms. "You never let anyone into your bed. That space is sacred. Like the holy grail of Sage intimacy."

"She has a point," Luca adds, not even trying to hide his amusement.

I groan. "Look, I didn't mean for any of this to happen. I didn't expect him to show up again, and I didn't expect him to stay." Josie sips her coffee with a knowing look.

"But you didn't ask him to leave either, did you?"

I stay quiet. And in that silence, everything I've been trying to deny hangs between us — the smile I can't suppress, the way my stomach flipped when I saw his post, the comfort of him making coffee in my kitchen like he belonged there. I glance back at my phone screen, still open on his story. God help me… maybe he does belong there.

MAVERICK

I'm stretched out on Sage's back deck, soaking in the Melbourne morning sun, my espresso in hand. The cicadas are humming faintly; the air smells like fresh eucalyptus and garden soil, and her stupid little wind chime is playing a melody that somehow feels like her—light, chaotic, and completely unforgettable.

I posted a quick story to kill time, mostly because I wanted to mark the moment. Being here feels… grounding. Like I've stepped off the hamster wheel of press, podiums, and performance. For now, I'm just a guy on a deck, drinking coffee at the home of the girl who's taken over every corner of my mind. But I'm also a guy who wants to be in hiding.

I probably should've gone to a hotel. But the thought of waking up anywhere other than next to Sage made my chest ache in a way I don't fully understand yet, and I'm not ready to unpack. I glance inside the house. She's gone to work. Left in a flurry of nerves and rushed mascara. I promised to behave. I didn't mention the fact that her sheets still smell like her, and I could barely sleep last night because I kept replaying the way she curled into me like she didn't even mean to.

I know I've overstepped. She's private. Flighty, in a way I recognise all too well because I live the same way — dashing in and out of people's lives between cities, never landing long enough to plant anything real. But damn, with her, I want to try. So, I'm making plans. Nothing big. Just something… solid. A quiet dinner somewhere away from the chaos. I've messaged Luca for a few local suggestions; he's better connected than most agents I know. I've also been scrolling through ridiculous Airbnbs, wondering if she'd come with me for a night away. Something on the coast. Just us, no noise, no expectations.

I want to see her laugh again. That full-body, unfiltered laugh she gave me when I nearly dropped her takeaway container last night. I want to know how she takes her tea and what her favourite movie is. I want… more. And yeah, maybe it's mad to feel this way after so little time. But when you know, you know. At least, that's what everyone says. And for the first time in my life, I'm starting to believe that might be true. Especially if she comes home tonight and doesn't ask me to leave. The sound of her car pulling away was like the curtain dropping after the final act — quiet and… oddly intimate.

Sage left for work an hour ago, her perfume still lingering in the hallway, subtle but impossible to ignore. I'm sprawled across her lounge in nothing but sweatpants and a hoodie she tossed over the railing last night. Oversized and faded, it smells like her, that vanilla and coffee scent that has embedded into my veins. I should feel out of place here, in someone else's space, tucked away in Melbourne suburbia like I'm in witness protection. But I don't. Not at all.

It's the first time in months I haven't felt like I'm sprinting. Not down a straight. Not through airports. Not away from another set of flashing cameras or headlines that have already decided who I am before I open my mouth. For once, I'm still. And it's strange. I've spent so long letting the world write my story for me— letting them paint me as the golden boy with a god complex, the billionaire adrenaline junkie, the man who collects wins and women like trophies. And yeah… I played into it. More than I should have. More than I wanted to. Because it was easier to be the persona than to let anyone see past it. But right now? For the first time in a long time, I'm not that guy. I'm just me. Sage doesn't know that version. And somehow, I'm not entirely sure I want her to.

Her place is warm in ways I didn't realise I missed. There's clutter on the kitchen bench — receipts, mismatched mugs, lip balm, a lone earring. Her world is real. Lived in. Untouched by performance. And I want in. Whatever this is between us — it feels good. Too good to pretend it's just physical. Too real to keep running from it like she's a one-night mistake I keep reliving in my head.

I scroll back through my phone, fingers hovering over a contact I haven't used in a while — my assistant. I tap out a quick message.

> Me: Hey, push my next flight. I'm staying in Melbourne for a few days. I need time. Will explain later.

As I hit send, I spot one of Sage's notebooks on the coffee table. Scribbled lists inside: grocery items, cryptic half- thoughts, what looks like a pros-and-cons list titled

"Things I Don't Do (But Maybe Should?)" with the first bullet point:

Let people stay.

The second?

Let him in.

I smile. She's fighting this - us just as much as I am, and that makes me feel less insane for how hard I'm falling. I start the coffee machine, making a second espresso, and I text Ricci to let him know I'm lying low for a bit. Then I pull up a delivery app and order groceries, some fresh fruit, real coffee beans — no more of these coffee pods, her favourite peanut butter, even that weird chilli oil I saw in her fridge. I don't know what the fuck I'm doing, but it feels right.

By the time mid-morning sunlight hits the kitchen window, I've made the bed, straightened the lounge cushions, cleaned up from Sage's last night veg out, and filled the house with the smell of something that feels like home. Feeling like I'm in my domestic god era and hoping she lets me stay. I guess I just have to prove I'm worth the risk.

SIXTEEN

SAGE

I walk up the front path with my head full of chaos. Work was a blur. Josie was relentless. And the second I opened Instagram and saw Maverick's story from my backyard, I knew I had lost any hope of keeping this low-key.

There's something dangerous about this… about him. Not in a scary way, but in this could wreck me way. I take a deep breath before unlocking the door. Part of me half-expects him to be gone; that would be easier, wouldn't it? Less complicated, less terrifying. But no, there he is—barefoot in my kitchen, sleeves rolled, sautéing something in a pan like it's his house and not mine.

"Hey, your home," he says like it's the most normal thing in the world.

"Yep. I do that sometimes," I mutter, closing the door with my foot. "What are you doing?"

"Cooking. Or at least trying to." He shrugs, flashing me that annoyingly charming grin. "Figured it was the least I could do after crashing here like some stray dog."

"I've had worse strays," I mumble, putting the groceries down. "So, this is dinner?"

"It's the starter," he says smugly, wiping his hands on a tea towel. "The main part of the plan comes later." I narrow my eyes at him.

"Plan?"

"Yeah. So… I made a reservation. Tomorrow night. Just the two of us. It's a small spot out by the coast—one of those hidden gem restaurants Luca recommended. You don't have to dress up or anything, just bring that weird sense of humour and maybe your hoodie, because it gets cold by the ocean at night."

I blink at him. "You made a dinner reservation for us?"

"I did," he says, suddenly less cocky, more earnest. "Look, I know this might feel… fast and messy. But I don't want to pretend that it's not happening. Like we're not happening."

I bit my lip hard. Because he's saying the thing I won't let myself say out loud. The feelings I've spent years avoiding.

"I don't do plans. Or feelings. I don't even do second dates." I finally say

He walks over, slow and careful, and brushes a strand of hair from my face. "Then let this be your first," he says softly. "Just one night. No pressure. No expectations. Just you and me, and some ridiculously expensive wine and probably overcooked pasta."

I swallow the lump in my throat. This is either the dumbest decision of my life or the best.

"Okay," I whisper.

And for the first time in a long time, I don't feel like running. So, I text Josie

> Me: He's in my kitchen. Cooking. Like it's the most normal thing in the world. Oh—and get this —he asked me on a date. An actual, real-life, capital-D DATE. I'm losing my goddamn mind. The only rule this man hasn't broken is number 2…

Group Chat: Sass, Snark & Secrets

> Josie: Ladies. Emergency debrief. Sage has entered her domestic era.

> Margot: Wait, what?! I blinked ONE day, and she's basically married now??

Me: Ok. First of all, NO. Second… maybe. Third, you're both dramatic.

Josie: Don't you dare try to downplay this. He's COOKING in your kitchen. COOKING, Sage. With herbs. Fresh ones. Probably from the pot on your windowsill.

Margot: This is beyond one-night stand territory. This is "he might have a drawer soon" energy. Have you checked your bathroom? Is his toothbrush there?

Me: No drawer. No toothbrush. Just… a dinner reservation and very distracting forearms.

Josie: Girl. That's how it starts. Forearms, food… feelings. Next thing you know, you're soft launching him on your Insta story with a "he did good" post and a photo of the pasta.

Margot: Have you told him you're emotionally allergic to intimacy yet?

Me: No… But I think he's figured it out. He keeps looking at me like he's trying to talk me off a ledge I didn't know I was standing on.

Josie: Because you are. You've got trauma. Walls. Spiked emotional fences. And he's out here playing gardener. Watering everything. Making himself useful. Pruning your bullshit.

Margot: Honestly, if he keeps this up… I might need to propose for you.

Me: STOP.

Josie: We're not saying marry him. We're saying…maybe let yourself date him. With actual feelings and, you know, sex that's followed by breakfast and not an escape plan.

Margot: He flew from Japan to see you. Girl, the last man I dated couldn't even be bothered to cross the Yarra.

Me: Yeah. I know. It's just… scary. When something feels this good this fast, it usually means it's about to fall apart.

Josie: Or it means it's finally something real. We've seen you survive pain. Let's see you enjoy happiness for once.

Margot: Preach. Now, tell us what you're wearing to this dinner. And please, for the love of tequila, let him keep cooking.

SEVENTEEN

SAGE

Tuesday's workday flew by. I woke up with Maverick still in my bed and, for once, I didn't feel the familiar urge to untangle and run. We were cocooned in warmth, and that ridiculous scent of his cologne mixed with laundry detergent. It should've felt foreign, but it didn't. The office was quiet. Josie and I had lunch together — well, more of a debrief where she grilled me for information like a tabloid reporter. I gave her the highlights: the food was divine; I introduced him to Kath and Kim; and we fell asleep watching Season 1, Episode 2. Nothing scandalous. No X- rated chaos. Just… comfort. A dangerous word in my world.

Now it's after five, and I'm heading home—home to him. Maverick Carter, who's currently lounging around my house and planning our dinner date like this, is normal. Luca texted him restaurant recommendations, apparently. Since when are they, mates? I'm filing that away for tomorrow's interrogation. But right now, my head is buzzing, and my chest feels tight. I grip the steering wheel a little harder than necessary. What am I doing? Who even am I? I could easily turn right instead of left. Head to the bar, find a stranger, and fall back into the rhythm I know. One-night stands. No strings. No expectations and just escape, but something bigger stops me.

Him. His laugh. His patience. The way he looks at me — like I'm something more than a good time wrapped in sarcasm and emotional evasion. Shit. I might be falling, so why don't I feel like running?

The drive to the coast is quiet in a way that feels like something is building. Maverick has one hand on the wheel and the other resting casually on my thigh. I stare out the window, letting the blur of waves and trees settle my nerves. He doesn't push conversation, and somehow, that makes me more nervous. The restaurant Luca suggested is perched above the cliffs, with sweeping views of the ocean and fairy lights strung above the deck. It's romantic—too romantic. The kind of place where people propose or end things. I'm not sure which this feels closer to.

"I requested the table by the window," he says as we walk in. He places a warm hand on the small of my back as the hostess leads us to a secluded spot in the corner. It's intimate, candlelit, and deeply unfair. Why does he have to be so bloody charming?

"This is… nice," I say, smoothing down the hem of my dress like it matters.

"You sound like someone trying not to panic," he replies with a half-smile. Because I am.

Dinner is a blur of conversation. He orders oysters, and I pretend not to notice the way his eyes keep dropping to my lips every time I speak. We talk about racing, about Melbourne, about work, about Josie and Margot and Luca, and for a while, it's easy. Until it's not.

He leans forward, elbows on the table, and hits me with it. "Sage… I don't know what this is between us, but I know it's something. It's not just sex"

And there it is. The thing I've been side-stepping, ducking and emotionally dodging since the second he showed up on my doorstep with that cocky grin and that goddamn ruin-your- life mouth.

I stare down at my wineglass, swirling it like maybe it has the answers.

"I don't know either."

"You're not a 'don't know' kind of girl," he says, soft but certain. "You know what you want. You just don't think you deserve it."

Ouch. That hits straight in the chest. Too close. Too honest. Exactly the kind of read I never wanted him to have of me. "I don't know," I say again, quieter this time. "Because I'm not built for this. I'm the hit-it-and-quit type. I'm not made for… whatever this is."

"You're scared." His voice is steady. "And that's okay. But I'm not going to let fear decide for us."

I glance up—and he's looking at me like I'm not something to fix, but something worth holding on to.

"I'm not asking for forever," he says. "Just don't run. Stay long enough to see if this is real."

My mouth doesn't trust my heart enough to make any promises. But I nod. Just once. It's not much. But for me? It's everything. I won't run, at least not tonight.

EIGHTEEN

MAVERICK

I should be focused on the food, or the view, or how the wine is surprisingly decent for a place this close to the water. But all I can think about is the way she keeps tucking her hair behind her ear. The way her fingers tremble just slightly when she lifts her glass is because she's trying so hard to stay calm, to stay in control. But, she's unravelling in the most beautiful, quiet way, and I want to be the one she finally unravels with. I'd rehearsed what I wanted to say a dozen times on the flight back from Japan. I kept picturing her standing in the doorway in her sweats, eyes cautious, arms crossed like a shield. I don't want to break through her walls —I just want her to let me in.

When I ask her what this is, I see it immediately: fear. Not cold feet. Not disinterested. Just fear. Like she's standing on the edge of something good and bracing for it to disappear. She thinks I'll get bored. That I'll leave. She doesn't know I've already chosen her, and when she finally says she won't run— doesn't even say it, just nods with those wild eyes—I feel something shift. Not in her. In me. I've never wanted anything so badly, so carefully. Like if I reach too fast, she'll vanish. So, I won't. I'll slow down. I'll match her pace.

The drive back is quiet. She kicks off her shoes, legs tucked up in the passenger seat, and hums along to some Dolly Parton track playing faintly through the stereo. She doesn't say much, but she doesn't pull away when I reach over and lace our fingers together at a red light. I know she's scared. But I'm not. Not of her. Not of this. If it takes days, or weeks or years, I'll wait. I'm in this. And for once, I'm not racing toward a finish line. I'm just… here. With her.

When we get back to Sage's place, she's halfway out of the car before I even cut the engine. I jog around to meet her, opening the passenger door like some overeager teenager who doesn't want the night to end.

Inside, she kicks off her shoes, and before I can second-guess myself, I'm there, hands on her waist, pulling her flush against me. Her back melts into my chest, her head tipping slightly as I lower my lips to the delicate skin at her neck. I kiss a trail from her jawline to her shoulder—slow, deliberate, reverent. She turns in my arms, and I meet her halfway. The kiss that follows isn't soft; it's fire. All tongue and teeth and want. She's on her tiptoes; I'm bending to reach her, hands everywhere. Her shirt comes off in one motion, and the sight of that red lace against her skin nearly undoes me.

We're laughing breathlessly, bumping into the hallway wall, tangled in each other. She breaks away first, striding toward the lounge with a mischievous glance over her shoulder. I follow without hesitation. When she sinks into the lounge, I kneel in front of her, one hand gently tilting her chin up. Her eyes bright, blown wide, and vulnerable - search mine. No games. No masks. Just us.

"Sage…" I whisper, my forehead resting against hers for a beat longer than a breath.

"I'm in charge, alright?" I command, and she just nods. "Use your words, baby," I command again.

"I understand" is her sinful reply.

"You're going to sit there and let me fuck that pretty face so I can fuck all of those thoughts out of your head," I say as I pull out my rock-hard cock and groan as she traces it with her finger. Her lips are already puffy from that kiss.

"Open up," I demand. I watch as Sage's mouth waters before I put myself into that pretty mouth and pull her hair into a ponytail, wrapping it around my fist. I sink in, and start at a slow pace, not going all the way in to help her adjust. I pull her hair tighter as I start to pound into her mouth - my pelvis hitting the tip of her nose, my cock is so deep. Damn, my girl can take a cock. A moan rumbles from her throat, vibrating around my cock, and my rhythm stutters. Jesus Christ. That pretty mouth is ruining me.

"That's it. Fuck, your mouth feels so good," I groan, threading my fingers through her hair, guiding her—slow, then faster, chasing that high.

"You're such a good girl, taking me like this. letting me use you like a toy. You deserve a reward"

Her hands brace against my thighs, nails digging in as I thrust deeper. She's gagging around me now, tears at the corners of her eyes, and I know I'm pushing her to the edge. I can feel it. I'm right fucking there. But I don't want to come like this, not yet. Not without seeing her fall apart first. I pull out with a gasp; my cock is slick and twitching.

"Fucking hell, Maverick," she pants, wiping her mouth with the back of her hand, all messy and flushed and looking like my next snack.

I don't give her a second to recover. I flip her over fast, grabbing her hips, tugging her panties to the side. She's soaked. Soaked from just sucking me off, and that alone makes me groan.

"Fuck, baby. This pussy's begging for me." She looks over her shoulder with a smirk

I slide in with one slow, punishing thrust, she arches, moaning loud enough for the neighbours to hear. My rhythm is relentless, rough, deep, desperate. I'm too far gone now, gritting my teeth as her ass bounces back against me. I watch as her back curves, fists clenched in the fabric of the lounge. She's so close, I can feel her flutter around me, getting tighter, more erratic.

"Maverick!" she cries out, shattering with a scream that sends me straight over the edge.

"Fuck, Sage." My voice is raw, breathless.

I pull out, barely hanging on as she grabs my cock, giving me three rough pumps, and I'm coming hard, all over her back, a puddle of hot mess that leaves me groaning and dazed. She's trembling, her legs weak under her, and I collapse beside her, chest heaving.

"That… was unreal." I pant, brushing a strand of hair from her cheek, watching her catch her breath with that blissed-out smirk that says she knows exactly what she just did to me, and then, like gravity can't bear to keep us apart, we fall into each other again. Skin on skin, heat building with every passing second. Kisses deepen. Moans melt into the walls. This is not just lust; it's something heavier, sweeter, more dangerous.

Later, as we lie absorbed in each other on her bed, her head on my chest, her breathing even and slow, I realise something. This isn't just a night. It's not just a break between races. It's the start of something I'm not ready to lose. And for once, the thrill isn't in the chase; it's in the staying.

SAGE

It's Saturday morning, and I wake up to the sound of Maverick on a call in the kitchen—his voice low, crisp, clipped in that way he gets when he's all business. I pull the covers tighter around me, not quite ready to face reality. Not yet, because reality means time is running out. He's leaving again soon. Another city, another race. The tight little bubble we've been living in is about to burst, and I'm not sure what we're supposed to be when that happens.

I eventually get up and pad down the hallway, the scent of fresh coffee pulling me toward him like a tether. He sees me and smiles—genuine and warm, like I'm the best thing he's seen all week.

"Morning," he says, already handing me a mug before I can ask.

"Are you always this chipper before 8 a.m.?" I grumble playfully.

"Only when there's coffee, and you're involved." He kisses me lightly, one hand resting at the small of my back like he always has to be touching me, and I lean in because pretending not to care is exhausting. And right now, I don't want to pretend. We fall into a peaceful rhythm — him packing for the weekend; me scrolling emails and trying to ignore the growing ache in my chest.

"You leave tomorrow?" I finally ask, my voice quiet. He pauses, turns to look at me.

"Yeah. The team needs me in China for briefings. Race week starts on Monday."

I nod; eyes fixed on my mug. "Right. Of course." There's a beat of silence, then his hand is on mine.

"But I'm not ready to leave this," he says softly. "You."

That single sentence shatters whatever resolve I had left. I look up, blinking back the sudden sting in my eyes.

"I don't know how to do whatever this is, Mav."

"Neither do I. But I know it's not nothing, and I don't want to walk away from it like it was."

I swallow hard, trying to find the right words. "You'll be back on the road. You have a team, sponsors, fans; your whole life is somewhere else."

He brushes a strand of hair from my face. "Doesn't mean you can't be part of it."

That one line sits heavy in the air between us because part of me wants to believe it. The other part knows what happens when I let myself fall, but for once, maybe falling isn't the end. Maybe it's the beginning.

MAVERICK

I hate packing. Not because it's tedious, but because this time, it feels like I'm putting distance between me and the only place I've wanted to be in a long time. With Sage. Everything about her—her laugh, her sarcasm, the way she hoards the blanket at night- it's in my blood now, and I don't know how to leave it behind without losing a piece of myself. I haven't told her yet, but I've already arranged for her to fly out to China next weekend. Just for the race. Just to see, just to feel what it might be like to have her in my world, not just on the edges of it. She doesn't know it yet— but I'm not planning on letting this end with a flight.

TWENTY

SAGE

Monday afternoon, and the office aircon is on full arctic blast, I've got a half-eaten protein bar on my desk, and I'm pretending to focus on a spreadsheet that I haven't touched in the last ten minutes because my phone just lit up and it's his name on the screen.

> Playboy: Hey, Love. I know I left yesterday, but I'm already thinking about when I can see you again. I want you here. With me. In China. Flights are booked. Details below. No pressure—unless you say no. Then, all the pressure.

A boarding pass image follows. Departure: Friday, Melbourne to China, Return: Monday morning. Seat: Business class. Of course. I stare at the message, rereading it three times, like the words might morph into something less terrifying. Less… significant. 'Hey, Love' indicates this isn't casual.

But then I remember how he looked at me the night before he left. He kissed me like he was memorising it. How he said, it doesn't mean you can't be part of it, and maybe I want to be.

> Me: So, if I say yes, do I get one of those ridiculous team polos and a headset? Also, you forgot to include what snacks will be on board. Priorities, Playboy.

His response is immediate.

> Playboy: You'll get everything you want, Trouble.
> Just say yes.

I stare at my screen, heart pounding like it's about to punch through my ribs, and then, I do something completely insane.

> Me: See you in China.

I submit my leave request. Friday and Monday — a neat little, long weekend wrapped in something that feels suspiciously like emotional danger. My boss, naturally, has questions.

"A bit last-minute, don't you think?" he asks, leaning on the edge of my desk like he owns the place. Technically, he kind of does. I give a vague answer about needing a reset, time off, blah blah blah, but my cheeks burn, and I know I'm a terrible liar.

By Wednesday, I've tried to recall my leave form no less than six times. Hovered over the cancel button like it might save me from… what exactly? A man who booked my flights, cooked me dinner, kissed me like I mattered?

Wednesday night rolls around, and I spiral into my usual comfort chaos: obsessive cleaning and sloth-mode movie marathons. My lounge has a Sage-shaped dent in it, and I'm defending it like it's a safety net. I'm not moping. Definitely not. I do not mope over men. Not even ones with smirky smiles and hands that know exactly how to hold me.

Josie honks from outside; she's dragging me to dinner. I owe her a catch-up. I've been avoiding her for a week, even though I already know she's coming in hot with the questions. I slide into her car, and she wastes no time.

"Tell me, bitch, and don't withhold." I sigh.

"What's there to tell? I worked, he cooked, we watched TV, talked about our lives and what we're doing… and we fucked. Pretty much in that order."

Her eyes narrow. "And?"

I glance out the window too casually. "andhebookedmeaflighttoChinafortheweekend."

"Are you kidding me?" Josie practically yells. "You're going, right?"

I hesitate. "I don't know. Feels… official. Like, people will see us. How will he introduce me? What even am I to him? What if I get there and it all unravels?"

Josie gives me the kind of look only a best friend can— equal parts love, exasperation, and silent *you're doing that thing again* telepathy. She doesn't push, not really. She just says the things I'm afraid to hear. "You're going to stand him up, aren't you?"

"If I'm being honest… probably." My voice is small. "I think an easy break is best. We're not anything yet, and calling it now would be cleaner. Less risk."

She doesn't argue. She just lets me sit in the silence I'm so desperate to avoid. That's the thing with Josie. She knows when to push—and when to let me stew in my nonsense until I talk myself into or out of something.

Thursday hits like a brick. I drown myself in spreadsheets, blast through emails, and even work through lunch. Anything to avoid the conversation I should be having with myself. It's late when I finally head to my car. I check my phone, expecting a 'where are you?' from my boss or another spam email. Instead, it's a message from Margot.

Margot: See you in China, bitch.

I stop dead in my tracks, reread the message twice. GOD. DAMN. IT. JOSIE. I knew she'd call in the big guns. She played the Margot card. Which means… I have to go.

THE SHANGHAI AIR IS THICK, humid, and filled with anticipation— and not just for the race. My stomach hasn't settled since the plane touched down. I've replayed every scenario in my head: Maverick is too busy to notice me. Maverick is having second thoughts. Maverick, not having second thoughts and sweeping me into some dramatic paddock kiss, ends up on the internet forever. Margot finds me before I can talk myself into getting back on the plane.

"Look who finally got her ass out of Melbourne," she grins, arms wide and full of chaotic love. Her lipstick is fire truck red, jet-black hair cascading down her shoulders, her sunglasses oversized, and her suitcase— of course—is Louis Vuitton.

"You were the trap," I say, hugging her tightly. "Josie called you in."

"Obviously," Margot smirks. "Because you're a self- sabotaging little menace, and we all know it. Now that you're here, you look hot, and you're not allowed to overthink anything until at least Monday. Deal?"

"Deal," I mumble, lying through my teeth.

Margot and I head toward the circuit's VIP area—passes in hand, looking like we belong even though I feel like I've stepped into someone else's life. There are sleek cars, beautiful people, media swarming like bees, and the constant echo of engines in the distance.

I spot him before he sees me. Maverick. Standing next to his car, deep in conversation with Ricci and another one of the engineers. His race suit is half unzipped, tied around his waist, revealing a black fireproof undershirt clinging to muscles I am very familiar with.

My breath catches. My knees? Weak. It's embarrassing, honestly. Margot nudges me.

"Go. Say hi. I'll find a champagne flute and pretend I'm part of a WAG documentary." I hesitate. He looks good. Too good. And this is his world. Where he's confident, focused, in control. I'm the outlier here, the plus-one to something I never thought I'd be part of.

Then his head turns. His eyes land on me. And that smile. God, that smile spreads across his face like I'm the first thing he's seen in colour all day. He blurts something to Ricci and breaks away, jogging toward me, unbothered by the media watching, the humidity, or the spectacle.

"Sage," he says, voice low and a little breathless. "You came."

"I did."

And then he's kissing me, not shy or careful. It's possessive, warm, and a little desperate. Like he's been waiting for this moment since he left my bed. I melt into him before I remember we're in public.

"Mav," I whisper, pulling back. "We're kind of in front of everyone."

"Good," he says simply, brushing my hair behind my ear. "Let them see."

Suddenly, I don't care about who's watching. I don't care about the media, or labels, or what I'll say if someone asks what we are. Because whatever this is, it's starting to feel real. And for the first time in a long time, I'm not running because I feel like I'm exactly where I want to be.

MAVERICK

I've driven circuits all over the world, chased adrenaline across continents, but nothing—and I mean nothing — prepared me for the gut punch of seeing Sage standing trackside, looking like sin wrapped in sunshine. Her hair is a little windblown. Her Eyes scanning for something... me, hopefully. She's here. She came. For a second, the world mutes. The cameras fade. Ricci's briefing is just background noise. My eyes are on her, and suddenly, every lap, every podium, every interview was just a warm-up for this moment. I don't even tell Ricci I'm leaving. I just start walking — no, jogging — toward her like I've forgotten I'm supposed to be calm and composed and laser-focused on a race.

"Sage," I say, and her name already tastes like relief. She looks up at me, unsure, but those walls I've come to recognise —the ones she holds up like armour—they're softer today. Cracked, maybe. So, I do what I've wanted to do since the moment I left her bed: I kiss her. Right there. Public and proud. The media be damned. She pulls away just a little, like she remembers where we are before I do.

"Maverick ... we're kind of in front of everyone."

"Good," I tell her. "Let them see."

Let them see that she's the reason I've got fire under me today. Let them know that maybe I didn't land P1 in Japan because my mind was back in Melbourne, wondering if she read my note, wondering if I'd ever get to see her smile again. She's smiling now. And I swear I'd give up a thousand podiums to keep it on her face.

For the rest of the day, I'm buzzing. I should be focused on qualifying and Ricci while he keeps running over strategy and tyre choices, but my brain is split: 80% race mode, 20% Sage. Okay, maybe 60/40. When I glance up into the VIP section and see her standing next to Margot, watching me, my chest tightens. Not from nerves. From the sort of ache that comes from wanting someone. Not just for the night but for the stretch of life in between. I've never introduced a girl to the paddock before, not like this. I've never wanted to. But Sage? She fits here without even trying. Like she belongs. Qualifying ended in P2. Not bad, I could've done better if I wasn't trying to spot her in the crowd on every lap.

After the team debrief, I sneak away. I find her near the back of the hospitality tent, drink in hand, looking like trouble. "You're distracting," I tell her, leaning in close, stealing another kiss.

"You're the one who kissed me first," she fires back, cheeks flushed.

"Not sorry," I grin.

She shakes her head. "I don't know why I feel so comfortable here. With you"

"Because it's real," I say simply. "And I'm not letting you run." She doesn't reply—not with words — but she doesn't leave either. That's enough for now.

<h1 style="text-align:center">TWENTY-ONE</h1>

<h2 style="text-align:center">SAGE</h2>

Maverick shows up at my hotel room with takeout, two beers, and that smug little grin like he knows I'll let him in before he even knocks. Which, annoyingly, I do. He sets the food down on the coffee table and plops next to me on the lounge, way too comfortable for someone who has a race tomorrow. I stare at him, waiting for him to act like a driver in race week — focused, distant, wired.

Instead, he stretches his arm behind me and says, "I missed this."

I raise a brow. "Shanghai hotel lighting and lukewarm dumplings?"

He grins wider. "You. Looking at me like you want to kiss me but you're still pretending you don't." I don't kiss him. Not right away.

We eat. We sit. We talk. He tells me about the setup challenges on the car, about Ricci's obsession with balance and weight distribution. I listen. I don't understand all the tech stuff, but I like how he talks when he's passionate. Like every word matters. Then the silence comes. That comfortable, dangerous kind of quiet where there's nothing left to say, and everything left to feel. He runs a hand down my arm, slowly, testing. I shift and close the space between us and press my lips to his like they've been waiting for hours. His hands are on my hips instantly, warm and certain, grounding me. We don't sleep together—not fully — but he holds me like we've been doing this for years. Like my presence in this bed is a given, not a question.

"Why me?" I whisper in the dark. He doesn't hesitate. "Because you make me feel like it's not all just about the next win."

Race days are chaotic. Even from the paddock, I can feel it—the energy, the pressure, the noise. Maverick is a different version of himself now, Focused, Tense. He nods to fans, smiles for the cameras, but I can tell he's already in the car, already flying down straights and braking late into corners.

Margot hands me a headset just before lights out. "Watch him work," she says. "This is art." The formation lap starts. Maverick's voice crackles through the team radio—calm, confident. I bite my lip, heart pounding like I'm the one on the grid.

When the lights go out, he's lightning. Quick off the mark, aggressive into turn one. The car moves like it's an extension of him — sharp, fluid, untouchable. I don't breathe for the first ten laps. Mid-race, the commentators praise his strategy. He is holding P2, saving tyres, waiting to strike. I can't stop smiling. This man is steel and fire in equal measure. Then, on lap 43, a window opens. He goes for it. DRS open, and he dives down the inside. Clean. Bold. Perfect. P1. The crowd erupts. So, do I. By the last lap, he's ten seconds clear. When he crosses the line, I'm on my feet before I realise, I've even moved.

He did it. Maverick Carter. Shanghai Grand Prix Winner. He spots me from across the barrier after the interviews. Helmet still in hand, sweat-soaked and grinning like a madman. Without thinking, he runs straight to me, pulls me over the barrier, and lifts me into his arms.

"You're insane," I laugh, burying my face into his neck.

"Yeah," he says, "I think I am." And then, in front of God, country, and the entire Formula 1 circus… He kisses me like the checkered flag meant nothing if I wasn't there to see it.

Walking through the paddock is a whole new vibe now. It's like we've turned the entire Formula 1 operation on its head. PR reps whisper. Engineers glance. Other drivers nudge each other. Ricci gives me a wink as he walks past. Maverick handles it like he handles a race start — head held high, focus forward, no apologies. At one point, a journalist shouts, "Who's the girl, Carter?" He just smiles. "Someone worth winning for." He doesn't give them more, doesn't need to. The mystery is part of the game now. And me? I try not to combust every time someone stares. I try to stay small, out of the spotlight, like I always have, but Maverick keeps pulling me into his orbit. Light brushing touches. A thumb across my lower back. A grin like he knows exactly what he's doing to my insides.

The photo's everywhere instantly.

"Maverick Carter, victorious in Shanghai, helmet off, champagne-soaked… and kissing a mystery blonde in the paddock like he'd just won her, not the Grand Prix." Turns out the F1 media circuit is just as fast as the cars.

"Carter's Surprise Flame?"

"Who's the Woman Behind the Win?" "Maverick's Mystery Girl Breaks the Internet,"

By breakfast, my phone is blowing up. Josie sends me five articles, three memes, and a text that reads: **I TOLD YOU THIS WOULD HAPPEN, followed** by a skull emoji.

Margot's contribution is more concise.

> Margot: Queen. Your soft launch failed
> spectacularly. Congrats on the hard launch.

Speaking of Margot - I have no idea what she has gotten up to here in Shanghai. She seemed to take a shine to Ricci, though.

I should be panicking. Hiding. Dying of second-hand embarrassment, but I'm not; plenty of time to do that on the plane. But right now, Maverick's right there beside me at the hotel table, hair still damp from the shower, eating eggs like he didn't just explode both our lives with one kiss. He scrolls through the headlines with a smirk.

"You, okay?" he asks without looking up.

I nod, sipping my coffee. "You just set feminism back a decade. I'm now known only as *'mystery girl'.*"

He leans in close. "Not a mystery to me."

I roll my eyes. "You're impossible."

"I'm yours," he corrects, brushing a kiss on my cheek like he hasn't already made global news with his mouth.

It's quieter now. Breakfast is done, and my bags are packed. Shanghai glitters below us as Maverick sits on the hotel balcony in sweats and a team tee, legs stretched out, a beer in one hand and my foot in his lap.

"I know this is a lot," he says softly.

"You think?" I tease, curling into the blanket around my shoulders. He chuckles, the seriousness creeping in.

"I didn't mean to blow it all up. But when I saw you after the win... I just had to."

I shake my head. "It's okay. I'm not mad. Just... still catching up." He turns to me, expression unreadable.

"You're not just a moment for me, Sage. I need you to know that. This... whatever this is... It's not casual to me."

I exhale. "That's the scary part, Mav. I don't think it's casual for me either." A pause. Then he reaches for me, pulls me gently into his lap.

"I'll go at your pace," he whispers into my hair. "Fast or slow. I don't care. As long as we're going somewhere together." And for the first time in a long time, I let myself lean all the way in, not just into his chest. Into the future.

MAVERICK

China was a success. On paper: a win. Maximum points. The team is elated. The sponsors are thrilled. Off paper, I kissed Sage in front of half the paddock and the entire internet. I know I shouldn't have done it; the PR team will be in a spin, and Sage, fuck, she's spiralling. I could see it in the way her shoulders stiffened, in how she blinked just a little too fast after we pulled apart. I don't regret a damn second of it. But now? Now I'm alone again, hurtling toward Bahrain with a pit crew, a schedule and a head full of thoughts I can't switch off.

I said goodbye to Sage at the airport, trying not to look as gutted as I felt watching her walk through security. She didn't cry, of course, not that I expected her to. She's too strong for that. Too composed. But I saw the way her fingers lingered at her necklace, the subtle shift in her smile. She didn't want to leave either.

Margot disappeared right after - something about Colombia, a writing deadline, and a new lover with questionable tattoos. That girl is chaos in vintage sunglasses. Sage swears she keeps secrets like a vault, but I think she operates like a smoke bomb—distracting, explosive, and gone before the dust settles. Now I'm headed to the desert. Bahrain, then Saudi Arabia. A triple-header grind. Long days. Sweat- soaked nights. Engine noises, track walks and media briefings. I don't mind the pressure. I've lived in it long enough to wear it like skin. But this time, there's a whisper of something softer, pulling at me.

I keep checking my phone like a teenager. Wondering if she's messaged. If she's made it home, if she's thinking about that night on the hotel balcony, my hands on her hips, my breath caught between her thighs. The team is buzzing on the flight; everyone's high from the win, jokes flying, predictions being made. And yeah, the Sage questions start the minute someone brings out the snacks.

"Is she your girlfriend now?" "Mate, when did you get romantic?" "Is she coming to Bahrain too?"

"Damn, she's a babe. Where've you been hiding her?"

I wave them off. Give them a smirk and deflect with humour. I can't help it; I want to keep her close, protect what we have before the world chews it up, and it ends before it's even begun. This industry isn't kind. It takes what you love and makes it currency. But Sage? She's not part of the show. She's the only real thing in my world that is built on speed and money. Still, part of me wants to scream her name on every podium. Claim her so loud the sky hears it. But not yet. Not until she's ready. So, for now, it's helmets on. Focus up. One more race closer to the break. Closer to her, and if I close my eyes tonight and picture her curled up on my pillow back home… That's nobody's business but mine.

TWENTY-TWO

SAGE

The flight home from China felt longer than the flight there. Not because of the time—though the jet lag was unforgiving — but because I left part of myself behind. With him. Maverick. I hadn't expected to feel it so sharply, the ache of missing someone who technically isn't even mine. We hadn't defined anything. No labels. Just long glances, late-night whispers, stolen kisses… and now, silence. Not the bad kind, he has messaged, they've been short and sweet though. A photo of his breakfast. A wink before bed. But still. The silence between those check-ins is loud.

I landed in Melbourne late Monday night and instantly hit the ground running. I immediately regret not taking an extra day off. It's Tuesday, and I'm already late. Coffee in hand, hair in a claw clip, an inbox with forty-seven unread emails and my mind going around in circles… oh, also my boss, Phil, is standing near my desk like a human pop-up ad.

"Sage," he says, like it's a warning and a greeting in one. "Rough weekend?" Oh god. He saw the kiss.

"It was… a weekend," I reply, sliding into my chair with the grace of a collapsing lawn chair.

He smirks. "Well, social media had a field day with your… international diplomacy." Jesus. That's what we're calling it now?

"Just keep the gossip at a dull roar, alright?" I mutter.

Unfortunately, the office has the energy of a pack of seagulls fighting over a chip. Everyone saw the clip of Maverick, in full racing gear, pulling me in like a scene from a Netflix special. The kiss that set Twitter on fire. Group chats exploded. Apparently, someone even started a TikTok fan page. I can't handle this. I had one co-worker say, "You kissed Maverick Carter? Like… with your face?" No one is getting work done today. Especially not me. I need to end this now, before it gets any bigger.

I'm not built for this kind of life, not really. It doesn't take much for the anxiety to creep in, or the depression to wrap its hands around my heart and squeeze. I work hard, damn hard, to keep it all in check. It's why I have rules. Boundaries. Why I don't do commitment, why I crave control. My independence isn't just something I like—it's survival. I keep my circle tight, my world quiet, because the noise gets too loud too fast. And when it does, I unravel. Not dramatically. Quietly. Privately. The kind of unravelling that looks like nothing on the outside but feels like a storm on the inside. But this? These public kisses, headlines, all the eyes watching me like I belong to someone else's world—it's the kind of chaos I don't need and yet… Here I am, trying to hold steady while everything around me spins.

BY THE TIME the weekend rolls around. I'm exhausted, mentally and physically, and I'm curled up on the couch in an old pair of sweats, watching the Bahrain Grand Prix, clutching a throw pillow like it might hold me together, while Josie and Margot blow up my phone with texts. Their words blur between laps and the ache in my chest.

Josie: They just mentioned you in the commentary. "Carter's mystery woman."
Mystery?? You're half the grid's wallpaper now

Margot: Honestly, kind of iconic. You're the Jane Birkin of pit lane.

Me: I hate everything.

The camera pans to him on the starting grid. Calm. Focused. Gorgeous, of course, annoyingly so. He's talking to his engineer, nodding, helmet in hand. But I can tell there's tension behind his eyes. Maybe it's race nerves. Maybe it's… me. I want to turn it off, pretend I don't care. But I care so much it hurts. He races like the wind owes him something. Fast. Surgical. By lap twenty, he's leading. By lap forty, he's unstoppable. I don't breathe until he crosses the finish line.

> Josie: He did it! AND LOOK AT HIM LOOKING FOR YOU IN THE CROWD

But I'm not there. I'm a thousand miles away, hiding behind a screen, watching a man who makes my heart race… and wondering if I'm brave enough to keep up.

Then my phone buzzes again.

> Playboy: Two down. One to go. You still watching, Trouble?

I stare at the screen, bite my lip… and smile.

> Me: Always.

TWENTY-THREE

MAVERICK

Saudi Arabia is chaos wrapped in sand and luxury.

The Jeddah track is brutal, high speed, and razor-thin margins. It's a street circuit that doesn't forgive mistakes, and this time around, I feel like I'm carrying more than just the weight of performance. Even though I'm sitting at the top of the championship, the pressure is on from the team to stay there. The media's still circling like vultures since China. Every press conference includes some version of:

"Who's the girl?"

"Is this your first official relationship?" "Will she be joining you this weekend?"

I shut it all down with a smile and a shrug.

"Just trying to win races," I tell them. But my jaw tightens every time Sage's name stays trapped behind my teeth.

We haven't spoken much this week. A few texts. One late- night voice note she sent that I've played more times than I'll ever admit. Her voice, soft, tired and smiling, "Good luck this weekend. Go do your thing." God, I miss her.

The paddock is a buzz. My engineers are laser-focused, Ricci's hyped on espresso and spreadsheets. Everything is locked in for a podium push.

But me? I'm distracted. Not by nerves. By her. By wondering if she's watching again. If she wants to be part of this madness. I'm also worried that what happened in China will make her run for the hills. Thankfully, there's some new gossip making its way through the paddock this weekend. Some rival team member's girlfriend apparently unfollowed someone, and now Twitter thinks there's a full-on scandal. I don't care; I just hope people aren't using Sage's name, as it belongs to the media, because that makes my blood boil. I want to protect her, not that she needs protecting. I want to wrap her up in silence and privacy. But she deserves more than that. I see a message flash across my phone during a team meeting:

> Trouble: You look good in red. Kick their asses
> this weekend.

Four words. And I can breathe again. After a track walk and dinner with the team, I sit alone on the balcony of my hotel room. Jeddah's lights are glittering like fallen stars across the water. I scroll back through our texts. I almost call her. Almost.

Instead, I send:

> Me: Wish you were here. This city's loud, but it's
> nothing without you in it.

She doesn't reply right away, and that's okay. I just hope she does reply. Race prep starts early tomorrow. I'll strap into the car, chase the podium, and try not to think about how good her name sounds when I whisper it in the dark.

SAGE

The race is halfway through when everything stops. I'm on the lounge, coffee long gone cold, heart already tight from nerves. I've watched every race since China. Quietly. Alone. Not because he asked me to, but because I need to. Because watching him gives me something I didn't realise I was missing, it gives me hope. And then it happens. The commentators' tone shifts that sharp edge of panic in their voices. The timing screen flashes red. yellow flags. Then the slow-motion replay. Maverick's car spins out of

Turn 13. The rear slides. Contact with the barrier. Carbon fibre explodes across the track like glittering shrapnel. No, no, no. My breath catches as the camera cuts to his cockpit, smoke, debris and then the words I didn't want to hear:

"That's Maverick Carter. He's gone into the wall. Hard."

I don't realise I've stood up or that tears are already forming. They cut to his radio. Static. Silence. My stomach sinks. I'm waiting, waiting for anything — his voice, a thumbs up, a groan…anything, anything that will start my heart.

Then, finally — a voice. "I'm okay."

Two words. Shaky. Groggy. But alive. I drop back onto the lounge and bury my face in my hands. The relief is messy. So is the fear, and I feel it all at once. They replay the crash again and again like it's entertainment, and all I can think is: That's his body in that car. That's his life. I can't go through this again……..

My phone lights up.

> Josie: You saw that, right? You, okay?? He's
> okay. He's okay.

> Margot: Girl. Breathe. DNF but walked away.
> Cars totalled, though. You texting him?

I stare at my phone. Fingers frozen. I want to text him. But what do I say?

"Glad you didn't die?" "Hey, how's your spine?" None of it feels enough.

So instead, I send the truth.

> Me: You scared the shit out of me. Please tell me
> you're okay. Really okay.

Three dots appear. Then vanish. Then reappear. Finally

> Playboy: Hurts like hell. But I'm breathing. Wish
> you were here.

I close my eyes.

Me too, Mav. Me too.

I've packed a bag before my brain catches up with my body. Jeans. Hoodie. Toothbrush. passport. It's all thrown together in a whirlwind of panic, adrenaline, and something deeper I'm not ready to name. Maybe I'm running to something instead of from it for once.

I call Josie on the drive to the airport. "Tell me I'm not being insane."

"You're absolutely insane," she says.

"But also — it's about bloody time." I laugh, but it comes out tight, breathless.

"He crashed, Jo. I watched it live. He could've—"

"I know," she says gently. "And you realised you don't want to waste any more time."

Yeah. That. Josie knows why this hits me hard; Maverick doesn't, and I don't want to tell him. Not yet anyway.

At the check-in counter, I buy the first ticket I can get to Jeddah, not even asking about the price. My hands shake as I hand over my card. This isn't me. This is some new, brave, possibly delusional version of me. I think I like her. I'm at the terminal, so I text him.

> Me: Don't freak out. Just… don't make any plans for tomorrow. I'm coming to you.

There's a pause. Then

> Playboy: Wait. What? Are you serious?

> Me: Deadly. You scared me. And I don't want to be afraid from a distance anymore.

Three dots.

> Playboy: You have no idea how much I needed to hear that.
>
> You just made this the best DNF of my life.

I smile for the first time since the crash; it feels real. I don't know what will happen next, I don't know how this ends, but I do know one thing: I'm done pretending that this is casual. I'm flying halfway across the world for a man who feels like gravity, and for once… I'm not afraid to fall.

MAVERICK

The triple-header is over. Thank God.

I hit a wall in Jeddah — literally, and now I'm under strict orders to rest and recover. Physically, I'm bruised and stiff. Mentally, I feel like I've been cracked open. Maybe that's what happens when the person who haunts your thoughts suddenly appears in your hotel room like it's the most natural thing in the world.

She's here. Sage. Sitting across from me at the low coffee table, typing out an email to her boss asking for two weeks off. Her bag is still half-unpacked in the corner, the most chaotic collection of clothes I've ever seen — a hoodie, jeans, two pairs of boots, a random sequin top, and absolutely no warm- weather gear. But none of that matters. Because she came. She looks up from her laptop, catching me staring. That soft, crooked smile of hers makes something in my chest relax. She knows something's changed between us. Hell, I think we both do.

Sage closes her laptop and leans back, biting her lip like she's building courage. "So… what do you want to do for the next two weeks?" She asks, voice lower, almost shy. God, she has no idea.

"I want to go home," I say, simply and clearly. "To Monaco. And I want you with me."

She freezes. Her eyes narrow as if she's doing mental gymnastics.

"Monaco?" she echoes. "Of course, you live in Monaco." The eye roll she throws in makes me laugh.

"Bougie, I know," I grin. "But it's quiet and private, and I want that with you."

She doesn't say yes, she doesn't say no either, but I've learnt that when she starts mentally rearranging her life to make something possible, it's her version of a maybe that leans toward yes. I book a jet not because I'm flashy, but because I want this to feel easy. Safe, and because I'm hurting physically from that damn wall. I make sure it's stocked with tequila, the good kind, and snacks Sage loves, yeah, I may have asked Josie for a list.

When we board, she's on FaceTime with Josie and Margot.

"Can you believe this man?" she yells, half-laughing. I hear Josie yell back, "Girl, MARRY HIM!"

Sage rolls her eyes but doesn't deny it. That's a win. Once she hangs up, she flops into the seat across from me and goes quiet. Not cold. Not closed. Just… processing. I can tell she's trying to keep a distance. Like if she lets herself get too close too fast, the spell might break. But she came to me, and that's something. I motion for her to come sit with me. She lets out a soft, dramatic sigh, but she moves. When she's close enough, I grab her by the hips and pull her down into my lap. She settles there with a sort of wary comfort, her guard lowered — just a bit. I trace her lips with my thumb, tilting her chin up until our eyes meet. One kiss. Slow, deep, steady. It's not about the sex anymore. It's about knowing she's here. That she came through the fear. That maybe, just maybe, I've proven to her that I'm worth the risk. When we part, she stays curled against me, her head on my chest. Eventually, she shifts to lie across my lap, her cheek resting against my thigh. I thread my fingers through her hair gently until her breathing slows. She's asleep in minutes, and that? That's my favourite version of her — safe, soft, and entirely at peace. If this is what hitting a wall gets me… I'd do it all over again.

SAGE

Monaco. What the actual hell?

This place doesn't look real; it's like someone sketched a postcard and turned it into a city. Everything is bright and clean and glittering with quiet wealth. Not loud wealth. Not Melbourne-footy-WAG energy. Monaco whispers wealth in your ear and makes you feel underdressed even in your best outfit, and here I am… with him.

We step off the private jet (yes, private jet, still not over it), and I immediately regret everything in my bag. This is not a hoodie-and-docs kind of destination, but that's exactly what I packed, and Maverick, the smug bastard, is grinning like it's the best entertainment he's had in weeks.

"Don't say a word," I warn him, holding up a finger as I yank my over-sized hoodie down.

"I didn't," he says, hands up like he's innocent. "Yet."

His place is… insane. It's not flashy. It's just him. Sleek lines, deep blues and greys, framed photos of races and teammates and moments that clearly mean something. There's a view of the marina from the living room and a balcony that looks like it was built for late-night wine and sex. I can already picture us there. That's dangerous. I drop my bag by the doorway and wander in like I'm trying not to disturb the air.

"You actually live here?" I ask, eyeing the giant sectional lounge and open-plan kitchen that looks straight out of a Netflix cooking show.

"Yeah," he says, coming up behind me, wrapping his arms around my waist. "It's not much—"

"Don't finish that sentence," I interrupt. "You live in Monaco, Maverick. That's not a 'not much' situation." He laughs and presses a kiss to my temple.

God, stop being so perfect — that's what I want to say, but I don't because a part of me likes it. More than likes it, and that's what scares me. I spend the afternoon unpacking my very limited wardrobe, wondering how the hell I ended up here. A week ago, I was sitting at my desk, convincing myself I didn't care that he kissed me in public. Now I'm in Monaco, contemplating a nap on his designer lounge. This is not my life. But it is for the next two weeks. And maybe, if I can silence the voices in my head and if I let myself, maybe longer. Maverick orders food (of course, he has the best sushi place on speed dial), and we eat out on the balcony, the air crisp but not cold, the stars just starting to show themselves. He tells me stories about races and rivalries, about sneaking his buddy Drew into the paddock at sixteen and getting caught by a former world champ. I laugh so hard I nearly choke on my wine.

There's no pressure. No expectations. Just us. When the night gets quiet, and I find myself barefoot in one of his hoodies, curled up against him on the lounge, I realise I haven't thought about running once since I landed. Maybe I don't want to. Not this time.

"Feels better now that you're here."

TWENTY-FIVE

SAGE

Post-lunch haze settles over us like a blanket—lazy, sun- warmed, and deceptively soft. Mavericks in those grey sweatpants — the ones that should be illegal. He knows what they do to me, and I'm curled into his side, letting some trashy reality show play in the background, not really watching. His hand is in my hair, mindlessly stroking, and everything feels quiet. Easy. Good. Then his phone buzzes, and he stiffens beneath me. Not noticeably, maybe not to anyone else—but I feel it. A subtle tightening in his chest, his breath catching like he's already halfway somewhere else.

"Team," he mutters, barely above a whisper. He shifts me gently, with practised care, like he's done this before, peeling himself out from under me and disappearing out onto the balcony with a speed that doesn't match the mood. I don't mean to listen. But I don't exactly try not to either.

"I said I'll handle it." His voice is low, sharp around the edges. "No, I haven't told her yet. Because it's not the right time and frankly none of the team's business. Just—back off, alright?" Then a beat. Silence. I can practically hear a breath tighten in his chest. "…I know what I'm doing."

When he comes back inside, he's wearing a version of his face I don't quite recognise. Smiling, light, offhanded, like nothing happened as I imagined it. He kisses the top of my head, tosses his phone on the kitchen counter, and mutters something about being out of milk. But something in the air has shifted. It's subtle at first. A little quieter. A little more carefully. He still pulls me into his arms at night, still kisses me like I'm air, but there's a sliver of distance threaded between us. Not cold. Not cruel. Just withheld. Like, something is occupying his mind that I'm not invited into.

By dinnertime, I've had enough. We're walking along the marina—sun setting, boats bobbing gently in the water, the whole thing obnoxiously romantic. Josie would've gagged. Margot would've demanded a photo. I stop in my tracks, my fingers tightening around his.

"Who was on the phone?" He looks at me like I've slapped him. Not because he's surprised by the question—he's surprised I asked it.

"Sage…"

"Don't 'Sage' me." I cross my arms, holding his gaze. "I heard you. You're hiding something, and I don't do secrets well." He exhales. Runs a hand through his hair like he's trying to untangle his thoughts.

"They want me to clean things up," he says eventually. "PR. The team. After the crash. After the photos of us."

"Clean things up." The words hit like a stone. He winces. "They think I'm… distracted. Or that you are. Or both.

They want control back. They don't like unknown variables, and you —" he breaks off. "You're not part of their plan."

"So, I'm a problem," I say, my voice quiet but steady. "A complication."

"No." His answer is quick, fierce. "You're not a problem, Sage. You're mine." That should soothe something in me, but I'm still standing here, wondering if the world I've only just dipped my toes into is a world that's already trying to spit me out.

We walk home in silence. His hand holds mine, but loosely. Neither of us is sure whether to hold tighter or let go. That night, I didn't sleep. I lie beside him, watching the shadows shift across the ceiling, listening to the rise and fall of his breathing and wondering if this is how the unravelling begins. Quiet. Gentle. It's almost like love sneaking up on you when you're not paying attention.

MAVERICK

I wake before Sage. It's still early, just past six; the sky outside is a dull wash of grey blue. Sage is lying beside me, on her side, facing away, the sheet tangled at her hips like she'd been restless all night. I don't think she ever really fell asleep. Neither did I.

There's a kind of silence between us now. Strained, like a breath held for too long. The kind of silence that's waiting for one of us to flinch first. I shift onto my side and watch her. Her hair's a mess, falling over her bare shoulder. There's a tiny crease in her forehead, like even her dreams weren't kind to her. I used to know exactly how to smooth that tension away, my mouth on her neck, my hand on her thigh, some whispered joke that made her eyes crinkle and her lips soften.

But last night, she didn't lean into me when I reached for her. Didn't meet me halfway. And I knew. I fucking knew. She'd heard more than she let on. I scrub a hand down my face and stare up at the ceiling, listening to the ocean beyond the window. It's like there's a clock ticking inside my chest now. Not the countdown before a race, kind. Not adrenaline. Something slower. Heavier. Sage stirs beside me, and I turn my head just in time to see her shoulders shift, her body inching closer — but not all the way. Like instinct pulled her in, but whatever was still sitting in her gut stopped her from reaching me.

"Sage," I say, voice gravelly from sleep. She hums. Not turning over. Not speaking.

"I didn't lie to you."

Still nothing. "They want me focused. They want the media off my back. They think anything that doesn't fit into their little curated image is a distraction. That means you. And I hate that." I swallow. "I hate that I didn't say something sooner."

Her voice, when it comes, is quiet. "So why didn't you?" Because I was afraid. Because I knew how it would sound.

Because I didn't want to see that look in your eyes — the one that told me you were already building walls between us. But I don't say any of that.

"I thought I could fix it before it touched you."

She finally rolls onto her back, eyes open now, staring up like she doesn't want to meet my gaze. "Too late for that."

Fuck. I sit up, scrub my hand down my face, and stare down at her. "I don't want to protect a brand. I want to protect you. You're not a distraction. You're the only thing in my life that feels… real."

She turns to look at me then, eyes tired but fierce. "I don't need protecting, Maverick. I just need honesty. I can't handle when things get complicated, and for two people who have been fucking for less than 3 months, this is feeling complicated." and there it is. That line in the sand, the truth hanging between us.

I nod, jaw tight. "Okay. No more secrets."

She doesn't answer right away. Just holds my gaze like she's trying to decide if she believes me. If I've earned that trust back. And I realise — I might have to do more than promise it. I slide back down, shift closer, wrapping an arm around her waist. This time, she lets me. Her hand finds my chest, resting there. Not holding on, not yet — but not pulling away either. It's not fixed. But maybe it's not broken beyond repair. Not yet. Monaco feels different with Sage here. Lighter. Like the walls of my penthouse, once a quiet sanctuary, now hum with the sound of her laughter, her playlists, the way she taps her fingers on the kitchen counter when she's thinking. It's subtle, but everything's shifted. She's only been here for 3 days, and already my place smells like her — that scent that I associate with peace, that undercurrent of Sage I can't quite name but would recognise in a heartbeat. But something's still off. Of course, it is that she's questioning her place again.

I clock it over breakfast. She's quieter than usual. Her eyes flick up to me while she's eating her toast, but they don't stay. She's chewing on something that isn't food — and not just her lip. That's her tell. And I've seen it before. I give her space, hoping she'll bring it up when she's ready. She doesn't.

Later, as we walk through the marina — I'm showing her my favourite corner cafes; the gelato stand I swear by, the street where I crashed my first scooter when I was seventeen. I expect her to laugh, to tease me, but she's not really present. Her smile doesn't reach her eyes. By the time we're home, I can't ignore it anymore. She disappears into the bedroom while I make us drinks. When I come in, she's by the balcony, arms crossed, gaze fixed out at the harbour like it holds the answers. I hand her the glass. She takes it but doesn't drink.

"Talk to me," I whisper.

She turns, finally meeting my eyes, and there it is — the storm she's been hiding all day.

"This place," she says, voice quiet but steady. "It's not real life."

I furrow my brow. "What do you mean?"

"This… us. Here. In this beautiful apartment, with silk sheets and zero responsibilities — it's not sustainable. It's not who I am." Ah. There it is. The pushback. The retreat.

"It doesn't have to be some fantasy," I say carefully. "It can just be… us, figuring it out. Together." She looks at me like I've said something impossible.

"I don't know how to do that, Maverick." I move closer, slow and deliberate. "Then let me show you."

She shakes her head, a bitter smile playing on her lips. "And what happens when you go back to the races, and I go back to Melbourne, and we're both just… ghosts in each other's inboxes?"

I reach for her hand. She lets me. "Then we figure out how not to be ghosts."

She lets out a long sigh. It sounds like surrender. Not to me — but to the possibility that this might actually be real.

"I didn't come here to fall for you, but here I am fighting my feelings every step of the way," she whispers.

"I didn't plan to crash into a wall either, but it got me here." That earns me a faint smile. I pull her in. She lets me. We just stand there, wrapped around each other in the middle of the too-expensive, too-perfect apartment that suddenly feels just right because she's in it. I don't know where we go from here. But I know I'm not letting her walk away without a fight.

TWENTY-SIX

SAGE

These two weeks are almost over, and I'm already dreading the goodbye.

Monaco has been a dream, the kind you don't want to wake up from. Ocean views and quiet mornings. Maverick is in the kitchen making coffee in nothing but boxer briefs. Lazy afternoons tangled in each other, followed by dinner on terraces that smell like salt air and rosemary. We've only got four days left before I head back to Melbourne, and he flies to Miami for the next race. Four days before the bubble bursts. I should soak up every second of this, but I feel myself pulling back. Retreating. Preparing for the fall. I'm too hard to love. Maverick has a photo shoot today — some sponsor thing he couldn't get out of. He asked me to come, but I made an excuse. I needed space. And after that phone call, I needed a full-blown escape.

So, I decided to wander around Monaco on foot. Take the cobbled streets like they might answer all the questions spinning in my head. I walk along the harbour, watch yachts I'll never understand the price tag of, and slip into a cafe with a view and a damn good croissant. And then I call Josie.

"Hey, Mrs Carter, how's the luxury life treating you?" That's it. That's all it takes. The damn bursts.

"It's not real, Josie. I'm not cut out for this. I got a phone call yesterday from someone on his team — asking if I'm going to travel with him this season. Like some glamorous plus-one. It's like I'm his wife or publicist or whatever title I'm supposed to have, and before that, he got a phone call from the team telling him I was a distraction and that I'm not media-trained. He needs to clean it up. And I panicked. Completely. I didn't even know what to say. Because I can't do this. I'm not built for this life. I don't belong here. This isn't me."

I stop to take a shaky breath. Josie doesn't interrupt — she never does when I need to unravel. "I mean, look at where I am, Jo. Monaco. With him. Everything is perfect, and that's the problem. I don't know how to function perfectly. I'm waiting for it to fall apart. Or worse… for me to ruin it." There's a pause on her end, then a soft sigh.

"You haven't ruined anything, Sage. You've just never had safe before. You don't know how to stand still in it." I blink, letting that sink in.

"You're not running because it's wrong," she continues, You're running because it might actually be right, and that scares the shit out of you." I let that sit. It makes my chest ache — because she's right.

"But", Josie adds, "you don't have to decide your entire future today. You just have to decide if you want this, if you want him, this life, what-ever shape it takes — more than you want the comfort of your escape plan."

I look out over the marina, sunlight flickering off the water, and I think about Maverick — the way he looks at me like I'm not broken. The way he doesn't ask me to be anything but myself. "I don't know how not to run," I admit.

"Well," she says gently, "then maybe it's time to let someone catch you."

I let myself back into Maverick's apartment, Josie's words still swirling in my head like a storm I can't shake. Maybe it's time to let someone catch you. She's right. I hate that she's right. And worse—I'm scared she's right. My brain is a mess. Spinning. I need a shower. And a margarita. Preferably both at once. I toss my keys on the kitchen counter and wander toward the bedroom, toeing off my shoes as I go. But when I push open the door, I stop cold. Mouth agape. Laid out on the bed like something out of a maga-zine is a sleek black dress with pearl straps, paired with matching black heels and a Chanel bag that probably costs more than my mortgage repayments. Tucked beneath the strap is a folded note in his unmistakably clean, confident handwriting:

Sage,

I'm picking you up at 7. Shower, pamper, and put this on. I think it's time we made some decisions.

Can't wait to see you in this. My girl

— M.

My girl. God, this man.

I clutch the note to my chest for a beat longer than necessary. I know I should question this—his certainty, this life, all of it—but instead, I'm floating. He sees me, he thinks about me. Knew exactly what I'd need before I even asked. With a dreamy little sigh, I undress, peeling off my wrinkled clothes and slipping into the ensuite. I take my time, have a full body shower, shave, exfoliate, and I even use a face mask I found in his guest bathroom drawer (bless his assistant) and moisturise until I feel brand new. By the time I slide the dress on, I swear it sighs against my skin. It's elegant and dangerously fitted, hugging me in all the right places like it was made for me. I glance in the mirror. Jesus. I look… hot. Like, rich-wife-hot. I twist for a better look and pause—panty line. Nope. Not tonight. I slide them off, toss them on the floor, and just as I'm slipping on the heels, there's a soft knock.

"Sage, baby, you in there?" Maverick's voice slides through the door like silk.

I swallow hard at the *'baby'*.

"Yeah, come in." The door cracks open. He steps in, and the moment his eyes land on me, he freezes.

"Damn," he breathes, gaze trailing from my eyes to my lips to the way the dress clings to my hips.

"You're… you're perfect." He walks toward me slowly, reverently, like he's scared I'll disappear. He reaches out, his hand brushing the small of my back—and then pauses. His eyes flick downward.

Shit. My panties. Still on the floor. Black lace in a sea of cream carpet.

He arches a brow, a smirk tugging at the corner of his mouth. "You planning on needing a quick escape, or…?" I roll my eyes.

"They were ruining the lines of the dress. Fashion sacrifice."

He closes the distance, hands framing my face. His thumbs brush along my cheekbones — gentle, grounding. He kisses me soft and slow, and I melt like wax under a flame. We stay there for a moment, just breathing, touching, not saying anything. It's calm. Safe.

"Remind me to personally thank whoever designed that dress."

Eventually, he pulls back just enough to whisper, "You ready?" I nod, heart full and eyes wide. For dinner? For the conversation? For everything? Maybe not. But I'm starting to believe that doesn't matter. Because if Maverick Carter is offering me a place beside him—in his world, his life, his heart—maybe, for once, I don't have to run. Maybe, for once, I'm already home.

MAVERICK

I've driven the streets of Monaco a thousand times but tonight feels different. She's in the car beside me — quiet, composed, her legs crossed in that dress I picked out like I knew exactly how it would cling to her. Because I did. Knowing she has no panties on is making my cock strain against the zipper of my pants and it's making this drive unbearable. My hand is on her thigh, so I move it up higher, brushing the tip of my finger over her pussy just to tease her a bit and she's soaking the passenger seat of my G-Wagon. I wanted her to feel powerful in it. Desired. Fucking undeniable, mission achieved. I'll have to deal with the no panties later.

Sage hasn't said much since we got in the car, but I catch the way she keeps running her fingers along the pearls of the dress, like they're made of questions. We pull up to a restaurant tucked into the cliffs—one of those places, where the clientele is whispered, not advertised. The hostess greets me by name and leads us through a low-lit dining room, all arched stone and candlelight, to a table by the glass windows overlooking the water. It's intimate. Intentional. I'm making a statement without saying a word.

"I've never seen you like this," Sage murmurs once we're seated, scanning the room.

"Like what?" I ask, lifting a brow. "Subtle," I smirk.

"I save subtlety for things that matter." Like her, the unspoken hangs between us, thick and sweet and terrifying.

We order. She lets me pick the wine because Sage knows it feels good to surrender something small. When the bottle arrives, I pour for both of us, watching her over the rim of my glass as she sips.

"Do you like it?" I ask. She nods. "It tastes expensive."

"It is."

She laughs softly. "Figures." There's a beat of silence as we both lean back in our chairs. I watch her. Not just the way she eats or smiles or fidgets, I'm watching the edges of her, like I'm trying to memorise who she is at this moment.

Sage clears her throat. "So, what's this dinner about?" My gaze doesn't waver. "You."

The way I say it—simple, direct—makes my heart lurch. "This dress, this restaurant… it feels like a send-off," she

says lightly, trying to keep it from sounding like a goodbye. "It's not." I lean in, hands resting on the table. "It's the opposite."

My pulse ticks up. "Okay…"

"I know I sprung a lot on you. Brought you here. Took you away from your life. Your job. You're everything." I pause. "But I also know you didn't hesitate when I needed you."

She glances down at her wineglass. "You didn't run," I whisper. "That means something to me." She finally meets my eyes. There's something vulnerable there—something raw and real that catches me off guard.

"I wanted to run," she admits. "You know that."

"I do." I nod. "But you didn't. If anything, you ran to me, and now, we've got a few days left before everything goes back to reality. Before I'm back in a car going 300km/h and you're back at a desk trying to forget all this happened."

"I won't forget," she says, more defensive than intended.

I smile, but it's soft. Touched. "Good. Because tomorrow night, I want to talk. Really, talk, I want us to decide about what's next. About us." The word lands like a stone in water.

"Is there an us?" She whispers.

I reach across the table and take her hand again, warm and steady. "There is an us, Sage. The only question is what kind we want to be."

The rest of dinner passes in a blur of delicate food, lingering glances, and slow, teasing smiles. But beneath it all is a steady hum of anticipation, like we're standing on the edge of something bigger. On the drive back, neither of us says much. We walk straight to the bedroom door; I brush her knuckles with my lips and then pull her into me for a kiss, and then, without thinking, I throw her over my shoulder and barge into the bedroom like a god damn caveman.

"This is for dripping all over my passenger seat," I say as my teeth drag down her ear.

SAGE

Maverick throws me on the bed like a man possessed. His eyes are dark, jaw tight, and he kneels over me like a man starved. He growls something about his passenger seat while dragging his teeth down my neck. I don't have time to catch my breath before he's pulling me upright with firm hands, kneeling in front of me like he's about to unwrap the most decadent gift. My dress slips off one strap at a time, his fingers careful, reverent almost. Then the zipper. He drags it down slowly, eyes locked on mine, like he's burning this into his memory. He lifts the dress over my head, and just like that, I'm bare before him. No bra. No panties. Just skin, nipple bars and goosebumps all over.

"Fuck," he breathes. "You really don't play fair, do you?" He lays me back down, and the worship begins. His lips trail from my collarbone to the swells of my breasts, then lower, skipping the places I desperately want him to touch. His tongue circles my nipple, slow and filthy, before he sucks hard, groaning as he flicks the barbell with his tongue. I arch for him, pulse hammering.

"You like that?" he murmurs against my skin, fingers already moving south. I can only moan, desperate and aching. When his fingers spread me open, Maverick lets out a low, guttural curse.

"Look at this pretty pussy," he mutters. "So wet for me already."

He dips one finger in, then two, slick sounds echoing in the room. My head falls back as he fucks me slow and deep, curling his fingers just right.

"You're dripping," he groans. "This tight little cunt's been waiting for me all day, huh?" My hips roll without permission. I'm needy, frantic. Every nerve in my body is on fire.

"Come for me, Sage. Show me who this pussy belongs to." The second he adds a third finger and hits that sweet spot,

I break. Back arched, body trembling, thighs clenched around his wrist, I come hard and messy all over his hand. But I'm not done. Not even close.

"I need more," I whisper. "Mav—please—"

He chuckles darkly. "Yeah, you do. That's my good girl." He doesn't make me wait. He positions himself between my thighs, the tip of his cock already rubbing against my soaked folds. My breath stutters. His cock is thick, heavy, flushed red and leaking. And all mine.

"Eyes on me," he says, grabbing my chin. I do. And he pushes in— slow, steady, torturously deep.

I moan loudly. My nails claw at his shoulders, grounding me as he fills me to the brim. "Fuck, Sage," he groans. "You feel like heaven." I whimper, legs wrapping around him. He starts to move, grinding into me with filthy purpose, hitting that spot that makes my brain short-circuit. The rhythm builds faster, deeper, until I'm teetering again.

He shifts my leg up over his shoulder and drives deeper. Slap. Slap. Slap. The sound is obscene. Soaked skin. Rough breath. The raw scent of sex. His thumb finds my clit again, pressing and circling. Evil man.

"You gonna give me another one, baby?" he growls.

I nod frantically, and then I'm gone. Screaming his name, as I come apart under him again, pulsing around his cock like it was made for it, me. Maverick breaks apart, he groans like a man possessed, snapping his hips one last time before burying himself deep and spilling inside me. Hot, thick, endless. His cum is leaking out of me as he pulls out and sits back on his knees watching it with pride, like he just painted a goddamn masterpiece. He collapses on top of me, breathing heavy.

"Jesus Christ," he mutters. "You're gonna kill me."

I laugh breathlessly, totally ruined. He wraps an arm around my waist and pulls me close, pressing a kiss to my sweaty forehead. We fall asleep like that — wrecked, sated, tangled in each other and smelling like sex.

I'm awake before Maverick this morning, out on the balcony, taking in the view. I don't know if I'll ever see it again. Maverick steps out behind me, two coffees in hand. He hands me one, then leans against the railing, close enough to touch but leaving a space between us. That space feels suddenly symbolic.

"I don't want to lose this," he says softly, eyes fixed on the horizon. "I don't want to lose you." My heart thuds hard. I wasn't expecting him to dive right in like that.

"But?" I ask because I know there's a but coming. "But we can't stay in this bubble forever. You go back to Melbourne, and I go to Miami. The season ramps up again. Press, races, flights, chaos."

I nod. "And all we are left with is late-night FaceTimes and stolen weekends. If we're lucky."

"I hate that," he says, jaw tightening. "I hate that being with you feels like something I have to fight for. It shouldn't be that hard."

"But it is," I whisper. "Because our lives don't match. Not really."

He turns to face me then, fully. "They don't match right now. But they could. If we wanted them to." I look at him, at this man who's handed me a fantasy and somehow made it feel real. "Are you saying you want me to move here? To Monaco?"

"I'm saying… I want you in my life. Every day. However, that works." I sit with that for a beat.

"And what about your life? The media. The paddock gossip. The constant spotlight. I'm not built for that, Maverick."

His eyes search mine. "Then we keep it ours. Private. Quiet. Protected. I'll do whatever I have to, Sage. I'll take the heat; I'll handle the noise. I just need to know you're not going to run." That cuts deep. Because I run. It's what I'm best at. I take a sip of wine, trying to steady the war inside me.

"And what happens when it gets hard? When I mess up?

When it's not perfect?"

"Then we figure it out. Together."

It's such a simple answer. So painfully simple. And maybe that's the point — maybe love doesn't have to be complicated to be real. I let out a shaky breath. "Okay. Let's try." Maverick blinks.

"Yeah?"

I nod. "I'll go back to Melbourne, sort things out. Talk to my boss. See what flexibility looks like. Maybe we will find a rhythm or something in between."

His smile is instant — wide and boyish and so full of relief I nearly cry. He pulls me into him, arms tight around my waist. "You have no idea how badly I needed to hear that."

I lean into his chest, heart pounding. "Just… promise me one thing."

"Anything."

"When it gets hard, don't shut me out. Don't protect me by pushing me away."

He pulls back just enough to look into my eyes. "Never. We're in this now." And just like that, we've made our decision. Together.

TWENTY-EIGHT

MAVERICK

That's it. Two weeks of domestic bliss, gone just like that, evaporated with the closing of a taxi door and the whoosh of an airport departure gate. I walked Sage to check in, kissed her goodbye at security and watched her disappear into the crowd. She turned around once, caught my eye, and gave me that soft, sad smile that kills me every time. Then, she was gone.

Now I'm heading the other way — to the private terminal, to the jet, to my job. The contrast couldn't be sharper. I nod to the team. No small talk. I slide my AirPods in and crank some music, and drop into my seat by the window. Outside, everything moves. Fuel trucks, cargo trolleys, engines roaring on the tarmac. But inside? All I can feel is stillness. Stillness and her absence.

We had two weeks. Fourteen days that felt both infinite and not nearly enough. Lazy mornings. Coffee in bed. Grocery runs. Sun-soaked balcony kisses. The way her laugh echoes off my kitchen walls. Her scent on my pillow. The way she looked when she thought I wasn't watching. It was everything I didn't know I was craving. And now it's gone.

Miami was a disaster. DNF. Mechanical failure. Barely made it to ten laps. Spent the rest of the race weekend simmering in frustration, missing her so viscerally it almost made me reckless. My engineer said I seemed off. Understatement.

Italy was better. P4. Decent points for the team. Clean race. But even then, crossing that line without someone waiting on the other side — someone who knows me, not just the number on the garage wall — made the result feel flat.

I don't tell anyone how I feel. Not my engineer. Not my trainer. Not even Drew. It's easier to keep my head down and pretend I'm fine. I text Sage. FaceTime her between sessions. Late-night calls from hotel beds where I lie under sterile lighting and dream about her curled beside me. But dreams aren't enough anymore. It's going to be two months. Two long, relentless, pitiless months without Sage.

I'm embarrassed about how much I miss her. Desperate isn't a good look, but that's what I am. I crave her. Her voice. Her touch. The way she grounds me when everything else is moving too damn fast. I'd give anything to go back to those quiet Monaco mornings. And Monaco is next. The crown jewel. My home race. My city. It should feel exciting. It should feel like something to look forward to.

But right now? All I can think about is how empty my apartment's going to feel when I walk through the door, and she's not waiting for me. And I know I can't ask her to come. She has a job. A life. Responsibilities. She can't just drop everything for me, even if that's all I want. She's not mine to keep in a glass case, to fly around the world on a whim. She's her. Independent. Fierce. Beautiful. She said she was going to work some things out in Melbourne, and I really hope she is. So, I suffer through another result. Another lonely race. Another night staring at the ceiling, wondering what the hell I'm doing. What's the point of chasing the world if I don't have her to share it with?

SAGE

It's been two months. Eight weeks. Fifty-six days of pretending like everything's fine. I'm still in Melbourne. Still at my desk. Still sipping lukewarm coffee in meetings, I don't care about. I answer emails. I go to dinner with Josie and Margot when she's in town. I fold laundry. I listen to Mav's voice through my phone at night and try not to let the space between us swallow me whole.

We talk every day. Text. Call. FaceTime. He tells me about practice sessions and tyre strategy, about post-race dinners and frustrating interviews. I listen. I tell him about office politics, Josie's latest date, and the supermarket being out of milk. We keep talking, but it's not enough. I miss him. And it's not just the sex — though, Jesus, I miss that too. It's him. His presence. The way I feel when I'm near him. Like, my world stops spinning so violently.

This afternoon, I cracked. I called Margot and Josie. Emergency wine night. I didn't even need to say anything when I walked into Josie's apartment — they just handed me a glass and cleared the lounge.

"So," Josie says, sipping her rosé like it's tea and we're at a garden party instead of a borderline emotional intervention. "Are you finally ready to admit you're completely and devastatingly in love with him?" I blink.

"Wow. No warm-up. Just diving straight in, huh?"

Margot kicks her feet up on the coffee table, already halfway through her glass. "There's no point sugar-coating it, babe. You've been a ghost since you got back. You flinch every time the word 'Monaco' comes up."

"I don't flinch," I say too quickly.

Josie raises an eyebrow. "You do. And you also avoid his name like it's cursed."

I sink deeper into the cushions. "Because I miss him, okay? I miss him so much, it's like this physical thing. I walk around all day pretending like I'm fine, and I'm not."

Margot softens. "So why don't you do something about it?"

"Like what?" I exhale. "Quit my job? Pack up and move to a city where I don't know anyone, where he's away more than he's home. Be the mysterious girlfriend who floats in and out of the paddock but has no identity of her own?" I pause.

"This man has come into my life and broken every rule I've put in place, rules to protect myself. We've been having sex, unprotected, and we still barely know each other. I'm not ready for that"

Josie leans forward. "Or… be the girl who takes a chance on something real. On someone who makes you feel safe. Who clearly loves the shit out of you."

"He hasn't said that, I murmur.

Margot shrugs. "He doesn't have to. That man would launch himself into a wall for you." I smile, despite myself. "He already did, technically."

Josie giggles, then grabs my hand. "Look. You're not choosing between your identity and him. You're choosing what kind of life you want. You can still work, Sage. You can freelance, consult — hell, launch your own brand. You're smart and capable, and you're allowed to change the plan."

I stare down at my wine glass. The idea terrifies me, but what terrifies me more is waking up a year from now, still here, still aching for something that slipped away because I was too afraid to leap.

"I'm scared," I whisper.

"That's how you know it's worth it," Margot says. "You're not running away; we won't let you. This time, you're running toward something." There's a long silence.

And then Josie, ever the chaos queen, smirks. "Also? You'd be doing a public service by going and taking Maverick Carter off the market permanently." I laugh. I laugh. And for the first time in weeks, I feel like I'm breathing again.

TWENTY-NINE

MAVERICK

I can't take it anymore.

I know I told her I'd give her time. Told myself I'd be patient, supportive and calm. But it's been weeks. Every conversation skirts around it. She tells me about her day; I tell her about mine, and we both pretend like there's not a giant fucking question mark hanging over us. I can't keep walking around like I'm not waiting for the floor to drop out from under me. So, I call her. It's early in Melbourne, and she sounds tired when she answers.

"Mav?" she says softly, sleep-worn and a little breathless. "Is everything okay?"

I hate that she's worried. I hate that I've made her panic. But I can't back down now.

"Yeah, baby. Everything's okay." My voice is too hopeful, too tight. "I just wanted to talk. Properly talk. No more holding back." She's quiet for a beat.

I hear her sigh, like she's bracing herself. "Maverick, I can't... I'm on my way to work, and this isn't something I want to do over the phone."

"Sage," I say, my voice lifting, strained, "Just give me ten minutes. Just the rest of your drive. Please. This has to be done over the phone because I don't know when I'll see you again." I pause, and the next part falls out before I can stop it. "If ever."

There's a sharp inhale on the other end. It sounds like she's trying not to cry. "Just tell me," I continue, softer now, "am I here waiting for you? Waiting for something that isn't going to happen? Or are you coming to me? Are you working out a plan?"

There's silence. Then…

"Maverick," she says, and the way she says my name already sounds like surrender. "I need time. These things take time. I have to decide if I'm really going to give up my independence — the one thing I've worked so damn hard for — for something that feels a little too close to love. And love is… fucking terrifying."

Her voice is breaking. I can feel her unravelling through the line.

"I'm not normal," she chokes out. "I'm loaded with trauma. My flight instinct is stronger than my fight. Everyone I love leaves — my mum… dead. My dad barely talks to me. The rest of my family? They only love me because they feel obligated. All I really have in this world is Josie and Margot."

She pauses, and when she speaks again, she's crying — quietly, like she's trying to keep it together behind the wheel.

"I'm a mess, Maverick." She says it flat. No sugarcoating. "I drink too much. I use sex to shut my brain up. I'm a slut. It's my coping mechanism. I sit in my grief like it's a damn armchair and I have no real intention of getting out of it."

I say nothing, just let her continue. "My highs are reckless, and my lows are brutal, and I live in the lows more than I care to admit. I push people away. I ruin good things. It's what I do. I'm better alone because that's how I survive."

I breathe hard, feeling the ache settle in my ribs.

"I'm hard to love, Maverick, I've been told time and time again. I don't think I even deserve it. Happiness? Forever? That's not me. I'm not someone you build a life with—I'm the wild story before the real thing shows up." My jaw flexes. But still, I don't interrupt.

"You deserve someone soft. Certain. Someone who doesn't flinch when you get close. Someone who can love you the way you love, fully, fearlessly. I don't know how to do that. I can't give you what you deserve." She sighs.

"You don't want my heaviness, Mav. You don't deserve it."

I can't speak. Not right away. My chest is so tight I swear I can feel my heartbeat in my throat. I asked her to be honest. And now I've got it — all of it. The truth of her, stripped bare. She lays it all out like she's daring me to run. But I won't. I won't even flinch. I'll just pull her closer and make her feel wanted.

There's silence at both ends. A heavy one. She misreads it. "See?" she whispers through a sob. "I'm too broken for your world."

"Baby," I finally manage, my voice rough. "You're not broken. You're human. You're brave enough to carry all this and keep going. But you don't have to carry it alone. I don't want you to give up your independence for love. I want you to have both. I want us to figure out how to hold space for all of it — your past, your future, everything." She says nothing. I think she's still crying.

"I don't need soft, Sage. I don't need polished or perfect. I sure as hell don't need a woman who's got it all figured out. I need something real. I need raw. I need you." My words are slow but deliberate; I'm hoping they'll ground her. "You tell me you're messy? So am I. You say you're not built for forever? Good. Let's just start with tomorrow and figure the rest out later. You don't owe me some neatly wrapped version of yourself, Sage. You just have to stop trying to push me away every time you feel like you're not enough because you are enough. Even when you're low. Even when you're mean, or wild, or stuck in your own damn head—you are enough." I exhale the breath I didn't know I'd been holding.

"I'm not here for the fantasy, baby. I'm here for you. All the broken, brilliant, fuck-it-I'm-done parts. So, unless you can look me in the eye and tell me you don't want this—don't want me—I'm staying right here. I'm staying in this fight. And for the record," I add gently, "I want your heaviness. I want every piece of you, even the messy parts. I want a one-way ticket on your hot mess express. "

Then I chuckle softly, trying to lighten the air just a bit. "Also, did you just throw the word love in there? Are you trying to tell me something, babe?"

She laughs, just a small one, but it's enough. "Maverick," she says, steadier now, "the first time I tell someone I love them, it will not be over the phone." Damn. I thought I had her there. But then her voice changes; she's strong again, confident, the version of her I fell so hard for.

"Listen, babe," she says, "I've gotta go. I'm already late, and my boss lives for this stuff. But thank you… for listening. For letting me unload. Can we pick this up again later?"

"Of course," I say. I'd wait a thousand lifetimes for her, but I don't say that part. "Can I just ask you one more thing before you go?" I hear the hum of the ignition cut and her car door slam,

"Go on."

"The British Grand Prix is coming up," I start, pacing now, nervous as hell. "It's my home race. My favourite race. My family, friends, everyone will be there… and I want you there with me. You don't have to be in the public eye — we can keep it private. I'll hide you away in the hospitality suite. Just say yes. Bring Josie and Margot if it helps. Just… come." I ramble. I beg. I let it all pour out. She sighs, and it's hard to tell whether it's a no or a maybe or a goddamn yes.

"I'll think about it," she says finally. "I'll talk to the girls. I just… need time, Maverick. Okay?"

"Okay." I swallow my disappointment. "Baby… have a good day."

"You too. Good luck this weekend. I'll be watching." Then she's gone. The line goes dead. And I'm left staring at the ceiling, wondering if that was the beginning of the end… or the start of something real.

THIRTY

SAGE

After that phone call with Mav, I just sat in my car for a full ten minutes, just staring out the window, gripping the steering wheel like it could hold me together. I wanted to turn the ignition, drive home, curl up in bed and pretend none of this was happening. But if I didn't do it now, I knew I never would.

So, I walk into the office, drop my laptop bag onto my desk, and just sit while my thoughts are a riot, slamming into each other, but beneath all that chaos is this stillness, this certainty. I want to be loved by Maverick Carter, God; I want to. But wanting isn't the same as being capable of loving him back, and Maverick Carter deserves everything, and I'm afraid I'll only ever be half of anything. Unless I try, I should try. Fuck it! That's it. I'm doing it. I stand up and make my way over to Phil's office. He had the door cracked open, probably hoping someone would come in with gossip or coffee. Or both.

I knocked once. "Sage," he said, eyes lighting up like he expected something juicy. "Come in." I step in. Calm. Clear and weirdly, at peace.

"I'm quitting," I say, my voice steady. "This is my two-week notice. I'll send through the formal resignation this afternoon, but I wanted to give you a heads up."

His smug little smirk faltered for half a beat before he covered it with fake understanding.

"Is this because of the driver? The one you were caught kissing in China?" There it is. I knew that was coming. Of course, he couldn't resist.

I tilt my head and level him with a look. "No, Phil. It's not. I need a change. And if I don't force myself to make that change, I'm going to be stuck here forever. And if it was about that driver, that wouldn't be any of your business, anyway." Mic. Drop.

I turn and walk out without waiting for a response. God, that felt good. Liberating. Like shaking off years of fear and self-doubt in one sentence. But the truth? That was the easy part. The hard part was Josie. Margot, I wasn't worried about; she lives out of a suitcase and probably has three flights booked for next month. But Josie? She's rooted. Solid. Constant. She's home.

At lunch, I pull out my phone and send a message to the real estate agent:

> Me: Hey, I'd like to list my house for rent. I'm moving overseas. Can we talk about timing later today?

I hit send before I could talk myself out of it. That's it. It's real. Shit.

I text Josie next.

> Me: Sorry I missed you today—wild day. Can you come over tonight? Drinks? Need to talk.

Then to Margot:

> Me: You're still in the country, right? Come over. I have news.

I stared at my phone screen, my reflection faint in the black glass, and let reality settle over me. I'm leaving. I open my contacts and scroll to the one I'd been avoiding, Dad. My dad and I haven't been close since Mum died. He changed after we lost her, and I get it; grief does that. But it wasn't just grief... he shut down. Became someone I don't even recognise.

The man who raised me, the one who used to show me how to fix my car and take me riding on the weekends, is gone. What's left is distant. Cold, it's like being around me, is just too much for him now. And I know parents are human. I know they break too. But I still believe your kids should always come first. No matter what. And with my dad… I've not felt like a priority for a while now. Hell, I barely feel like his daughter anymore.

I hadn't told my family about Maverick yet. Haven't even hinted, I'm sure they've heard whispers, even though my name hasn't been mentioned, they'd still recognise me from the photos. But if I was going to do this right, I needed to tell them now. No dramatic last-minute airport calls. No secrets.

I hit dial before I could chicken out. "Hello?"

"Hey, Dad, it's me," I said, already wincing at how dry my mouth was.

"Sage, is everything okay?" I inhaled slowly.

"Yeah. I mean… sort of. I wanted to let you know I'm moving. To Europe."

A beat of silence. Then — "Europe?"

"Yeah. I've been seeing someone. He's based there, and I just... I want to try. I need to try." He says nothing for a moment. I brace for the speech. The passive-aggressive concern. The guilt. But instead, he said softly,

"You're running away again, are you?"

"No," I whisper. "I'm running toward something." Another pause. Then he sighs.

"Okay. Thank you for telling me, and Sage?"

"Yeah?"

"I hope it makes you happy. Really."

When I hang up, I stare at the screen again, dazed. It was all falling into place—and yet, nothing feels solid. It's like walking into the ocean, unsure of how far the floor drops off.

Tonight, I'd tell the girls, and then, I'd pack up my life. Fuck, I'm really doing this.

THE CORK POPS on a bottle of Prosecco just as Josie walks through the door, kicking off her heels like she owns the place. Margot's already perched on the lounge; legs tucked under her in some boho linen jumpsuit that only she could pull off on a Wednesday night. There's a candle burning on the kitchen bench, and the faint hum of Fleetwood Mac playing in the background. It's cozy. Comforting. Exactly what I need for the conversation I'm about to drop like a grenade in the middle of girls' night.

"Alright, woman," Josie says, plopping down next to Margot and grabbing the flute I pour for her. "You've been cagey as hell and avoiding me all day. What gives?"

I swallow a nervous laugh and pass Margot her glass, then grab mine.

"Okay. First of all, thank you both for coming. And second of all, you're not allowed to yell at me."

Josie narrows her eyes. "If you start with some vague 'I've been doing some thinking' monologue, I swear to God, I will tackle you before the sentence ends." Margot just sips her Prosecco like she's waiting for the drama to unfold, a small, amused smirk pulling at her lips.

"This is about Maverick, isn't it?"

I blink at her. "Wait, how—?"

"I have instincts," she replies, raising her brows. "And you've had 'existential crisis disguised as a European fantasy' written all over you since you got back."

I laugh, but it's a little watery. I sit down, tucking my knees under me on the armchair. "I handed in my notice today. I'm moving. To Europe."

Josie stares at me. The kind of stare where her brain is buffering. Margot's jaw drops and then quickly morphs into a proud, beaming smile.

"You're what?" Josie finally squeaks.

"I'm moving to Monaco." I take a deep breath. "I've already told my landlord I'm putting the house up for rent. And I've started the visa process today. Maverick asked me to share his life with him. I don't know what I'll do yet, exactly career-wise, but even though I'm scared as hell, I know I need to go."

Margot practically whoops and launches off the lounge to wrap me in a hug. "YES. Yes, girl! Oh my God, I'm so proud of you. Screw the rules, go chase the hot race car driver and your European dreams."

Josie still hasn't moved.

"Jo?" I ask gently. "Say something."

She blinks hard, then grabs her Prosecco and takes the most dramatic gulp I've ever seen. "So… you're just leaving? Like leaving, leaving? What about our brunches and bottomless mimosas and bitching about Phil?" "

I laugh, tears already welling. "You can bitch about Phil to Margot. She knows him."

"Yeah, but it's not the same," Josie huffs, getting up and throwing herself on top of me in a clumsy hug. "Ugh, Sage. You're my person. And now you're gonna go live this bougie- ass Monte Carlo life and forget all about your broke- ass Melbourne roots."

"Never," I whisper, hugging her tighter. "You're both stuck with me. We are just gonna have a time difference now." We sit like that for a minute, wrapped in arms, sniffling into each other's hair—until Margot claps her hands

"Okay! I give us ten more minutes of emotional sobbing, and then we're ordering Thai, and I'm teaching you both how to say *'bitch'* in French."

Josie sniffles and raises her glass. "To bitches in Monaco."

"To bitches in Monaco," we all say, and clink our glasses together.

The night turns playful. We blast music, scroll through expensive European apartments we can't afford, and start a shared Pinterest board titled Monaco Babe Vibes. Josie insists on helping me pack when the time comes, even though she'll throw a tantrum over every pair of heels I try to leave behind. Margot's already plotting visits that align with race week- ends. It hits me in a quiet moment, watching them laugh on the floor of my home, surrounded by takeout containers and half- finished drinks. I'm scared, but I'm also ready. For love. For change. For something entirely stupid and new.

THIRTY-ONE

The two weeks went by quickly. The British GP is this weekend, and I'm all packed and ready to go. Actually, my entire life is packed up and on the way to Maverick's apartment in Monaco. I haven't told Maverick yet, even though we speak every day. I've got this plan to surprise him at the Grand Prix. The girls are coming with me, so they are in on the surprise, a part of it anyway. The three of us are on the way to the airport - Josie took a bunch of annual leave; she deserves it, and Margot, well, this is the norm for her. Maverick organised a jet for us because he was holding out hope that I'd come, but because I wanted to surprise him, we are flying commercial, economy unfortunately, because, well, I don't have his credit card… yet.

This flight is long, but the drinks are flowing, and Josie's already halfway through charming the flight attendant into giving us the good snacks. Margot's got her noise-cancelling headphones on and a face mask that screams do not disturb unless the plane is crashing. I, on the other hand, am two mini bottles of vodka deep and trying not to overthink every-thing. Keyword: trying.

Because I'm somewhere over god knows where, and Maverick Carter is the only thought in my head. It's ridiculous. I'm picturing his damn smirk. The way he says my name — like it's a promise and a challenge all at once. The way his hands know exactly what to do, and his eyes don't miss a thing. I sip my drink and stare out the window, like the clouds are going to offer up answers. They don't, of course, they don't. God, I miss him. UGH! What is happening to me?! It's not just the sex, though; let's be clear, the man is a goddamn menace in bed. I miss his laugh. His stupid early morning kisses. The way he looks at me is like I'm more than a distraction or a fling. Like I'm real. Like I matter. Which is terrifying, honestly, because falling for someone like Maverick? That's not in the plan. That's the kind of risk that can break you wide open. And I'm not sure I'd survive it twice. I down the rest of my vodka and pull the scratchy airline blanket tighter around me.

We've landed at Heathrow — three women, slightly drunk, borderline delusional, and running purely on adrenaline and poor decisions. Josie is arguing with the customs officer like it's her day job, Margot's got her sunglasses on inside like she's famous, and I'm dragging my suitcase with all the grace of a baby giraffe learning to walk. We booked a hotel close to the track because, for once, we were smart. The moment we got to the room, we collapsed like dramatic starlets after a press tour. Alarms set. Game faces are pending. Day one of the plan kicks off tomorrow. And I'm fucking spiralling. I keep asking the same question on repeat, like it's going to change the answer: 'What the hell am I doing?', but it's too late now. I'm in England. I'm jobless. Technically homeless. Emotionally… Well, let's not even open that box.

I'm going to his home Grand Prix, so I'm probably going to meet the Carters. His family. His friends and we haven't even labelled this yet, and I can already feel the spotlight turning toward me like a heat lamp.

"Carter's mystery girl returns!"

"On again, off again—can Maverick focus with her back in the picture?"

"Career crash incoming?"

I hate how easily the headlines write themselves. He's had a rough few races. Luck hasn't exactly been in his corner. But there's still time left in the season. Right. There has to be. Because if I've burned down my entire life to be here, if I've risked everything, then I need to believe this isn't just a story that ends with bad timing and broken pieces. I need to believe this is the start of something real. Preferably, though, after a sleep.

The sound of Josie snoring softly in the next bed pulls me out of my anxious, sleepy haze. My heart is already racing, and I haven't even gotten out of bed yet. It's Friday—Free Practice Day, surprise day and somewhere in the paddock, Maverick Carter is pacing, wondering why I've gone radio silent.

I roll over and pick up my phone. Five missed calls. Three voice notes. Ten texts.

> Playboy: Hey, baby, just checking in—are you okay?

> Playboy: Sage, it's been a day. You always answer. I'm kinda freaking out here, call me.

> Playboy: Okay, this silence thing is cruel. What's going on?

His last message was only thirty minutes ago.

> Playboy: I'm going mad not hearing your voice. Please, just text me. Anything.

God. This man. He'd probably charter a plane to Melbourne if he didn't hear from me by tonight. I sit up and stretch, the nerves instantly tightening in my stomach. Josie grumbles and throws a pillow over her face. Margot's already up, in her robe and sipping a disgusting green juice she somehow got her hands on.

"You're really doing it, huh?" she says, arching a brow as she scrolls on her phone.

"Too late to back out now," I mutter, brushing hair from my face and checking myself in the mirror.

"Remind me again why I thought surprising an international superstar unofficial fuck buddy boyfriend-thingy at the most high-pressure race of his season was a good idea?"

"Because", Josie says from under the pillow, "you're a little unhinged."

"Thanks," I say with an eye roll. She pops her head out and grins.

"It's a compliment."

We spend the next couple of hours getting ready like we're about to rob the Crown Jewels. Outfits are laid out with military precision, makeup bags explode across the hotel room like we're filming a Vogue tutorial, and Josie is applying eyeliner like it's a contact sport. We're not just getting dressed—we're staging an entrance.

We've already roped in a co-conspirator: Annabel, Maverick's assistant-slash-unwilling-accomplice. She's both terrified and thrilled to be part of *Operation Sage Surprise,* and honestly, same. Annabel has pulled strings I didn't even know existed—VIP paddock passes under fake names, wristbands smuggled into our hotel in an unmarked envelope like we're in a spy movie, and a plan to sneak us through the media zone into the driver's area just as the first practice session ends. Everything is choreographed down to the minute, and yet, I'm pacing the room like a bride before a runaway wedding. Because it's not just nerves. It's him. It's the fact that in a few hours, Maverick Carter will open the door and see me standing there.

As we pull up to Silverstone, the energy hits me like a wall. Fans everywhere. Flags, signs, roaring engines and distant cheers. This isn't just a race—it's his race. His home turf. The one that matters most. I check my phone one more time.

> Playboy: Whatever's going on, just know I love you. I really, really love you. And I miss you like hell.

I gasp.

Josie leans over my shoulder. "Oh, my God. He dropped the L-bomb."

"He typed it," I correct, heart pounding. "It's not official if it's in iMessage."

"Girl," Margot cuts in, "you flew to a different continent for this man. It's official. Now claim what's yours."

I'VE BEEN WANTING to send Maverick a spicy picture for a while. Good thing it's part two of the plan. So, I may or may not have had one (okay, two) prepared for this exact moment. It's the perfect distraction, and after not replying to his calls or texts for the past 30 hours, this is my way of answering… with style. Opening our message thread, I scroll past the increasingly concerned (and adorable) string of missed calls and voice notes. My heart squeezes for a second, but then I shake it off. He's about to get the surprise of his life, and I need to enjoy this moment. I attach two photos: one in a sultry red lace set, the other in vibrant orange. One of his team colours, the other a cheeky nod to his old team, just to mess with him a little.

> Me: Which one looks better?

I hit send, take a deep breath… and look up. Because I'm not just texting him from afar—I'm standing outside his driver's room in the paddock, watching through a narrow window where he's lounging with his phone in hand.

I watch his brows furrow as he opens the message. His jaw clenches. He zooms in, swiping between the two, studying each like it's a priceless piece of art. His eyes darken instantly, the effect deliciously visible even from out here. The way his body tenses, the way his lip's part like he's biting back a groan, it's so hot I have to clutch the window frame just to stay standing.

Maverick runs a hand through his hair, tugging it in that signature move of his that usually means he's stressed, but right now? Oh no. He's something else entirely. He leans back, still staring at the screen like it holds the answers to the universe. He shifts in his seat, his race suit half undone, hanging at his waist, and I can see the effect I've had on him. Holy hell.

"Fucking hell," I hear Maverick groan; it's almost primal.

I'm biting my lip so hard it might bruise. I know I shouldn't be watching him, not like this, not when he thinks he's alone, but I can't look away. He's unguarded, raw in a way I've never seen him before, all because of two little photos. His jaw is tight, breath shallow, chest rising and falling like he's been sprinting. I watch as he palms himself through his pants, slow and deliberate, and when he finally frees himself, God, it's like

I've been punched in the stomach. Thick, hard, achingly ready... all for me.

He's gorgeous like this, head tilted back, hips shifting up into his own grip as his hand moves in slow, hungry strokes. Every motion is for those pictures. For the version of me that only he gets to see. His eyes are locked on the screen, and the look on his face — wrecked, desperate, completely undone — makes heat bloom low in my stomach. Still no reply. But his body is telling me everything I need to know. He looks so good it hurts. I should turn away. Give him back his privacy, but I can't. I'm transfixed. Watching him stroke himself over me, watching him fall apart for me, and then he mouths something as he comes, hard, thick strings shooting all over the lounge in his driver's room. It's hard to make out, but I know that whisper. That name.

Sage.

That's my cue. I tear my eyes away and walk briskly to the door, cheeks flushed, heart pounding like I'm about to go into battle, leaving a puddle on the path behind. I knock once, then twice. On the other side of the door, I hear a thud, some scrambling, and then silence. Footsteps. The door creaks open. Maverick stands there shirtless, breathless, wild-eyed and completely still.

His voice, low and stunned, breaks the silence. "Sage? You've got to be kidding me." I smirk, trying to play it cool, but my heart is racing.

"Surprise," I whisper, looking up at him through my lashes. He doesn't say anything, just pulls me into his arms like he's afraid I'll vanish if he lets go.

THIRTY-TWO

MAVERICK

There's a knock at the door.

I nearly fall over trying to pull my suit back up, around my hips. My chest is still heaving, my body flushed, and my mind completely wrecked from the high of those damn photos Sage just sent. Red lace. Orange lace. I didn't even get a chance to reply before I lost every ounce of composure I had left. Who the hell is knocking?

I wipe the sweat off my forehead, grab a towel and toss it over the mess I've just made on the lounge. The knock comes again, softer this time, but persistent. I check my phone, just in case Sage sent another photo. I open the door cautiously, still adjusting my suit around my waist, and then I freeze. It's Sage. In the flesh. Hair wild from the British wind, cheeks flushed from either nerves or laughter or maybe both, and this look in her eyes I haven't seen since Monaco. A look that says: I'm here.

"Sage?" I say, like my brain doesn't believe what my eyes are seeing. "You've got to be kidding me?"

"Surprise," She shrugs, a smirk tugging at her lips. "I didn't like the idea of you jerking off to my photos alone."

I choke out a laugh, half-stunned, half turned on all over again.

"Jesus, woman. You almost gave me a heart attack."

"I thought you'd like the surprise."

"I love the surprise," I say, stepping aside and tugging her into the room, shutting the door behind her. The second it clicks shut, I spin her into my arms. "You're really here?"

She nods, her voice barely above a whisper. "I'm really here. I also enjoyed the show". She winks…. Wait, was she watching me? My heart pounds. I grip her hips like I'm afraid she'll disappear again, but she doesn't move. She just stares up at me with those eyes, so full of mischief and vulnerability and, damn it, maybe even something deeper.

"Why didn't you tell me?" I ask, brushing my hand over her cheek. "I've been losing my mind."

"Because I wanted this moment," she says, tipping her head toward my chest. "To see your face. To feel it… not through a phone screen. I wanted you to know that I'm here, with you in every way" Her hands slide around my waist, her fingers tugging at the fabric of my race suit. I kiss her again, slower this time. Like I've got all the time in the world. Like I'm finally kissing my future.

The British Grand Prix weekend always feels like a fever dream — fast-paced, over-packed and overflowing with pressure. But this year? It's pure madness. Not because of the media. Not because it's my home race, but because Sage is here. She's here, really here, and the minute I kissed her yesterday, my world tilted. It hasn't tilted back. Now it's Saturday qualifying day, and the paddock is in chaos. Cameras flash, team radios scream, Ricci is losing his mind over tyre strategy, and my mother's cornered me outside of the hospitality tent.

"Maverick Carter," she yells, hands on her hips, brows arched.

"Where is she? Did she come?"

I blink. "What?" Yeah, I might have been hopeful and let it slip to Mum that Sage might be here.

"The girl. The one who's finally made you look human again instead of like a brooding, overpaid robot." I rub a hand over my face.

"Mum, maybe now's not the—"

"Oh, don't you dare," she snaps. There's a gleam of excitement in her eyes. "You've been sulking for weeks. I saw the photos and heard the rumours, oh and don't think I haven't noticed the concerning lack of Instagram thirst traps. This girl must be something."

I don't get a chance to answer because suddenly, Sage appears, the timings like a damn rom-com. She's in jeans and one of my older team jackets that I swear she stole from my place in Monaco, hair tucked under a cap, sunglasses on, but it's her. Every molecule of me recognises her even in a crowd of hundreds.

"There she is, that's her, right?!" Mum declares like she's just spotted royalty. Sage hesitates, but then she sees me and smiles — nervous, genuine, beautiful.

I grab her hand and tug her forward. Press my lips to her ear and whisper, "I'm sorry".

"Sage, this is my mum, May. Mum—Sage." They shake hands, and I prepare for an awkward pause, but it never comes.

"So, you're the one who finally got through this thick- skulled boy's ego," Mum says, pulling Sage in for a quick hug.

Sage laughs, and I swear I melt right there in the gravel. "It wasn't easy," she teases, shooting me a look. "Took a few international flights and a lot of emotional blackmail." My mum loves her already. I can tell.

My dad gives her a quiet nod, his version of approval, and then grunts, "Hope you've got earplugs. These races are hell on the ears." She nods politely.

"Don't worry. I've been to one or two now."

My sister Eden is also here with her husband, Lachlan, and the kids in tow. Ziggy's already halfway up a tree, and Bowie's clinging to her dad's leg like she's part of his outfit. Chaos, as always. I glance over just in time to see Sage step into their orbit, totally unfazed. She smiles at Eden and Lachlan, introduces herself with that confident charm of hers and then, without hesitation, drops down to her knees in front of the kids.

"Hey there," she says gently, meeting them at eye level like it's the most natural thing in the world.

"You must be Ziggy and Bowie." Ziggy eyes her with immediate suspicion, then looks at me.

"Is she your girlfriend?" Sage just laughs, tossing a glance over her shoulder.

"Depends on who you ask," I murmur, and just like that, Bowie's tugging on the sleeve of Sage's dress, showing her some sparkly rock she found on the ground like it's a diamond. I don't even realise I'm smiling until Eden elbows me.

"She's a keeper," she whispers. Yeah. She really is. The whole thing is surreal. She's blending in like she's always been a part of this, like she belongs here. With me. But that's the easy part. The hard part is qualifying. We're on the back foot after yesterday's setup struggles, and every lap matters. The pressure's high, Ricci's voice is buzzing in my ear, and I'm gripping the wheel like it owes me rent, but every time I pass the pit straight and catch a glimpse of red in the garage, her red jacket, her grin, I drive harder.

We qualify for P2. Not pole position. But close enough to fight tomorrow. The team's ecstatic. The media's rabid. The chaos of it all makes my head spin, but through it all, I find her. After all the debriefs, the media obligations, the chaos, I find Sage tucked into a quiet corner of the garage with Josie and Margot laughing, arms crossed, eyes on me like I'm the only thing that matters. And I know. This race weekend might be madness, but Sage is my calm in the storm.

SAGE

It's Race Day, and I wake up to the sound of engines roaring in the distance and my heart hammering just as loud. Josie is passed out next to me, one leg flung over the covers, snoring softly like we didn't just sneak into bed four hours ago after a team dinner turned into a tequila-soaked celebration. Margot's already dressed, sipping espresso and muttering something about timing and pit walls and logistics like she works for the damn FIA. And me? I'm trying not to puke. It's nerves. Pure stomach-churning nerves. Maverick's race days feel like they belong to another planet. He's a different version of himself — laser- focused, intense, dialled in so tightly that I wonder how he breathes. I love him in that mode. But today is different. Today, I'm here. Not just watching from a screen or texting him good luck between meetings. I'm here on his turf, in the chaos, in the heartbeat.

I throw on jeans, a black tank, and that same red team jacket I wore yesterday. The one that still smells like him. Pull my hair into a low ponytail and throw on my sunglasses to hide the nerves sitting in my eyes.

The moment we step into the Silverstone paddock, it hits me. The buzz. The tension. The sheer weight of what this means for him. It's electric, alive, and somehow suffocating at the same time.

"Breathe, babe," Margot says, linking her arm with mine. I nod, pretending I can.

The team ushers us into the garage's hospitality area. Everything and everyone is moving so fast — media, mechanics, engineers, friends, family. Everyone has a job. Everyone has a purpose, and mine, I guess, is just to be here. I catch a glimpse of Maverick through the glass helmet in hand, suit zipped to the neck. He looks like a warrior walking into battle. Controlled fury in motion. My chest swells with something too big to name. He turns. Sees me and smiles. The kind of smile that cuts through the engines, the chaos and the nerves. The kind of smile that belongs just to me. I press a hand to the glass. He mirrors it with his own, palm to palm, separated only by the barrier between us.

"Come back to me," I mouth. He nods once. Firm. Certain. Then he's gone, helmet on, visor down, walking out like he was born for this.

The girls and I are watching from the garage with the Carters, headphones tight over our ears as the grid forms. It's Maverick's home race, and the crowd is wild—flags waving, chants echoing, a sea of Union Jacks and team colours. My hands won't stop shaking. The lights go out, and the world erupts. Twenty cars launch into the first turn like missiles. Maverick holds P2 through the chaos of Turn 1, then dives into an early battle with the leader. He's aggressive. Smart. The last of the late breakers. My heart's in my throat the entire time. I don't breathe for forty-four laps. The pit stop is clean. Strategy's perfect, but there's traffic, and tyre degradation, and a rogue yellow flag that throws everything sideways with ten laps to go.

Then…then he makes a move. A risky, wild, textbook Maverick Carter move. He takes the lead with four laps left and holds it. The entire garage is on its feet. Josie is gripping my arm. Margot's swearing into her comms even though she's not actually talking to anyone. I'm frozen. Eyes locked on the screen. Hands clutched in front of my mouth. When he crosses the line—P1, arms raised, the British crowd exploding — I break. Tears flood my eyes before I can stop them. Relief, pride, joy, all colliding into one unstoppable wave. He did it. He fucking did it, and then the realisation hits: he's going to come find me. I wipe at my eyes just in time to see him leap from the car, helmet off, smile wide, sweat glistening. With cameras in his face, the team swarming around him, everyone losing their minds. But he doesn't care about any of it. His eyes are on me. He jogs past the cameras, past the pit wall, past his own damn team and wraps me up in his arms, spinning me off the ground.

"You stayed," he says into my ear.

"I stayed," I whisper back. He kisses me. Right there. On the track. On camera. In front of everyone, in front of his family, and for once, I don't care about the headlines. Because this? This is everything I feared and everything I never want to live without again.

THIRTY-THREE

The race is over, and the summer break has officially begun, and yeah, P1 at my home Grand Prix was everything I'd hoped it would be. But somehow, that didn't feel like the real win this weekend. Having her here, my girl, my Sage, that's the victory I'll replay in my mind long after the checkered flag fades from memory.

The weekend has been pure chaos. I've barely had five minutes alone with her since Friday. She's been with the girls, doing whatever it is Aussie women do when they say things like *'one last horah.'* I don't know what that means, but I know this: tonight, she's mine. Fully, completely, uninterruptedly mine. We climb into my G-Wagon, and everything feels easy. Natural. No need to fill the silence. My hand settles on her thigh like it always belonged there. I take the long route out of the circuit, the one that avoids the crowd and gives me more time with her. Just to feel her here beside me. "Where are we going?" She asks, eyes soft with curiosity.

"My house", I say. "I want you all to myself tonight. No team. No chaos goblins, no interruptions," She smiles at that soft and secret and sinks back into the seat like she's home.

When we get inside, I barely get the door closed before I've got my hands on her, my mouth on hers. The kiss is raw and all-consuming and weeks overdue. I don't want to stop. I want to devour her, memorise her, tell her about every minute I've missed her, even though I thought about nothing but the way I'd hold her. But then her stomach growls. Loudly. We both laugh, heads resting against each other, catching our breath.

"Alright, alright," I say, backing up, "that's my cue to feed you." She offers to help, but I shoot her a grin and toss a kitchen towel over my shoulder.

"Hell no. Sit that sweet ass down and let me cook." She smirks but listens. Good girl.

The silence is easy. Comfortable. Until I ruin it by asking the one thing that's been burning a hole in my chest since she got here.

"When's your flight home?" I keep my eyes on the stove. "I'm on break now. Figured I'd fly back with you for a bit." Silence. I glance up just as a slow, smug smile spreads across her face.

"About that," she starts, teasing like she knows exactly what she's doing to me. My heart stutters.

"I'm not going home." Another pause, another hit to the chest. "I quit my job three weeks ago. My house is up for rent. My things are already boxed and on their way to Monaco, and I'm—". I don't let her finish.

My lips crash into hers, and I kiss her like I've been holding my breath for months because I have. I press her against the kitchen bench, pouring everything I'm feeling into her mouth. This is real. This is happening. She breaks the kiss, just slightly breathless, like she needs to say one more thing, and I know from that look there's a "but" coming. There is always a but coming.

"Mav," she says softly, "I'm scared. Like… shitting-myself scared."

I wrap my hands around her waist, grounding her.

"Babe, I'm here. Every step of the way. We'll make a plan. We'll find you a job if that's what you want. Hell, I'll even buy you your own apartment, so you never feel like we're moving too fast—" That laugh.

That deep, belly-laugh that starts in her chest and shoots straight to my dick.

"No, Maverick. That's not why I'm scared." Another pause. My world holds its breath. "I'm scared because I'm in like with you. So, fucking in like with you, and it terrifies me. Like, I'm disgusted with myself for how much I like you."

She grins as she says it, big and bright and honest. That's it. That's all it takes. I sweep her up in one move, toss her over my shoulder while she squeals and laughs, and head straight to the bedroom. I'm done waiting. She's mine now. And nothing or no one is going to keep me from loving the hell out of her.

SAGE

I'm over his shoulder, giggling like an idiot. His arm is locked around the back of my thighs, carrying me through the hallway and up the stairs of his London townhouse like he already owns me. Maybe he does. I don't even care. It's stupid how easy this feels. How much I want this. I want him. He kicks open the bedroom door like a man on a mission, and suddenly we're surrounded by soft shadows, warm light, and the faint scent of whatever cologne he always wears, the one that drives me completely out of my mind. He drops me gently onto the bed, climbs over me, and just looks. It's reverent. Soft. Like he's trying to convince himself I'm really here. That this is really happening.

I'm not sure when I stopped laughing — maybe sometime between Maverick's shoulder bumping into the wall and his over-the-top dramatic bedroom entrance — but I'm giddy, nervous, high on him. On this. He drops me onto the bed like I'm made of glass, but climbs over me like he's starved.

His arms bracket either side of my head, his eyes scanning every inch of my face like he's trying to memorise it. It's quiet, charged. My heart hammers in my chest, too full of everything as his thumb brushes the edge of my jaw, and I swear my heart stutters in my chest.

"You're really not going back?" he whispers.

I shake my head, unable to speak with the lump in my throat.

"Nope."

"You're really moving to Monaco? You're really going to give us a chance?"

"Yeah. I am."

He leans down and kisses me like the world is ending, like the only thing that matters is my mouth on his, his hands in my hair, his body pressing into mine. I feel like I've waited forever for this. For him, and somehow, it still feels brand new. I let my fingers slip beneath the hem of his shirt, slide up the warm skin of his stomach, and smile against his lips when he shivers under my touch.

"God, I've missed this," I whisper.

"You've ruined me," he murmurs into my neck, his breath hot and trembling.

"I've been walking around with a permanent hard-on for weeks."

I let out a breathy laugh, "Poor thing."

"I'm serious." He lifts his head. "You don't get it, do you? You turned my whole life inside out, and I wouldn't change a single thing." That hits somewhere low in my stomach. I swallow hard.

"You still sure about me? Because I'm not exactly low maintenance." He laughs—laughs—like that's the most ridiculous thing I could've said.

"Sage," he says, resting his forehead against mine. "I've seen your chaos. I want all of it. Every complicated, fiery, emotional, incredible part of you." My eyes sting. No one's ever said that to me before. No one's ever meant it. I reach up and touch his cheek, my thumb brushing the scruff on his jaw.

"Okay, but just remember that when I inevitably cry over some old playlist or yell at you for breathing too loudly."

He grins. "Can't wait."

I tug him down again, kissing him like I want to imprint the moment into my bloodstream. His hands slide under my thighs, pulling me closer, anchoring me to him. It's hungry and hot and tender all at once. This isn't just lust. Not tonight. This is what it feels like to be chosen, and I choose him right back. Every stubborn, charming, insanely talented piece of him has worn me down, and I don't know where this new life will take me. I don't know what job I'll end up with, or if I'll ever feel truly at home in a country that's not mine. But this? Him? This feels like home. He leans down, brushing his lips against mine once, then again, slow, careful, like he's still not convinced I won't vanish if he moves too fast. But I don't. I pull him in. I kiss him like I'm trying to quiet every doubt I've ever had. We've kissed before, obviously. But this? This feels like a promise. He kisses me like he means forever.

My fingers slide back up under his shirt, over warm skin and firm muscle. I tug it up, and he lets me pull it off, tossing it to the floor like we've done this a thousand times. Maybe we have, in dreams I never dared say out loud. He kisses me again, and it's deeper now, hotter, messier. His body pressed between my thighs, his hands greedy and reverent all at once. It's not just want. It's a relief. It's home.

Maverick kisses his way down my body, slow and torturous. It's killing me. I'm desperate for him, dripping ready. My hands are pulling at his hair as I feel Maverick's moans vibrating against my clit while he laps at my pussy with insatiable hunger. It's delicious the way his tongue glides through my slick folds, swirling his tongue around my clit while he lets out soft grunts that only push me closer to the edge. I'm squirming—completely, deliciously undone. My hands are grabbing at anything I can reach: the sheets, his hair, his back, the hand locked around my thigh like it owns me. And honestly? It does. Maverick's holding me in place, like he knows I'd try to escape the intensity if he let me. The pleasure is building hot, fast, overwhelming. There's definitely no need for reverse cowgirl with Maverick. He's a one-man wrecking crew. I'm so close, I can barely think. One flick of his tongue and I'm going to combust, be reduced to absolute rubble. And of course, he knows. He always knows.

That smug grin spreads across his face as he does it, slow, devastating, and precise. My whole body jerks, hips stuttering, thighs trembling around his head like I'm riding a lightning bolt. Maverick groans like he's starving and I'm his personal feast. He licks his lips, cocky and wild-eyed, like he's already planning round two. My moan catches in my throat as he yanks down his boxers in one rough movement, his cock already thick, flushed, and ready. He strokes it lazily while his eyes roam every inch of me like he's taking mental snapshots, committing me to memory. Then swiftly and seamlessly, he flips me onto my stomach. My cheek hits the cool sheet as he spreads my legs with firm, greedy hands. Rough but gentle. Like he knows I'll break, but he wants me to.

I gasp when he slides his fingers inside me, slow and filthy. The wet sound of it makes me blush and moan in the same breath.

"Fuuuck, baby," he groans, his voice ragged. "This is gonna be quick."

"Yeah?" I pant, glancing back at him. "You are sensational."

Then he presses his cock against my entrance, thick and hot and pulsing.

"Get up on all fours, Sage." There's a wicked grin in his voice. Bossy. British. Fucking lethal. I obey; how could I not? He grabs my hair and pulls me back against him until I'm arching. My heart is pounding out of my chest.

"Are you gonna be a good girl for me?" he growls into my ear.

I whimper, "Yes."

"Answer me properly, Sage." His voice goes steel.

"Yes, Maverick," I moan louder, my whole body begging for it.

His thumb finds my clit expertly and relentlessly, and then he's inside me. One long, slow thrust that has my eyes rolling back in my head. The stretch is insane. So thick, so deep.

"That's my girl," he groans, breath ragged. "Always taking me so fucking deep." He lets go of my hair, one hand wraps around my throat, the other hand grabs my hip, holding me steady as he pounds into me, deeper each time. It's almost too much.

"Fuck, Sage," he rasps, the sound nearly a whimper. "You feel like heaven." I'm gone. The pressure is blinding; my body is right on the edge.

"I'm… gonna come," I breathe, voice shaky.

"You can come," he pants, slamming into me, "but you better come screaming my fucking name." The dominance in his voice tips me over. My hand flies to my clit, circling fast.

"Yes, Maverick… yes—fuck—"

His voice is guttural now. "Show me how you like it, baby."

"FUCK, Maverick!" I scream, the orgasm ripping through me like a freight train.

"MAV…rick—"

It ends in a broken whisper as I pulse around him, clenching so tight I send him over the edge. His cock twitches, then I feel it hot and messy, his spilling deep inside me as he collapses over my back, panting, sweating, wrecked.

We stay like that, breath tangled, skin stuck together. He finally pulls out, and I shiver at the emptiness as I feel his release start to leak out. Then, like an absolutely obsessed man, he slides a finger through my folds and pushes his cum back in, only to shove his finger between my lips. The taste of us coats my tongue as I suck, heat tearing through me so fast it makes my head spin

"Maverick!" I gasp, jerking from the overstimulation. He just groans and flops beside me, wild hair, flushed cheeks, and that smug, sexy grin. I turn my head to face him, still panting, legs jelly, and then he says it, soft and simple, like it's just a fact of life.

"I love you, Sage. I fucking love you." and just like that, my whole chest cracks wide open.

"I'm scared." He stills, looking down at me like I've just said something sacred.

"Of what?"

"Of how fast this is moving. "

His breath catches. He thinks I'm going to run.

"I've never felt this way before," I whisper. "It's terrifying." His thumb brushes along my cheek.

"Then let's be terrified together." God. This man.

I smile through the sting in my chest and try not to cry. "You're going to regret saying that when I'm five lattes deep and crying over some documentary about abandoned dogs." He grins, lowering his lips to my neck.

"I'll stock tissues and lattes."

I laugh, this stupid, helpless sound and wrap my arms around his shoulders. I'm not sure when I decided to stop running. Maybe when I told him I wasn't going back. Maybe when I got on that plane. Maybe when he kissed me like he was done pretending, he couldn't breathe without me. But I'm here now. I'm in this. With him and whatever comes next… I'm not scared to face it anymore, not with him by my side.

THE SMELL of coffee drags me from sleep before the sunlight even does. For a second, I'm not sure where I am. The bed is too big. The room is too quiet. There's no tram clanging outside, no alarm blaring to remind me to get up for work because there is no work. Then I roll over, and there it is. His side of the bed is messy, warm and empty, but his hoodie is draped over the foot of the bed like a lifeline. London. Maverick. Last night. A grin stretches across my face before I can stop it. I pull on his hoodie. It smells like him and feels like safety, and I pad out into the kitchen, still half-asleep and probably a mess.

He's standing at the stove shirtless, wearing only grey sweats and bedhead, flipping something in a frying pan like he's been up for hours. When he hears me, he turns around with the cockiest damn smirk. He knew what he was doing. He knew that those grey sweatpants would make my stomach twist and my cunt clench around nothing. His ass always looked so good, and don't get me started on his thighs. I find myself staring, almost drooling over that outline of his dick. Who am I?

"There she is. Sleeping Beauty."

"I am definitely still asleep," I mumble, rubbing my eyes and making a beeline for the coffee mug he's already poured.

"I used the fancy beans. I thought it might soften the trauma of waking up somewhere new." I take a sip and groan.

"Okay. Fine. You can stay."

He laughs and turns back to the pan. "I've been downgraded from a one-night stand to roommate already?"

"No, you've been upgraded from international sex god to domestic sex god." I slide up onto one of the barstools and yawn. "It's a good look for you. What are we making?" He flips the pan with too much flair.

"Eggs. Toast. Maybe bacon, if you promise not to judge how much I eat."

"I've seen how much you eat."

"Wow. I pour my heart into these eggs, and you come for my appetite."

I giggle into my mug and glance around the space. It's sleek, warm, and impossibly clean. Like him, in a way. Calm on the outside, warmth underneath.

"So…" I toy with the rim of the mug. "What happens now?"

He glances over his shoulder. "Now? We eat. Then we lie around in bed for a disgusting amount of time, have a few more orgasms, maybe plan our future and maybe nap in the middle of it all. Depends on how hard the toast hits."

I roll my eyes "You know what I mean."

He plates the food, sets one in front of me, then leans on the counter across from me. "You mean the fact that you dropped your whole life to be with a man who hasn't even told you how he found out your name yet?"

I grin with a mouthful of toast. "Exactly."

"Well," he says, walking around to stand behind me, wrapping his arms around my waist. "Then I guess I'd better take you on a date and tell you before you realise, I'm a terrible investment."

I tilt my head up. "Maverick?"

"Yeah?"

"This is already the best investment I've ever made."

He kisses the top of my head and whispers, "Good. Because I plan on giving you serious returns." I wrinkle my nose.

"Was that a finance joke?" He groans and buries his face in my neck.

"I'm losing my touch." I laugh and feed him a bite of my toast.

"You're not. You're just in love."

He chews, swallows, and then presses a kiss to my cheek. "Yeah, I really fucking am."

THIRTY-FOUR

Group chat: Sass, Snarks and Secrets.

Josie: Welfare check! S you alive, or fucked to death? Also, bitches. LAST night in London. I expect heels, lashes, and at least one poor decision.

Margot: Hahaha, I'd be sad, but I hope it's the second one. What a story to tell, and yes, I'm already manifesting a tequila blackout and a mysterious bruise I can't explain.

Margot: Sage Davidson, died at the hands of Maverick Carter's god-like dick.

Josie: Okay, that's going on her headstone.

ME: OMG, will you two STOP! I'm alive.... Just ;) I have a dress that should be illegal. Zero chest support, maximum chaos. So, I'm down.

Josie: Yes. That's the energy. No thoughts, just hot. Hot Mess express behaviour but make it a relationship. Mrs. Caaaarrrter.

Margot: If we don't end the night dancing on furniture or getting politely kicked out of a private club, what was it all for?

Me: Nope, stop that Mrs. Carter shit. BTW his house here in London is holyfuckballs.

Josie: invite us over then.

Margot: Yeah, I want to snoop through a world champ's house.

Josie: M, you can't tell people you're going to snoop. **We can just do it while we go to the "bathroom".**

Margot: ;)

Me: No snooping, you demons.

Margot: You're the demon, the sex demon.

Josie: Can I have your little black book now?

Me: If you can find it.

Margot: Yeah, J, Score!

Margot: Margaritas and Karaoke.

Me: Oh, I'm so in! I guess y'all can get ready here. Let me check.

Both: AHHHH we're going to the fuck pad.

Me: *eye roll* Yeah, all good to pre-game here.

Josie: Bring a spare pair of panties just in case you "accidentally" end up at Mavericks.

Margot: Spoiler alert: all her panties are already there.

Me: Shut up. But also... yes.

Josie: Alright, ladies, pre-drinks at 7, regrets by midnight, and someone PLEASE hold my hair back this time.

Margot: Only if you promise not to flirt with the bartender while puking again.

Me: London won't know what hit it. Let's go out with a bang. Literally.

MAVERICK.

The girls have taken over my house, and honestly? I kinda like it. It's like glitter, tequila, and poor decisions exploded everywhere. My kitchen smells like citrus body spray and hot girl summer. Eyelashes are stuck to random surfaces like confetti. There's a bottle of Patrón sweating on the counter, and someone's country playlist is blasting like we're hosting a rodeo in Notting Hill.

I'm not going out with them tonight. Can you imagine the chaos if I showed up? The paps would have a field day, and I want them to enjoy their last night in London, not get dragged into my circus, but I am playing chauffeur. Which, let's be real, might be the most dangerous part of the evening, especially if Sage looks anything like I think she will. I yell up the stairs, already regretting it

"You lot ready yet?"

"Coming down now!" Sage shouts back and then, one by one, they descend like some kind of sexy girl gang sent from hell to test my self-control.

Josie's in a leather set that could cause accidents. I think her skirt qualifies as a belt. Margot's wearing… honestly, I think it's just a bra with ambition, and then, then there's Sage. Sweet. Actual. Hell.

She walks down in this strappy little leather dress that clings to every inch of her body like it was stitched by sin itself. I nearly pull a hamstring trying not to sprint back upstairs and throw on a button-down just to crash their girls' night. Jesus. She's unreal in sweats. But this? This is criminal. Actually, can I get this dress outlawed? Who do I talk to about passing legislation? I swallow hard and throw my keys in the air like I'm chill.

"Alright, come on, all of you—into the car."

The girls all scream, "Let's go, girls!" like a damn Shania Twain tribute act as they pile into the G-Wagon, makeup shimmering under the dome lights. Sage climbs into the front seat, legs crossed like she doesn't know she's murdering me slowly. I cannot. Stop. Looking.

My eyes keep drifting down her thighs. She keeps catching me, smirking like the smug little menace she is. I should not be allowed to drive in this condition. We make it to the club somehow, and they start piling out like it's prom night. But I catch Sage's wrist before she disappears into the crowd.

"Enjoy, baby," I say, low and playful.

"Oh, I will," she replies, flashing me a look that could burn down cities. I eye that damn dress one last time.

"You know… I'd prefer that on my bedroom floor. Maybe I should come, just to make sure every bloke in there knows those tits have been claimed."

She gives me a wide-eyed, fake innocent smile. "Oh, Mav…" she purrs. "You know we haven't labelled this yet, right? It's not official until it's official." Then she winks. WINKS.

My jaw drops. I blink at her, stunned into silence, which she clearly enjoys because she spins around with that wicked little hip sway, hair bouncing, while Josie and Margot cackle behind her like backup minions hyping the main villain. She glances back once, blows me a kiss, and vanishes into the crowd. I'm sitting here, hands gripping the steering wheel, dick rock hard, ego wounded, respect through the roof. Yeah… she's coming home to me tonight. And when she does, she's getting punished for that *'not official'* bullshit. Right after I get control of this boner in my pants. God help me on this ride home.

I'm trying to ignore the obvious tent in my pants as I hit the call button for Drew on the way home. If I'm going to be alone tonight, at least I could get a mate over and distract me with beer and banter… and try not to think about Sage in that dress. Not that it was going to work.

"Carter, mate! What's happening?" Drew singsongs through the car speakers.

"Not much," I reply, adjusting my seat like that's going to help.

"You free tonight? Thought you might want to swing by for a drink. The house is covered in glitter and terrible music, so it basically feels like a nightclub at this point."

"If only you had called an hour ago," he groans. "Just got to the club with some of the boys. You should come out, man." I laugh. "Yeah, not risking that. The media's been breathing down my neck. One photo and they'll have me married with twins by morning."

"More headlines, huh? What's the story this time, Playboy Carter is tamed by a mystery woman?"

I grin, shaking my head. "Something like that." He whistles.

"Well, shit. Didn't think I'd live to see the day. Playboy Carter pussy whipped." I cringe.

He's not wrong. "Shut up. Come round tomorrow. I'll fill you in."

"Deal. Later, lover boy."

The line goes dead, and I'm left alone with my thoughts and a hell of a problem in my pants.

By the time I get home, I'm still rock-hard just from replaying Sage stepping out of the car like a damn supermodel with legs for days and a smirk that promised trouble. That dress should be illegal. Hell, I'm going to file paperwork to get it banned. Or at least, demand she only wears it in my bedroom.

I make it up to the shower, stripping off like I'm on a mission. The second I step under the water, all I can think about is her—her voice, her scent, the way she blew me that cheeky little kiss like she knew exactly what she was doing. Water warming, I strip off and watch as my cock points straight at the mirror, God damn it - I jump under the water with a rainfall shower head, this shower is made for two, but it's just me tonight. I grab my cock and start stroking, slowly at first, but as the pressure builds, so does my speed. My left hand is pulling up and down on my cock, my right hand is keeping flat on the tiles, keeping my balance - eyes are closed, picturing Sage in that dress as she left my car… definitely keeping that in the spank bank. Three more long, hard strokes and I'm there, shooting my load all over the shower tiles - checking over my shoulder to see if she is watching again. By the time I step out, steam clinging to my skin and heart still pounding, I know one thing for sure: Sage better come home to me tonight because the next time I see her in that dress, I'm not letting her leave the room.

SAGE

"Maverick definitely went home and jerked it thinking about you in that dress," Josie practically yells over the music, zero shame, full volume.

"Absolutely not," I shot back, raising a brow. "He has some self-control… I think."

Margot nearly spits her drink. "Babe, did you see the tent situation happening in his pants the entire drive? The man looked like he was smuggling a damn baguette. You lucky bitch." I bite my lip, trying and failing not to smile. She's not wrong. Maverick could be in a GQ spread wearing boxers, and I'd still have to fan myself.

We're at least four margaritas deep each, and the DJ is killing it. There's a strobe light situation happening, someone's dancing like they're in a music video, and I'm seriously debating asking the DJ if he takes requests. If he plays the Kath & Kim theme song, I might cry from joy. Nights like these are why I love these girls. Josie and Margot are the calm in my chaos, or, more accurately, the chaos I choose repeatedly because it makes life ten times more fun.

Margot nudges me with her elbow and nods toward a group of guys lingering near the bar. Tall, rugby-built types. One in particular — dirty blond hair, white tee, some kind of fancy- ass designer pants can't seem to take his eyes off Josie.

"Should we gently shove her in his direction?" Margot whispers with a grin.

"Too late," I smirk. "Looks like he's making a move."

We watch, barely containing our laughter, as Designer Pants struts over like he owns the bar and says something to Jo. It's loud as hell, so we can't hear a word, but next thing we know, we're trailing behind the two of them toward a VIP table like tipsy little ducklings.

"You good, J?" I ask, the smugness practically dripping from my voice.

She shrugs, completely unbothered.

"Just wanted to see what all the fuss is about with British men."

Cheeky minx. I raise my glass in solidarity. God, I love my girls. Tonight's going to be a memory, and tomorrow's probably going to come with a hangover, and a voice note from Maverick demanding a private encore of this outfit. And honestly? I'm so okay with that.

We decided to call it a night around 1 am—mostly because it looked like Josie was two seconds away from experiencing a very hands-on introduction to British dick right there on the dance floor. Maverick said to call him when we were ready to come home, but I wasn't about to wake him to chauffeur our glitter-drenched, tequila-soaked asses around. So, we pile into a taxi — instead, myself, Margot, Josie, and… Designer Pants. Yes. He's still here. And apparently very attached to Jo's mouth.

I shoot Mav a quick text, though, a casual:

> Me: Hey, Playboy, might be a strange man in your kitchen tomorrow. Don't freak. He's probably harmless. Also, hot. X

That should do it. As we slide into the back of the taxi, Mr Fancy Pants climbs in after me, and that's when I see it — a flash. Like, paparazzi- level flash.

"Did someone just take my photo?" I ask Margot, half- laughing, half- scanning for TMZ. She shrugs.

"Maybe it was your secret admirer. Or maybe Designer Pants is famous, and we just hitched a ride with the next Prince Harry. Could be worse." Honestly fair.

Margot and I continue our party in the backseat like we're auditioning for a reality show. Meanwhile, Josie has fully entered another dimension, one where she's the only girl in the universe and her lips have a strict no Sage policy.

"Jo."

"JO."

"JOSIE!"

Nothing. Unless I grow a six-pack and a penis in the next five seconds, I don't stand a chance at getting her attention. Thankfully, Maverick's house isn't far. Margot has passed out against the window, mid-snore, and Josie and her flavour of the night are practically dry humping before the car even stops. We stumble out. I yank Margot out of the cab like a drunk toddler and watch Josie already tangled up with whatever his real name is on the footpath.

I punch in Mav's gate code like I own the place. We all shuffle in, heels in hand, dignity somewhere back at the bar. That's when Mr Fancy Pants speaks.

"What the fuck are we doing at Carter's house?" he whisper-yells. I freeze mid-step and whip around.

"Wait… you know Maverick?" Margot and Josie go still. This is suddenly very interesting.

"Yes," he replies, wide-eyed. "I'm Drew. We've known each other since primary school. My jaw drops.

"Wait, Drew? Mavericks mentioned a Drew once." He eyes me suspiciously.

" How do you know Maverick, and why do you know his gate code?"

Before I can even answer, Josie swoops in, smug as hell. "Because she's the future Mrs. Carter."

"JOSIE," I groan. "Stop. I'm not." But it's too late. Drew's face lights up like a Christmas tree.

"Shit. You're the girl? His girl?!" I smile, drunk and a little smug.

"Yeah. I am. I'm his girl."

Drew whistles low. "Well… this is going to be fun. Let's just not tell Mav I'm crashing here tonight. I'm guessing he didn't picture our first meeting happening post-make-out marathon with your best friend in the driveway."

"I know he didn't," I laugh. "But hey, I enjoy watching him squirm. It's hot."

Drew and Josie disappear down the hall, clearly ready to continue their... marathon. Margot barely makes it to the lounge before she face plants into sleep. And me? I tiptoe upstairs, quietly praying Maverick's still awake. I push open the bedroom door and peek in.

"Sage?" His voice comes through the dark, rough and sleepy.

"Yeah, babe. It's me."

Dress off, heels kicked into a corner, I give my face a quick wipe with a makeup wipe that probably expired last year and crawl into bed, naked, of course, curling up next to the man who's absolutely ruined me for anyone else. He's warm. He smells like heaven, and when his arm pulls me close, sleep is the last thing on my mind.

MAVERICK

I'm half-asleep when I hear the door creak open.

"Sage?"

Her voice answered, soft and sweet, "Yeah, babe, it's me" and fuck, that did something to me. Even in the dark, I could feel her presence fill the room, like everything just fell back into place the second she walked in.

She kicked off her heels with a little thud, and I caught the quiet rustle of her shimmying out of that goddamn dress— the one that's been driving me fucking insane since she stepped into the living room hours ago. I don't even need to look to know she's naked. I know her. Know the way she moves when she wants to be touched. Know the brief pause she takes before sliding under the covers, waiting, checking to see if I'm asleep. I'm not. I reach out and catch her wrist, tugging her straight into me, and the second her bare skin touches mine, I'm hard again. Instantly. Painfully. She's warm and soft and mine, and the second she curls her thigh over me, I growl low in my throat.

"You're killing me, baby," I murmur, lips brushing her ear.

She hums, smug. "I know."

I flip her onto her back in one motion, settling between her thighs. Her skin's still warm from dancing, flushed and a little dewy, and she smells like tequila and coconut and what I think is sweat. Fucking heaven. My hand drags down her chest, slow and teasing. I take my time with her breasts, circling her nipples with my thumb until she arches up into me, gasping when I suck one into my mouth.

"Maverick," she breathes, already writhing.

I move lower, licking and kissing my way down her stomach, nipping at her hipbones, her thighs. She's already wet. I haven't even touched her properly yet, and she's dripping for me.

"God, Sage," I groan, mouth hovering just above her cunt. "This for me?" She nods, but I want words. "Say it."

"Yes. It's for you, Mav," she whispers, voice wrecked.

I dive in like a starving man. My tongue finds her clit, and I circle it slowly, then fast, then slowly again until her hands are in my hair, pulling, tugging, nails dragging down my scalp like she's coming apart. She's loud when she comes, fuck hopefully this house is big enough to drown the sound, and I feel it ripple through her as she gasps my name again and again, thighs clamping around my head like she doesn't want to let me go. But I'm not done. I kiss my way back up her body, grip her thighs, line my cock up with her entrance, and slam into her in one hard, deep thrust. She cries out, nails raking down my back, and I swear I see stars. She's tight. Wet. Fucking perfect. And I have no patience left.

"You were such a tease tonight," I pant against her mouth as I start to thrust. "That dress? That look you gave me before you walked away like you didn't know I'd be jerking off thinking about it two minutes later?"

She laughs breathlessly, wrapping her legs around my waist. "You jerked off, didn't you?"

"Hell yeah, I did. I couldn't wait. But this—" I pull out and reach my hand down to cup her pussy and kiss her hard. "This is so much better, though."

I pound back into her, hips snapping against hers, watching her fall apart all over again. Her second orgasm hits fast, her body clenching around me like a vice, and I fucking lose it, gripping her waist, burying my face in her neck, and spilling deep inside her with a groan that shakes the walls. When it's over, we're both sweaty and gasping, tangled together in a mess of sheets and limbs. She's quiet for a minute, fingers tracing lazy circles over my chest.

"You're gunna be really smug about this in the morning, aren't you?" she mumbles. I grin in the dark, pressing a kiss to her forehead.

"Hell yeah, I am. I just made you scream my name loud enough for your friends to hear."

She laughs, soft and sleepy. "They definitely heard." I smile.

"While we are on the topic of your friends, who's this supposed mystery man?"

She laughs, "Josie's very own British sex-god."

I pull her closer and nuzzle into her shoulder. "Hmmm, good for her."

I WAKE up to the smell of coffee and the distant sound of someone talking in my kitchen. It's Not Sage. Definitely not Sage. She's still wrapped around me like a very naked, very satisfied little octopus, her leg slung over my hip and her arm across my chest. Her hair's a mess, mascara smudged under her eyes, lips swollen from everything I did to her last night. She looks like sin. My sin. And I'm about two seconds from dragging her back under me and making her late for whatever plans she had today. But the voices downstairs get louder. Both familiar, one of them too fucking familiar. I frown. No way. I ease Sage off me, grab a pair of sweatpants from the floor — no shirt, no dignity and pad downstairs like I'm walking into battle.

The second I round the corner into the kitchen, I stop dead. Drew is standing in my kitchen, wearing a pair of my sweatpants that I'm assuming he got out of the laundry and is helping himself to my cereal like he owns the place

"Drew?" He turns mid-bite, spoon halfway to his mouth, eyes wide.

"Maverick!" We both stare. I blink. He blinks. Then his face breaks into a wide, sheepish grin. "Surprise?"

"What the actual fuck are you doing in my kitchen?" He sets the spoon down slowly, like this is a hostage negotiation.

"Well… funny story, really. Met this hot Aussie last night—a bit wild, absolute freak on the dance floor - followed her home. Didn't realise her best friend was your girl. Or that her bed was in your house." Oh, the British sex god Josie brought home.

"You're telling me you fucked Josie. In my house."

"I mean… yeah?" He shrugs. "Would've been rude not to."

I scrub a hand down my face, torn between laughing and tossing him out the nearest window. Instead, I open the fridge, grab the orange juice, and drink straight from the bottle.

"Did you know whose house it was before or after you got here?"

He grins. "After. But Sage handled it well. Very welcoming. Honestly, mate, you've got a good one there."

I glance toward the stairs, where I can still hear soft footsteps and Josie's laugh echoing down the hall. "Don't I fucking know it."

Drew watches me, curiosity glinting behind the smugness. "So, it's serious then?"

I exhale, nod once. "Yeah. It is."

He whistles low. "Damn. Playboy Carter, out of the game."

"Playboy Carter is dead and buried, mate."

He chuckles. "So, when's the wedding?" I glare at him. He holds up both hands in surrender. "I'm kidding! Mostly."

I lean back against the counter, arms crossed, and nod to where Josie's voice is coming from. "Did she at least rock your world?"

He groans dramatically. "Bro. You have no idea. I think I saw God."

I snort. "That'll do it."

We stand there for a moment, two half-dressed idiots in a million-dollar kitchen, before I shake my head and grin. "You're cleaning whatever the fuck mess you two made last night, and don't eat all the cereal. That's Sage's favourite."

Drew salutes me with his spoon. "Yes, sir. Respectfully fucking your houseguest, reporting for duty." I sigh. This man is going to be the death of me, but at least breakfast will be entertaining.

SAGE

I'm halfway down the stairs when I hear Drew's voice and Maverick's very unimpressed grunt in response. Josie is behind me, looking way too smug for someone who had sex within five feet of a trophy cabinet. Margot follows us into the kitchen, hair in a pineapple bun, wearing one of Mav's t-shirts. Drew's sitting at the island shovelling cereal into his mouth while Maverick looks like he's trying not to throttle him with his bare hands.

"Well, good morning, lovers," I say, leaning against the doorway.

Josie blows me a kiss, then tosses a wink towards Drew. "Thanks for the hospitality, babe. Five stars. Would bang again." Mav mutters something that sounds suspiciously like *'never inviting anyone over again.'*

Drew grins, unfazed. "I told you the perfect hostess. And her best friend? Quite the woman." Josie takes a sip of her coffee like she didn't just make the entire room blush.

"You can write that in my Google review."

Margot slides onto a stool and snags a piece of toast off Maverick's plate, because apparently, personal boundaries don't exist in this house anymore.

"You boys having a little bromance reunion?" she teases.

Maverick shoots me a look. I shrug. "Don't blame me. I tried to tell them we should keep it low-key last night, but nooo—Josie had to find herself a surprise best friend with abs and a god complex."

Josie beams. "Guilty."

Drew raises his cereal bowl in salute.

Mav sighs and rubs his temples. "I need a stronger coffee. Or a tranquilliser."

The girls cackle. I can't help but laugh, too. But honestly? I think Maverick loves this. The girls take their breakfast into the backyard, Drew following them like a golden retriever in Maverick's sweats - not the grey ones, thankfully. I stay behind, grabbing a bottle of water from the fridge and padding upstairs, the hardwood cool beneath my bare feet.

Maverick's already there when I walk into the bedroom, shirtless, perched on the edge of the bed like he's been waiting for me. Maverick. Me. A messy bed and a little vulnerability. His eyes meet mine, and just like that, everything else fades.

"I missed you last night," he says, voice low and a little rough. I smile as I walk toward him.

"Missed you too." He pulls me onto his lap without hesitation, hands warm on my thighs as I straddle him. I lean in, brushing my nose against his.

"I take it that the bromantic breakfast went well?"

He snorts. "I swear to God, if I find one more half-naked childhood friend in my house…"

I laugh, then let the sound soften as I brush my fingers through his hair. There's a pause. A shift in the air. He looks up at me, quieter now. "You really told him you're my girl?"

"I did," I whisper. "Because I am." Something shifts behind his eyes. A flicker of that cocky grin, but there's something else now—something heavier, deeper. His hands slide up my sides, slow, possessive.

"You know what that does to me, Sage?" I smirk.

"I've got an idea."

He pulls me closer and slides his hips down, wrapping my legs around his in one smooth motion, my body covering his, his mouth already finding the curve of my throat.

"Well then," he murmurs, lips hot against my skin, "Let's see if you're right." And just like that, we forget about the leftover tequila, discarded heels, cereal bowls and half-naked houseguests. Because this—me and him, tangled up in each other, in this messy, wild, beautiful chaos. This is the only thing that matters. Maverick's body moves with mine, all heat and tension and muscle, his teeth grazing my ear, sending goosebumps down my spine. He sits me up, reaches to the floor and gently pulls the dress I wore last night over my head and down my shoulders. What is he up to?

"You wore that dress out…" he murmurs, voice thick with desire. "Knowing exactly what it'd do to me."

"I didn't wear it for them," I whisper, arching up into his weight. "I wore it for you."

A growl rumbles in his chest, and then his mouth crashes into mine — hungry, hot, claiming. His hands are everywhere, gripping my hips, hands sliding up my crumpled dress, pushing it down so my tits pop out, and he lets out a groan, "Fuck, Sage…"

I tug at the waistband of his sweats, fingers sliding underneath, brushing the hard line of him. He's already rock hard. Maverick hisses between his teeth, hips jerking into my touch.

"You gonna show me what that dress did to you?" I tease, breathless.

"Yeah, baby," he rasps, yanking the sweats down his hips and kicking them off. "But first…"

He shifts his body lower so I'm riding his face, spreading my legs with a touch that's confident, reverent, and just a little filthy. He drags his tongue over the inside of my thigh; eyes locked with mine.

"…I want a taste."

My head falls back as he licks up my centre, slow and purposeful, like he's savouring every second. His tongue flicks against my clit, and I cry out, hips bucking, hands in his hair. Maverick doesn't let up; he groans like I'm his favourite fucking meal and he's starving.

"You're so wet, Sage," he breathes against me. "Just for me"

"Always for you," I pant.

He sucks gently, fingers sliding inside me, curling until my vision blacks out. I come hard, soaking his face, moaning his name like a prayer, thighs trembling around his head, but Maverick doesn't stop. He keeps licking, keeps punishing me with his fingers, drawing out every aftershock until I'm twitching and gasping, oversensitive and absolutely wrecked. When he finally pulls back, his lips are shiny with my juices, and he's grinning like he just won the Grand Prix.

"You're a menace," I say, breathless.

"You love it," he replies, moving my body down.

He grips himself, sliding the head of his cock through my slick folds, teasing me. "You ready?"

I wrap my arms around his neck, pulling him closer. "Always."

He thrusts into me in one smooth stroke, and we both groan. He's big, thick and fucking perfect. The stretch between my legs burns in the best way. He holds still for a beat, forehead pressed to mine, breathing hard. "Fuck, Sage… you feel so good."

"Move," I beg, nails digging into his back.

His thrusts are deep, hard and relentless; I pick up his rhythm and start riding his cock in response. The headboard taps the wall. The bed creaks. My name tumbles from his mouth over and over like a chant, and I can't get enough of him, of us. Every grind of his hips sends me spiralling closer to the edge again. His hands palming my titis, my legs are shaking, pleasure coiling tight in my core.

"Gonna come again," I gasp. "Maverick—"

"Let go, baby," he pants, fucking me harder. "I've got you."

I shatter, riding him all the way, crying out, clinging to him like I'll float away. He follows seconds later, hips stuttering, coming with a deep, broken groan against my neck. We collapse in a tangled heap, sweat slicked skin and shaky breaths, his arms locked around me like he's never letting go.

"Okay," I murmur after a long moment, "that dress is definitely destroyed."

He chuckles, kissing my shoulder. "That was the plan."

THIRTY-SIX

SAGE

It's barely 10 a.m. and I've already had two orgasms, good ones, and my house — correction, Maverick's house — is an unhinged cocktail of chaos, luggage, leftover glitter, and a half- naked man still in the kitchen.

"Drew, I swear to God," Maverick yells, "Take my damn pants off and go home."

"I should just stay. I'm coming around for a beer this afternoon anyway," he argues, holding up a piece of burnt toast like it's a shield. "Also, I enjoy seeing domestic Maverick in action - could've done without hearing it though." He says with a wink.

Josie appears around the corner wearing a deeply satisfied smile. "Amen to that," she says, smacking Drew's ass on her way to the fridge. Margot's in the middle of sitting on her suitcase, trying to get the zipper to close while cursing in three languages and sipping an iced coffee. Total icon.

"What? I packed last night," she grumbles.

"When you were drunk. Why is there a single high heel, a vibrator, and a ladle in your bag?"

"You never know what international customs are into," Margot replies with a shrug. I'm laughing, but it's that kind of tight, high laugh that sits a little too close to something else. Something heavier.

They're leaving. My girls. My chaos wranglers. My reality checkers. My tequila-fuelled therapy team. And I suddenly feel like the air in the room has changed.

"Hey." Margot drops onto the lounge beside me, luggage forgotten. "You, okay?"

"Yeah," I lie, because it's instinct. Then I groan and bury my face in my hands. "No. Not really."

Josie flops down on my other side. "Talk to us, babe."

I sigh, chewing on the inside of my cheek. "It's just… What if this thing with Maverick is only good because it's temporary? Like a holiday romance. What happens when the novelty wears off and I'm still here, in his world, but I don't fit?"

Margot's face softens instantly. "You're not a novelty, Sage."

"You're the whole damn show," Josie adds.

"I know. I mean—thank you. But…" I trail off, heart thudding. "He's… Maverick Carter. He's used to supermodels, international travel, and having his life mapped out. I'm just… winging it. I don't even know what I'm doing when we go back to Monaco, let alone next year." They're both quiet for a second, which is how I know they're taking me seriously.

"Do you love him?" Margot asks softly.

The answer comes without hesitation. "Yes. Like, terrifyingly yes." I just haven't told him that yet.

"Then maybe stop trying to fit into his world," she says, "and realise he's already building space for you in it." I blink, swallowing the sudden lump in my throat.

"Damn it, Margot, when did you get so wise?"

"About three mimosas ago," she grins.

Josie nudges me with her knee. "And for the record, we've seen the way he looks at you. That man is gone. He's not going anywhere." I nod, sniffling and laughing at the same time.

"God, I'm going to miss you two idiots."

"We're going to miss you more," Margot says, pulling me into a hug that I melt into.

"But we're only a FaceTime meltdown away," Josie adds, sandwiching herself into the hug. "And if he ever fucks it up, we'll fly back and key his car."

"All of them," Margot confirms. "And shave his eyebrows in his sleep."

"I love you, lunatics," I murmur, eyes prickling.

"Good," Josie says. "Now help me pack. Before Drew steals all my undies," I laugh again, the pressure in my chest easing just a little. They're leaving… but I'm staying. And maybe that's the beginning of something, too.

MAVERICK

The front door clicks shut, and it's like someone hit mute on the world. No more Josie yelling across the house. No more Margot arguing with my smart fridge about the lack of coconut water. No more Drew wandering around like it's his damn house. Just silence. I walk back into the kitchen, where Sage is standing barefoot, leaning against the island, holding her coffee like it's anchoring her to the earth. The oversized hoodie she's wearing is mine. She must've grabbed it from my drawer this morning. She looks like she belongs here. Like this is what mornings were always meant to be. She doesn't speak, just watches me with those stormy eyes like she's waiting for something to crack.

"The house feels too quiet now," I say finally, rubbing a hand over my jaw as I stop across from her. She gives a small nod but doesn't look away.

"Yeah. It does."

"You, okay?" I ask, she hesitates. Just a flicker. But I caught it. "Sage."

She sighs and sets her mug down, crossing her arms over her chest. "I'm fine. Just… weird, I guess. They're gone. The last piece of home."

I step closer, slow, not wanting to crowd her, not physically. Emotionally? That's a whole other story.

"You can still leave, you know," I say, voice low. "If that's what you need. If this, us, ever feels like too much, or not enough…I'm more than willing to fly to Melbourne every chance I get, just as long as I get to be with you."

She shakes her head immediately. "That's not what I'm saying."

I nod once. "Then what are you saying?"

She looks up at me like she's searching for a way to say it without unravelling.

"I've just never… stayed. Not like this. Not long enough to picture things. Morning coffees. My clothes in your drawers. Your toothbrush next to mine."

I let that sink in. Let it punch me in the ribs a little, because fuck, I get it. I move to her, wrapping my arms around her waist, pressing a kiss to the top of her head.

"You're not the only one picturing it, Sage."

Her breath catches. "No?"

"Nah," I murmur, lips still against her hair. "I've been picturing it since you rocked up to my hotel in Jeddah." She laughs softly, pressing her forehead to my chest.

"Also, I believe this is my hoodie," I stated, while starting to lift it off her. "You're a thief."

"What's yours is mine", she says with a laugh. I lean back just enough to tip her chin up with my thumb. Her eyes are glassy, but her mouth is curved, soft.

"I want you here," I say. "Not just for now. For real. You don't have to know all the steps yet. We'll figure it out." She studies me for a second. Then she nods, slowly.

"Okay."

"Okay?"

"Yeah." Her smile breaks through. "I'm not going anywhere." And just like that, the silence doesn't feel so heavy anymore.

I'VE GOT to head into the factory today for a seat fitting, spec check, and the usual mid-season run-through. The team's been working around the clock on updates for the second half of the season, and it's my job to pretend like I understand the technical jargon while I sit in a very expensive chair and tell them my ass feels fine.

This'll be the first time, Sage, and I haven't spent the day together since Silverstone. The girls flew back to Melbourne, so she's solo in a brand-new city. I pull on jeans and a team polo, slide on my sneakers, and head downstairs. And there she is. Barefoot, hair in a messy bun, still sipping coffee like a goddess on vacation. Sunlight catches her skin just right, and for a second, I just stand there, completely fucking gone for her. I wrap my arms around her from behind, nestling my face into her neck.

"Hey, baby," I murmur, kissing her neck. She doesn't speak, just leans back into me like I'm her favourite place to land. "I've gotta hit the factory. A couple of things to sort out. I'll be back later this afternoon," I say, still pressed against her. "Don't get up to too much mischief while I'm gone."

She laughs softly. "Can't make any promises." I spin her around, tilt her chin up and kiss her, slow and deep, with just enough tongue to make her sigh against my mouth.

"Call me if you need anything," I say, giving her one last kiss… and a playful smack on that perfect ass. Then I head for the garage and jump into my car, already missing her.

The drive to the factory is a straight shot down the motorway, and I spend most of it picturing Sage barefoot in the kitchen, coffee in hand, completely at ease. I left my credit card on the kitchen counter as a subtle encouragement for a little London retail therapy, but I have a feeling I'll come home to her, wrapped in a blanket, deep into a Netflix binge, trying to find the closest thing to Kath & Kim.

I pull into my usual spot outside the factory, toss the keys to the intern who's trying to be helpful and walk through the front doors, greeting the reception staff with a smile and a wink and make my way down to the factory floor. Down on the floor, it's a buzz of activity — 100 + people elbow-deep in machinery and strategy.

"Carter," Benny, my team principal, says, clapping me on the back. "Looking good."

"Cars looking better, I hope?" I smirk.

"We'll see." He glances up from his tablet. "Don't forget about the event tonight. Bring a date, if you've got one…" Shit, I forgot about that.

Bring a date, if I've got one. I roll my eyes at that; he says it like the entire PR team didn't go into cardiac arrest when Sage showed up at Silverstone looking like she belonged in Vogue and ruined my bachelor reputation with one kiss. I dodge the topic and head for the changing rooms. I'm halfway into my race suit, standing in front of a mirror like an idiot, when I pull out my phone and text her:

> Me: Wanna make us "official" and come to a team event with me tonight?

> Me: No pressure. I know it's a big step. I'm happy to go solo if you'd rather not.

A few minutes pass. Then:

> Trouble: "Official," hey? What does being Maverick Carter's official girlfriend look like?

I laugh out loud. Cheeky.

> Me: Not much different to how it looks now, baby.

> Trouble: Okay, I'll come. Might be a good way to make some friends.

> Me: I can't wait to show you off. I'll be home by 5. Don't do anything I wouldn't do.

Seat fitting done. Body slightly numb as I say my goodbyes, thank the team and head out, but instead of gunning it home, I take a detour. Because Sage has nothing formal to wear. Her clothes are in Monaco, and tonight is a black-tie situation. And… I really enjoy spoiling her. I park outside one of the swankier boutiques in the city, march inside like a man on a mission, and somehow charm the hell out of the sales assistant. She shows me a red floor-length dress, corset back, V-cut neckline, and gold accents on the straps. Elegant. Sexy. Her. The only thing I ask.

"Can you make sure it's something she can wear panties with?"

The salesgirl looks up and raises an eyebrow. "You'd be surprised how often we get that question."

I get home, shopping bags in hand, and sneak upstairs like a man with a plan. The shower's running, so I lay everything out on the bed — the dress, matching heels and a brief note I scribbled on the boutique receipt: *Can't wait to see you in this. Or out of it. Love, M.*

I step into the bathroom and lean against the doorframe, watching. Sage is humming to herself, completely unaware I'm there. Water trails down her back, her hair pulled up into a slicked knot in her hands as she massages shampoo into it. She looks soft. Real. Like she belongs here.

"You coming in, or just going to stand there and be a creep?" She calls out without looking. Busted. I strip in record time and slide in behind her, arms wrapping around her as I rest my chin on her shoulder.

"So… we're official now?" She teases, tilting her face up.

I kiss her temple. "Do you want to be?"

She turns in my arms, eyes locked on mine. "Yeah, baby. I think I do." And fuck — I don't think I've ever wanted anything more than I want this girl right now. I lift her, press her against the tile, and kiss her roughly. We stay that way, embraced in one another until our skin prunes. Sage steps out of the shower, towel wrapped around her like a goddess and freezes when she sees the dress laid out.

"Maverick… did you buy me a dress?"

"Yeah, baby. It's a formal thing tonight. You've got nothing here and —" I shrug, suddenly nervous. "And I wanted to."

She walks over, fingertips grazing the fabric, and smiles, not the usual smirk she gives me when she's about to roast me, not the flirty grin she gets when she's got the upper hand, but a real smile. The kind of smile that reaches her eyes.

"It's beautiful. Thank you." She presses a kiss to my cheek, then whispers against my skin. "I can't wait for you to show me off."

THIRTY-SEVEN

SAGE

My heels click against the marble floor as we walk into the lobby of the venue, and I'm about ninety per cent sure I've forgotten how to breathe. The dress hugs every inch of my body just right, red fabric cinched at the waist, dipped low across my chest without veering into wardrobe malfunction territory, and the corset back Maverick couldn't stop eyeing in the mirror earlier is doing exactly what he hoped it would. My hair is softly curled and pinned loosely, my lips red to match the dress, a gold clutch in one hand and Maverick's hand wrapped tightly around the other.

The man looks like sex in a suit. Black on black, tailored within an inch of its life, and a quiet confidence that screams yes, I know I look this good and I'm still only looking at her. Which is exactly what he's doing. Staring at me like he hasn't seen me all day, even though we literally showered together an hour ago. "You're staring," I murmur under my breath.

"What do you expect? You wore that dress," he replies.

"You bought me this dress."

"Exactly," he grins. "I knew it'd ruin me."

We stop just before the doors that lead into the main event, where there's a red carpet rolled out, a few photographers already waiting, and media wristbands peeking from under suit jackets. My stomach does a slow, nervous flip.

"Are you sure about this?" I ask, looking up at him.

"The cameras. The gossip. The PR chaos you're inviting." His expression softens just slightly, enough to tell me that the Maverick Carter I know — that one underneath all the bravado and the teasing is still here, still looking at me.

"I'm sure," he says. "I want them to see what I see."

My chest tightens, but not in a bad way. In that full, heady way that happens when someone says something that might just rearrange your whole heart. He leans in, brushing a kiss to my temple. "You ready?"

"Ready as I'll ever be," I say, lifting my chin. We step out together. The lights are instant. Flashes are going off in every direction. Someone calls out his name, but Maverick keeps his hand on my waist, firm and grounding.

He smiles for the cameras, does the cool nod he's famous for, but every few seconds, he glances sideways at me, making sure I'm okay. Checking in without saying a word. I can hear the murmurs from reporters, the clicking of camera shutters, and then—

"Is this your official debut?"

"Is this the girlfriend?"

"Who's the woman on Maverick Carter's arm tonight?" He stops walking. Turns his body slightly toward me and, just loud enough for them to hear, says. "This is Sage. My girlfriend."

My heart skids. He said it. Out loud. I glance at him, but he's already looking at me like I hung the damn moon. A few more photos, a couple of smiles, and then he tucks me in close, guiding me through the entrance doors like the chaos outside never existed.

Inside, the room is warm and buzzing. Lights strung like floating bubbles across the ceiling, soft music humming underneath the chatter, and way too many beautiful people in one space. Maverick's hand slides down to the small of my back. He leans in, voice low and for me only. "You're the best thing I've ever walked into a room with."

My cheeks flush. My pussy is clenching, and my life feels like a whirlwind right now, and I'm not used to this level of attention, but in this moment right now, with his hand on my back and his words still curling down my spine, I feel like I belong. I feel like I'm exactly where I'm meant to be.

The drinks are crisp; the lighting is flattering, and somehow, I'm managing to keep my heels on. Maverick's hand hasn't left my body since we walked in, lower back, hip, the curve of my waist. It's possessive in the most delicious way. Like he knows all eyes are on us, and he doesn't care, as long as I'm close, and judging by the way he leans in close to whisper, he's having way too much fun with this.

"You know," he murmurs in my ear, fingers brushing just below the open back of my dress, "if you didn't put panties on, I'd already have you in a bathroom stall." My mouth parts slightly, breath catching in my throat.

"Classy," I reply.

He grins. "Never claimed to be." I give him a subtle bump with my hip.

"You picked this dress. You knew what you were doing."

"And now I'm dying on the inside because I can't take it off you…yet"

I sip my champagne, doing my best to look unaffected. "Maybe if you behave, I'll let you undo the corset before we get home."

He leans in, pressing his lips just behind my ear. "Behave? Baby, I'm trying so hard. But I'm going to lose." I feel it in my spine that slow, simmering ache that's been building since he showed up in the shower earlier. His voice, that heat behind his gaze, the way he's looking at me like he wants to ruin me and care for me in a hundred ways. We're interrupted by a couple of Maverick's teammates, all cheeky smiles and a good suit, who greet us with the kind of swagger that screams *fast cars and big egos.* One of them, Jack, I think? Turns to me.

"And who's this vision in red?" He must be the reserve driver because I'm pretty sure Maverick's teammate is called Liam. Before I can respond, Maverick's arm snakes tighter around my waist, his tone cool and casually possessive.

"This vision is mine."

Jack lifts both palms in surrender, smirking. "Easy, Carter. Just admiring."

"Well," I smile sweetly, stepping closer into Maverick's side, "you can admire from way over there." That earns a low chuckle from Maverick and a wink from Jack before he disappears into the crowd.

The moment they're gone, I glance up at Maverick. "Are you jealous?"

"Very," he says without hesitation, eyes dark. "But mostly just aware that if one more man looks at your ass the way he just did, I'm going to lose my job for throwing someone into the champagne tower." I blink, surprised, then laugh softly.

"You really are gone for me, huh?"

His mouth dips to my ear, voice low and barely controlled, "Baby, you don't even know. You have no idea how bad I've got it." The music swells, people move past us like glitter in the wind, but it's like we're in our own bubble. Heat and energy between us, electric.

He brushes my hip with his hand, deliberately slow. "I'm trying to behave. I swear I am."

"You're failing," I whisper, throat dry.

He dips his head, lips brushing my ear as he pulls my hand down to the crouch of his pants. "You feel how hard I am right now?" he murmurs. "That's your fault."

I gasp quietly and grip his arm. "Maverick."

"Meet me in five," he says, pulling back to look at me, fire dancing behind those stormy eyes. "We'll find somewhere dark. Just long enough to remind you what this dress does to me." I swallow.

"You're unhinged." I giggle

"Only for you, Sage."

Then he kisses me quickly, intensely and far too briefly before stepping away to talk to someone from his engineering team, like he didn't just whisper filthy things into my ear. My knees? Wobbly. My brain? Scrambled. My panties are wet, yeah, I might just slide those off. And, somehow, this is exactly where I want to be.

MAVERICK

She doesn't follow right away. Of course, she doesn't. She's going to make me wait. Make me sweat. God, I love her. I keep it casual, moving through the event like I'm not completely wrecked with tension. I speak to Benny. Shake hands. Nod. Smile. But my mind is on that dress. That mouth and the heat in her eyes when I whispered what I wanted. And then I see her. Sage. Moving toward me like a devil dressed in red. She doesn't even stop. Just glides past with a subtle flick of her fingers, a gesture that says: follow me now. I'm gone before I realise, I've actually moved. She disappears down the corridor that leads toward the service areas of the venue, dim lighting, no foot traffic, just the throb of distant bass from the main room. I catch up to her just before the corner, grab her wrist and pull her into the shadows. She lets out a gasp as I pin her against the wall, one hand braced beside her head, the other already finding the bare skin beneath her dress.

"You're playing a dangerous game, baby," I rasp, eyes locked on hers. "Walking around in that dress, giving me that look... What were you expecting to happen?"

"I was hoping," she breathes, "you'd stop talking and do something about it."

My hand slides up her thigh. Silky skin and heat, but no panties. Fuck.

"Jesus Christ, Sage," I growl, dipping my head to her neck. "Where did your panties go? I know I saw you put them on?" She smiles, devilish, puts her hand out and stuffs the red lace in the pocket of my suit jacket, yeah… I'm adding those to my collection.

"I thought I said you needed to behave," she whispers, breath hitching as I bite down gently on her collarbone.

I slide two fingers between her legs, finding her wet and ready. My body jolts with want, dick hard and pressing against my zipper with painful urgency. "You're fucking soaked," I groan, fingers moving slow and deep, just enough to make her hips twitch.

Her hands clutch my shoulders, lips parting as she lets out a soft moan. "You going to fuck me or make me come on your fingers? I don't care, as long as I leave here shaking" Oh, this woman. I yank the slit of her dress higher, undo my pants just enough to free myself and press the tip of my cock against her bare pussy. I pause, forehead resting against hers.

"You want this?" I ask, voice low, strained.

"Yes," she whispers. "Now. Please, Mav."

With a sharp thrust, I'm inside her — buried to the hilt. We both gasp. She clings to me, one leg wrapped around my waist as I grip her ass, holding her flush against the wall. I move slowly at first, letting her adjust, letting myself feel every inch of me. She's so goddamn tight. So warm. Every moan she makes is a reward. Every breathy whimper is a promise that she's just as undone as I am.

"God, you feel too good," I groan, thrusting harder now. "I'm not going to last."

"I don't care," she gasps, digging her nails into my back. "Just keep going. Just like that."

The rhythm builds; it's raw and desperate, our bodies colliding in the dark. Her moans turn into cries, my name falling from her lips. Then she clenches around me, tightening and pulsing.

"Maverick!"

That's it. That's the end of me. I bury myself deep and come hard, groaning her name into her neck as I lose it completely. We stay like that pressed up against the wall, gasping and shaking until the world slowly tilts back into focus. I kiss her softly this time. Just lips on lips, grounding us both.

"You, okay?" I murmur. She nods, dazed.

"Better than okay." I tuck her hair behind her ear, smiling like an idiot.

"Think anyone noticed we were gone?"

"Only if they're monitoring seismic activity in this building."

I laugh, pull back slightly and kiss her again.

"Let's go back in there and show them what official looks like."

She smirks, "Lead the way, Mr Carter."

And just like that, we slip back into the noise and the lights, like the power couple nobody saw coming. And now, they'll never forget us. And for the first time in weeks, I feel like I'm breathing again.

THIRTY-EIGHT

SAGE

Living in Monaco sounds like luxury, like a dream come true. Day drinking on yachts, marble floors, linen curtains dancing in the breeze. But to me? It just feels like a suitcase full of all the shit I haven't unpacked—literally and emotionally. Maverick and I are flying there today. My things finally arrived, which means I can stop living out of his drawers and start living out of my mess again. It should be exciting. A fresh chapter. Maybe even the beginning of something real. So why do I feel like I'm holding my breath?

He's in the kitchen right now, barefoot and shirtless, leaning over the counter, eating a protein bar like it's a life-or-death mission. I'm staring at him from the staircase like a weirdo, trying to make myself feel settled. Grounded. Like I belong in his world. But the truth is I don't. Not really. And I'm starting to wonder if I ever will. I slide into a chair at the table, watching as he downs his coffee and tosses me a wink. God, he's beautiful. That kind of stupid, unfair, movie-star hot that makes your stomach do tricks even when your brain is busy spiralling. He catches me watching and smirks as he knows. Of course, he knows. He always knows when he's getting to me. What he doesn't know is the pit that's been forming in my stomach. The one that tightens every time he calls me 'My Girl' or every time I catch my reflection and think, who even am I now? Because as much as I love waking up in his bed, wrapped in his arms and ruined in the best way possible, I don't want to disappear into him. I fought too hard for my independence. I clawed my way into adulthood through grief. I bought a house at twenty-two, paid off my car, worked a full-time job with a boss who absolutely sucked but still gave me a reason to get up in the morning. And now? Now I'm floating.

No job. No house. No structure. Just good sex, expensive wine, and a man who could buy me the Eiffel Tower if I asked nicely, and yeah, that sounds dreamy. But it's not me. I need something to call my own. A project. A purpose. A job, even if it's just part-time, or something stupid like making lattes or designing stupid little graphics. Anything that reminds me I still exist outside of him.

I haven't told Maverick any of this yet. I should. I need to. But every time I think about sitting him down and opening my mouth, the words get stuck in my throat. The last few months have just been about sex. This is the longest amount of time we've spent together. I'm not complaining. I'd never complain about sex with Maverick, never. I just feel like it's never the right moment to talk about the past. Because what I'm afraid of telling him isn't just that I feel lost. It's why I feel this way.

I became a 'slut' because of grief. Because the last man I let myself love couldn't handle my grief and couldn't understand my need for independence that came with it, and left me alone when I needed someone to love me the most. That's not exactly something you drop over morning coffee. How do I explain that to someone like Maverick Carter? That I spiralled after my mum died and my ex left me, that I went numb and chased any distraction I could find, kisses in club bathrooms, one-night stands with strangers who didn't ask questions. Anything to fill the space where love used to be.

How do I tell the man that I'm falling for all of that? He'll run, I know he will. Everyone else did. It's a hard juxtaposition. One I haven't figured out how to hold yet. One, I'm not sure I ever will. But I know I can't keep carrying it on my own. He deserves to know, and if we're really going to make a serious go of this—whatever this is—then I have to give him the whole truth. Even the ugly parts. Even the part where I'm scared. Scared of losing myself. Scared of being too much. Scared that he'll look at me differently once he knows the full story. But maybe—maybe if I tell him, and he stays, then I'll finally believe this thing between us is real. Maybe I'll start to believe I belong in his world. Maybe I'll start to believe that love doesn't have to come with conditions, that those who truly love you don't leave.

I pick at the edge of my sleeve as Maverick walks past me, brushing a kiss across the top of my head like it's the most natural thing in the world. His hand lingers at the back of my neck for a beat too long, and my body reacts before my mind can keep up. Safe. It's the first word that floats through me. Even with everything I'm wrestling with, being with him feels like safety that I haven't known in years.

"You good, baby?" he asks, standing behind my chair now. I tilt my head up, and he's looking down at me with those ocean blue eyes, scanning me like he knows something's off but isn't sure if he should ask yet. I nod. Lie.

"Yeah. Just tired." He doesn't push. Just runs his fingers gently along my shoulder before heading back into the bedroom to grab the last of our things. I stare at the grain of the table, my heartbeat loud in my ears. I want to tell him. I need to. But the truth feels like a wall I don't know how to climb. He comes back with our bags, tossing his duffel near the door and running a hand through his messy hair. He's wearing a plain white tee and charcoal joggers, but somehow, he still looks like sin and power wrapped in a GQ cover.

"Car's outside. Ready to go?" he asks. I nod again. Lie again.

He grabs my suitcase, and we head out to the car in silence. It's not the comfortable kind. It's the kind that echoes in the wrong places. The kind where words are supposed to live. The driver loads our bags, and I slide into the back seat beside him, the leather cool against my legs. Maverick takes my hand like he always does, like it belongs there and laces his fingers through mine. I let him.

We drive in silence for a while, the London skyline blurring past, the airport getting closer. His thumb strokes lazy circles into my skin, and my eyes sting from how soft it feels. How undeserved it feels. I don't realise I'm crying until a single tear slides down my cheek. He notices instantly.

"Sage." His voice cuts through the quiet, low and immediate. He shifts to face me, one hand still holding mine, the other reaching to cup my cheek.

"Hey, what's going on?"

I shake my head. "It's nothing. I'm fine." But the tremble in my voice betrays me.

"No, baby." His hand slides to the back of my neck, grounding me. "Don't do that. Don't shut me out."

I bite the inside of my cheek. My throat burns. "I don't know if I belong in your world," I whisper. It's out before I can stop it. He stills beside me.

"What do you mean?"

I glance over at him in the backseat, the hum of the car the only sound between us. My pulse is high and tight, my throat is dry, but I can't keep this inside anymore. It's building, pressure behind my ribs, swelling in the corners of my eyes.

"I don't think I can do this anymore," I mumble. His head turns sharply. I see the flicker of confusion first, then the heartache hits him. Sharp. Immediate. A crack he can't quite hide. "These last few months have been amazing… life-changing even," I continue, my voice trembling as I speak. "But we barely know each other, Maverick. And now I'm going to be unpacking boxes in a place that isn't mine, trying to playhouse in your world like it makes any sense. It feels backwards."

He looks away, eyes dropping to his hands. I watch him exhale slowly, like he's trying to keep the disappointment from showing. But I see it. I feel it. I press on, even though it hurts.

"That call you got from your team back in Monaco when they said I wasn't a good fit. I heard enough to know they weren't wrong." My laugh is bitter, self-deprecating. "I'm not someone they can polish into a media-friendly girlfriend. I don't wear designer, I don't do reformer Pilates or whatever the fuck the WAGs of the grid are doing these days. I drink cheap tequila, I eat leftover pizza, and I spiral when life gets too quiet." I pause, trying to catch my breath, my voice thick with everything I've tried not to say.

"I'm not built to be someone's picture-perfect plus one. I'm a fucking mess, Mav, and you're going to see that soon, and it'll get too hard, and then I'll be back to doing what I was doing before you turned my world upside down." He shifts, pulling his hand from mine. The warmth of his touch disappears, and he leans his elbow against the door, fingers at his temple as he stares out the window.

Silent. Thinking. Regrouping.

Not a single word leaves his mouth. And somehow, the silence hurts more than anything else he could have said. I sit there beside him, the space between us growing with every second, my chest hollowing out under the weight of what I've just said and what I might have just broken. His jaw is tight; his eyes are focused on something far outside the window. He doesn't look at me again for the rest of the drive, and all I can do is sit in the storm I just created.

We arrive at the airport. The car stops in front of the jet. Does Maverick own this thing or something? Who am I kidding, of course he does. Everything in his life is luxury, everything except for me. He still hasn't spoken, he just opens the car door and helps with the bags, I slide out and stand by the stairs like I'm waiting for an invitation, Maverick steps besides me, puts the bags down and grabs my hand, fingers intertwined I squeeze his hand and he leads me up the steps into the plane, without saying a word.

THIRTY-NINE

MAVERICK

I don't look at her. If I do, I'll say something reckless, or I won't say anything at all, and that might be worse. Instead, I stare out the window, watching the cars blur past. My fingers twitch against my thigh, wanting to reach for hers, but I don't. Because she said she can't do this anymore, and it's not like I didn't see it coming. With the way she's been pulling into herself most of the day, the restlessness in her bones, the weight in her eyes when she thought I wasn't looking. I noticed, of course, I fucking noticed. I just didn't know it would sound like this. Like goodbye. Like, I'm not enough for her to stay.

We pull up to the airport, and I move to open the door. I slide out first, silent, my shoulders tight. I follow the driver and help with the bags, nod a thank you and walk up beside her, grab her hand, and our fingers intertwine. She gives me a little squeeze, and we board the plane together in silence. The moment the door closes behind us, I speak.

"You think I give a fuck about what anyone else wants?" My voice is quiet, but it lands heavy in the space between us. She pauses halfway to her seat.

"You think I care if you do Pilates, or wear designer shit, or play nice with the media?" I keep my tone even, but the edge is there.

"You think I'm with you because I want someone to look good on my arm at a gala?" She turns, finally facing me, something sharp flickering in her eyes.

"You don't get it, Mav. This isn't just about you choosing me. It's about me choosing myself. And I don't know how to do that when I've suddenly been picked up and dropped into a life that doesn't feel like mine." Her voice breaks, and I feel it like a hit to the ribs.

"I knew who I was before you," she adds. "I worked for what I had. I had built something, was building something and, yeah it wasn't glamorous, but it was mine."

I take a step toward her. Then another. "I don't want to take that away from you, Sage. I never have." My voice softens. "I just wanted you in my life. However, you came. However messy it looked." She blinks, like she doesn't quite believe me. So, I keep going.

"You want to find a job? I'll help. You want your own space; I'll buy you an apartment. You want to scream at me for wanting to share my life with you? Scream. Hit me. Walk away if you need to." I pause. "But don't say this thing between us isn't real just because it's hard." She looks away, blinking fast, jaw tight. "If you want me to walk away from all of it right now, I will." My voice is steady, but my heart's pounding.

"I'll retire now, Jack can take the seat, and finish the season. Hell, win the damn championship for all I care. None of it matters if you're not in my life." She says nothing, but I can see her eyes searching mine like she's waiting for me to take it back. I don't.

"I'll move to Melbourne. You want to work, chase something for yourself? I'll back you every single step of the way. No matter where we are, no matter what it looks like, if we're doing it together, I'm in 100%." I move closer. Her jaw's tight, her fingers twitching like she's holding onto the edge of something sharp. "You're it for me, Sage. And maybe you're not ready to say those words yet. That's okay." I swallow hard. "I'll wait. A year. A lifetime. However long it takes, I'll wait to hear them." She's still quiet. Too quiet.

"But if you need to go," I add, softer now, "if you walk out that door, I won't stop you." My throat tightens, but I push through. "It'll wreck me. But I'll let you go."

I pause. Let it hang there. Because it's the truth, the ugliest and most honest kind. "I love you, Sage. So goddamn much it hurts." And for the first time in my life, I hope love is enough. "Yeah," I whisper. "We barely know each other. But what I do know is I haven't been myself in years. Not really. Not since I started playing the part they wrote for me and then you came along, with your cold pizza, your big opinions and your fire… and fuck, Sage, you made me feel like me again."

She closes her eyes. I step closer, brushing my hand over her arm. "You don't need to fit into my world, Sage. I want to build something that fits us. Not the media. Not my team. Just you and me." She opens her eyes slowly, and I see the war still waging behind them. But she hasn't run yet. So, I keep holding on. "So, let's figure it out together," I say. "I'll fight for you, Sage. But you've got to fight for you, too.

Sage is sitting across from me on the plane, curled in on herself like she's trying to disappear into the seat. Her arms are wrapped around her middle, and she hasn't looked at me once since we took off. She's doing that thing where she shuts down, goes quiet, not angry, just distant. Fragile. It reminds me of that first flight from Jeddah to Monaco. The way she sat just like this, like getting too close might crack something open she didn't want to show me. Except this time, it feels heavier. More personal. Like maybe I'm the thing she's afraid of now, and that thought fucking hurts. I watch her for a second, watch the way her fingers twitch against her thigh like she's holding something back. Words. Emotions. Everything. I can't take it. I unbuckle my seat belt and stand. Her eyes flick up in surprise. I don't say a word. I just walk over, slide one arm under her legs and the other around her back, and lift her straight off the damn seat. She gasps.

"Maverick, what the hell are you doing?"

There's that fire. Good. Still in there somewhere. I ignore the look she gives me, the half-glare, half-heartbreak that somehow still makes her the most beautiful thing I've ever seen and settle back into my seat with her in my lap, one arm wrapped tight around her waist. She stiffens for a second, resisting it, resisting me. But I breathe her in, let my face rest in the crook of her neck, and slowly, her body softens. I speak quietly, just for her.

"I love you," I say. "And I'll chase you to the ends of the fucking earth if I have to." Her breath catches.

She says nothing, but she doesn't move either. Just rests her head against mine like she's tired of fighting everything—me, herself, this whole damn situation. We stay like that for the rest of the flight. No talking. No fixing. Just the quiet rhythm of her breathing against my chest, like maybe that's enough for now. Maybe it has to be.

SAGE

The car ride from the airport is quiet. Not uncomfortable, exactly. Just… muted. Like we've both said, all we can do for now. I rest my head against the window, watching as the city flickers past in soft light. Monaco is stupidly beautiful. Golden cliffs, glimmering water, the smell of sea salt in the air, even from behind the glass. It should feel like a dream. But it doesn't. Not yet. I still feel like I'm wearing someone else's life. And it's a size too big. Maverick said he'd give it all up. The racing. The spotlight. The whole damn empire just for me and God, part of me wanted to let him. Just say yes and wrap myself in him like some selfish fairytale ending. But I can't. I won't because if he walked away from the thing that sets his soul on fire… for me? I'd never stop wondering when he'd resent me for it. I'd never stop punishing myself for asking him to dim his own light so I could feel safe in the shadows. I love him. I do. That truth lives like a fist in my throat. Pressing, aching, ready to be let out. So why the hell can't I say it? Why can I scream his name in the dark, but choke on three little words in the light? Maybe because if I say it out loud, it becomes real. Permanent. Exposed. And I've spent too long surviving behind walls to know how to live outside of them. But I want to. For him… I want to try.

Maverick hasn't let go of my hand since we stepped off the plane. His thumb moves over mine, steady and grounding. He's giving me space without stepping back, and I don't know how to ask for that kind of gentleness without breaking down, so I just hold on tighter. We pull into the underground parking beneath his building, where the concrete is polished and even the damn lighting feels expensive. Maverick shifts the car into park and glances at me.

"You, okay?" I nod. He doesn't push. He just kisses the back of my hand and gets out of the car, walking around to open my door like we haven't just had one of the heaviest days of our relationship. Like, I didn't nearly end it before we left the UK.

I step out into the cool underground air. The sound of my shoe echoes against the walls. The suitcase I'd packed weeks ago, filled with all my real clothes, my everyday life, sits in boxes. The elevator ride up is silent. I lean into Maverick's side, and he wraps his arm around me. I can feel his heartbeat against my temple. He smells like home and adrenaline and worry, and somehow, all at once, I feel safe and overwhelmed.

The doors open, and his apartment greets us bright, sleek, and expensive. It looks more like a luxury suite than a home, but there are boxes everywhere, my boxes. Signs of me, of us. I step inside slowly, like I'm testing the floor beneath me. Maverick sets my suitcase down by the wall and doesn't say anything. Just watches me as I take it in again, this time knowing I'm not a guest. I'm supposed to live here.

"Come here," he says softly, holding out his hand. I go, because that's the only thing that's felt easy lately. He pulls me into him, arms around my back, chin resting on my head like always.

"Whatever we need to figure out," he murmurs, "we'll do it together. You don't have to carry it on your own." I nod against his chest, and for the first time all day, my eyes sting. I still don't know how I fit into this world. But right now, I'm standing in his arms in the middle of Monaco, and it feels like a place I might want to stay.

It's dark by the time the boxes are cleared out, and I step out onto the balcony, wrapped in one of Maverick's hoodies that hangs halfway to my knees. Monaco glows below like it's made of diamonds. The harbour is still; the water catches every shimmer of light. The air is cool and smells faintly of salt. It shouldn't be comforting, but somehow, it is. Behind me, I hear him moving around, closing cupboards, turning off lights, and the soft thud of his footsteps on the polished floorboards. I sip the wine he poured for me earlier, the glass cold in my hand, and try not to overthink everything I haven't said yet. It's a lot. I hear the sliding door open, and a moment later, Maverick's behind me. His arms slide around my waist, his body pressing close. He's warm and steady and shirtless, and it takes everything in me not to melt into him completely.

"You're quiet," he murmurs into the curve of my neck.

"I'm thinking."

"Dangerous," he teases gently, lips brushing my skin. "Want to tell me what about?"

"I wanna fuck about it," I ask, teasing as his grip tightens.

"You what?" he says with a smirk across his lips. "I won't let you get out of talking to me with sex."

I turn to face him. He's looking at me like he sees all of it — the fear, the stubbornness, the part of me that's still halfway out the door. He lifts a hand and cups my jaw, his thumb brushing over my cheek. I nod, my throat thick, but before I can spiral into my own thoughts again, he kisses me—softly, deeply. The kind of kiss that anchors and reminds me, I'm not alone in this. We stand there like that for a while, wine forgotten, the city humming beneath us, and when he finally takes my hand and leads me inside, I follow without hesitation. We don't talk much. We strip slowly, quietly. Not like we're racing to get to the sex, but like we're undressing all the heaviness of the day, piece by piece. When he lays me down on his bed —our bed now—I feel it again. Safety. The closeness. The quiet certainty of him. And when he moves over me, when he whispers that he's here and not going anywhere, I believe him. Even if I'm still figuring out how to believe in myself.

FORTY

I blink, and just like that, the break is over. Three weeks goes way too quickly.

One second, I was living in a dream waking up next to Sage every day, cooking dinner together every night like we were playing house, pretending that the world outside didn't exist, and now I'm shoving race suits into a duffel bag and prepping to fly out for the Dutch Grand Prix. Whiplash, honestly. We've got a double header, Netherlands and then Italy, thankfully, we're still racing in Europe though. Close enough to not feel like I've been flung halfway across the world and left my heart behind on a damn patio chair in Monaco. She's not coming with me this time, even though I'd love to see her in the paddock, wearing my team colours, grinning at me from behind the pit wall, but I get it. She needs space. Time to settle. Time to breathe and maybe even miss me a little.

It's Wednesday morning, and I'm flying out tonight. She's in the kitchen, barefoot in one of my oversized shirts, a crime, truly making breakfast while FaceTiming with Margot, who I think is in New Zealand right now. Time zones, chaos, and Sage? Apparently, not an issue. She's glowing. Her hair's a mess, her laugh is echoing off the marble countertops, and she looks so goddamn at home in my house, and it makes my chest tight. I lean against the doorway for a second, just watching her. Fully soft. Whipped. Whatever, I've accepted it. When she finally hangs up the call and turns toward me, she slides a plate of blueberry pancakes and a mug of coffee across the island like she's been doing it her whole life. Like we've always been us.

"Your highness," she says, mock-curtsying.

"My domestic goddess," I counter, smirking as I hop up onto a chair at the breakfast bar.

She slides in next to me, and I immediately pull her closer, dragging her chair until her thigh's pressed to mine. Why? Because I can. Because I want to. Because being apart for four days already sounds like psychological warfare, and I'm trying to soak her up while I can. We eat in calm silence, the kind that doesn't need filling. I take a bite of pancake, nudge her with my knee, and ask, "So, got any big plans for the weekend?"

She looks at me sideways, with that wicked glint in her eyes, and sips her coffee like she's about to ruin me.

"Oh, I was thinking I'd go out," she says casually. "You know, see what other billionaires Monaco has to offer." I nearly choke on my pancake.

"Is that right?" I shoot back, trying to sound unaffected but grinning like an idiot. She shrugs, innocent as hell.

"You know, keep my options open. You did say you like a challenge." She winks, and that slow, sinful grin spreads across her, the same one that had me unravelling like a damn amateur the day we met.

God help Monaco if she goes out, and God help any billionaire stupid enough to look at her because even though I've got a race to focus on, my head's already here. With her, I don't think that's going to change soon. No one knows this yet, not even Sage. I guess it's the part of me that I'm kind of hiding, but depending on the outcome of this season, if I win that ninth championship, I'm thinking about retiring. Most people are expecting me to see out my three- year contract. I will if I don't win, but watching Sage here in my house, our house gives me that extra fire I need to win number nine, so I can spend my days with her.

THE EXCITING THING about Zandvoort is that it's loud, chaotic, and fans that are packed shoulder-to-shoulder, flares already staining the air orange before we've even hit the track. It smells like burnt rubber, fried food, and adrenaline. Normally, I thrive in this shit. Today? I feel a little... off. Not bad. Just... missing something. Or someone. The garage is buzzing, the engineers in their rhythm, the crew is in formation; the car looks damn sexy in its fresh livery, but my mind is half a country away in Monaco, wondering if Sage actually went out last night or if she stayed in, raiding my snack drawer and yelling at Netflix. I wouldn't blame her either way. She's still trying to find her footing, and I respect that. But God, do I miss her.

"Yo, Mav," Benny claps me on the back as I'm pulling my balaclava over my head, "media wants a soundbite before you go out." Right. The event. The photos. The fact that I'm now very publicly taken. I walk up to the mic, smile tight, arms crossed in my race suit.

"Yeah, the car's feeling good. The track looks solid. Excited to see what we can do today."

The reporter smiles, leans in like she's already bored with the basics.

"And how's life off-track, Maverick? Big change for the man once dubbed Formula One's most eligible bachelor."

There it is. I smirk. "Let's just say I'm not so eligible anymore, and I'm better for it." Quick, clean. They can twist it however they like. Sage will see it online in a few hours, probably with some unhinged headline, and I hope it makes her laugh. Or maybe blush a little. She does that cute thing where she tries to hide behind her hand when she gets flustered. Drives me insane.

Helmet on, visor down, the world goes quiet. It's just me, the car, and the track now, but even as I rocket down the straight at full throttle, everything humming beneath me like a living beast, I find myself thinking: She should be here. I'd love for her to be here.

Practice sessions are over. I had a quick dinner in the hospitality suite and went over the strategies for tomorrow's qualifying, as I'm currently leading my teammate in the points, so I get the preferred strategy tomorrow, so that's a win this weekend already. I'm on my way back to the hotel. My car is swamped by fans on the way out of the track, so it's a slow exit. My phone buzzes the second I walk into my suite. Sweat still clinging to my skin, hair a mess, adrenaline finally bleeding out of me.

Trouble: Saw your interview. 'Not so eligible anymore,' huh? That was sweet... for a guy who just ghosted me all day.

I grin, thumbs already flying.

Me: I didn't ghost you. I was just driving very, very fast. Also, I look hot in the fireproofs. Admit it.

Trouble: No lies detected.

Me: How's Monaco?

Trouble: Lonely. Your shower pressure rocks, though. I organised your spice rack too.

Me: You're perfect. Can I call you before I crash?

Three dots. Then her reply

Trouble: Always.

And just like that, I'm not so tired anymore.

Qualifying. P2. Not bad. Could've been better, but I'll take it.

The media gauntlets behind me, the debriefs done, and I'm finally alone in my hotel room with nothing but room service, sore muscles, and the constant ache of not having Sage here. I drop onto the bed, phone already in hand, checking for messages. One from Drew - something about his rugby team in Ireland. Two from Mum, God love her and then finally Sage. The preview stops me cold.

Trouble: Photo Attached.

I tap it open, and Jesus Christ. She's sprawled out on my bed, our bed, wearing my team shirt and absolutely nothing else. Legs bare, skin glowing in the golden evening light streaming through the window, one finger in her mouth and the smirk of someone who knows exactly what she's doing to me.

> Trouble: P2's nice, babe. But I'm hoping for gold before you get home. So, I thought you could use a little motivation…

My hand's already gripping the back of my neck, heat shooting through me like I'm back on track with the throttle wide open. I call her. Immediately. She picks up on the first ring, voice all syrupy smug.

"Well, hello."

"You're going to kill me, trouble," I growl.

"I was going for inspire, but okay."

"You are lying in my bed in my shirt with nothing underneath, which is not inspiration, Sage. That's fucking torture."

"Still not hearing a thank you…" she responds

I groan, dragging a hand down my face. "You're the worst. And by worst, I mean you're everything I've ever wanted and quite possibly my actual downfall." She laughs, low and smug.

"You should've seen the second photo I almost sent."

My dick twitches at just the idea. "Send it."

"Only if you're alone." I swing off the bed, lock the door, close the curtains, and drop back onto the mattress.

"Now I am."

There's a beat of silence, and then — Ding. This one's filthier. Her legs are parted just enough, the hem of my shirt hitched high, a teasing hint of her bare heat between her thighs. One hand's still on her stomach, the other slipping just low enough to drive me insane.

"Fuck, baby…" I mutter, palming myself through my sweatpants, already hard.

"You like it?" she purrs.

"You know I do. You're going to ruin me."

"That's the goal," she whispers. "Now tell me what you'd do if you were here."

I shut my eyes, sinking back into the pillows as her voice curls into my ear like smoke.

"I'd start by dragging that shirt over your head so I can see all of you, your skin flushed from teasing me, nipples already hard. Then I'd spread you wide and lick you slow, just to make you squirm. No rushing it, not tonight."

"Maverick…" she breathes, voice already ragged.

"I'd slide two fingers in, right here…" I imagine it, my hand now wrapped tight around my cock, stroking slowly. "And my mouth on your clit, sucking until you come so hard you scream my name."

She gasps. I can hear her shifting, the soft rustle of sheets, the breathy, shaky way she exhales.

"Then I'd flip you over, pull your hips up, and slide in deep, so deep just how you like it. No teasing. Just all of me."

"Oh my God," she whimpers.

"Say my name."

"Maverick. Fuck—baby, I'm—"

"I've got you," I whisper. "Come for me, Sage." She moans loudly, and I don't hold back either. I come hard, spilling over my hand with a grunt, heart pounding like I'm back on the starting grid.

For a few seconds, we're both silent. Just breathing. Then she giggles.

"That should count as some kind of team support, right?" She says, breathless and smug. I laugh, breath still shallow.

"If I win, it's all you."

"You'd better. I'm not done ruining you yet." God, I fucking love her.

THE LIGHTS GO OUT, and I launch. It's chaos. Tight. Aggressive, but I get the jump and pull ahead. Clean. Precise and fucking perfect. P1. Now I just need to hold it. Every lap is a war against my tyres, my neck, my own damn heartbeat. The Dutch fans are a blur of orange in the stands, engines screaming in my ears, sweat pouring down my back. I block out everything but the track. Focus. Feel. Breathe, and then the checkered flag waves, and it's mine. The win. The crowd is roaring, and the team is screaming in my ear.

"You did it, Maverick! You fucking did it!" I let out a guttural yell, fist pounding the wheel as I coast around for the cooldown lap. My voice is hoarse. Fuck, I've never wanted to get home faster in my life.

I CLICK OPEN the front door at 1 a.m. It's quiet, but I know she's awake. I can feel her. It's that kind of heavy quiet that tells you something's off, like the air's thicker somehow. My duffel drops to the floor by the door, and I toe off my shoes, listening for her. Sage. Then I hear the barely there hum of the microwave, the faint buzz of the TV, and the sound of soft breathing. Not asleep, just... tired. I round the corner and find her exactly how I expected. Curled up on the lounge like she's trying to fold herself smaller, my hoodie drowning her, glass of wine untouched now, her heat pack clutched to her stomach like it's the only thing anchoring her to the earth and my heart cracks, just a little.

"Sage," I say softly, stepping into the room like it might spook her. "Hey, baby." She looks up at me, eyes glassy, lashes heavy, hair a mess, and still the most beautiful thing I've ever seen.

"Your home," she says, voice scratchy and low. She tries to sit up, but I'm already kneeling in front of her.

"Don't move. I got you." I take the wine glass from her hand and set it aside, brushing a strand of hair from her forehead. She leans into the touch, her body melting in a way that tells me she's been holding tension for hours. Days maybe.

"Bad one?" I ask, already knowing the answer.

She nods, a breath catching in her throat. "Endo's being a bitch. I feel gross and pathetic and bloated and like I might cry at literally any moment."

"You're not gross," I murmur, kissing her temple. "And crying is allowed. I'll even join you if you want." She lets out a half-laugh, half-sob, and it punches me right in the gut.

"Come here," I mumble, my hands already beneath her thighs. She doesn't argue. She's too exhausted to put up a front, and maybe that's a good thing. I lift her, careful and slow, carrying her into the bathroom like she's something precious because she is. She rests her head against my shoulder, a quiet exhale slipping from her lips. I set her gently down on the toilet lid and crouch in front of the tub. Turn the tap. Run the water hot, her kind of hot like she's training to live in hell someday. "The devil likes it hot, right?" I glance back at her and raise a brow. She doesn't answer, just gives me a small, tired smirk. That's enough. She's still in there. I stand up and reach for her hoodie.

"Arms up." She doesn't move at first. Then, slowly, she lifts them. I peel the hoodie off, stealing a glance at her body because, well, I'm still me and even now, hurting and worn out, she's still unreal, but I don't linger. This isn't about that.

I slide her pants down next, tracing my hands down the backs of her thighs as I go. She shivers a little, from the contact or the fatigue, or the pain, I can't tell which. Once she's undressed, I scoop her back up and lower her into the tub. She hisses at the heat at first, then sinks into it with a relieved groan. I grab a towel, fold it, and sit beside the tub on the tiled floor. I'm not going anywhere. She leans her head back against the porcelain edge, eyes closing for a moment.

Her voice is quiet. "I didn't want you to see me like this."

I shift closer, elbow on the side of the bath. "I want to see you like this. In every way." She turns her head, resting it against the rim to look at me. Her expression is unreadable for a second. Then she snorts softly.

"You're really ruining the whole Playboy fantasy, Carter."

"Good," I murmur, brushing my knuckles over her damp arm. "Means I'm doing something right."

That gets a soft laugh out of her, and just like that, I feel her unravelling some of that sharp, tight tension in her body, giving way to something looser, something closer to comfort. Her hand finds mine beneath the water, our fingers linking across her stomach. I stay like that, tracing the back of her hand with my thumb, until the question that's been sitting in my throat finally works its way out.

"How long have you had endometriosis?" She opens her eyes again.

"Since I was fourteen." Fourteen. Jesus.

"That's young," I say, voice low. She just nods. "Has it always been this bad?"

"Sometimes it's worse. I've ended up in hospital more than once."

That hits harder than I expected. Hospital. Worse than this. I already hate watching her in pain. The idea that it's only a glimpse of what she's lived through makes my chest tight.

"Baby," I whisper, shaking my head. "That's rough." I take a breath, watch her chest rise and fall with mine. "How often do you get these attacks?"

"They just come. No real pattern. Usually worse at the start of my period, but honestly, it messes with everything. My body. My energy. My brain." I nod, giving her the space to keep going. "Sometimes I'll just… drop. No warning. I had one at work once. Ended up on the floor of a toilet cubicle, vomiting from the pain. Josie found me thirty minutes later. I couldn't even move." Fuck. That image settles deep and cold in my gut. I can picture her curled up on a shitty bathroom floor, no one knowing. No one helped.

She continues, quieter now. "It's not just a bad period, Mav. That's what most people think. But it's more than that. It affects every part of my life. Some women can't have kids because of it." That one lands. Not because it scares me, though, maybe it does a little, but because of how she says it. Like she's used to people walking away because of it. I don't know if she wants kids. I don't know if this is her way of warning me, pushing me away before it can get that far… nah, I'm not going anywhere. I shift closer, lean in, and press a kiss to her damp shoulder.

"Thank you for telling me," I say. "You don't have to hide any of this from me. I'm your partner, Sage. That means all of it. The pain, the hard days, the ugly parts, too." She doesn't speak right away. Just looks at me like maybe she's trying to memorise this moment like it's something she never thought she'd get. Then she smiles, soft and quiet and full of something that aches in my chest.

"Thank you for listening," she says. I squeeze her hand, and we sit there like that — her in the bath, me on the floor, linked by fingers and silence and the quiet hum of something real growing between us. Whatever this is… It's not fragile anymore. It's solid. We sit there like that for a while — no talking. Just the quiet thrum of something strong growing between us.

FORTY-ONE

The water's starting to cool, but I don't want to move not because I'm still in pain, but because Maverick is right here, sitting on the bathroom floor like there's nowhere else in the world he'd rather be. He hasn't let go of my hand. His thumb keeps brushing over my knuckles in this steady, grounding rhythm. Like he's reminding me he's still here, even if I stop talking. I tilt my head toward him. He looks tired, like he's been carrying more than just me tonight, but his eyes are soft, steady. Focused entirely on me and that? That undoing feeling starts again in my chest. Not the sharp, stabbing kind that took me down earlier. This is something gentler. Something that terrifies me in an entirely different way. He saw it all, the whole ugly reality, and he didn't flinch. Didn't pity me.

"You know you didn't sign up for all this, right?" I murmur, my voice barely above the water. "The random flare-ups. The crying. The part where I feel like a liability in my body."

His gaze doesn't budge. "Can you tell me about your mum?" I wince. I knew this conversation was coming, and I'm vulnerable, so I guess now's as good a time as any.

"She was killed in a car accident about 9 years ago now." His eyes sink. "That's why I came to you in Jeddah, my trauma response kicked in, and I didn't want you to be alone like my mum was"

"She was in her car, and another car was speeding in the wet and lost control. Mum was thrown from her car and left to die on the side of the road" Maverick doesn't move. His hand's resting over my heart now, warm and steady, like he knows it's working overtime. Like he can feel the cracks under my skin.

"There's more," I say, and my voice is rougher now. Sharper. "God, there's so much more." It's word vomit now. He doesn't say anything, just waits. He's good at that, better than anyone I've ever met. Patient in the quiet. Present but never pressing.

"I did everything," I say. "The funeral, the house, the insurance paperwork, the flowers, the fucking catering. My dad couldn't speak, and my brother kept disappearing into his room with a bottle of something. He was so young, barely an adult, and everyone else, family, friends, neighbours, they just watched me do it. Like I was supposed to know how to pick the right coffin and guess if Mum would've preferred lilies or white roses." I exhale.

"And I did it. All of it. I kept it together because someone had to. I didn't cry. Not once. Not until the night after the funeral, when everyone had left, and the house was silent, and I finally—finally let myself fall apart."

Maverick's grip tightens around mine again, and I can see his jaw working overtime like he's trying not to react too much, but it's killing him, anyway.

"I went back to Melbourne a week later," I continue. "Because Uni was starting again, and I needed something to hold on to, I needed to adjust to my reality on my own, and no one told me not to. But then, suddenly, I was the bad guy." I laugh, dry and hollow. "Apparently, I'd 'abandoned' them. Left my dad and my brother behind. They say I 'ran away' and that I should've stayed. I should've put them first. Never mind the fact that I'd already spent weeks putting everyone ahead of myself. Never mind the fact that I couldn't breathe in that house anymore without seeing her everywhere." I shake my head, mouth pressed tight.

"They didn't say it to my face. Not at first. But I heard them. The whispers, the guilt trips. Someone even said, 'Your mother would be disappointed you ran.'" Maverick mutters something under his breath, sharp and angry, but I keep going. I need to get this out.

"I didn't run. I did what I had to do to survive, and I survived, only just. And no one fucking thanked me for it. Not once." The tears are silent now. They're not violent or dramatic. They just slide down my cheeks like they've been waiting years for permission. "I never talk about this," I whisper. "Not with Josie. Not with Margot. Not even with my family."

"You don't have to carry it alone anymore," Maverick says, voice low, a little rough. "I've got you, Sage."

He turns me, lifting me out of the bath and into him now, his hands firm on my hips, grounding me. "You did what no one else could. You held your family together when you were still breaking yourself. That doesn't make you a bad guy. That makes you a fucking hero."

I let out a shaky laugh, wiping my face with the sleeve of his hoodie. "I don't feel like a hero."

"You don't have to," he says. "You just have to let someone see the real you. All of it. The strong parts, the broken parts. I want it all."

I lean in, kissing him. Soft and slow. Not to distract, but to say thank you. To say I see you too in the only way I know how, when words fail, and for the first time in a long time, I don't feel like I'm bracing for impact. I feel like maybe, just maybe, I can exhale. I don't cry too often over any of this, not anymore. I think all my tears have dried up. His, however, slide down his cheek.

"Baby, you've carried that for so long. I'm so sorry I put you through that in Jeddah," His eyes red "Let me carry some of it for you, so you don't have to do it alone, He repeats, and I shrug, suddenly finding my knees very interesting "You think that's not part of loving someone?" he asks quietly.

"I don't know. Maybe."

Maverick huffs. "I love you, Sage," he says, inching closer until he's sitting me back on the toilet lid and starts sliding my pants back on. "The real one. The one who drinks tequila on a Tuesday has seven unique personalities and would probably kick my ass. The one who lets me hold her when she's hurting." He continues, and I blink hard.

"You're going to make me cry again."

"That's alright," he says, not looking away.

"I'll hold you through that too." God. This man. I reach out with my free hand and brush the hair back from his forehead. He tilts into the touch as he needs it as much as I do. "I don't think I've ever let anyone see me like this," I admit.

His jaw flexes, just slightly. "I'm honoured."

It's such a Maverick thing to say — so simple, so sincere. I shift, carefully, so he can pull my pants all the way up and over my bottom. He moves instantly to steady me, hands gentle on my arms.

"Bedtime or lounge time?" he murmurs.

I nod. "Bed, only because I want you in bed." His brow lifts, surprised, but then a slow grin tugs at his mouth.

"You sure you're up for that, trouble?" I lean in, pressing my lips just beneath his jaw.

"I didn't say I was starting anything," I whisper. "I just want your arms around me. Your warmth." His breath catches. Then he's standing, wrapping the rest of me in a towel, careful like I'm something break-able, which only makes me feel stronger. Safer. We move to the bedroom in silence. He helps me into one of his shirts, then slides in beside me, pulling the blanket over us. I curl into him, head tucked beneath his chin, one leg slung over his hip. His heart is steady beneath my ear. So is his hand, resting over my lower stomach like a quiet promise. I don't tell him this, but I've never felt more wanted in my life.

I wake up to warm hands sliding under the hem of my shirt. His fingers graze my bare thigh, slow and aimless, like he's been doing it for a while and only just realised I'm awake. I hum, eyes still closed. "If you're trying to cop a feel, there are more efficient ways."

He laughs quietly, the sound low and sleepy against the back of my neck. "I wasn't copping a feel. I was admiring."

"Big difference?" I cock a brow

"Massive." He presses a kiss to my shoulder. "Appreciating the view without disturbing the masterpiece." God, he's such a menace. A sweet, half-naked, devastatingly hot menace.

I roll over slowly, muscles still sore from yesterday, and not the fun kind of sore, unfortunately, and I catch his face in the soft morning light. Hair a mess, eyes hooded with sleep, stubble brushing against the pillow.

"I thought you had an early meeting today," I murmur, curling a hand against his chest. He's all warm skin and lazy confidence; the kind of man who makes a bed feel like gravity.

"Cancelled it."

My eyebrows rise. "Seriously?" and he nods, casually.

"Needed to make sure my girl woke up okay."

"Still on the my girl train?" He shrugs one shoulder, pretending to play it cool.

"I figured, I earned at least partial custody." I laugh, then grimace slightly as my stomach tightens with the motion. He notices, instantly, concern flickering behind his eyes. I press a hand to his jaw.

"It's okay. Just sore. Still upright. Still functional."

He leans in and kisses me, featherlight. "Still sexy as hell."

"You trying to sleep with me, Playboy?" He grins.

"Always." I curl into him, leg slipping between his.

"You're clingy in the mornings, aren't you?"

"You say that like it's a bad thing."

"It's not." I pause, then whisper against his collarbone, "It's nice."

He kisses me again, this time deeper, slower, more like a promise than a tease. My body might still be recovering, but my heart is wide awake and sprinting. When we finally pull apart, I trace a lazy line down his chest.

"So, what's the plan for today?"

"Whatever you want."

"Dangerous words."

"I'm into danger," he says with a wicked grin, flipping me gently onto my back, hovering above with a spark in his eyes. "Especially when it comes with bed hair and a smart mouth."

I raise a brow. "Pretty sure this smart mouth is the reason in here right now." He laughs, dips his head, and presses a kiss just below my jaw.

"Oh, baby. That and so much more."

It's just after 10 a.m. and Maverick's already trying to convince me to skip breakfast for brunch in bed. Which, in theory, sounds divine until I remember he doesn't believe in brunch unless it's delivered and accompanied by a blowjob. I pull the oversized sunglasses down over my face, toss my hair into a messy bun that says effortless but took at least fifteen minutes, and grab my tote bag like I have somewhere important to be.

"Let's go, Playboy. I want coffee that doesn't come from your kitchen." He trails after me, half-dressed in a navy linen shirt that's only buttoned halfway, and shorts that are probably more expensive than my car.

"You're bossy before caffeine," I smirk.

"And you're brave for talking back to me before I've had it"

He laughs and catches up, slipping an arm around my waist as we step into the sun-drenched street. Monaco looks like it was filtered by a Vogue editorial: yachts glittering in the harbour, women who look like models walking dogs that probably have Instagram accounts, and streets so clean they sparkle.

"I could get used to this," I say, gesturing at the view.

"You mean waking up here next to me every morning?" I roll my eyes.

We walk into a little cafe on the corner, one of those places with outdoor seating and tiny espresso cups that cost more than a bottle of my favourite tequila. The hostess clearly recognises Maverick and clearly wants to suck him off. I give her a polite smile that says, " Don't even think about it, and link my arm through his.

He leans down, murmuring in my ear, "Jealous?"

"No," I reply breezily. "Possessive. There's a difference."

"God, I love you."

I raise a brow. "Don't distract me with declarations of love, Playboy." He orders two coffees, a latte for me and an Americano for himself, a basket of pastries and something else in rapid French that I hope is food and not a room reservation. We sit. We eat and flirt shamelessly.

"So," I say, biting into a croissant, "how long until someone takes a sneaky picture of us and sells it to a gossip site?"

"Probably already happened", he shrugs

"And how long until someone takes a sneaky picture of me sucking you off under this table?" With his mouth open wide, looking at me, I take a sip of my coffee and look at him over the rim.

"Feeling lucky, Playboy"

He grins. "You're unbelievable."

FORTY-TWO

MAVERICK

Back on the road. Italy this time.

I got home Monday morning just long enough to exhale, sleep with Sage curled into me and pretend for a minute that real life didn't include weekly departures. Now it's Wednesday, and I'm packed again. The season doesn't let up, and neither does the ache I feel every time I have to leave her behind. We've got a week off after this race, then Baku, then the States. A blur of cities and circuits. She's not ready to travel with me yet, and I'm not about to push it. But damn, I wish she were coming.

I sling my duffel bag over my shoulder just as the bathroom door opens and steam rolls out like a movie scene. She steps into the room wrapped in a towel, hair dripping, skin flushed from the heat. She looks like heaven. And hell. And everything in between. I drop the bag and pull her into me, burying my face in her damp shoulder. I don't want to let go. Not now. Never. She looks up at me, her eyes soft and unreadable. I tilt her chin and press my mouth to hers, slow and deep, like I can imprint the kiss on both of us until Sunday.

"I've got to go, baby," I whisper against her hair. "Car's here."

"Stay safe," she says, voice thick. "I'll be watching. I'll see you Sunday night." She walks me to the door; towel still clutched around her like armour. I pause, hand on the doorknob.

"I like, like you. Don't have too much fun without me," she says with a cheeky grin that does nothing to make leaving easier. I smile, brushing one last kiss to her lips.

"I won't. And Sage? I love you." Then I'm out the door.

Somewhere between the freeway and the airport, my phone lights up with a message from a group chat I don't remember being a part of.

Group Chat: 2 Horn Bags and a Sex God

…Jesus Christ.

Maverick changed the group name to "M&M&J."

Josie changed it back to "2 Horn Bags and a Sex God." Guess that names staying.

> Josie: Hey Sex God, how's it hangin'?

> Margot: Preferably low, heavy and keeping our girl walking funny

> Me: Not sure what "it" is referring to.

> Margot: You know exactly what we mean.

> Josie: SO. M and I had a thought. Dangerous, I know. Sage's 30th is next weekend. We want to surprise her; could we stay at your place?

> Josie: I half-promise not to have sex in your guest room again.

> Margot: She absolutely will. Also dibs on the good towels.

> Me: Hold up, Sage's birthday is next weekend?! Why the hell didn't she tell me?

> Margot: Because her mouth's been busy. With you.

> Me: …accurate.

Josie: OMG I CANNOT

Me: Yes. Of course. You can stay. Flights are on me, and I'll put you up in a hotel for the first few nights. Just don't tell her; it should be an actual surprise.

Josie: Best. Bestie. Boyfriend. EVER.

Margot: Ugh, she's so lucky. Also, Josie said to invite Drew.

Me: No.

Josie: C'mon, give the man a chance.

Me: Nope. Drew will give you a rash.

Margot: Don't worry, J

Me: You people are feral.

Josie: And you'll love us. Soon enough

Me: That's the most terrifying part.

Great, now I've got two chaos goblins flying into Monaco to plan a surprise party for the woman who's taken my heart. This is going to be... something.

THE GARAGE IS loud and chaotic in that strangely comforting way race weekends always are. Headsets crackling, the whir of drills, the scent of fuel and adrenaline thick in the air. It's home, even if it never stops moving. But I'm off again today, again. Not technically, my lap times are clean, my car's running fine, the team's happy, but I know myself, and this isn't me at 100%, and it's because Sage isn't here. I've raced for years without her. I've travelled more miles than I can count solo. But now? Now I know what it's like to wake up next to her, wrapped in my arms, stealing the blanket and drooling on my chest like it's her full-time job. And it's messing with my head not having her grounding energy right now. I pull my helmet off after FP2 and run a hand through my hair. Sweat clings to my neck, the back of my race suit sticking to my spine. My engineer says something about corner 9, but it barely lands.

My phone buzzes.

> Trouble: Saw your practice. You looked hot. Not as hot as when you made me come against the wall the other night, but close.

Jesus. I cough-laugh and discreetly angle the screen away from the mechanics. She's going to be the death of me.

> Me: I'd like to formally lodge a complaint. You can't send that shit while I'm in a race suit - it hides nothing.

> Trouble: Can't? Or shouldn't?

> Me: Both. I'm seconds away from risking a helmet cam ban just to FaceTime you in the driver's room.

> Trouble: Mm, imagine the scandal. "Apex's golden boy caught sexting in Ferrari country."

> Me: They'd forgive me if they saw you.

> Trouble: Flattery will get you everywhere. Even in my pants when you get home.

My heart kicks like I'm going to turn one blind. Yeah. I'm gone for her. I tuck the phone away as the team debrief starts. I manage to focus, but the corner of my mind is somewhere else entirely — Monaco with Sage. She's wormed her way in, and I'm not even mad about it.

After the meeting, I stop by the Apex's hospitality coffee and catch sight of a few reporters hovering nearby. They've been circling all weekend, waiting to ask about Sage, the girl who's now permanently tied to my name in the media. Let them ask. They don't know her as I do. And honestly, I hope they never get close. Because she's mine.

Back in my hotel room that night, I lay on the bed in compression shorts, staring at the ceiling, phone balanced on my chest. My body's tired but wired, typical on a Friday night before qualifying. I FaceTime Sage. She answers on the third ring, fresh out of the bath, hair wet, oversized tee hanging off one shoulder. I groan, loud and obnoxious.

She grins. "You called me just to suffer, didn't you?"

"Pretty much."

"Is this your 'I'm tired and want cuddles' face?"

"I don't have a face for that."

"You absolutely do. You're making it now."

I flip the camera and show her the pillows stacked on the other side of the bed. "You think I'm not pathetic enough to build a fake you out of hotel linens?"

She snorts. "You are so lame."

"Don't tell anyone. I have a reputation to uphold." She blows me a kiss, and I catch it like the idiot I am. My chest loosens for the first time all day.

"Go kick ass tomorrow," she says softly, voice curling around me like a blanket.

"Then come home to me." "Always."

SAGE

My heart's in my throat, and he hasn't even started the damn engine yet. I'm curled up on the lounge in his apartment, still wearing one of his shirts because apparently, I've become that girl who steals her boyfriend's clothes and talks to his plants like they're old friends. (For the record, Gerald the fern is thriving.)

The broadcast is already running, pre-race coverage full of slow-motion shots of cars and drivers and an annoyingly handsome man with a jawline that could slice bread. Maverick. My Maverick. Standing next to his car like he's posing for a movie poster, visor still up, with that slight furrow in his brow like he's already thinking ten steps ahead. It's ridiculous how attractive I find him when he's working, focused, locked in, jaw clenched like he's about to go to war in a carbon fibre rocket. Damn, that race suit really does show everything, and I mean everything. Don't mind me, I'm just over here drooling over the outline of my man's dick.

The lights go out. The grid launches, and I forget to breathe for, like, the first eight laps. He's so fast. I knew that. Obviously. I've watched the races, been in the paddock, and heard the stories. But watching him from here, from our lounge with my knees hugged to my chest and his scent still clinging to my skin, it hits differently. I'm not just watching a driver. I'm watching him. The man who makes me blueberry pancakes, kisses my shoulder in his sleep and holds my hair when I'm doubled over in pain. Every overtake has my stomach in knots. Every radio crackle has me gripping the blanket tighter. Every second he's not in P1 feels like a personal attack. But when he takes the lead halfway through the race? Yeah, I scream. Out loud. To no one. The neighbours probably think someone's being murdered here, but I don't care.

By the time the last laps roll around, I'm practically pacing. "Come on, baby," I whisper. "Hold it, hold it…" And he does. He wins. He fucking wins. I drop to the floor like some dramatic old-school sports fan, face in my hands, tears pricking the corners of my eyes—because I'm so damn proud of him I could burst. His name is everywhere on the screen, the crowd roaring, the team losing their minds. But all I can see is that smile breaking across his face when he climbs out of the car and throws his fist in the air. He's glowing and, fuck, I love him. Yeah, I really should tell him.

I'm still on the floor when his message comes in

> Playboy: Did you scream my name? Tell the truth.

> Me: I screamed so loud I scared the neighbours.

> Playboy: I can't wait to get home.

> Me: Neither can I. Come collect your reward, champ. I've got plans for that trophy.

> Playboy: … Now I'm going to be getting on the plane in a permanent state of arousal. Thanks.

> Me: Anytime, baby. Win again in the next race. See what I do with two trophies.

I close the messages and sit back on the floor, heart still racing like I'm the one who just crossed the finish line. He makes me feel everything. Terrified. Exposed. Wildly alive and for once, I'm not running from it.

I'm cleaning up after making myself a late dinner, and yeah, I'm still wearing his t-shirt when I hear the door slam shut. I barely have time to turn before he's on me. Maverick drops his bag where he stands, strides across the living room like he owns the place, which, technically, he does, but right now he's giving me that look, the one that says he owns me too.

"You're wearing my shirt," he growls, voice low, breath still heavy from the flight, his pants clinging to his thighs and his shirt to his chest, outlining everything.

"Yeah, and I didn't feel like pants," I smirk, leaning back against the kitchen bench. "I was busy screaming your name and scaring the neighbours." That smirk on his face sharpens.

"Yeah? You liked watching me win?" I nod, slowly.

"Almost as much as I like seeing you right now, all sweaty, tired and cocky as hell."

He closes the space between us in two steps, grabs my hips and lifts me onto the bench without warning. I gasp, my hands grabbing at his shoulders instinctively.

"Tell me what you'd do with the trophy," he murmurs, burying his face in my neck, dragging his teeth over that spot he knows makes my knees weak.

"I said I had plans," I breathe, wrapping my legs around his hips, pulling him flush against me. I can feel him already hard, pressing into me through the thin fabric of my underwear.

"I hope those plans involve screaming my name again."

"Only if you earn it, champ."

That's all it takes. He crushes his mouth to mine, all tongue and teeth and filthy heat. He kisses like he races, ruthless and precise, like he knows exactly where to touch to make me unravel. His hand slides under my shirt, his shirt and cups my breast, thumb flicking over my nipple until I whimper.

"I missed you," he says, breath hitching against my collarbone.

"Every damn night. I'd close my eyes and picture this: your legs around me, your mouth on mine, those god damn metal bars through your nipples and that fucking look you give me right before you come." I reach between us and tug down the waistband of his pants. He hisses when I wrap my hand around him.

"Missed this?" I tease, stroking him slowly. "Or just missed coming home to someone who won't stroke your ego?"

"Don't need you to stroke my ego when you're doing that," he groans, rutting into my fist.

"But fuck, Sage—yeah, I missed this. Missed you." I slide back on the counter, legs parting wider.

"Then shut up and show me."

He doesn't hesitate; he pushes my underwear aside and sinks into me with one deep, perfect thrust. We both moan, bodies snapping tight, the heat between us molten and immediate. There's nothing slow about it; he takes me like he's racing the clock, hips snapping, his hand at the back of my neck keeping me steady while he fucks me into the marble.

"You feel so good," he groans against my skin. "God, baby, I'll never get enough of this." I cling to him, nails digging into his back, my thighs shaking.

"Harder," I whisper, voice wrecked. "Don't hold back; I want all of you." His eyes darken.

"Be careful what you ask for, sweetheart." And then he really lets go. He fucks me hard, relentlessly, focused and filthy, worshipping every reaction I give him. The bench rattles. My moans turn to cries. His name leaves my mouth like a prayer, over and over and over. When I fall apart, it's not quiet. It's violent and raw. He follows me seconds later, still inside me, forehead pressed to mine, panting like he just crossed the finish line again.

He doesn't move right away, just stands there, watching me as our heartbeats sync up.

"Welcome home," I whisper, cupping his cheek. He kisses me slowly this time, reverent.

"That's the best finish line I've ever crossed."

FORTY-THREE

MAVERICK

It's Sage's birthday. Not that she knows that I know yet. She was still in bed when I left for my morning run, all wild bed hair and bare legs, one arm stretched across my pillow like she was claiming territory. I kissed her shoulder before I left. She stirred. Mumbled something about coffee and orgasms and rolled over. My girl's got priorities. There's no race this weekend, which means I've got nowhere to be and all day to spoil her. I've planned it down to the last detail — not a massive party, she'd hate that, but a solid little surprise. Margot and Josie flew in two nights ago. They're tucked away in a hotel around the corner, hiding like chaos goblins. Drew's with them, too, yeah, I'm not touching that.

I round the last corner of my run, shirt soaked, legs burning in that good way, and there she is. Sage. Perched on the balcony like she's starring in a goddamn perfume ad, golden in the morning sun. Hair messy. One leg pulled up onto the chair. Coffee in one hand, phone in the other. No bra. Fuck. Me.

I shoot her a text:

> Me: Hey, birthday girl. What would you like for breakfast?

I pause at the corner, watching through the trees like a perv. She reads it. Frowns. Then grins, biting her lip.

> Trouble: Bloody Josie.

> Trouble: But since you asked, your dick and a margarita, in no particular order.

I laugh so hard I nearly pull a hamstring. Dirty little menace.

> Me: Let me see what I can do

I slip inside the building and take the stairs two at a time. My heart's already racing, but for a whole different reason now. Back in the apartment, I head straight for the kitchen. Sage is still on the balcony, AirPods in, chatting on FaceTime, probably with family. She's animated, smiling, totally unaware. Good. She won't hear a thing.

I throw some ice in the blender, tequila, margarita mix, and lime. Hit blend. The second it's done, I strip top to toe. Running shorts, briefs, socks, all of it in a pile on the floor. Yeah, we're doing this properly. I pour the margarita into a tall glass, and, with one idiotic, very on-brand decision, I slide my dick into the drink. Cold. Fucking hell, Sage better appreciate this.

She's still distracted as I walk onto the balcony, bare-ass naked, holding the margarita glass like it's room service. Her gaze lifts. She freezes. Call forgotten. Eyes locked on me. Or more specifically, on the fact that I'm serving her birthday drink like this. She sets the phone down slowly, standing.

"You didn't," she whispers, grinning, eyes wide. I raise a brow.

"You said a margarita and my dick. I'm just being efficient."

She saunters over, pure sin wrapped in a sleepy morning smirk, one brow raised like this guy cannot be serious.

"Oh, you are lucky your dick is pretty," she mutters, and then Jesus, she reaches out, wraps her fingers around my cock and pulls me out of the glass like she's reclaiming stolen property. I'm halfway to groaning when she lifts the glass and tips a little of the liquid right onto the head of my cock. Then licks it off. One slow, maddening swipe of her tongue.

"Holy shit, Sage."

She hums like she's tasting fine wine. "Mm. Smooth. A little salty, but I'll allow it."

I drop the glass to the table and haul her in fast, my mouth crashing into hers.

"You're unbelievable," I mutter between kisses, already rock hard.

"And you're about to be fucked. Right here. Right now."

"Happy birthday to me," she purrs.

Her lips crash into mine, all tongue and tequila, her fingers still wrapped around my cock like she owns it, and honestly, she does. I back her up until her ass hits the little cafe table, and I lift her onto it without breaking the kiss. She gasps when the stone hits the back of her thighs, cool against her warm skin. I spread her legs and step between them, grinding against her; she's slick from that ridiculous margarita stunt.

"Your trouble," I murmur into her mouth. She smirks, reaching up to twist her fingers into my hair.

"You're the one who put your cock in my cocktail, Playboy."

I groan, dragging my mouth down her neck, across her collarbone, until I find what I want, those perfect, pierced nipples. God, those things drive me insane. I suck one into my mouth hard, tugging the barbell with my teeth, and she arches with a cry, one hand slapping down on the table for balance.

"Mav—fuck."

"You love this," I whisper, licking across to the other one. "These little metal bars… You know what they do to me?"

"I got them for me," she pants, breathless. "But I love how they ruin you."

I drop to my knees in front of her like a goddamn worshipper. She's soaked and swollen, that pussy practically begging for my mouth. I drag my fingers up her thighs, parting her wider, and press one slow kiss to her inner thigh before I finally taste her. She jerks forward with a cry, threading her fingers through my hair and pulling me closer, grinding her hips against my face. I groan against her, tongue relentless, alternating between slow licks and fast flicks that make her whimper. When I slide two fingers in, she clenches around me, thighs trembling on either side of my head.

"Maverick, I'm gonna—"

"That's right, baby. Come for me. Right here. Let the neighbours hear."

Her whole body locks up, then shudders, and she comes hard, moaning my name loud enough that I wouldn't be surprised if Josie and Margot heard it through their hotel walls. I don't give her time to recover. I stand, grip her hips, and line myself up, still rock hard, still wet with margarita and her.

"Pass me the drink, Mav?" she breathes.

"Fuck," I grit. She slides off the table and grabs the glass, naked and flushed and laughing breathlessly. I follow her movements. She pours the margarita between both of us. I bend down and give her pussy one more slow lick and suck up all the liquid.

"Delicious", I say with a smirk. I grab her like a goddamn animal, throwing her on the lounge. She's on all fours now, looking over her shoulder at me with a grin, that wicked, ruin- your-life grin.

"C'mon, Playboy," she purrs. "Give me my present."

I pull her hips closer with shaking hands. "Oh, I'll give you the whole fucking gift bag." And then I'm inside her in one deep, perfect thrust. I wrap my hand around her neck, pressing gently. Sage always goes wild for a hand necklace. She cries out, arching back into me. Her hair falls around her shoulders, skin flushed, those tits swaying with every movement as I set a rhythm hard, deep, relentless. She takes it like she always does — hungry, wild, moaning my name. Her fingers dig into the lounge, her hips pushing back into my hips, her whole body is lit up. I reach around to palm her breast and tug one of the bars as I thrust harder. She loses it.

"Fuck, Mav—I'm going to come again."

"Do it," I growl into her ear. "Come on, my cock, baby. Squeeze me." And she does legs shaking, voice breaking, her whole body trembling around me as I thrust through it, chasing my release. A few more strokes and I'm there too, groaning her name into her shoulder, clutching her so tight I think she might bruise. We collapse together in a tangle of limbs and sweat and laughter, breathless and messy, so goddamn happy.

"Best. Birthday. Ever," she murmurs.

I kiss her shoulder. "Good thing it's not over"

. . .

SAGE

It's my thirtieth birthday, and I know Josie told Maverick. The sneaky little bitch. Am I mad about it? Absolutely not. Because starting my day with a cocktail-soaked dick and a screaming orgasm on a sun-drenched balcony? Yeah. No notes. If I want to spend my birthday getting absolutely railed by a man who worships my body like it's a damn religion, then that's exactly what I'm going to do. It's my birthday, and I'll scream if I want to. Literally.

Still, Maverick's been cagey since I got off his face this morning, and that usually means he's plotting something. But whatever. Plot away because while he's being secretive and sexy and sneaking around the apartment with that devil grin on his face, my phone's been painfully dry. No texts from Josie or Margot. Those bitches better be in witness protection or a coma, because if they've just ghosted me on my dirty thirty, I will burn everything to the ground. At least my dad called. Briefly. But it counts, I guess. Even Maverick's mum called. May Carter, queen of the Carter family. I assume Maverick gave her my number, and honestly? Not mad. It made me weirdly warm. Still suspicious, though.

"Sage, baby?" Maverick calls from the bedroom, his voice low and loaded. I grin. Round two it is.

"Coming," I yell, already heading for the door, "in more ways than one, I hope."

"Damn, baby," I hear him mutter, and it makes my hips sway harder. I step into the bedroom and stop short.

On the bed is a dress. Another one. He's turning this into a habit, buying me things. Not that I'm complaining. It's stunning. White. Strapless. A corset bodice with draped satin that looks almost... Bridal. My stomach does a slow, traitorous flip.

"This is gorgeous," I say cautiously. "But where are we going?"

"You'll find out soon," he smirks.

"Shoes are in the box. Oh, and don't bother with underwear." He winks. I swear to God. This man is chaos and temptation wrapped in muscles and horsepower. But damn, he is fine. I slip into the dress and the heels while ignoring the anxiety clawing at the edges of my chest and wait.

He knocks, then pushes the door open and stares. Like I've physically punched him in the throat with how hot I look.

"Wow," he breathes. "Sage… you look…" His voice drops. "Fucking incredible."

He grabs me by the waist and kisses me so hard I lose all sense of gravity. "As much as I want to stay and tear that dress off with my teeth," he mutters into my neck, "the car's here." And now I hate him a little. Tease.

We pull up to a restaurant high in the cliffs, the same one he brought me to back when I first came to Monaco. The view is obscene. Dripping in romance. The whole thing screams proposal. My heart thuds. Then I see the white dress. The twinkle lights. No other guests, just staff. I swear to God if that bulge in his pants is a ring box and not his semi-erect dick, I'm going to be so mad. Cue full-blown panic. Oh, my God. He's going to propose. He's going to propose, and I'm not ready, and he's going to leave when I say no, and my life is going to implode in a very expensive dress with no panties on—

"Happy birthday, Sage!!" I freeze. Around the corner come Josie and Margot, dressed like goddamn birthday Barbies, drinks in hand, screaming like we're back in uni. And… is that, Drew? That motherf— Josie. And… wait. Is that Maverick's mum? This woman has met me twice, and she's here in Monaco for my birthday? I suddenly can't breathe. The lump in my throat is embarrassingly real. I'm trying so hard not to cry.

"Surprise, baby," Maverick whispers, pulling me into his chest, pressing a kiss into my hair. "Happy birthday."

I say nothing. I can't. So, I just wrap my arms around him and breathe him in. Okay, fine. I might cry just a little. But only because this man makes me feel like I matter. Like I'm loved. Like maybe turning thirty isn't a funeral for my twenties, but the beginning of something even better.

Still…I lean up and whisper in his ear, "If you ever make me think you're proposing in public again, I will murder you."

He laughs. "Duly noted, birthday girl."

Apparently, Maverick invited every person who's ever seen me naked or cried with me in a bathroom and Drew. So, obviously — best party ever. Josie and Margot are fully loaded tonight, both dressed in sequins like disco balls with boobs. I don't even ask where the outfits came from.

Margot's already drunk half a bottle of tequila deep, and Josie's pulling out temporary tattoos and yelling, "IT'S A VIBE!" while trying to stick one on Drew's forehead that I'm 80% sure it says "Daddy."

May Carter — bless her heart is holding her own with a gin martini and giving Josie fashion advice like she's on the Met Gala red carpet. I overheard her say, "You remind me of a younger me, except louder," and Josie wept. The playlist is also complete chaos, Dolly Parton one second, Cardi B the next, then someone throws on ABBA, and it's all downhill from there. Margot is sobbing to "Dancing Queen", and Drew is air-grinding next to her like a human traffic hazard.

Meanwhile, Maverick is across the room watching me with that look. The one that says you're the only one I see, even in a room full of people, drinks, and utter chaos. His gaze is hot. Heavy. Possessive. I know that look, and so does the very bare, very needy little situation between my legs. I take my drink and saunter over like a woman with an agenda. Because I am. I grab him by the front of his shirt, pull him down to my level and whisper in his ear

"You said no underwear. So, either you get me off in the next ten minutes, or I do it myself in this ridiculously expensive bathroom."

He chokes on his drink. "Bathroom. Now."

We slip out like teenagers ditching an afterparty. I half- expect someone to wolf-whistle, but we make it down the hallway unnoticed. Maverick pulls me into the private staff bathroom, marble walls, dim lights, big mirror. Perfect. The second the door locks, his mouth is on mine, hungry and hot, teeth dragging over my lower lip. He spins me and pins me against the counter, hands sliding up my thighs and under my dress.

"You've been dripping for me all night, haven't you?" he growls, sliding two fingers straight into me like he already knows the answer.

"Fuck, Sage, you're so wet," he groans against my neck. "All for me?"

"All. For. You," I pant, grabbing the counter as he pumps into me. His other hand tugs the top of the dress down, freeing my nipples, and he groans when he sees them.

"I'll never tire of these," he says, sucking one into his mouth, teeth grazing the barbell, tongue teasing the tip until I'm trembling.

"May, I'm gonna—"

He drops to his knees. That man has no shame.

He drags my leg over his shoulder and buries his face in me like he's starving. "Such a desperate little thing," He mutters against my cunt. His tongue is relentless, teeth scraping, moans vibrating through my whole damn soul. I bite my knuckle to keep from screaming because my girls and his mum are literally fifty feet away, but fuck, he's too good at this, and when he looks up at me, his mouth shiny and smug as hell. I'm gone.

"I should've served your birthday margarita right from here."

I let out the filthiest moan known to humankind, and Maverick stands, flips me, and pushes me over the counter. My hands splay across the cold marble as I feel him line up behind me.

"I'm going to ruin this dress."

"You better." He thrusts into me hard and deep, the stretch perfect and punishing. With one hand on my hip, the other slides around to pinch one of my nipples, twisting the metal until I jolt with a cry.

"Mav—fuck—"

"You love it when I fuck you like this," he grits out. "Bent over in expensive places, wearing my gift, while you're dripping down your thighs."

"Yes," I moan, head falling forward, watching our filthy reflection in the mirror.

He reaches down, rubs my clit in tight circles and, boom, the orgasm hits like a freight train. I gasp, legs shaking, walls clenching so hard he lets out a guttural curse and follows me over the edge, burying himself deep and pulsing inside me. We both pant, still pressed against the counter, catching our breath.

"You know," I mumble, breathless, "if this is thirty… I might survive it." He chuckles against my back, hands still wrapped around my waist.

"Oh, baby… thirty's just getting started."

We are back in the apartment now. Maverick took his mum back to her hotel. Honestly, it's for the best; she does not want to be around the apartment tonight.

"Alright," Josie says, slamming a shot glass down like she's about to call war crimes legal.

"New birthday rule: every time someone mentions Maverick, we take a shot."

Margot groans. "I like my liver, Josie."

Raising my margarita, "I like my orgasms, but here we are—discussing Maverick again."

Josie narrows her eyes at me. "YOU just said Maverick. SHOT."

Damn it. We throw back our shots. Mine is tequila, Margot's is something unidentifiable and green, and Josie has what I'm 90% sure is straight gasoline. She doesn't even flinch, sociopath.

"Okay, my turn," Margot says, eyes gleaming.

"Never have I ever… hooked up somewhere public in the last twenty-four hours."

My mouth drops open, "You bitch."

"You're the bitch! You're the one who snuck off with your race car sex god during your own party!"

"DID YOU JUST SAY, 'RACE CAR SEX GOD'?" Josie yells.

"She did. SHOTS." I scream. We drink again. I'm warm, flushed, and not responsible for anything that happens next.

"Okay," I say, grinning, "my turn. Truth or drink. Josie: What's the wildest thing you've ever done during sex?"

Josie doesn't even blink. "Used a curling iron handle. Not turned on. I'm not a monster,"

Margot chokes on her drink. "You… WHAT?"

"It was clean!"

I wheeze into my glass. "Josie. You need therapy."

"Probably," she says cheerfully. "But do I look like a woman who's making good life choices?" Absolutely not. Her crop top says, 'Horny but Healing', and I'm pretty sure she lost one shoe on the walk back to the apartment.

Margot leans in close. "Okay, Sage, truth or drink: would you marry Maverick if he proposed tomorrow?"

I freeze. My heart skips a beat.

"…is this tequila laced with a trap?" They both stare at me. I down the shot.

"OH MY GOD," Josie screams. "You didn't answer!"

"She's terrified!" Margot cackles.

"You'd say no!"

"I didn't say no!"

"You didn't say yes!"

"I said nothing!"

Josie throws her arm around me. "We'll be there no matter what, babe. Whether you get married or run to Mexico and fake your own death."

Margot clinks her glass to mine. "To messy choices and women with nipple piercings."

"Cheers, sluts," I laugh, grinning as we down another round.

Across the room, I catch Maverick watching me from the other side of the lounge, completely ignoring Drew, one brow raised, lips twitching. He knows we're up to something. He just doesn't know what. Yet.

"Josie," I whisper, "Want to dare me to give Mav a lap dance?"

"I thought you'd never ask."

FORTY-FOUR

MAVERICK

I should've known something was coming the second I saw the three of them whispering like witches at a coven meeting.

Sage's dress is barely holding on, Josie's lost a shoe, and Margot looks like she's about to commit a felony for fun. I should've known. But I didn't. So, when the music cuts and I hear Pony by Genuine starts to play… I freeze.

"Oh, fuck no," I mutter, already moving.

Too late. Sage is on the goddamn table. My girlfriend. My beautifully unhinged, drunk on tequila, chaos goblin of a girlfriend. She's barefoot, margarita in hand, hair wild, eyes locked on me like I'm prey, and then she starts to dance. Like, actually dance. Grinding her hips, licking salt off her hand, downing the tequila shot she pulled out of nowhere, and then throwing the lime over her shoulder. The girls lose it. Phones are out. I hear Drew somewhere behind me yelling, "GET HER, BRO. THIS IS HOW IT STARTS. THIS IS HOW WOMEN RUIN YOU."

She crouches low and crooks a finger at me. Goddammit. I walk toward her, trying to keep my dick from announcing itself to the room. It's not working. My cock is on a full PR tour. Sage grins and hops down right into my lap when I sit in the nearest chair like an idiot. She straddles me. Grinding. Moaning. Laughing against my mouth like a goddamn tease. Everyone's watching. I should care, but I don't. My hands are under her dress, gripping her bare ass.

"Sage…" I growl. She leans in, lips brushing my ear.

"It's my birthday, baby. Are you going to spank me or just sit there like a little bitch?" Christ.

I stand up, throw her over my shoulder and walk straight into the bedroom to a chorus of "WHOOOO!!!" and a "MAV'S GONNA CLAP THEM CHEEKS!" from Josie.

The moment the bedroom door slams shut, she's on me again. Dress around her waist, bare because, of course, she listened when I told her not to wear underwear. My fingers brush her slick heat. She's still soaked from the quickie at the restaurant, and she gasps, clutching my shoulders. Her nipple piercings brush against my chest, and I lose every last drop of sanity I have. I pin her against the wall and slide inside her in one smooth thrust.

"Fuck, Mav—" Her legs lock around me. My hands grip her thighs. I pound into her like I've been waiting my whole life for this moment.

"You want to put on a show?" I growl, fucking her hard enough to make the picture frames rattle. "You want to dance like that in front of everyone? This body's mine, baby. You don't tease the man who owns you like that." Sage gasps and scratches her nails down my back.

"Then fuck me like you mean it."

I do. I fuck her on the wall. Then on the bedside table. Then over the dresser and by the time we stumble exhausted onto the bed, she's still got tequila on her breath, but I'm not stopping until she screams.

Later—much later—we lie there, tangled and spent. Finally sated. Her dress is on the lamp. My shirt is on the TV, and her phone buzzes with a message from Josie that says: "You dead? Or just paralysed from dick?" Sage shows it to me and giggles.

I smirk and kiss her temple. "Both."

I WAKE up to the unmistakable sound of hell. Someone's groaning. Something crashes—glass, maybe? A pan? And then a very familiar voice yelling, "Where the fuck is my bra, Drew?!" Josie. Yep. This is home. Sage is curled up on my chest, naked, warm, tangled in the sheets and snoring just the tiniest bit. Her thigh is thrown over my hip. Her nipples catching the sunlight. We're both covered in what I'm hoping is lime juice as I gently brush the hair off her face.

"Baby,"

She groans. "No. Don't wake me unless you've got coffee. Or your dick. Or both." Tempting. But there's chaos happening out there, and I need to do a damage assessment before someone sets the place on fire with a toaster.

We both eventually drag ourselves up and wrap ourselves in the nearest clothes. She pulls on my shirt; God damn, she's a vision and shuffles out of the bedroom like we've just survived a natural disaster. We make it to the kitchen and freeze because Drew— fucking Drew—is completely naked, standing at the counter, eating a banana, like this is some nudist resort in Ibiza. He turns to look at us casually, like we're the ones being weird.

"Mornin'," he says through a mouthful of banana. "You got any Gatorade?"

Sage blinks "Why are you naked?"

Drew shrugs. "Didn't feel like pants. They were... sweaty." I cover Sage's eyes like I'm shielding her from solar radiation.

"Put your dick away, mate. This isn't the Olympics." He laughs and just keeps chewing. Still fucking naked.

From the lounge, Margot yells, "If anyone touches my nachos, I will commit actual homicide." Nachos, what the fuck? She must've cooked those last night. Sage peeks around my hand, eyes still on Drew.

"Do I need to know why there's a traffic cone in our bathtub?"

"Nope." Drew practically yells as a "Definitely not" comes from Josie.

She sighs and leans her head against my shoulder. "You know, this might actually be the best birthday I've ever had."

I press a kiss to her temple and tighten my arm around her waist. "Even with the naked rugby player?" She smirks.

"Especially with the naked rugby player."

Drew winks. "Anytime, princess."

"Jesus Christ," I mutter, and Sage just laughs, warm and messy and content. And somehow, standing in our tequila-soaked, absolutely destroyed apartment with a naked man in the kitchen… I've never felt more at home.

———

SAGE'S BIRTHDAY weekend nearly killed us, and by killed, I mean we drank enough tequila to pickle ourselves. Josie nearly fell off the balcony, Drew was naked for 36 hours straight, and we saw things that should've never been seen. My mum flew back to London the next morning. She'd invited herself (classic May Carter), but honestly? I'm glad she came. I think it meant more to Sage than she let on.

Now the real world is calling. Baku's next, then the States. Austin, Brazil, Vegas, Qatar and Abu Dhabi. It's full throttle from here to the end of the season. I already know it's going to suck being away from Sage again. We haven't talked much about what comes next, but I feel that weight in my chest already.

I'm zipping up my suitcase, bigger than my usual duffel, because the end-of-the-season schedule is brutal when I spot another suitcase on the bed. Sage's. I raise a brow, unzip it. It's packed. Full. Organised. Even has the cute little packing cubes she swore she'd never use.

"Babe?" I call out.

"Yeah?" She yells from the kitchen, casual as hell.

"You going somewhere?" I ask, poking my head around the corner.

She strolls in like she owns the place—which, let's be real, she kind of does—and grins at me like she's about to drop a bomb.

"Yep," she says, popping the 'p'. "With you. If that's okay?" I blink. Once. Twice. She's coming with me. For real?

"Wait… seriously?" I say, stepping toward her.

"Seriously," she says, and I don't give her another second before pulling her into a kiss that says finally. That says thank you. That says don't ever leave my side again, you infuriating, tequila-soaked, perfect human. She wraps her arms around my neck and leans in, that smirk playing at her lips.

"I'll be in Baku with you, and Margot's flying out to meet us in Austin, so you won't get too distracted."

"Distracted?" I raise a brow, pulling her tighter. "You mean like… right now?" She grins, and it's pure trouble.

"Don't start something you can't finish, Playboy."

"Oh, baby," I murmur into her neck, "I always finish." She laughs, that full-bodied, sexy laugh that gets me every damn time.

"I want to be there when you win the championship, but I need to go back to Melbourne for my cousin's wedding, so I'm going to fly out after Mexico and then meet you in Qatar. I miss the Las Vegas and Brazil race weekend, so that sucks," she whispers, but the words hit me square in the chest. She means it. I can see it in the way her brows pinch together, how her mouth twists in that way she does when she hates something but knows she can't change it. I nod, slowly, because what the hell else can I do? She has a life too. A family. Commitments that don't revolve around race calendars or podiums or whatever chaos my world spins into next.

"Okay," I say, trying to sound casual, even as every muscle in me rebels at the idea of her not being there.

FORTY-FIVE

SAGE

So, here I am… in Baku. Azerbaijan, baby. Never thought I'd end up here unless it was by accident or via an Instagram ad promising cheap spa retreats. But no, I'm here on purpose, riding shotgun on the Maverick Carter chaos train, now boarding for the rest of the season. And I'm loving it. Sort of. Okay, I mostly love it.

The travel's been smooth, the weather's stunning, and the skyline looks like a futuristic fever dream. But holy hell, race weekends are intense. It's like a three-day music festival but with fewer bathrooms and more testosterone. Maverick's been in full driver mode since we landed. Serious, focused, and sexy as hell in that race suit. I mean… come on. The way that suit hugs his ass? Criminal. I tried to behave myself, really; I did. But he walked out of the paddock after practice yesterday, helmet under one arm, sweat glistening on his neck, smirking like the cocky bastard he is, and I swear to God, I nearly dragged him into a hospitality tent and gave the team a show they'd never forget.

"Later," he whispered in my ear. "I want you screaming my name louder than the engines," and I almost blacked out.

Today is qualifying, and I'm pretending to be a functioning adult in the paddock lounge, sunglasses on, hair perfect, drinking something fizzy and pretending I'm not thinking about last night when Maverick very enthusiastically welcomed me to his race calendar. Spoiler: I screamed his name louder than the engines.

Josie texted me five minutes ago:

> Josie: I see you on TV. Stop pretending you're innocent. We all heard about the sex in Monaco. Also, your man is HOT.

I smirked and texted back:

> Me: He's in pole position every night, babe.

The track's buzzing, the cars are firing up, and Maverick is heading out for Q2. I catch his eye on the screen just for a second, but I know he's looking for me. Always does. Gives me that stupid smirk that tells me he's about to risk it all. I press my fingers to my lips and blow him a kiss, even if he can't see it. Because no matter where the hell we are in the world, I'm right here. His girl. His home base. His race suit groupie with a dirty mind and an excellent ass. Let's go, baby. I barely have time to sit back down after Q3 before Maverick's name flashes up on the leaderboard: P2. Not bad. Not pole, but close enough that I know he'll still strut around the paddock like he owns the joint. My phone buzzes with a message from Margot, who clearly caught the broadcast from wherever she's currently sipping rosé:

> Margot: Your man's looking spicy. Is it the car, or is he just horny again?

> Me: Why not both?

I make my way down to the motorhome, flashing my pass like I belong here now because I do. I've been here long enough to know where everything is, how the schedule works, and which hospitality staff will sneak me an extra pastry if I wink at them. Maverick finds me before I find him. Still in his suit, peeled halfway down so it hangs from his waist. His fireproof undershirt clings to his chest like a second skin, and I'm hit with a full-body memory of what that chest felt like pressed against my back last night.

"Hey, speedy," I grin, stopping just short of him. "P2 looks good on you."

"P1 would've looked better," he mutters, pulling me in by the waist, "but I've got better things to do than mope."

"Oh?" I tease. "Like what?"

He doesn't answer. Just dips his head and kisses me like he didn't just spend the last hour dodging walls at 300km/h. His tongue slides against mine, slow and claiming, and I make a very undignified noise against his mouth. I barely notice when he backs me into the side of the trailer wall.

"Someone's still running hot," I murmur when he finally pulls back.

"You wearing anything under this little skirt?" he asks, voice low and dangerous, eyes dark with want.

"Wouldn't you like to know."

"Oh, I'm about to find out." He lifts the hem without warning and grins when he discovers the truth: no underwear, just bare skin.

"Mav—someone could see—"

"No one's looking but me," he says, already sliding his hand between my thighs. "And I'll be quick. Like a pit stop."

"You're disgusting."

"And you're wet." God help me, he's not wrong.

He spins me, presses me to the side of the motorhome and pushes my legs apart with his knee. His fingers find me first, his bulge is pressing right up against me and—

"Twenty seconds," I gasp. "That's all you get."

He laughs, low and dangerous in my ear. "Don't threaten me with a good time."

And when we're done — all sweaty, smug, and breathless, he tugs my skirt back into place and kisses my temple like he didn't just fuck me against a motorhome.

"Your trouble, Playboy," I say, adjusting my hair in the reflection of his visor.

"Baby," he smirks, tossing me a water bottle, "you love it." He's not wrong.

. . .

I DON'T KNOW what I was expecting from an Apex team dinner, but it wasn't this. We're at some rooftop restaurant overlooking the Caspian Sea, the entire team gathered to celebrate a double podium. Maverick finished P2, and his teammate Liam snagged P3. The champagne's been flowing since the cooldown room and hasn't stopped.

The place is swanky, with string lights hanging above us, a breeze rolling in from the water, and way too many men still wearing their team polos like it's a uniformed cult. I'm seated next to Maverick, who's got one hand resting high on my thigh because he owns and judging by the number of staff who nod when he speaks, he might as well own this place as well.

He leans in close, murmuring in my ear, "Right now I'm imagining how fast I could get you off under this table" I shoot him a warning look, but my thighs clench all the same.

"Behave."

He smirks, "I'm literally never going to do that." He kisses the side of my neck, and I swear if I weren't already tipsy, I'd be halfway there just from the way he murmurs into my skin. As dessert shows up, Maverick's fingers drift higher under the tablecloth, and I shoot him a look.

"Stop it." I glare,

"I'm not doing anything."

"You're about to make me moan into this crème Brûlée."

"Good," he says with that smug smile.

I grab his wrist and whisper, "If you keep this up, I'm going to drag you into the coat closet before the espresso even hits the table."

His pupils dilate like I just offered him pole position. "Check, please."

FORTY-SIX

MAVERICK

Having Sage on the road with me is like racing with a loaded gun in my chest. Every moment feels like I'm seconds from detonating in the best kind of way. She's been with me since Baku, so for about two weeks, one race week, one travel week and now another race week and somehow, instead of the novelty wearing off, it's only getting harder to concentrate. She walks into the paddock like she owns the whole damn sport, always in jeans that hug her ass, sunglasses that scream bad decision incoming and a mouth that whispers filthy promises that I'm constantly cashing in. The entire grid knows she's mine now, not because I've said it out loud but because I can't keep my hands off her.

We're in Austin now, it's loud, hot and chaotic. Texas energy is next level, and the fans here don't sleep. Neither do we, apparently. I've had about four hours of shut-eye since we landed, and most of it was interrupted by Sage's mouth somewhere on my body. She's lying on the hotel bed, wearing one of my T-shirts. Honestly, she just lives in them now and nothing else, legs tangled in the sheets, scrolling through her phone like she's not the single biggest distraction I've ever had to face in my entire damn career. I button up my race day outfit halfway and pause in front of the mirror, glancing back at her.

"You coming to the track now or later?" I ask, tossing her one of my caps. She looks up, smirks.

"Why? You need your good luck charm?"

"No. I need you there to remind me not to punch that rookie from Maclean if he stares at your ass again." She laughs. A full-body laugh. God, I love that sound.

"It's not my fault your rivals have good taste."

I walk over and climb onto the bed, pinning her with my knees on either side of her hips. "If they had good taste, they'd know not to look at what they'll never get."

She grins, eyes flicking to my mouth, then back up to my eyes. "That mouth going to kiss me or just make threats?" So, I kiss her like I'm trying to memorise it.

"Wish me luck," I whisper, pulling back just an inch. She tugs the zipper of my jacket up to my neck and smooths it down my chest.

"Go make 'em cry, champ." I leave her there, a cocky grin on her lips that are still puffy from mine.

The energy is insane at the track. Every American fan wants a piece of me, and for once, I don't care if they get it. I've already got the one thing I want most in my corner. The guys tease me because I'm grinning like an idiot every time I catch sight of her on the pit wall, wearing my team jacket like she's always belonged there. After FP3, Margot shows up loud and wild as always, sunglasses on and a beer in hand, even though it's barely noon. She and Sage disappear for an hour and return with suspiciously satisfied smiles.

"Do I even want to know?" I ask as we walk back to the hospitality unit.

"Nope," Sage says sweetly, brushing her fingers down my arm. Having Sage with me on the road? Dangerous. Distracting. A dream come true, and I don't want to do another race without her.

RACE DAY in Austin feels like I'm stepping into a pressure cooker with a tequila chaser. It's loud. Hot. Fans are screaming. Engineers are barking into headsets. The grid is vibrating with nerves and adrenaline. There's smoke in the air, bass from some pre-race DJ pumping through the paddock, and somewhere in the chaos... Sage. I haven't seen her since this morning, when she woke me up with her mouth and then casually strutted off into the shower, completely naked and covered in... well, me. Before she left for the bathroom, she whispered,

"Win today and I'll let you do anything you want to me. Lose, and I'll do whatever I want to you." Either way, I'm screwed and not in a good way.

Now I'm getting strapped into the car. Helmet on. Visor down, and through the wall of engineers, media and photographers, I catch a glimpse of her. Pass hanging around her neck, sunglasses pushed into her hair, her mouth tugging up in that little grin that says I dare you to lose, baby. God. I'd race backwards while blindfolded for that woman. The lights go out, and I launch. The race is brutal, tyre degradation is hell, overtakes that should've been illegal, and some back marker nearly took me out in Sector 3. At one point, I'm screaming into the radio and thinking about quitting it all to be Sage's pool boy, but then I hear her voice over the team radio — literally.

The engineers patched her in for five seconds as a joke. She just says, "Eyes up, champ. Bring it home."

Fastest lap. Clean overtake. I'm back in the zone. We finish P1. Just. The team is losing their minds; I'm punching the air and screaming into the radio like a lunatic. I don't even care that I'm covered in sweat and half deaf. Because I know what's waiting for me in Parc ferme. I pull into the spot, kill the engine, rip my gloves off, and she's already there, hopping over the barrier like she's part of the damn pit crew. She throws herself at me before I can even take my helmet off. Legs around my waist. Arms around my neck. Her mouth crashes into mine, and the crowd roars harder than the engines.

"You did it," she breathes, kissing me again. "I knew you would."

"You said I could do anything I wanted to you," I growl, hands full of her thighs. "Hope you blocked out the whole night." She just smirks.

"You'd better hydrate first, champ. You're going to need stamina."

The podium is a blur. Champagne. Screams. American flags are waving everywhere. But the only thing I see is her watching me like I'm the only thing that matters. Like I'm not just Maverick Carter, the race winner, but hers.

Back in the hospitality suite, she's sitting on the edge of the counter, drinking something alcoholic straight from the bottle, legs swinging, still wearing my team gear and a dangerous smile.

"Ready for round one?" she asks.

"Baby," I say, already unzipping my suit, "this is going to be a fucking marathon." And just like that, the race day ends the only way it ever could in chaos, victory, and in her.

Sunlight's sneaking through the curtains, warm and golden, casting a soft halo over the tangled mess that is my girlfriend in bed. Her hair wild, legs kicked out from the sheet, one arm flung across my stomach like she owns me because she does. I shift, trying not to wake her just yet, not because I don't want her awake, but because damn, I enjoy watching her like this. Wrecked from the night before, totally relaxed, not a trace of the fire she threw at me when she was riding me like a damn victory lap. She's got the faintest smirk tugging at her lips, like she knows exactly what I'm thinking, and maybe she does, because she lets out a little hum, eyes still closed.

"Are you staring at me again, Playboy?"

"Always," I murmur, dragging my fingertips down her back. "You're my favourite view."

She peeks one eye open, smiles lazily, voice still scratchy from sleep— and maybe the screaming.

"Ugh! You're so obsessed with me."

"Obviously," I grin, leaning in to kiss her shoulder.

"Have you met you?" Her laughter warms the room. She stretches catlike, which does insane things to my ability to think rationally. Sheets slip down, giving me a full view of those tits that I swear are designed to ruin me.

"Round four?" she teases, quirking a brow.

"You're dangerous," I say, already rolling on top of her, kissing down her neck. We make out like we've got nowhere to be because today, we don't. No races, no meetings, no flights. Just me, her, and a ridiculous amount of room service waiting to happen.

Eventually, she wriggles out from under me, stealing the sheet as she walks toward the window, completely naked and not even a little shy. She throws it open, soaking in the view of Austin, her silhouette lit up in gold.

"You know," she says over her shoulder, "this whole post- race glow- up? Big fan."

I grab the hotel phone with one hand and watch her like I'm never going to stop.

"Room service. One full breakfast spread. And two mimosas."

"Make it three," she calls.

"Make it four," I correct, smirking. She turns back to me, eyes sparkling.

"God, I love you." I practically yell. And just like that, I'm gone for her all over again.

FORTY-SEVEN

SAGE

Travelling with Maverick is... a total experience. Like, sure, there's the private jet and the VIP treatment and the whole being-ferried-around-like-a-celebrity part. We're barely on the plane, and he's already halfway into my seat; his hand slides onto my thigh. Like it's always been his place to touch, whispering something utterly inappropriate in my ear while a flight attendant pretends not to notice. His palm is warm, his smirk smug, and he's wearing those goddamn grey sweatpants that make my pussy clench around nothing.

"Tell me again why you're dressed like a walking thirst trap?" I ask, flicking the waistband of his pants and raising a brow. He leans closer, lips brushing my ear.

"So, you'll stay distracted and not notice when I sneak my hand under your blanket mid-flight." My jaw drops a little, not from shock, but from the sheer audacity.

"You're unbelievable."

"You love it," he grins, teeth flashing. I do. I swat at his chest, and he feigns injury dramatically, draping himself across me like a man defeated. His hoodie smells like his cologne, and he's warm and devious and all mine. We're heading to Mexico, another city, another race, and I'm finally here with him. Out in the open. No more hiding. Just Maverick Carter and his chaotic, brilliant, adrenaline-fuelled world... and me, right in the thick of it.

I settle back in the seat, slipping my fingers through his as he rests his head against my shoulder and watches the window as the clouds roll past in cottony streaks beneath them. A new country is waiting. Mexico - the home of tequila, here we come, and honestly, they're not ready for us or me at least.

The moment we step off the plane, it hits me, the warm, thick air and the kind of energy you can feel in your bones. Mexico doesn't just welcome you; it grabs you by the hips and says let's dance. Maverick throws his arm around my shoulders, and I don't even care that I'm jet-lagged and wearing yesterday's hoodie. I've never felt more seen, more claimed.

"You ready?" he murmurs into my ear as we move through the private terminal. Sunglasses on, hair a little messy from the flight, but Maverick still looks like a goddamn magazine cover. It's rude, honestly.

"Ready as I'll ever be," I say, even though my stomach is doing gymnastics. Security meets us outside, already whisking Maverick toward the waiting car. It's sleek, black and just dramatic enough for someone with a reputation like his. I slide in beside him, and he immediately laces our fingers together, his thumb brushing slow, calming strokes over my knuckles. The ride to the hotel is smooth until we hit traffic and Maverick gets handsy, smirking when my breath hitches. Thankfully, I redirect his attention before the driver has a heart attack.

We pull up to the hotel, and it's ridiculous. Floor-to-ceiling windows. Private elevator. A suite that overlooks the ocean.

"Jesus," I breathe, spinning slowly in the middle of the room.

"Like it?" Maverick asks, clearly smug.

"It's alright," I tease. "Could use a few more shirtless drivers lounging by the pool." He steps in behind me, hands on my hips.

"Give me two hours," he murmurs.

"I'll meet you there."

"Are you going to behave yourself?"

His laugh is low, wicked. "Not even a little."

This is my last weekend with Maverick until Qatar. I'm flying back to

Melbourne late Sunday night to attend my cousin's wedding. I'm a bridesmaid, so I have dress fittings and a hen party to attend in the lead-up.
Maverick's not coming; it's too much for him to fly there and back before a
race weekend. I would have loved to introduce him to my family, but
maybe another time. I'm bummed to be missing the Vegas Grand Prix,
though, hello, it's Vegas! So, I'm trying to make the most of this weekend,
soaking in Maverick while I can. What if I can't come back to him… what
if my heart decides it's too hard to love again? Have I told him this? Nope,
of course not, why would I? He needs to win; he's so close to winning his
ninth championship, I can't be the distraction his team thinks I am.

MAVERICK

By the time I get back to the hotel after an afternoon of media and
debriefs, I'm itching. Not just for a win this weekend but for her. We've got
four races left after the weekend, and for two of them I'll be going solo.
I'm already counting down the minutes until Qatar.

Every interview, every flash of the camera, every handshake with a
sponsor and all I could think about was Sage. Probably lounging by the
pool in that tiny bikini she definitely packed on purpose, sipping something fruity, looking like summer. She's leaving for Melbourne on Sunday
night; she's a bridesmaid in a few weeks and has a few things to do while
she's there. She'll miss Brazil and Vegas, but that's probably a good thing;
somehow, Sage and Vegas don't seem like the best mix. Sage will meet
me in Qatar, or so she thinks. I told her I couldn't make the wedding when
she asked me if I'd want to come a few months ago, but with some planning, I've been able to make it happen. It's only going to be a quick trip
for me, though. I'll fly in on Thursday night, meet Sage at her family
home on Friday, attend the wedding and then fly out Sunday with her. I
hope.

When I unlock the hotel room door, it's dim inside. Music low. Something slow and not playing by accident. I step in and close the door
behind me.

"Sage?" I call. Then I see her standing on the balcony, back to me,
bathed in golden hour light, wearing nothing but one of my button-downs.

Bare legs. Hair down. Holding a glass of wine, like the moment was curated just for me. I groan. "You waiting for someone?"

She turns around, smug as hell. "Depends. You planning on leaving this hotel room?"

"Absolutely not."

I'm across the room in seconds. She meets me at the balcony door, eyes blazing. I grab her by the hips, hauling her into me. That glass of wine hits the table without ceremony as my hands go straight to her thighs, lifting her onto the railing. Her legs wrap around me. I grind against her, already hard and aching from nothing more than the sight of her.

"You've been teasing me all day," I say as she murmurs against her neck.

"You like it."

"I like what comes next more."

I undo the buttons of her shirt - my shirt — one by one, slow and deliberate, until her nipples are peeking through, hard and begging for attention. I run my tongue over one, watching her body arch up, then the other, flicking the bars just to hear her hiss.

"Mav," she gasps.

"Yeah, baby?"

"I want you. Now." I don't need more than that. I drop to my knees right there on the balcony, hands gripping her thighs as I spread her open. No panties. God bless her apparent hatred of anything pant-related. I drag my tongue over her slowly, savouring the way she trembles under my mouth. Her hands go straight into my hair, tugging hard like she's trying to keep herself grounded. But I want her to come undone. I slide two fingers inside her, curling just right, mouth working her clit as she starts to shake. She's close. So close.

"Come for me, baby girl," I growl against her.

And she does. Loud and unfiltered, back arching off the railing, legs trembling around my shoulders. I stand and pull her into me, kissing her like I need her to breathe. She tastes like tequila and sunshine and mine.

"Your turn," she whispers, already dropping to her knees. "Jesus, Sage—"

She unzips my pants slowly, that evil grin playing on her lips as she frees me from my jeans. Her eyes lock on mine as she drags her tongue up the length of my cock, teasing the head with a wicked flick before taking me deep, her lips stretched tight, eyes glassy with lust. My hand fists in her hair, hips twitching forward as she takes me deeper, hollowing her cheeks like a goddamn professional.

"Fuck, baby—" She moans around me, sending vibrations straight through my spine, and I swear I black out for a second. When I can't take it anymore, I pull her off gently, lifting her back into my arms.

I carry her to the bed, pinning her wrists above her head, my hands locked tight around them, and her eyes—fuck, her eyes are daring me to lose control. She's panting beneath me, chest rising with every breath, her nipples glistening and swollen from my mouth, those piercings catching the light and making my already rock-hard cock twitch. I take one between my fingers and pinch.

"You know what these do to me, don't you?" I growl, grinding my hips against her, the friction making her whimper.

"You got them pierced, knowing one day I'd find them. You were waiting for this." She bites her bottom lip, deliberately slow.

"Maybe I just like the way it feels…"

I curse under my breath and crash my mouth back to hers, hot, open, wet. Tongues tangling, teeth clashing. I release her wrists, and my hands are everywhere, palming her tits, sliding down her stomach, gripping her thighs. She's already soaked, and when I slide two fingers through her slick heat, she moans against my mouth.

"Fuck Sage," I mutter. I pull my fingers out, and I sit back on my knees for a second, just long enough to take her in naked, flushed, glistening and spread out like a goddamn feast. I run my hands up her legs, spreading them wider, settling between her thighs. I kiss my way back up her trembling body, my cock hard and heavy between us, and when I slide into her, she arches instantly, a strangled cry slipping out as I thrust harder and deeper until her fingers dig into my back. Sage's lips brush my ear.

"I loooike you", she whispers, barely audible, like a secret. Did she go to say, 'I love you' and then catch herself… I'll find that out later. I kiss her softly this time, reverent, pouring every unspoken word into her mouth.

"I love you, Sage. So goddamn much." And then I lose myself in her completely, our bodies moving in sync, tangled in sweat and whispers and the kind that makes the world disappear.

"Maverick—fuck," she pants, clutching at the sheets, and when we come, it's not fast or frantic — it's breaking, quiet, shaking, chest-to-chest collapse. I don't pull out right away; I just hold her, breathing hard. Hands in her hair.

"I'm never going to get tired of fucking you raw like this' I whispered into her hair before I rolled off her, pulling her into my side, pressing soft kisses down her neck.

"You know what kills me about you, Sage?" My voice is low, uneven, my breath still ragged from the way her mouth just undid me. I tilt her chin up, force her eyes on mine. "You don't give a damn about the headlines, or the trophies, or whatever the hell people think I am. You just see me. Do you know how rare that is? Every other woman wanted the champion, the lifestyle, the chaos that comes with my name. But you—" My thumb drags across her swollen bottom lip, and it nearly breaks me. "You don't want any of it. You call me out, you cut through my bullshit, you don't let me get away with anything. And I need that. I need you." Her chest rises against mine, heat coiling tight, and the words tumble out before I can stop them. "You make me softer in ways I didn't think I could be. Your laugh feels like home. Your stubbornness makes me respect you more than anyone I've ever met. And your strength…" I shake my head, pressing my forehead to hers. "It makes me want to be better. You don't need me, Sage. And that's exactly why I can't stop needing you. With you, it's not about fame, or image, or money. It's just raw. Real and terrifyingly simple. You're my peace in a world that never fucking slows down."

FORTY-EIGHT

SAGE

I wake up to the scent of Maverick, sex, sweat, and a hint of whatever cologne clings to his skin. My thighs ache in the best way, my hair's a knotty mess, and I'm pretty sure I still have faint imprints of his fingers on my hips. Ten out of ten. I would do that again and likely will before breakfast. He's sprawled beside me, one arm tossed over my waist, chest rising and falling with the kind of peace only found after hours of... let's call it cardio. I turn my head just enough to watch him sleep, and yep, still annoyingly hot even unconscious. Jaw rough with stubble, lips swollen from everything we did to each other last night, hair an absolute disaster. I'm not fixing it because I love him rugged. I stretch, wince slightly and bite my bottom lip. Jesus. Did he have to ruin me that thoroughly? Four rounds, at least two locations, a margarita in the middle and one very aggressive moment that left a bite mark on my shoulder. I glance down. Yup. There it is. Possessive little shit.

I shift slowly, trying to ease out from under his arm without waking him, not because I'm shy or sneaking off. No, I'm just on a mission. For coffee and maybe an icepack. Possibly a celebratory pastry. I feel like I've earned something covered in frosting and loaded with sugar. But as I roll away, his grip tightens around my waist. A sleepy groan rumbles from his chest. "Where do you think you're going?" he mumbles, voice wrecked and rough with sleep. I smirk.

"To file a complaint with hotel management." He cracks one eye open.

"You going to tell them you got fucked too good?"

"I might."

"You begged for round four."

"Allegedly."

He groans again, rolling onto his back and dragging me with him until I'm sprawled across his chest like some victorious jungle cat. His hands wander to my ass. Of course they do.

"You, okay?" he murmurs, a little softer now, brushing my hair back from my face. I nod, kiss his jaw.

"More than okay."

"Three weeks without you is going to suck"

I raise a brow. "After last night? I think my pussy needs a break. "

He grins. "Oh, is that so?" He leans in and kisses me slowly, sweetly, and a little lazily and just when I think we might be heading for another round, my stomach growls loud enough to shake the walls. Maverick pulls back and laughs, deep and low.

"Breakfast?"

"Shower first," I say, sliding off the bed and tossing him a wink over my shoulder.

"And you're joining me, champ. My legs still don't work properly." He watches me walk away, all cocky and unbothered, until I disappear into the bathroom.

"You're going to be the death of me, trouble," he calls after me. I grin.

"Yeah," I say. "But what a way to go."

Turns out, being the girlfriend of a Formula 1 driver is like dating a very sexy hurricane. One minute you're sipping a latte on a balcony in the Mexican sun, and the next you're being whisked through the pit lane like you belong there, which, according to the team, I do now. And I kind of love it.

The paddock in Mexico is chaotic, hot, loud and full of impossibly attractive people in race suits. And then there's Maverick in his race suit, heat waves rising off the tarmac, sweat on his neck, jaw locked in focus, and every inch of him screaming, 'don't touch me, I'm working', except for the way his eyes always find mine. Yeah. I'm ruined. Fully, enthusiastically, willingly ruined.

I've got my paddock pass, my sunglasses on, and my very best do n't-mess-with-me-but-also-look-how-hot-I-am outfit. Maverick keeps saying I don't have to dress up for these weekends, but baby, I am arm candy now. Let me live. Friday's practice is smooth, Saturday's qualifying even smoother. Maverick clocks in P2, which means he's broody but not unbearable. I've learned the difference. If he's storming through the hospitality suite without talking, stay out of his way. If he's muttering under his breath but still squeezing my ass when he thinks no one's looking. We're good.

After qualifying, he pulls me aside, tugging me into a quiet hallway between the garage and the team's lounge.

"I want to win tomorrow," he says, voice low, fingers at the back of my neck. "Not just for the points." I blink up at him.

"Why then?"

"Because you're here," he says, mouth brushing mine. "And everything feels better when you are."

Oh. Well, then. My knees might have gone a little wobbly.

"You're such a show-off," I murmur, biting back a grin. "Only for you, baby."

He kisses me, quick and deep and entirely inappropriate for a hallway anyone could walk into. When we part, I feel drunk on him.

"You're not allowed to hit the wall tomorrow," I tell him, smoothing a wrinkle on his suit.

"I have plans for you before I go."

"Oh, yeah?" he asks, eyes dark.

"Yup. They involve very little clothing and possibly whipped cream." His jaw clenches. I swear, I could weaponise the effect I have on this man.

"I'll win the fucking race," he growls.

"Good," I purr, stepping back. "Now go make me proud, champ."

Race day in Mexico tastes like metal and nerves. It doesn't matter that Maverick is calm. Doesn't matter that he winked at me before stepping into the garage, that he kissed me like he wasn't about to go full gladiator mode in a carbon fibre rocket. My heart's still in my throat, even after being on the road with him for close to a month. I'm still not built for this. At least, I didn't think I was. But here I am, paddock pass swinging against my chest, sweaty palms wrapped around a bottle of water that I keep forgetting to sip, standing just behind the team pit wall.

"This is insane," I murmur, eyes on the grid.

Ricci laughs. "You're only just realising that now?"

Mavericks in the car, helmet on, hands on the wheel. The crew swarms around him like bees, and I swear I can feel his focus from here. He's not my Maverick right now. Not the man who sticks his dick in margaritas. Not the one who tells me he loves me with his mouth, dragging across my collarbone. He's something else entirely — sharp, brutal and breathtaking. I hate it, and I love it. The national anthem plays. The grid clears. The engine roars to life, and my soul lifts out of my chest. I catch one last glimpse of him on the screens before they switch to race cam.

It's lights out. The start is chaos; it always is, but Maverick is P2 off the line. He's behind the Havoc car, aggressive as hell, already pushing harder than he should on Lap 3. I start pacing by Lap 5. By Lap 12, I'm chewing on my lip like it might save my life.

Team radios are on a low volume, but I can hear the engineers muttering in clipped voices, updates flying between strategy and pit. "Box this lap," someone says. I don't know if it's for Maverick or his teammate. I hold my breath anyway. Someone whispers beside me. "He's looking good." I nod like I believe them, but inside I'm a hot mess. He overtakes the Havoc car on Lap 18, bold and surgical, and I lose my damn mind. Literally scream. I don't even care that people are watching.

"Let's go!" I yell, jumping like an idiot. I swear, even one mechanic cracks a grin. From then on, it's a blur. Strategy, pace management, a safety car that nearly gives me a stroke and thirty-seven minutes of me doing every possible superstitious thing I've never believed in before.

It's finally the last lap. Maverick crosses the line first. I watch it on the monitor and feel my legs give out, joy and adrenaline crashing through me like a damn wave. He's won. He won. My boyfriend just won the Mexican Grand Prix, and suddenly, every nerve, every minute of terror, every second of watching a man I love risk everything… feels worth it.

"Let's go!" I scream again as the whole garage erupts. Mechanics are high-fiving; the team boss is hugging someone aggressively. It feels like I'm drunk, and maybe I am. Because Maverick just took that checkered flag again, like he was born to, and I've never been more in love.

MAVERICK

The champagne's barely dry on my race suit, and I can still taste victory in the air. Mexico delivered. Another podium, another high, but the only thing I'm hungry for now is her. I've been scanning the crowd since I stepped off the podium, but she's not in the sea of celebration. No smug smirk. No Sage. That can only mean one thing: sight, she's waiting for me somewhere quiet. I slip out of the craziness, nodding at a few engineers and brushing off another camera crew. I know where she is. I head straight for the back hallway behind the garage, the one the team doesn't use much, tucked out of sight, and there she is leaning against the wall, arms folded, legs crossed. Still in that little black top and those tight jeans that make my brain short- circuit. She raises an eyebrow like she's unimpressed.

"You took your sweet time, Playboy," she says.

"I had to make sure the fans got a good view," I grin, stalking toward her. She pushes off the wall, sauntering toward me, fingertips teasing the collar of my fireproof shirt.

"You're all sweaty and smug."

"You like me sweaty and smug."

"I like you silent and naked," she says, dragging my suit down my waist in one slow motion.

I press her back against the wall before she can get another jab in, lips on hers, fast and hungry. Her fingers slide into my hair, yanking me closer as she kisses me like she's starved. The heat between us is instant. Her mouth is hot, her body hotter, and even though we're barely hidden behind the paddock chaos, I don't care. She's moaning softly against my lips, tugging my suit lower, her hips rolling up against mine.

"I've got twenty minutes before I have to leave for the airport," she whispers, breathless.

"Then I'd better make it memorable."

I hook an arm around her waist and lift her onto the storage bench behind us, her legs wrapping around me like it's second nature. Our bodies move in sync, grinding, kissing, breath catching, and even with clothes mostly on, it's a mess of heat, pressure and need. We don't go all the way. Not here. Not like this. By the time we pull back, her lipstick is smudged, her top is askew, and I'm panting like I've just done another fifty laps.

She fixes her shirt with a grin, like she hasn't just ruined me in under ten minutes "Good luck dealing with that without me." She kisses me once more, slow and lingering, then slips away down the hall like she didn't just wreck my entire day in the best way, and just like that, she's gone. Off to Melbourne. Back to reality. I lean against the wall, still buzzing, still tasting her on my lips. God help anyone who tries to interview me now.

———

I'M on the team plane. I decided to fly to Brazil with the team. It didn't make sense to use my plane without Sage; it feels emptier without her. Don't get me wrong, the team plane is just as nice as all private jets, endless snacks and entertainment and seats that turn into beds, it's all here. But she isn't, and now everything's just a little too quiet. I've done this a thousand times. In and out of countries, through time zones, hotel rooms and media days that all blur together. I used to love this part. I used to have a different woman in every country, too, the movement, the rhythm, the control. Now, all I can think about is Sage asleep next to me with one leg thrown over mine and her cold toes tucked against my calf. Or her stealing half the minibar and acting like she didn't. Or having her climb on top of me at 30,000 feet, telling me she's bored. God, I miss her already.

I scroll through my photos like a loser, stopping on the one from this morning in my hoodie, like always, sitting on the edge of the bed with her hair still wet with a coffee in hand, smiling at me like she didn't just break me in half last night. She said we had twenty minutes before she had to leave. We used nineteen, and now it's just me and a calendar that looks like a goddamn endurance test. I've got Austin in the rearview. Mexico was fireworks. Brazil's up next, and Vegas after that. We're closing in on the championship, but everything feels a little off-kilter without her around. Like I've lost my edge, and the distraction of Sage is all I want.

The guys were giving me shit after the race, asking where Sage was, winking like they didn't all see the wet patch on my race suit after the garage incident. I haven't come in my pants since I was a teenager; it was half of me and half of her. Yeah, I heard the rumours. Let 'em talk. They wish they had someone like her. I kept thinking about what she said before leaving:

"Go win the thing. I'll be watching."

Damn right she will, and when I do, she better be trackside in that tight little dress and nothing under it. I close my eyes and let the jet engine hum around me, Sage's voice echoing somewhere in the back of my head. I'll see her soon. I just have to get through a few more cities, a few more press conferences and a few more lonely nights in cold hotel beds. Then I'll fly straight to her, or better yet, bring her straight back to me. Because travelling the world is cool. But waking up with her next to me forever? That's what I want more than any title.

FORTY-NINE

SAGE

It's cold. Not just weather-wise, although Melbourne's late spring seems to have missed the memo about warming up, but everything feels cold after Mexico. I'm staying with Josie in her apartment, and jet lag is a bitch, so it's dark and quiet as I step into the living room, oversized hoodie swallowing me whole. His hoodie, of course. The black one he loves to wear, which I stole while I was packing the other night, the one that smells like his cologne if I bury my face in the hood and breathe like a lunatic. Which I did. Twice. This morning. Okay, maybe three times.

I drop onto the lounge and scroll through the photos from a race day like a lovesick groupie. There's one of him on the podium, champagne-soaked and grinning, hair a mess from the hat, waving like a goddamn rockstar. I zoom in on his eyes. They always give him away sharp, focused… and lit up in a way that makes my chest ache a little too hard. He was looking for me in the crowd. I know he was, because he always does.

Now I'm back in Melbourne for the first time in months, trying to prepare myself for my cousin's wedding and the onslaught of my family, trying not to mope about the 3 weeks without Maverick. I've got dress fittings, a hen's party and quite a few 'cocktails and chaos lunches with the girls' to keep me busy. I'm sure there will be plenty of questions flying at me, too. I let out a breath and stretch my legs out. There's a chill in the air, and my legs are bare, just his hoodie and my knickers, because apparently, I'm torturing myself for sport now. God, I miss that man.

He's so close to the world title now, it's all coming down to the last four races, and I promised I'd be watching the ones I'm missing. I will be watching. Probably from under a blanket, wearing his hoodie, with one hand in a bag of chips and the other... well. That'll depend on how well he's driving.

My phone buzzes.

> Playboy: Miss me yet, trouble?

> Me: Only every second since I left. You wearing my panties under your race suit yet?

Three dots appear instantly.

> Playboy: Not yet. Maybe you'll have to come to Brazil to make sure I do?

Oh. Oh, this man. I grin, flop sideways on the lounge, and type back with one hand.

> Me: Might need some convincing. Playboy: Challenge accepted.

I bite my lip, smirking at the screen like a total cliché. My legs kick up on the couch like I'm sixteen again and my crush just texted me back. Except my crush is a six-foot-something weapon of a man who could make a nun wet, and I've already done very dirty things to him in at least four countries. So, a slightly different vibe. Still the same butterflies. I shoot back:

> Me: What kind of challenge are we talking about here? Because if it doesn't involve you on your knees, I'm not sure I'm interested.

> Playboy: Oh, baby, I'll be on my knees. But so will you.

Jesus Christ. I short-circuit a little. My thighs clench on instinct, and I have to physically stop myself from launching my phone across the room.

Me: You trying to kill me before the next GP?

Playboy: Just making sure you're sufficiently distracted while I count down the hours.

I curl deeper into the couch, hoodie pulled over my knees, suddenly very aware of how much I miss him. I wonder what time it is in Brazil. If he's already in bed. If he's thinking about the way I sound when I ride his face. God, now I'm thinking about it. And I'm thinking about going. To Brazil. To him. And I wish I could go. To Brazil. To him.

It wouldn't be the first spontaneous trip I've taken in the name of questionable decisions and truly life-changing orgasms. But I can't go. I can't let my cousin down; she's the closest thing I have to a sister, and I'm honoured to be her bridesmaid. I glance at the time, it's Midnight here. Early morning in São Paulo. I picture him in bed, sheets dusting his sweet ass, hair a mess, and that lazy smirk he gets when he's winning on and off the track. I sigh and tap out a message.

Me: Make sure you book a soundproof hotel in Qatar. I want to celebrate your wins loudly.

It's a promise. A hint. A distraction. Something to hold on to. His reply comes back instantly.

Playboy: Done. Hope you're ready to scream my name.

I let out a soft laugh and drop the phone beside me, heart aching in the best kind of way. I miss him like hell, but I love him harder than I've ever loved. Challenge delayed. Not denied. Maverick finishes fourth in Brazil. No podium. No champagne. No smug grin through the national anthem. But still points. Still solid. It doesn't shake his championship standing too much, but I know him. He's going to replay every lap in his head like it's a crime scene and he's searching for evidence. I watched the entire race from Josie's lounge, curled up with a pillow clutched to my chest like it could absorb my stress. She gives me a look at one point, like, Girl, chill. But I can't, not with my heart living somewhere in Maverick's car, apparently.

Watching the race from the lounge feels different. Colder. Quieter. Like I'm too far away from the action but still way too emotionally involved. Being trackside, you feel it every rev, every cheer, every heartbeat. On the TV, it's just angles and commentary and a delay that feels like torture. But when I saw him get out of the car, safe, upright, pissed off, but walking, I finally exhaled. I hadn't even realised I was holding my breath until then. Classic me, my trauma response doesn't just knock—it kicks the damn door down. The second he's out there driving, and I'm not beside him, my mind jumps straight to worst-case scenarios. It's irrational; I know that. But it doesn't stop the anxiety from creeping in. Maverick knows this about me. That's why, even though I watch the race live, he still texts me the second he gets his phone back. No delay, no excuses, just a simple message that lets me breathe again. He gets it. He gets me, but I can't wait for that message today, so I snapped a photo of the screen, his face half-shadowed by the helmet, eyes stormy under the brim of his cap. Still devastating. Still mine.

I send it to him with no caption. He'll know what it means. He always does. My phone buzzes a few minutes later.

> Playboy: Still sexy even when I don't win, huh?

I smirk. He knows exactly what he's doing.

> Me: Always. But I'd reserve your gloating for when you're naked.

Three dots appear. Pause. Disappear. Reappear.

> Playboy: I'm counting down the hours, trouble.

I toss my phone beside me on the lounge, ignoring the teasing look Josie shoots me as she walks in with a fresh drink.

"She's got that 'my man's still hot even when he's losing' look on her face," she mutters, flopping next to me.

"I do not," I say automatically, but my stupid smile betrays me. She narrows her eyes.

"You miss him." I pause.

"Yeah. I really do." And I do. It's not just about the race or me not getting to be there for the post-race debrief and the late-night hotel... celebrations. It's everything in between. The quiet moments. The ones he doesn't post or even talk about. The way he wraps himself around me like he's trying to hold on to more than just my body. Like he's holding onto peace.

Josie sighs dramatically and passes me her cocktail. "Here. You're pathetic. Drink this."

I take a sip and groan. "What is this?"

"Doesn't matter. It'll numb your sad little sexless vagina until your man can ruin it again." She's not wrong. About any of it. Because I miss him, his hands, his mouth, his goddamn ego, but mostly, I just miss the way he looks at me like I matter. Like I'm not just part of the chaos, but the calm in it and maybe that's what scares me most. Because Maverick Carter isn't just a fast driver with a dirty mouth and a perfect dick anymore. He's the man I've fallen for. Hard.

FIFTY

MAVERICK

Fourth place. Not the worst finish of my season, but it leaves a bitter taste in my mouth. Brazil is always chaotic, tight corners, unpredictable weather, and a crowd so loud it feels like the entire country is breathing down your neck. I usually thrive in it. Eat it up. But today… nothing clicked. Not like it should've. Not like it needed to.

The car felt twitchy. The rear end is loose as hell. Couldn't get the tires to settle, couldn't find clean air when I needed it most. Pitted too early. Got caught in traffic. The strategy was solid on paper, but in practice. It just didn't land. I'm pissed, and there is no way around it. Not at the team, they did their job. Not even at myself, really. Just… pissed that I couldn't squeeze more out of the car. Pissed I didn't have her here. Maybe that's soft of me. Maybe I've gotten used to looking for her in the crowd when I climb out of the cockpit. Maybe that's the problem. Because when I stepped out of the car today and didn't see her, it hit harder than I expected.

I'm still standing there, helmet under my arm, visor up, sweat drying uncomfortably against my skin while the post- race buzz hums around me, engine noise, team radios, fans screaming from the grandstands. But all I want is her voice in my ear. Sage texted me a photo from Josie's place. Me on TV. No caption, just my face staring back at me from a screen across the world. I'd know her silent messages anywhere. That's Sage. She doesn't need to say it. I feel it. And I feel the gap she's left in my space like a phantom limb. Back in the motorhome, I down two bottles of water, ignore the media debrief for another five minutes, and fire off a reply.

> Me: Still sexy even when I don't win, huh?

Her answer? Effortless. Flirty. Dangerous.

> Trouble: Always. But I'd reserve the gloating for when you're naked.

Fucking hell. That woman. I grin despite myself. Suddenly, the sting of missing the podium dulls just a little. I want to tell her to get on the next flight to meet me in the middle of the night somewhere between Las Vegas and the hotel bed I plan to ruin. But I won't. Not yet.

She's doing something real in Melbourne, and I respect that. Doesn't stop me from wishing she were here, though. Doesn't stop me from scrolling back through the photos in my phone until I land on one, I took of her bare-faced, wrapped in my hoodie, flipping me off with a grin while stealing my fries. Fuck. I miss her, and as I walk into the media room, lights blinding and questions flying, all I can think is this would've felt easier with her hand in mine. I'll bring it home in Vegas. The last race without Sage, the last week without Sage. I fly out of Vegas the Monday after the race and land in Melbourne early Tuesday morning. I can't wait to see her.

VEGAS. Loud. Fast. Flashy.

This track feels like a fever dream, neon lights bleeding into the night sky, straights so long you could question every life decision before you hit the next corner, and crowds that don't stop screaming even when the engines do. It's also the latest race on the schedule, an 11 pm race start. Whoever thought that was a good idea should probably put the bottle down.

It's a circus. But it's also the last actual shot to lock this in. My title.

I've got to finish P3 or higher here and in Qatar, and I can wrap the championship up in Dubai with no contest finish any lower or DNF in the next two races, and it's going to be a three -way race to wrap up the championship. I can feel the pressure thumping in my chest long before I get in the car. Not nerves. Never nerves. Just the magnitude of it all pressing in from every direction.

The Strip is buzzing, cameras are everywhere, and I'm supposed to act like it's just another race. It's not. Not with everything on the line. Not with her watching from the other side of the world again. I hate that she's not here. But she's with her family, and I get it. Doesn't mean I like not having her here.

She's still with me in a way, though. Every time I slip into the cockpit, I can hear her voice in my head, all sass and sweetness, all tangled up. Her laugh from our hotel room in Austin. The quiet sigh she makes when I trace her spine with my fingers. That look in her eyes when I told her I wanted forever.

The race? Yeah, that was a blur. P1 in qualifying, held it through the battle. Every lap I was fighting like hell, tyres screaming, strategy on a knife's edge. One mistake and it would've slipped through my fingers.

But I didn't fuck it up. I didn't fuck the race up either; I crossed the line first. P1. Heart pounding. Radio crackling with the team screaming in my ears. I let my head drop back in the cockpit. Let the crowd noise wash over me. The camera's flashing. Fireworks burst across the skyline like the universe was in on the celebration. But all I wanted was her.

I'm back in the garage, champagne in my hair. I grab my phone.

> **Me:** I told you I'd bring it home. Where's my prize? It takes her all of thirty seconds.

> **Trouble:** Winner! I've got plans for that trophy and your mouth.

Fuck me. I grab a towel, wipe off the worst of the sticky mess, and laugh like a madman. Let the city party; I've got a plane to catch.

. . .

SAGE

I'm at my cousin's hen's party, music pumping, heels kicked off, dancing like I have more than three tequila shots coursing through my bloodstream. (I do. Maybe four. Honestly, who's counting) So then, why am I hiding in the bathroom, perched on the edge of a bathtub, streaming the Vegas Grand Prix with the sound off like it's my dirty little secret. Because I'm completely and pathetically obsessed with the man currently leading the damn race. My very own fast- driving, smug-smirking, orgasm-delivering menace.

We're leaving Melbourne tomorrow morning to head a few hours north for the wedding in my hometown, yay… honestly, I'm planning on staying tipsy the entire week. Feels like the only viable survival strategy. Between my nosy aunts, the chaos of bridesmaid duties, and not having Maverick's hands or mouth anywhere near me, I'm dangerously close to becoming feral.

Who the fuck am I? This isn't me. I don't do the bathroom hideout thing. I don't get soft over a man in a fireproof suit. And yet… Here I am, refreshing the live standings like a groupie with a Wi-Fi addiction, hoping to see his name first. Ugh, this is embarrassing. But this is the last weekend without him. Thank. God. Because come Tuesday morning, I'm flying to Qatar, my passport's ready and my legs will be shaved, and if he's not waiting at that hotel with nothing but a margarita and that crooked grin, I will riot. Until then… I guess I'd better go rejoin the bridal chaos before someone sends a search party. You'd better win tonight, Playboy. Because next week, I'm your prize.

FIFTY-ONE

MAVERICK

It's way too early, and I haven't really slept. I went and celebrated the win for a few hours last night, and now I'm here at the airport, still wired from the win. Sage face-timed me after the formalities were all said and done, still out at her cousin's hen's party, looking incredible in that slick, almost slip-like dress. Yeah, I'm going to make her come in that dress.

So here I am on the first flight out to Melbourne, and I haven't told Sage a thing. She thinks I'm staying in the States doing some sponsor bull-shit. I let her believe it. Let her tease me on the phone last night while I lay in a hotel bed alone, jerking off to the sound of her voice because I couldn't fucking wait to see her again.

Fourteen hours in the air is enough time to convince myself this isn't too much. That showing up during her cousin's wedding weekend like a man possessed is romantic and not borderline insane. But Sage. She's it. The girl who turned my life on its head — not because she tried to, but because she is honest, fiery and fucking beautiful. She's chaos on legs I'd crawl across continents for.

The seatbelt sign dings off, and I glance out the window. Melbourne's skyline is just starting to glow on the horizon, and I've never cared less about jet lag. My phone buzzes with a message from her.

Trouble: What time is it in the US? I grin.

Me: Early. Can't sleep. Might have to take a nap before dinner.

Trouble: Poor baby. You need someone to wear you out?

My cock twitches in my jeans. This woman.

Me: Already packing for Qatar?

Trouble: Still deciding. Depends on whether my boyfriends worth the airfare.

Me: He is. You should see him, sexy as hell and totally obsessed with you. International sex god, really.

I tuck my phone away as the wheels touch down. No driver. No entourage. Just me, a bag slung over my shoulder, and one mission: get to Sage. I look like shit. And apparently, everyone knows it.

"Hey, Mav! You look like shit," Josie calls out with a grin the second I step into the arrivals hall.

"Wow," I mutter, dragging my bag behind me, cap pulled low, and hoodie yanked over it. "Great to see you too, Jo. Really warms the heart."

Margot snorts from beside her, sunglasses on and a coffee in hand. "You do look like a raccoon that lost a street fight. But like… a hot raccoon?"

"Thanks. That's what everyone wants to hear after a fourteen-hour flight — that I've got rabid woodland animal energy."

They laugh as I slide into the back seat of their car, keeping my head down. I'm not taking any chances — one photo, one Insta story spotting, and this entire plan goes to hell. I'm wrecked. Vegas adrenaline is still lingering somewhere under the surface, but my bodies in shutdown mode. My brain's just repeating one thing: Sage. Her face when I show up. Her mouth when I kiss her senseless. Her hands when she—okay, yeah, I'm officially sleep-deprived and horny. Margot's saying something up front, but her voice is a blur as the hum of the road kicks in. I sink into the seat, hoodie pulled tighter, cap down low, and let myself drift. Just a quick nap. Then tomorrow… I'm hers.

I wake up as we pull into Josie's driveway. The thirty- minute drive from the airport wasn't nearly long enough. I'd barely shut my eyes before we were here, it's the kind of exhaustion that settles in your bones — the price of racing, red-eyes, and missing your girl like hell. We pile out of the car, Josie humming some chaotic pop song under her breath while Margot laughs at something on her phone. I just keep my head down and follow them inside. I need sleep. Proper sleep.

Margot shows me to the guest room — Sage's room, apparently. The second I walk in, I know it. Her scent lingers in the sheets, subtle but unmistakable. That warm, sweet note that drives me fucking insane. It hits me like a punch to the gut and a kiss to the throat all at once.

I shut the door behind me, strip down to my boxers and dive into the bed. I bury my face in her pillow and breathe her in like an addict. God, I miss her. I miss everything. I fall asleep fast; it's probably the best sleep I've had in weeks. When I wake up, it's dark. The house is alive with muffled sounds — Josie talking loudly on the phone, her voice bouncing off the walls. I swear she's yelling Drew's name. Mental note: Ask her about that later. Could be entertaining.

I check my phone. Three missed calls and a stream of texts from Sage. I smirk. Guess I'm pulling a her-in-Silverstone moment and making her sweat. It's fair play. Also, a couple of missed calls from Mum. Shit. I'd better call her soon before she sends an MI6 search party. I roll out of bed and wander toward the back deck. Margot's out there with a glass of wine, the breeze lifting her hair, her phone in her lap. She grins when she sees me.

"Well, well. Sleeping Beauty's awake."

I groan and stretch. "That bed smells like her. I'm not even ashamed."

"There's pasta on the stove if you're hungry," she says with a wink.

"Starving," I mutter, turning on my heel and heading inside. I load up a bowl — Sage-style, none of that tiny-portion bullshit, grab a beer and head back out to join Margot. We eat in silence while Josie's inside, pacing and half-shouting into her phone. I raise a brow at Margot, but she just sips her wine like it's above her pay grade. Then her phone buzzes. She checks the screen and smirks.

"Sage," she mouths, then holds up a finger. "Be quiet. I'm putting her on speaker." I nod and keep my mouth shut.

"Sage, how's it going up home? Punched anyone out yet?" Margot asks, laughing.

Sage sighs dramatically. "God, I want to. If one more person asks me when I'm getting married and I quote 'to that sexy car driver', I swear I'm going to rip someone's throat out."

My pulse kicks up at the sound of her voice. I try to clamp down a laugh and press my beer to my lips instead. Hearing her like this — raw, honest and just a little feral — makes me miss her even more. Not jumping into the conversation is actual torture.

Margot rolls her eyes and gives me a look. "Never say never, Sagey baby," she says into the phone. "You might've finally found the person you'd let in long enough to build a life with." She winks at me. I flip her off. She just smirks.

Sage groans. "Ugh, you sound like Mrs Carter. You and she both are trying to marry me off to Maverick and have me barefoot and pregnant before the year's out." I raise a brow. She's talking to my mum now. Margot looks at me knowingly and keeps her voice light.

"Babes, no one's trying to marry you off. We just want you to be happy. And we can see how much he loves you. You're scared — but honestly? I don't think you need to be." She pauses, then adds with a cheeky grin, "That boy is pussy whipped." I let out a low growl, half insulted, half proud. Not wrong. Sage laughs, softer now.

"You're both unhinged," Sage replies.

Margot stands, stretching like a cat. "Alright, I'm gonna love ya and leave ya. I've got a date with Mr Rosé and a hot bath."

"Dirty," Sage teases. "Night, M. Love ya."

"Love you back." The call ends, and Margot glances at me, smug. "You better be worth the meltdown she's clearly trying to avoid."

I meet her gaze evenly. "I am." And I will be. Every damn time.

"Mr Rose?" I asked, Margot curiously.

"None of your business", she replies.

"She's going to leave, isn't she? She's going to realise what she's left behind and leave me?" I ask, staring straight ahead, voice low like saying it too loud might make it true. My heart's pounding like it already knows the answer. Margot glances at me, soft but steady.

"For the first time in a long time," she says, "I don't think she is."

I want to believe her. God, I need to believe her.

"She doesn't let herself fall," Margot adds, her tone quieter now ", Not anymore." I look over at her, and she gives me a small smile.

"The last time she did was six years ago. A guy named Tim. Josie and I used to call him Tim-Tim, nice but dim." Despite everything, I let out a quiet snort as Margot shrugs, like she knows exactly how ridiculous it sounds now.

"They were together for over two years. Everyone thought they were endgame. Marriage. Kids. The whole deal. They were together when her Mum died. He held her through that, but after her Mum died, Sage just… disappeared inside herself. She bought her house, thinking maybe that would help her cope with her new reality, take her mind off the pain she was feeling, and the plan was for Tim to move in with her." Margot pauses, eyes unfocused like she's watching something in the distance that only she can see.

"But she wasn't herself. She was grieving. Lost. Not the loud, fire-cracker Sage you now know. She was quiet. Withdrawn, Josie and I were scared, honestly, we thought we might lose her, too."

My chest tightens.

"And when it came time to move in," Margot continues, "Tim said he'd only do it if she pulled herself together. Said it was time to stop mourning. Time to 'move on.'" She says it with air quotes, her disgust barely masked. I feel like I'm going to be sick.

"That's when she left him. Told him love wasn't supposed to have terms and conditions, and if he really loved her, he would support her through grief, not try to push her out of it. Sage locked herself in that house for a night. Josie and I found her on the bathroom floor the next morning."

I shut my eyes. My poor girl. My strong girl.

"That night, she threw out every photo of him. Got her hair done the next day. Bought herself a new little black book, got her nipples pierced and said she was done letting men break her. Swore she would never cry over another man," Margot lets out a soft laugh, fond and aching all at once.

"And just like that, she was back. Sassier. Stronger. But harder, too." She looks at me, "And now she's here. With you." I don't say anything. I can't. My throat feels thick, and my heart's in pieces. So that's what she's been carrying.

It all makes sense now — the way she hesitates when I talk about the future, how she flinches when things start feeling too good. She's not scared of me. She's scared of what it'll cost her if she lets herself believe in us and I disappear. It's like she's waiting for me to put conditions on my love, like he did.

Margot stands, stretching. "I'm going to bed." She leans down, kisses me on the top of the head like a big sister or maybe a quiet warning.

"Look after our girl," she says softly, but it lands with the weight of an oath. Then, as she heads for the hallway.

"Oh, and fair warning. The wedding… there's a chance Tim Tim, nice but dim, will be there." My jaw tightens. That name again. The one tied to everything Sage never deserved. I force a small smile, keep it polite. Controlled.

"Night, Margot. Don't worry, I've got her, always."

FIFTY-TWO

SAGE

I'm lying in my childhood bedroom, wrapped in a scratchy old doona that smells vaguely of lavender and nostalgia, staring at the ceiling like it holds the answers to all of life's existential romantic dilemmas. Spoiler: it doesn't. This house holds so many memories. The good kind, the kind that wraps around you like a warm blanket on a chilly night. I see echoes of Mum everywhere: in the chipped paint on the hallway door, she always promised she'd fix, in the garden she used to fuss over, in the laughter that used to live in these walls. Back when it was Mum, Dad, my brother and me. Back when things made sense.

But walking through it now… it aches. The happy memories feel like ghosts, and reliving them doesn't bring comfort; it just makes the loss louder. Some days, I wish I could forget. Other days, I wish I could go back, and then there are the days, dark, ugly days, where I wished I'd followed her. Left this grief behind instead of drowning in it. I know how that sounds. But I've learned to live inside this sadness. I've built a rhythm in it. It's familiar. It's mine. Most people don't understand that—and honestly, I've stopped trying to explain. I've learned that happiness and sadness can live side by side.

It feels unfair sometimes that I still get to be here. That I get to love and laugh and celebrate things like birthdays and weddings and people falling in love when Mum doesn't. When she can't. It makes every bit of joy feel jagged, like I'm stealing moments that should've been hers too. There's a gaping hole in our family, and it's impossible to ignore. Maybe that's why I keep my distance. I love them, really, I do, but it's hard being around them when I'm still stuck in this grief… and it seems like they've moved on. My dad, especially, is already remarried, and while I don't begrudge him and his healing, it still hits me like a punch to the gut every single time.

I'm supposed to be sleeping, not trapped in these thoughts. Tomorrow's another full-on day of pre-wedding chaos: hair trials, table arrangements, more people trying to measure my body while yelling over each other and sipping mimosas at inappropriate volumes, and I am excited, I guess. But also? I'll be glad when it's done. I love my family, but they're a lot. We laugh hard, drink harder and throw around unsolicited opinions like confetti. Especially when it comes to the topic of him, about my love life.

"Maverick? The F1 guy. Isn't he way out of your league?"

"Are you seriously dating?"

"Wait—is this some kind of PR stunt?"

"Oh, come on, Sage, he dates models. Like, genetically engineered women."

It's all said with that wine-soaked curiosity that pretends it's playful but still manages to burrow under your skin. I try to laugh it off.

"We'll see," I tell them, while tossing back Prosecco as a distraction. But it sticks. Of course it sticks. Especially since he hasn't answered my last few texts. Or the two calls. Not that I'm counting. Not that I'm panicking. The doubt starts to creep in. I tell myself he's busy. It's the end of the season; the pressure's high. But it doesn't stop me from unlocking my phone and refreshing his Instagram like some love-sick teenager, and then there it is. A photo he just uploaded. It's him.

Wearing my hoodie, the soft grey one he wore when he flew back from Japan. Hair a mess, coffee mug in one hand, the other tucked into the pocket like he's trying to keep something steady. Barefoot in my kitchen. The caption 'Home looks different these days.' I blink. My chest aches. Like physically. Heart, lungs, ribs, all of it squeezed tight. I remember that night in Austin. Him looking at me like I hung the damn stars. Saying—

"I'm not proposing."

"Then what are you doing?"

"Just... letting you know how serious this is for me."

And I kissed him. I haven't said it yet. Not out loud anyway, those three words that keep clawing at my throat every time he holds me, every time he tells me he loves me, and I say— "I know." With a smile. A guarded, traitorous smile. I love him. God, I do. So why the hell can't I just say it? Maybe because it makes it real. Or maybe... I'm scared, he's everything I want, but I'm scared he's going to put conditions on his love, too. I've never really trusted that I could keep something so good, but looking at that photo—him, my hoodie, my kitchen, with that caption, maybe I already have. Maybe it's time I stop running from the truth that's been quietly screaming in my chest since Monaco. I love him. I love him. And I think I'm finally ready to say it. My thoughts are broken by sunlight streaming through the gauzy curtains and a full-blown assault on my bedroom door.

"Sage! Get up and get drunk!" Charming. .

The bridal party has taken over my childhood home like a glittery, wine-fuelled army. They've been camped out here all week and probably until the weekend ends. Tonight's the final sleepover before tomorrow's big 'I do's.' Apparently, the pre- wedding chaos needs an HQ — and lucky me, my old room still has glitter stickers on the wardrobe and a stuffed dolphin named Kevin on the shelf. I groan, roll over, and check my phone. Still nothing. No messages. No missed calls. No little heart-eyed selfies from Maverick. And just like that, my chest twists. I try not to spiral, but it's been days. We've had less radio silence during an actual race. So, of course, the little voice in my head kicks off. He's over it. Moved on. Got bored. Found someone taller, thinner, and less emotionally constipated. Nice work, Sage. This is why you don't let yourself get attached.

I throw my legs over the side of the bed, feet slipping into my fuzzy slippers, and tug on one of Maverick's hoodies. It still smells like him, only just, a faint smell of cologne, a bit of motor oil and poor decisions — which doesn't help. It's technically summer, but the mornings are still cool. So, I'm cozy and ready to pad downstairs toward the sounds of music, laughter, and champagne-fuelled chaos. The second I walk into the kitchen, a mimosa is shoved into my hand. Bridal energy. It's a lifestyle.

Breakfast has been demolished, and now we've migrated to the front lawn like some less-than-wholesome rom-com montage. There's food, sunshine and kids running barefoot through sprinklers. Everyone's pumped up, glowing and drunk on love and Prosecco. And I'm… here. Standing in cutoffs and Maverick's oversized t-shirt, pretending my heart doesn't feel like a bruised peach. Until I spot him. Fucking Tim. My ex. Still hanging around like a foul smell because he became best mates with the groom during our relationship, and I was too much of a people pleaser to put a boundary in place and make it a hard no or make Matthew choose.

He's swaggering toward me, beer in hand, smirk locked and loaded.

"Sage. Long time no see. You're looking… good." His eyes rake over me like he has the right.

"Tim," I say, tone cool. "Nice to see you too. Been a while."

"I saw some photos of you online recently," he adds casually, like he didn't have them bookmarked. "Kissing that F1 guy. What's his name again? Bit of a playboy, isn't he?" Ah. There it is. Jealousy is a funny emotion. Tim believes his god's gift to women, so therefore I couldn't do any better than him.

"People change," I say, levelling him with a stare. "You sure as hell did." He flinches a little, but pushes on, cocky.

"He won't love you, you know."

I pause, sip my mimosa slowly, then tilt my head. "Well, Tim, here's the thing — if I want to get my heart broken by a ridiculously hot international billionaire superstar with a monster cock who can make me come just by looking at me, I bloody well will."

He chokes on his beer, sputtering like a frat boy caught mid- bluff. I smirk.

"Big difference between you two. His ego isn't compensating for anything." He opens his mouth to reply, but I'm already walking away because I just spotted my car turning the corner. My car. The one I left parked at Josie's when I moved to Europe and behind the wheel? Oh, hell yes.

FIFTY-THREE

MAVERICK

I wake to the sound of chaos in the kitchen, pots clanging, cupboards slamming, voices overlapping. Josie's in a rush, high heels clicking on tile, and Margot's already making breakfast like she owns the place. I step into the kitchen, duffel bag slung over my shoulder, Sage's car keys in hand.

"Morning, ladies," I say, heading straight for the coffee like a man on a mission. Josie barely glances up as she finishes tying her hair.

"Hey, sex god. Big drive today?"

I grin. "Biggest one I've had in weeks." She kisses Margot on the cheek, grabs her bag, and tosses a parting shot over her shoulder.

"Drive safe, Maverick. Try not to break the town." Then she's gone.

I take a seat beside Margot at the counter, and she slides over a plate with an omelette that smells better than any hotel breakfast I've had all year.

"You sure about this?" she asks, eyes on me but voice soft, like she's trying not to poke the nerves too hard.

"Showing up to her childhood home? She's surrounded by family." I nod, even if my stomach is doing laps around itself. "I'm sure. I think… I think Sage will be okay with me being there."

She watches me for a beat, like she's weighing my words for truth.

Then she nods. "She might freak out a little. This is a big step for her. But I trust you to support her through it."

"I will. Thanks, Margot. I really appreciate how much you care about her."

"You're not so bad yourself," she says with a wink, standing to rinse her mug. "Now get going before they're all passed out on the lawn and covered in fairy bread and sausages." I laugh, finish the last bite of breakfast, grab the keys and head out.

Margot gave me everything I needed over breakfast, the address, the lay of the land, even a rundown of her cousins and their exes. I've booked a hotel for two nights in town, because once I've survived the family gauntlet, I need time alone with my girl. Badly.

The drive's not long, about three hours, but in Sage's tiny little Golf, my six-foot-five frame feels like a pretzel. I wouldn't trade it for anything, though. The car smells like her. There's a hair tie on the gearstick. Lip balm in the cupholder. It's her world, and I'm driving straight into it. I almost texted her five times. Just to say I miss you. But I didn't. I want to see her face, unfiltered, unprepared and glowing, when she sees me, and yeah, I'm nervous. I know how private she is around her family. I know she likes to play things close to the chest when it comes to us, not out of shame, but protection. This is her hometown. Her roots. A place where everyone probably knows everyone, and I'm about to drop in like a headline in human form. But I don't care. I just want to be near her. Let her see, I mean every word I said in Austin. That this is serious for me.

As I turn down her street, it all feels so her. The sleepy charm, the front lawns full of laughter and beer bottles and cousins running around barefoot, it's got history. It's got heart. And suddenly, I get it. Why she needed to leave after her mum died. Then I see her. Standing on the grass in denim cutoffs that hug her perfect ass and my t-shirt, talking to some guy. Some guy who's looking at her a little too long, raking his eyes up and down Sage's body. She's mid-sentence when she notices the car — her car — rolling down the road. Her eyes squint, then widen, and then she freezes. I pull into the driveway, shift into park, and kill the engine. Her mouth drops open like she can't believe what she's seeing, like I've stepped out of a dream she hasn't dared to admit she's been having.

I barely get the door open before she's moving, flying across the lawn like gravity doesn't apply to her anymore, and then she's on me, arms wrapped around my neck, legs around my waist, face buried in my neck like I'm home and she finally remembered where she left the key. I hold her tight. Because, God, I missed her. This was worth the drive and the flight. She doesn't say anything at first. Just clings to me like she's afraid I'll disappear if she lets go. Her face is buried in my neck, her breath warm and shaky, and I can feel her chest rising fast against mine. She smells like summer and sunscreen and faint traces of my cologne from the shirt she clearly stole weeks ago.

"I thought you weren't talking to me," she mumbles, voice muffled. "I thought you were ghosting me; you realised I was too much work." I pull back just enough to look at her. Her eyes are glassy; her cheeks flushed from the sun and surprise. She's blinking like she still doesn't quite believe I'm here.

"I wasn't ghosting you," I mumble. "I was flying across the world to crash your family's pre-wedding bender and remind you that I'm not going anywhere."

She lets out a half-laugh, half-sob and hits me not hard, but enough to let me know I scared her.

"You're an asshole." I grin.

"Missed you too, Trouble." Then she kisses me. Right there in the middle of the lawn. Not just a 'hi' kiss or a 'thanks for showing up' kiss, a full-body, pull-me-into-you-like-you 've-been-starving kind of kiss. The kind that makes the rest of the world dissolve around us. Until it doesn't. Someone wolf-whistles. A beer can cracks open. And then—

"Oh my god, is that the Formula One guy?!"

"Wait—is that actually him?"

"Holy shit, Sage brought the race car driver home!" I glance over Sage's shoulder, and yep, there they are. Her family. All of them. Staring like they've just seen a unicorn pull up in a Volkswagen. There's an older man in board shorts and Crocs who's holding a toddler on one hip and a sausage in tongs in the other like a weapon. A teenage girl is openly taking a video. And someone's grandma just muttered something that sounded like, "he's taller on TV."

Sage lets out a mortified groan and buries her face in my chest. "I'm going to die."

I stroke her hair. "Too late. You're dating a public spectacle now."

One of her cousins calls out, "He better be good to you, Sage, or we'll key his stupid fast car!"

And yet, through all the laughter and stunned stares, there's something warm in the air. Not judgment. Not resentment. Just the messy, loud, alcohol-soaked curiosity of people who obviously love her deeply, even if they don't show it. Sage finally pulls back from my chest and wipes at her eyes, smiling despite herself.

"You're insane, you know that?"

"I do. But I love you, so the insanity can be overlooked."

Her breath catches. Her lip's part like she might finally say it back. But then someone shouts, "Oi! Lover boy! Hope you brought sunscreen; it's a scorcher today!" and she shoves her face into my neck again, laughing and crying all at once. I hold her tighter, letting it sink in. This strange, beautiful chaos that raised the woman I'm completely gone for. And if this is the circus I need to walk through to get to her? I'll buy a damn ticket every time.

Once the whirlwind of introductions settles — names I didn't quite catch, hugs, beers shoved into my hand—that's when I catch him. The guy from before. Still staring at me like I've just crashed the party and insulted his mother. Arms crossed, jaw tight. That must be Tim. The ex. Interesting. Before I can dwell on it, Sage grabs my hand and tugs me toward the house with that quiet urgency that tells me she's barely holding it together. I follow her inside, grateful for the escape, and even more grateful when she leads me up the stairs.

Her childhood bedroom is exactly what I hoped it would be: tiny, chaotic, and pure Sage. Faded posters, photos pinned to a corkboard, a bookshelf crammed with everything from teenage vampire novels to feminist poetry. It smells like her, somehow like old perfume and summer. I sit on the bed, and she steps in between my legs like she's done it a hundred times. She looks like she's about to fall apart. Her hands roam over my face like she's checking I'm real, like this might be a dream, and she's about to wake up.

"You really flew in from the States?" she whispers. "You've got two races left. You should be focused on the championship." I lean my head against her chest, slow and steady.

"Baby," I say, quietly, "I'm right where I need to be." Her fingers tremble against my jaw.

"I convinced myself you were done with me," she admits, "because I hadn't heard from you in days."

I smile, even though it kills me, she thought that. Especially when she's standing there in my t-shirt.

"I'm so fucking obsessed with you," I murmur. "You're stuck with me, Sage." I pull her down into a kiss. Short but deep. Honest. Her lips are soft and warm, and it knocks the air out of me how much I missed her. How much she still feels like home. "I didn't text or call because I didn't want to ruin the surprise," I add, my voice rough against her mouth. "I'm sorry I made you feel like that." I kiss her again, slower this time. Hungrier. Three weeks without her is three too many.

Then I ask, "Who's the guy out front — the one who looked like I just kicked his dog?" She laughs against my lips.

"That's Tim. My ex, from, like, six years ago. I haven't really talked much about him."

My mouth finds her neck. She tilts her head for me instinctively, like her body still remembers every place I like to touch. I'm getting hard, fast, but I don't stop.

"Margot told me about him," I say between kisses. "Hope that's okay. She just wanted me to be prepared if he was around."

Sage smiles faintly. "Of course she did."

"He told me I looked good," she continues, her voice lower now. "Said he saw the photos of us. Said you're a Playboy. That you wouldn't love me."

That one hit. I flinch. Not because it's new — I've heard worse from strangers and the media, but because she had to hear it. From someone who once claimed to care about her.

"He doesn't know me," I say, my voice tightening. "He knows the headlines."

"I know," she says.

And then she hits me with this: "I told him, 'Well, Tim, here's the thing if I want to get my heart broken by a ridiculously hot international super-star with a monster cock who can make me come just by looking at me, I bloody well will.'"

I freeze and lean back just enough to stare at her. Then I grin wide and proud and completely in awe. "Hm. That's my girl." And in a blink, she's pushing me down onto the mattress with a look in her eye that says she's about to ruin me in the best possible way. But I catch her hands.

"Sage," I say, breathless, "Not here. Not in your childhood bedroom with all your family in earshot. I booked us a hotel for the next two nights."

She blinks. "You what?"

"I want you," I say. "But I want you all to myself. No interruptions. No one is yelling about BBQ sauce. Just you and me." She searches my face, then straightens. There's a fire in her now. Determined. Soft. Knowing.

She turns without a word and walks out the door. I grab my bag and what I'm hoping is hers and follow her. Because she's it for me, and I've waited long enough to find this, to find her.

FIFTY-FOUR

SAGE

The hotel is small, quiet, tucked away off the highway with soft lighting and a king bed that suddenly feels like the only thing that matters. We don't make it more than five steps into the room before his hands are on me under my shirt, in my hair, gripping my ass as he kicks the door shut behind us. I shove him back against the wall and kiss him like I need oxygen from his mouth. It's messy and wild, all teeth and tongue and weeks of restraint coming undone in a single breath. His hands are everywhere, like he can't touch me fast enough, can't get enough.

"You're wearing my shirt," he growls against my throat.

"It still smells like you." I arch into him. "I slept in it. Every fucking night."

He groans, deep and low, like it's killing him.

"Take it off," he commands. I do it slowly and deliberately, baring myself for him inch by inch. His eyes darken as I drop it to the floor.

"You're perfect," he murmurs, stepping forward. "I'm going to worship every inch of you."

He drops to his knees like I'm the altar and he's the sinner begging for mercy. His hands slide up my thighs, thumbs grazing the crease of my hips before he drags my shorts and panties down in one smooth motion. He kisses my inner thigh first, then the other. My breath hitches. My fingers curl in his hair.

And then, "Oh fuck, Mav—" His mouth finds me, hot and wet and unrelenting. His tongue moves like he knows every nerve ending, every desperate pulse inside me. He licks, sucks, teases, tortures, one arm locked around my thigh to keep me from running, the other sliding up to palm my breast. I fall apart, quick and messy, hips grinding against his mouth like I'm starving and he's the only thing I've ever needed. And he doesn't stop. Not even after I come the first time. Not until I'm shaking and whimpering and begging him to fuck me. When he finally stands, his mouth is slick, his pupils blown wide.

"You good?" he rasps.

"Need you. Now." He doesn't make me ask again. He strips in seconds, shirt, jeans, boxers, every inch of golden skin and muscle, and oh my god, he's so fucking big. He lines himself up, looks into my eyes like he's trying to see straight through me, and when he pushes inside, it's everything. I gasp, nails digging into his shoulders. He moves slowly at first, hips grinding deep, thick and stretching and perfect. My body moulds around him like it was made for this, for him.

"For weeks," he growls, "I've been dreaming of this pussy."

"Don't stop," I pant. "Don't you fucking stop."

He thrusts harder, faster, gripping my hips as the bed frame knocks against the wall. His mouth is at my neck, his teeth scraping, biting. I'm drowning in him, the smell of his sweat, the rasp of his voice, the way he fucks like he's trying to brand himself into my bones. I'm close again, so close it hurts. My body arches, trembles, and clenches.

"Come for me," he demands, voice low and guttural. And I do. With a cry that's half his name and half a broken prayer. He follows, hips stuttering, spilling deep inside me with a groan like he's been waiting his whole life to let go like this. We collapse together, tangled limbs, sweat-slicked skin, hearts hammering in sync. His lips brush my ear.

"Still think I'm not serious?" I smile, breathless.

"No. I know how serious you are now." And I think tomorrow, I'll finally tell him. I love you.

———

BY SOME MIRACLE, I make it to the hair and makeup chair with only one hickey visible. A strategic curl and a little foundation later, I'm officially bridal-party presentable, albeit sore in places I didn't know could get sore. I grin at the memory, worth it. The morning is a whirlwind. Steamers hissing, mimosa glasses clinking, nerves and lashes fluttering. Everyone's buzzing, but there's one thing, or rather, one person on everyone's lips. Maverick Carter. The fact that he showed up yesterday like some kind of cinematic fever dream. Is still rippling through the family like a gossip tsunami.

"Is he really staying for the wedding?" "I thought he was overseas?"

"Wait — like, the real Maverick Carter? The driver?" That one came from my cousin's future in-law, who missed the show yesterday.

My cousins' group chat is also apparently imploding, and at least two of the groomsmen are actively trying to get selfies with him in the background. Meanwhile, my Nan keeps making pointed comments like, "Well, at least he's polite," and "He's very handsome, isn't he?" Which is Nan-speak for he's growing on me. Emily, my cousin, is thriving. She winks at me every time someone else swoons over his accent or his jawline or the fact that he offered to carry in the wedding cake when it arrived.

"He's going to break the internet when someone posts a pic of him at the reception," she says over her glass of champagne, eyes glittering. "My wedding is about to go viral", I laugh, shaking my head, but there's a hum in my chest I can't shake. A soft, steady buzz of disbelief.

Because he's here. Because he chose to be here without being asked, he chose to step into the chaos of my family and the claustrophobia of my small-town history and just be in it with me. And last night… God. If there were any lingering doubts, he blew them right out of my body and replaced them with something terrifying and beautiful and undeniable. Love. The word is still stuck in my throat. Not because I don't feel it, I do, so much it aches, but because once I say it, there's no pretending anymore. No backpedalling. No hiding behind 'we'll see' or half-smiles. But maybe that's what I'm finally ready for now. Maybe loving him out loud is the only thing left.

.   .   .

THE CEREMONY IS GORGEOUS. My cousin looks radiant, her husband's crying, and standing at the back, tucked away but unmissable in a navy suit that was clearly tailored to ruin women, is Maverick. Watching me. Only me. He doesn't flinch when people stare. Doesn't shrink under the attention. Just stands there like he's carved out of stone and confidence, like he's exactly where he's supposed to be. When our eyes meet, he winks. My stomach flips.

After the ceremony, while the bridal party's getting herded away for a million photos in a field full of scratchy wildflowers and fake laughter, I keep stealing glances back toward the reception tent. And there he is helping my uncle set up chairs, high-fiving some kid who recognised him from the 'PlayStation', laughing like he's done this a hundred times. Like he belongs here. The speeches are done. The sentimental toasts, the matching satin dresses, the polite applause, and a few extra family photos are all wrapped up. Finally, now it's time to find my man. I scan the crowd, and there he is. Tall, unfairly gorgeous, lit up by the string of lights like the main character in every daydream I've had for the past week. Maverick and of course, of course, he's deep in conversation with my dad. Fabulous. I start weaving my way through the crowd toward them, trying to decide if I should interrupt or fake an emergency, when someone grabs my arm, hard.

"What the fu—Tim?" I snap, yanking my arm back. "What the fucking hell?"

"Sorry," he says, hands up like that makes it okay. "Didn't mean to be rough. Just figured we should catch up properly. We got interrupted yesterday, and I barely know you anymore."

"Yeah, Tim," I say, forcing a smile that could cut glass. "That's what happens when someone actively tries to disappear from someone's life. People change."

He shifts awkwardly. "I thought I'd see you more at family stuff."

"I avoid the ones you'll be at. Obviously."

His jaw tightens. "Look, Sage… I was wrong. What I said back then — I fucked up. I've regretted it ever since." I roll my eyes so hard I see the back of my skull. I can feel Maverick now. His presence is like gravity. He's close. Listening.

"I think we should give it another shot," Tim continues, clearly delusional. "You and me. We're practically family now. We'll be around each other all the time—" Before I can even launch a verbal grenade, Maverick is there. His arm slides around my waist, solid and certain. Calming. Tim's eyes flash to Maverick's hand.

"You can't seriously think he's for you. The guy's got a different woman in every country." Maverick's grip tightens. Ohhh, he's mad.

I lift my chin. "Listen carefully, Tim. Because I'm only saying this once. The night you put conditions on your love was the best damn thing that ever happened to me. I gave myself one night — one — to cry over you. For the two and a half years I wasted on someone who couldn't handle me at my worst." Tim tries to speak. I hold up a finger.

"The next day, I cut my hair, burned the photos, pierced my nipples and became everything you hated. I became myself again." His eyes drop automatically.

Maverick clears his throat. "Eyes up, mate. Those are mine now."

I lean in, eyes locked on Tim's. "You threw me away when I needed you. You couldn't handle my grief, couldn't accept that losing my mum wasn't something I could just 'get over.' Well, guess what? Her death is not something to get over. My mum is not someone I get over. She's not you. It's been real damn easy to forget you." Tim's standing there like someone just unplugged his soul. "And as for Maverick?" I add, voice sharp and a little psychotic. "Yeah, he might live a fever dream of a life, but I never doubt his love for me. He loves all of me, grief, trauma and chaos included. He loves the hot mess that is Sage Davidson. And yes… he does have a woman screaming his name in every country." I smirk. "Me."

Tim's mouth opens. Closes. He's got nothing. Maverick leans in, lips brushing my ear. "Let's get out of here, so you can scream it again."

And just like that, we walk away, leaving Tim to stew in his fragile ego and backwards take on love. I don't look back. I don't need to. Maverick, however, can't help himself and grabs my ass as we walk away, just as another fuck you to Tim. By the time we finally join the rest of the party, it's golden hour, and someone's put on a playlist that's just nostalgic enough to get the aunts dancing. Maverick finds the nearest bar, two drinks in hand. His eyes roam over my dress slowly, possessively, like he's mentally unzipping it.

"You look like fucking sin in satin," he murmurs, passing me a champagne. It's time.

So, I take his hand, pull him away from the crowd, away from the music and the lights and the chaos into the shadows of the marquee, where the fairy lights flicker like stars. And I say it.

"I love you, Maverick."

His eyes go wide. But not with surprise. Relief. Awe. Maybe even a little devastation. Then he kisses me softly and reverently, like I just gave him the thing he's been waiting to hear.

"You have no idea how long I've wanted to hear that," he whispers.

"Since London," I breathe, smiling. And then I kiss him again because it's my cousin's wedding and love is in the air and finally — finally — I'm not running anymore.

FIFTY-FIVE

MAVERICK

Did I just hear that? Did I just hear those words I've been waiting to hear? I love you, Maverick. She said it, the words I've been aching for. And I don't even hesitate. I lift her right off the ground, her legs wrapping around my hips like she belongs there. Because she fucking does. If we don't get out of here now, I'm going to fuck her right behind this marquee.

I lean in, lips brushing her ear. "Let's get out of here." She slides down, breath shaky, fingers lacing with mine, and we're gone, weaving through the wedding crowd and straight into the first taxi I can wave down. The second that hotel door clicks shut behind us, it's game over.

I've got her up against the wall like I've been starved. Because I have. Last night wasn't enough; it wasn't enough to make up for three weeks without her. Three weeks of my hand instead of her body. Three weeks of lying awake at night thinking about the way she sounds when she falls apart under me. I kiss her like a man possessed. I rip the zipper on that silk dress down and push it down her body. Fuck, she's not wearing anything underneath. I groan low in my throat.

"You did this on purpose." Sage grins, eyes dark, wicked. "You weren't supposed to see it until later."

"Oh, baby," I growl, hand sliding up her thigh, fingers finding her already wet and waiting. "It's later."

I slide two fingers into her, slow and deliberate. She gasps, arching against the wall, clenching tight around me like her body's been waiting too. Her head tips back, mouth open, and I'm gone.

"You feel that?" I murmur, voice low and rough against her ear as I pump my fingers deeper. "That's mine. All of you — mine."

I pull my fingers out, and she whimpers at the loss. I drag her to the bed and lay her out like a fucking offering. Her skin's flushed, lips swollen, pupils blown wide as she looks up at me like I hung the damn moon.

"Say it again," I tell her, hovering over her, my cock heavy and hard, pressed against her thigh. "Say it, and I'll give it to you."

She locks eyes with me, chest heaving. "I love you, Maverick."

I don't ease into her. I claim her. One rough, deep thrust and I'm buried to the hilt. She moans loud and raw, and I bite back a curse. She's tight, warm, and perfect. Taking every inch of me. I keep my pace steady, grinding into her just right because I want her to feel it, feel me, feel us.

"God, you're so cocky," she pants, voice high and trembling. I thrust harder, and her words break on a moan.

"Always so smug—" Again.

"Full of yourself—oh my God—" Again.

I grab her wrists and pin them above her head, grinding deeper, fucking into her with every ounce of control I've got left.

"Eyes on me," I growl. She opens them wide, glassy and desperate.

I lean down, kiss her softer, slower, just once, and that's all it takes. Her orgasm hits like lightning, ripping through her in waves. My fingers are pressing her clit, and she clenches around me, thighs trembling, voice breaking on a high-pitched cry that echoes off the walls.

"Shit—fuck—Maverick—" She screams as she soaks my cock. I lose it, growling into her neck as I come hard, hips stuttering, my whole body locking up. I pulse inside her, buried deep, panting against her skin. We don't speak for a long moment; we just keep breathing, high off the heat and the passion and everything in between. Eventually, I roll off and collapse beside her, a satisfied smirk stretching across her flushed face.

"I think you broke me," she purrs, stretching like a cat in the sun. I glance at her, raise a brow.

"You think I did."

"Oh?" Her voice lilts, teasing. "You've got more in you, Playboy?"

I flip her onto her stomach and give that perfect ass a firm smack. She squeals, laughing breathlessly, but her body's already reacting.

"You tell me." I kiss her spine and drag my fingers between her thighs again, still dripping with me. My cock twitches and hardens again at the sight of my seed leaking out of her.

"On your knees," I say, my voice pure gravel. She obeys, looking over her shoulder, hair wild, eyes full of sin. I slide into her from behind and lose my fucking mind. No holding back now. No, pretending this isn't everything I want. Skin slapping, moans echoing, my name like a prayer from her lips as I fuck her deep, hard, unrelenting. She takes all of me, greedy, perfect, filthy. It's like her body's built for mine. We don't stop until we're ruined. Until we're nothing but smelling of sweat and sex and exhaustion.

After a much-needed shower and round ... 5, I think, we crawl into bed, naked, and Sage is sprawled across my chest, legs tangled with mine, hair damp against my skin. She traces patterns on my stomach, voice soft and smug. "Worth the flight to Melbourne?"

I hum, already half-hard again just from her touch. "Worth the jet lag."

She lifts her head, biting her bottom lip, eyes sparking. "Think you've got one more in you before sunrise?"

I grin, dark and slow. "For you, Sage? I've got infinity."

Sunlight is leaking through the curtains, warming the sheets tangled around our bodies. Sage is tucked into my side, her face buried in my chest, one leg thrown over mine like she's trying to anchor me here forever. Her hair smells like sex and sleep and whatever shampoo she stole from the hotel shower. My hand traces lazy circles on her bare back, and she makes a little sound — a sleepy hum that curls around my chest.

"You awake?" I murmur. She nods, still pressed into me. "Unfortunately."

I kiss her forehead. "We've got to leave in an hour."

She groans dramatically and flops onto her back. The sheet falls away from her chest, and I can't help but grin. Fuck, she's unreal. I lean over, drag my lips along her collarbone.

"You're just trying to distract me," she mutters, eyes still closed.

"I don't need to try. You get distracted all on your own." She sighs; it's a mix of resignation and contentment.

"You know I've never brought anyone home like that before, right?"

"I figured." I prop myself on one elbow, watching her. "They were staring at me like I'd walked in naked with a keg under each arm."

She snorts. "You kind of did."

"You're not mad I crashed the wedding, are you?" She opens her eyes, finally, soft and honest.

"No. I needed to see you. Even if I didn't know it until you were standing there in the driveway."

My heart does that stupid squeeze thing again. I reach for her hand and thread our fingers together.

"I don't enjoy being away from you," I admit quietly. "Even when I'm supposed to be focused on winning." She looks at me until she lifts my hand to her lips.

We've packed up Sage's tiny Golf, loaded it with bags and whatever dignity I've got left after last night, which, let's be honest, isn't much. She absolutely ruined me in that hotel room. And now we're driving back to the house to say our goodbyes to her family like nothing happened, like I wasn't making her scream my name hours ago. I promised one of her aunties last night that we'd be back for Christmas. I said it with a smile; the kind you give someone's well-meaning relative. But I already know I'm breaking that promise because if I win this championship, I've got plans for a Sage-only Christmas. No cousins, no Tim, no distractions. Just us, snow or sun, wrapped around each other and no one else.

We pull into the driveway, and I glance over. Sage moves a little stiffly as she steps out of the car, hips still sore. That's my doing, and I'm not even sorry. But then my jaw ticks. Tim is still here. Still lingering like a foul smell. He's watching her again, the way a guy watches something he thinks he lost by mistake. Newsflash, mate, she's not lost. She's found, and she found me. I step out, come around the front of the car and take her hand. I don't say anything. Just lace our fingers together, grip tight enough to make a point. We walk past him without a glance. He doesn't deserve one. Sage leads the way across the lawn to her nan, brother and aunties. They're smiling, warm, and waving before we even get there. She pulls each of them into a hug.

"We just came to say goodbye," she says. "We're driving back to the city tonight and flying out to Qatar in the morning." Sages pauses. "I'm not too sure when I'll be back in the country, but I'll make sure I visit as regularly as I can," she says, almost regretfully.

"I'm also happy to fly you all over to visit us anytime, too," I say, hoping that didn't sound too braggy. I'm trying to help. They nod, hug her tightly with a mix of surprise and understanding on their faces. I step in, offer each of them a hug and a grin.

"Sorry again for the wedding crashing," I say, rubbing the back of my neck. Nan pats my cheek like I'm already family. Sage's aunty grins. "Good luck in Qatar. And bring her home for Christmas, you hear?" I nod, lying through my teeth with a smile. "Absolutely."

Her brother just gives us a sad-looking wave; maybe he hasn't really processed that his sister is no longer just a few hours away. Hand in hand, we head back toward the car. Her fingers melt into mine like they were made for me. Like maybe, despite the noise and travel and media, this whole thing might just be sold, we might just be solid.

The drive back to Melbourne is smooth, quiet, but full. We talk about everything. The last three weeks. The race schedule. Her family and the fact that her cousin apparently stalked my racing stats for three days straight before deciding she liked me, and through it all, my hand stays right on her thigh, skin warm under my touch. Eventually, my fingers creep higher, teasing between her legs. She looks over, gives me that smirk, the one that undoes me. I swear my cock twitches to life just from that look. She doesn't say anything. Just shifts slightly, like she's daring me.

"Don't test me, Sage," I mutter, voice low. Her smirk widens, and I have to pull my hand back.

"If I keep going," I add, "we're going to end up in a ditch and not in the sexy way." She laughs, victorious.

We roll into the city just as the sky starts to bleed orange and pink, and the skyline's bathed in gold. I stop to grab some takeaway — enough for

Josie and Margot, because they've probably earned a meal for hiding me for a few days. But truth be told, I've only got one thing on my mind. A night in. A night in her.

"God, I love you." I practically yell. And just like that, I'm gone for her all over again.

FIFTY-SIX

SAGE

The entire weekend feels like a dream I haven't fully woken up from. It started with the shock of seeing Maverick— my Maverick—pull up to my childhood home in my tiny Golf, looking like sin behind the wheel and completely out of place in my sleepy hometown.

One look at him and I swear my knees nearly buckled. My brain couldn't compute it. He was supposed to be in another country, prepping for the most important races of his life. But there he was, flying in like some impossibly hot, reckless knight in shining fireproofs to be by my side, and when I ran into his arms, it felt like coming home. The rest of the weekend passed in a blur of heat and tension and tangled sheets. After crashing my cousin's wedding like a scene out of a romcom, if romcoms ended with ripped bridesmaids' dresses and me screaming Maverick's name through the hotel walls. We were inseparable. We barely made it out of the reception without scandal. His hands were all over me, his mouth at my ear whispering things that turned my knees to jelly.

God, and the hotel… There are no words. Just sweat, skin and the kind of connection that felt bone deep. He didn't just make love to me; he claimed me. Again, and again. I said it— I love you—and he looked at me like I was the only thing keeping his heart beating. And when he said it back… I swear, I'll never forget that sound. The way he whispered it into my skin was like a vow.

Sunday morning, I woke up sore in all the best ways, cuddled in his arms and the sheets, his skin warm against mine. We move slowly. Lazily packing up, sneaking in a few kisses, brushing teeth while laughing over what the front desk staff must think of us. When we get to my nan saying goodbye, I try to stay composed, but there's this buzzing under my skin. Everyone's still reeling that Maverick Carter is here, holding my hand like he's got no plans to let go. Tim is still lurking, annoying as ever, but it barely registers. Not when Maverick's thumb is stroking over my knuckles, not when he leans down, and murmurs promises in my ear.

On the drive back to Melbourne, we talk like there's no time left. Catching up. Teasing. His hand stays on my thigh for most of the ride, occasionally wandering just high enough to distract me in ways that make me squirm. Yeah, he knows exactly what he's doing. We arrive at Josie's apartment just after sunset. I can tell he's tired—jet lag and a busy weekend clinging to him, but he still insists on grabbing dinner for the girls and me. Josie and Margot eye him like proud, nosy sisters, and he handles them like a champ. I'm so proud. After dinner, we curl up in the bed of Josie's spare room, his arms wrapped tight around me, my legs wrapped around his hips, his breath warm against my neck. He kisses the spot just below my ear and murmurs, "Get ready, baby. Qatar's going to be wild."

The next morning, we're up before the sun. It's early, but we're wired. The bags are packed, passports double-checked, and Maverick's team is coordinating everything from the car. I don't think they were thrilled about his impromptu visit to Melbourne. By the time we reach the airport, every-thing is starting to feel surreal again. I'm standing on the tarmac, about to walk on to the jet with a global racing superstar who also happens to be my boyfriend, and it hits me that this isn't just a fling. It's real. We're real. He keeps close to me the whole time, his hand low on my back, protective, possessive in the best way. He makes space for me in his chaotic, high-speed world without hesitation.

On the plane, I curl into his side, and he wraps his arm around my shoulder, eyes closed, head resting on mine. We're flying across the world together. Together. I glance up at him, and he opens one eye with a lazy grin.

"You good, baby?" I nod, heart full.

"More than good." He kisses my temple.

"Then buckle up. This championship? I'm winning it for you." And just like that, I fall in love with him all over again— 30,000 feet in the air.

QATAR IS HOT.

Like, sweat-in-places-you-did n't-know-you-could-sweat kind of hot. But it's nothing compared to the inferno that is Maverick Carter in a fireproof race suit with the top half tied around his waist, chest on display and a glint in his eye that says he knows exactly what that does to me. We land in Doha, and it's go-time from the moment we step off the plane. Maverick's team scoops him up like he's the crown jewel (which, let's be real, he kind of is), and I get a lanyard slapped around my neck that says 'Paddock Access–All Areas' which is basically code for girlfriend privileges. I flash it like it's a VIP pass to heaven.

The first day at the circuit is chaos and adrenaline and jet lag all rolled into one, but I'm thriving, also silently dying. Maverick keeps glancing over at me between meetings and briefings, and every time he does, I blow him a kiss or give him a cheeky wink. He smirks like he's trying not to drag me into the nearest motorhome. There is also a lot of pretending that I'm not absolutely dying every time he peels his helmet off after practice, hair messy, sweat dripping down his neck like sin. But I'm a grown woman. I can be mature. Professional, even. (…I lie.)

BY THE TIME race day rolls around, Maverick is locked in. Laser-focused. All smoulder and strategy and that intense, no- one-else-exists energy I've only ever seen when he's seconds from a lights-out launch. But even then, he still finds me. Just before heading to the grid, he comes over, helmet in hand, and pulls me in by the waist.

"You're my good luck charm," he says against my mouth, before kissing me slow enough that one of the engineers coughs and looks away. I fan myself dramatically when he walks off.

"I don't just bring luck," I mutter to myself. "I bring the full damn upgrade package."

The race is insane. Every overtake, every perfect corner exit, I'm screaming like a woman possessed. And when he crosses the line in first? I lose it. Literally jump up and down, arms flailing, cheeks hurting from how hard I'm smiling. I don't think I'd ever get sick of this feeling. He's pulled into parc ferme, and I wait, trying not to bolt like a lunatic toward the podium. But the second I see him unstrap his helmet and look for me—me —I'm moving. I barely stop myself from launching over the barrier.

When we finally get a moment alone post-press conference, he's sweaty and exhausted and grinning like the devil. I grab his face and kiss him, all tongue and teeth, and he groans into it.

"Think I earned some kind of victory celebration?" he teases. I raise a brow.

"Baby, I only packed lace, not gold." He blinks.

"White?"

"Red."

His jaw clenches. "Room. Now."

MAVERICK

Her leg is draped over mine like she's trying to claim the whole bed, and honestly, she can have it. Hell, she can have everything. My body feels like it's been hit by a freight train made of orgasms and profanity, and my brain is somewhere floating above us, still trying to catch up. I glance over, and she's just lying there, cheeks flushed, chest rising and falling slowly. Glowing. Literally glowing. I swear to God, the woman's skin has some kind of post-sex halo situation going on.

As Sage is flipping through the photos on her phone from her time in Melbourne, I'm watching over her shoulder. It's all her and the girls making ridiculous faces, one of me with my tongue out like a child hopped up on sugar. All cute, harmless shit. And then—

Boom. There it was. The photo. Not just sexy. Not just hot. Lethal. Black lace barely covering anything, heels on, lipstick the colour of the devil, eyes locked on the camera like she knew exactly what she was doing to me and everyone else who would die to see her like that.

"Are you fucking kidding me?" I blurted, I reach out and grab the phone, holding it up like it had personally offended me.

"What is this?"

Sage's face turned red instantly. "Delete it!"

"Delete it? Babe. I'm about to send it to myself and make it my phone background." She lunged for the phone, which I dodge like it was the last lap of a Grand Prix.

"Maverick!"

"Oh no, no, no," I smirked, backing away like I'd just uncovered the holy grail. "You've been walking around with an outfit like this, taking thirst traps like that and not sharing with the class? I feel betrayed."

"You weren't supposed to see that!" she hissed, hands on her hips now, completely naked of shame but still trying to front like she isn't about to combust.

"Sweetheart," I say, while stalking toward her, dropping her phone onto the bed, "You take one more photo like that, and I'll have to lock you in my apartment just to keep you safe."

Her breath hitched as I reached her, hands sliding up her waist.

"I'm serious," I add, eyes dragging down her body like I was already imagining her in that exact set, except this time, under me. "Next time you want a sexy photo, you come to me. I'll take it with my hands. My mouth. Maybe even my cock, depending on lighting."

"Maverick!" she squeaked, totally scandalised—which only made it worse. Or better.

I didn't give her time to respond. I dropped to my knees, buried my face between her thighs and show her exactly how I felt about secret lingerie photos without proper husband... uhhh boyfriend approval. Sage is soaked in seconds. Writhing and about to leave puddles on the hotel floor. Saying my name like it's a prayer and a threat. Her thighs lock around my ears, so tight it's also suffocating. If this is how I die, so be it. I stand up, my cock hard and leaking. Sage is a flushed mess. I drag the tip of my cock through her slickness, grinning like the arrogant bastard I am.

"Still want to delete the photo?"

She glared. "Shut up and fuck me."

She's already breathless beneath me, skin flushed and dewy from everything I just did to her, everything I plan to do again. I kiss my way up her body, slow and deliberate, tongue trailing a path across her ribs until I reach her perfect, pierced nipples. I give each one the attention it deserves. Sucking hard, teasing the bars with just the right pressure. Her body jolts under my mouth, a whimper slipping from her lips that makes my cock throb. I know she's sensitive here, and I use it shamelessly, pinning her down with pleasure. Her hands are in my hair, pulling gently, like she doesn't know what to do with all the sensation at once. I take my time, dragging it out, until she's panting beneath me and by the time I reach her mouth, she's wrecked. Beautifully wrecked. I kiss her like I'm starved, tasting her on my lips and groaning against her tongue.

"Taste yourself, baby," I whisper, lips brushing hers. "You like that?" She nods, dizzy and breathless, eyes fluttering open.

"Mmm. I want to taste you now." Damn. That voice? That look? I nearly lost it right there.

"You want my cock in that pretty mouth?" I growl.

"Yes, Playboy. Let me have it."

I brace myself, sliding my cock into her mouth with a hiss, her lips warm and wet around me. She meets my eyes as her tongue wraps around the head, slow and deliberate, like she's enjoying watching me fall apart. I grip the headboard to keep myself from thrusting too deep and because I'm barely hanging on. She's got her hand around the base, her mouth working the shaft, and her eyes look devilish as she palms my balls with the other hand.

"Fuck, Sage," I grit. "You keep that up, and I'm going to lose it."

She just hums, sending vibrations straight through my core, and I swear to God, I almost lose my balance and fall off the damn bed. I pull out before I paint the back of her throat, dragging her up for a kiss, tasting myself on her lips this time. She moans into my mouth, and I know she wants more. I line myself up and push in with one hard thrust, buried to the hilt in her soaked heat.

"Jesus—Sage—this pussy's unreal."

She's gasping, fingers digging into my back, and I move— deep, fast and relentless. I'm not giving her space to think, just feel.

"You're such a good girl," I groan, grinding in deeper. "Taking all of me like that." She clenches around me, that telltale flutter, so I wrap my hand around her throat because I know what's coming.

"I—Maverick—I'm—fuck—I'm gonna—"

"Come for me, baby," I whisper against her neck. "Let me feel you."

She cries out as she tightens around me, shaking under me in waves, and I can't hold back any longer. I bury myself deep and come hard, lost in the rhythm of us, the heat and the goddamn way she owns me in moments like this. We're both a mess, a sweaty, tangled, breathless mess. I roll onto my side, arm draped over her waist as I kiss her shoulder.

"Baby," I murmur, still high off her, "I'm never going to tire of your pussy or this body." She turns, eyes lazy and satisfied, and grins.

"Good. Because it's yours, Playboy." And yeah, you better believe I set that photo as my wallpaper. Lock screen and home screen. I've got priorities.

The sun's barely up, the light creeping through the sheer curtains in golden streaks. Everything's quiet, slow, the kind of morning you want to stretch out forever. Sage is curled up beside me, still half-asleep with one leg draped over my waist, one arm thrown across my chest like she owns me. And, yeah, she does. Her hair's a wild mess, mascara smudged under her eyes, lips kiss-bitten from last night. Beautiful. Fucking breathtaking. My fingers skim over her bare back, and she hums softly, snuggling closer.

"You awake?" I whisper, brushing her hair off her face.

"Mmhm." She doesn't open her eyes, just nuzzles into my neck.

"Don't move. You're warm."

"I'll stay right here," I murmur. But my hand is already sliding lower, tracing the curve of her spine, dipping to the swell of her ass.

"You're not staying still at all," she teases, voice sleep-rough and full of mischief.

"I lied."

She laughs, low and raspy, and I swear my heart stutters. I tilt her chin up and kiss her softly. Slow. Just lips. Then the tongue. She tastes like sleep and sin. I roll her gently onto her back, hovering over her without breaking the kiss.

"You, okay?"

"More than okay," she whispers, arching under me, completely bare and so damn soft.

I trail kisses down her jaw, her neck, then lower just like last night, but slower now. Reverent. Her nipple peaks as I take them in my mouth, warm and careful, tugging them gently between my lips. The ring is cool on my tongue, and she gasps, hips shifting beneath me.

"You know I can't be gentle with these for long," I murmur against her skin.

"Who said I wanted gentle?" she breathes. Goddamn. I kiss my way down her stomach, letting my hands explore every inch of her soft, sensitive and marked from where I held her too tight. I settle between her thighs and look up at her.

"Stay still," I say, voice thick. "Let me wake you up properly."

Her eyes flutter closed, lips parted, already undone before I even start. I drag my tongue slowly through her folds, savouring every sound she makes, every twitch of her hips. She tastes like heaven, like mine.

I flatten my tongue and lick her again, deeper this time. She moans, low and desperate, fingers gripping the sheets. I wrap my arms under her thighs and hold her in place, mouth working her in slow, lazy circles, like I've got all morning. Because I do. Her hips start to roll, chasing every flick of my tongue, and I know she's close when her breath catches. One more pass, and she's gone quiet, trembling, thighs tight around my shoulders as she rides the edge and then falls apart completely. I kiss her inner thigh and glance up, chin wet, pride in every inch of me. She's glowing. Wrecked. Beautiful. She looks down at me, flushed and breathless.

"That was... Jesus, Maverick."

I grin and crawl back up to kiss her.

"Good morning, baby." We've got one weekend left of the season, one weekend left destroying hotel sheets. One weekend left until we can spend all our days loving each other.

FIFTY-SEVEN

SAGE

Steam curls around me as I step into the shower, the hot water a relief on every muscle Maverick worked last night— and again this morning. My thighs are still shaking a little. Not that I'm complaining. I let the spray hit my back and tilt my head under, eyes closed, moaning quietly to myself. God, I needed this. I barely hear the door open through the rush of water, but the familiar scent of him hits me before I hear his voice.

"You started without me?"

I smirk as I glance over my shoulder. Maverick is leaning against the wall like a fucking movie scene—arms crossed, hair a mess, completely naked and already half-hard. Typical.

"Didn't realise you needed an invitation," I tease, turning back into the spray, making sure he gets a full view of my ass as I reach for the body wash.

"Consider this your reminder that everything on this body, including that peachy little ass, is mine."

"Possession is bold, Playboy," I say as I lather my hands, arching my back a little more just to make him groan.

"Wanna prove it?" He doesn't need another invitation. The glass door slides open, and a second later, his hands are on my hips.

"You're such a fucking tease," he growls against my neck.

"Who, me?" I purr, grinding back just enough to feel how hard he is. "Just enjoying my shower."

"Liar."

He spins me gently, pressing me against the slick wall with his body. His hands slide down my sides, slow and possessive, and his mouth captures mine in a kiss that's far too hungry for the morning. I reach down between us, curling my fingers around him, stroking slowly.

"Missed this already?" I murmur against his lips.

"Baby, I will never stop missing it." His mouth finds my nipple. The cool metal of my piercing contrasts with the heat of his tongue, and I gasp, knees nearly buckling.

"Maverick," I whimper, gripping his shoulders.

He moves lower, kissing a wet trail down my stomach. "Turn around," he orders, voice hoarse. I obey; palms braced on the wall. The anticipation burns hotter than the water. Then he's behind me, his cock sliding against me, teasing, not giving in yet.

"You're not going to—"

"Oh, I am," he cuts in, one hand wrapping around my hip. "But I like hearing you beg first."

"Maverick, if you don't—ah, fuck!" He pushes inside in one deep thrust, and I shatter.

The water, the heat, the slick sliding of his cock, everything is too much in the best way. He sets a brutal pace, one hand pressed to my lower back to hold me there, the other tangled in my hair.

"You feel that?" he groans into my ear.

"This pussy was made for me."

"Yours," I gasp, biting my lip. "Fuck, I'm—"

"Come. Let go for me, Sage." And I do. With a scream that echoes off the tile, I fall apart under him. He follows seconds later, hips jerking, a low growl vibrating against my skin as he spills into me, holding me close through it. The water keeps running, but neither of us moves. Eventually, he kisses my shoulder and whispers, "So breakfast? Or round two?" I look back at him, dripping and smug.

"Why not both?"

.   .   .

"WE'VE GOT one week left on the road and then a break until the season starts up again in March," Maverick says, casually sipping his coffee like he didn't keep me up half the night. He raises an eyebrow over his mug.

"Anything you want to do in the off-season?" I grin, swirling a piece of pineapple in my mimosa.

"Find a job." That gets his attention.

He blinks. "A job?"

"Yeah," I say, steady. "I mean, the whole jet-setting- around-the-world-with-my-hot-race-car-driver-boyfriend vibe has been amazing, don't get me wrong. Sex on balconies? Life- changing. But I need something of my own, Mav. Something to fill my days, something to challenge me… something that isn't just waiting for you to come back from the track sweaty and irresistible."

He smirks at that, but I see the flicker in his eyes. He's thinking, not resisting.

"I know you could support us both forever, and we'd live like literal royalty," I continue. "But I need to feel useful. I need something that's mine."

He leans back, arms crossed, eyes fixed on me like I've just told him I want to climb Everest in heels. Then he smiles. "Okay, baby," he says, voice warm, "I'll help you find something you love. Something that sets your soul on fire. All I want is for you to be happy. I know how much your independence means to you." I melt a little at that. He really gets it.

"And", he adds with a cheeky grin, leaning in to kiss the top of my head, "I cannot wait to see you in those sexy-ass pants again."

I raise a brow. "So, it's job-hunting with ulterior motives, huh?"

"Always," he says with a wink. "Motives... hard."

My eyes flit down to his lap. "Jesus, Maverick. Let me finish my mimosa before you pitch a tent at the breakfast table." He just shrugs, smug as ever.

"Not my fault, my girlfriend's a walking fantasy." I roll my eyes as my cheeks burn. Because the truth is, I love this man, and I love him hard. But I also love myself, and it's time to start chasing something of my own again and maybe in a very short skirt.

I stare down at the open suitcase on the bed, then back up at the pile of chaotic clothes I've somehow managed to throw everywhere but inside the suitcase. Maverick walks into the room shirtless, the towel from his second less fun shower slung low on his hips, smug grin like he just won something, and my attention immediately shifts…south.

"Are you trying to distract me?" I ask, eyes narrowing.

He raises a brow. "Distract you from what? You haven't packed a single thing."

I flip him off and sigh dramatically.

"Well, what do you pack for Abu Dhabi? I need something race-week glam, something post-race slutty, and maybe something that screams 'future CEO hiring material'… just in case."

Maverick walks over, pulling me in by the hips, lips brushing my neck.

"I vote for the slutty dress. The red one. Or the black one. Or anything that makes me want to bend you over the balcony."

I laugh. "That's literally everything I own."

"Exactly."

He drops a kiss on my shoulder and lets go, heading over to the side of the room where his suitcase is already packed and zipped, the overachiever. Mine looks like a hurricane made of lace and miniskirts tore through it.

"I can't believe it's the last race," I say as I fold a top and finally put it in the suitcase.

"Feels surreal," he agrees. "And exhausting."

"You've been unreal this season," I say, watching the muscles move under his skin as he pulls on a shirt. "I'm so proud of you."

He smiles, eyes softening. "Wouldn't have made it through without you."

"Oh please, I'm just the emotional support slut with a good margarita arm."

He laughs, walking back over and pulling me into him again. "You've been my calm in the chaos, Sage."

My chest tightens a little at that. His voice is quiet, raw. And honest. And God, I'm going to cry into my lingerie if I don't do something soon.

"Okay," I say, grabbing a silk bralette and tossing it at him playfully, "enough feelings. Let's talk about strategy. I'm thinking 'I'm not trying but still hot' outfits, and minimal underwear."

He catches the bralette mid-air. "Why pack any underwear at all?"

I grin and finally start folding properly.

"Abu Dhabi, here we come. One more race weekend. Let's end it with a bang." He leans in, voice low.

"Oh, baby… I plan to bang all weekend." He's dressed now, as he slaps my ass cheek.

"You ready darlin', cars here"

The plane hums around me, that steady white noise that usually lulls me to sleep within twenty minutes. But not today. I'm too wired. Too full of nerves and excitement, and something dangerously close to awe as I sit here, pretending to scroll through my phone while secretly stealing glances at the man next to me. Maverick is dozing with his arms crossed and his cap pulled low over his eyes. His calm, composed, and completely unbothered. Like he isn't about to go after his ninth World Championship. Nine. It sounds unreal in my head.

If he wins in Abu Dhabi, and let's be honest, it's Maverick fucking Carter, so of course he's going to win, he'll break every record. Cement his name in the sport's history like it was always meant to be there. He'll go down as the greatest of all time. And I get to love him through that. I get to be the woman in his corner. The one who sees the version of him the world doesn't. The loveable, fiercely loyal and annoyingly sexy version who leaves socks on the floor and makes margaritas better than I do. The man who told me I was his calm in the chaos. Who kisses me as if I matter and touches me like I'm made just for him. Oh God, my chest tightens. Because after this weekend… what happens? The season ends. The travel stops. The circus packs up and takes a break.

And Maverick and I…? We face real life. The not-on-the- road, not-wrapped-in-constant-adrenaline life. And as much as I want it, I want something steady, I want to find a job and build a little world of my own again… I'm terrified. Terrified of what happens when the momentum slows, and we're left with just us. Not to mention the eyes of the world that are constantly on us. The obsession with every woman tied to a driver, especially one who wins championships like they're party favours. I've tried to stay grounded. To stay, Sage. But there's a voice in the back of my mind that still whispers I'm not built for this world. That I'm just…

passing through it. But as that thought enters my mind, Maverick shifts beside me, and his hand finds mine under the blanket without opening his eyes. Like he just knows I'm quietly freaking out.

My chest softens. I look at him, all jawline and sleepy attitude, and I know. This is what I want. Him. Us. Whatever form that takes. Wherever it goes. Even if it scares the hell out of me. Because there's no one else I'd rather stand next to as he rewrites history and when he wins that title, because I believe with my whole damn heart that he will, and I'll be right there. Screaming. Crying. Probably trying not to flash my tits on live TV. But right there, all in for him. For us. I climb into his lap and, as I go to tell him I'm scared. Not that he'll lose, that he'll win and that everything will change. That maybe, once we actually settle down and the champagne's gone flat, I won't be enough. But when I open my mouth to speak, his hand grip my chin and pulls my mouth to his, and he just kisses me. Slow. Purposeful.

"Stop thinking, baby," he whispers against my lips. "You're mine, and I'm in this forever

The hotel in Abu Dhabi is ridiculous. Like gold elevator buttons and a chandelier bigger than my house, it's ridiculous. The kind of place where you expect Beyoncé to sashay past you in the lobby with zero security because even the walls are too rich to bother her. And I'm still standing there in travel sweats and slightly greasy hair, looking like someone who snuck in through the staff entrance.

Maverick's already halfway to the front desk, charming the hell out of the poor man checking us in — his sunglasses still on indoors, one hand slung lazily around my suitcase like it doesn't weigh more than I do. Of course, he looks good. He always looks good. Jet lag doesn't dare touch that man. I'm still adjusting to the aggressively cold air conditioning when I hear the shriek.

"SAGE!"

I whip around just in time to get tackled by a blur of curls, fake tan, the faint smell of gin and expensive perfume.

"Josie," I gasp, half-laughing, half-suffocating in her perfume cloud.

"Jesus, let a girl check in first."

"Oh, please, I saw that little stress crease between your brows from across the lobby. You needed a distraction." Before I can sass back, another pair of arms wraps around me from behind. Margot. Cooler, calmer, but still warm as hell.

"You look exhausted," she murmurs in my ear. "You were spiralling this entire flight, huh?"

"Define spiralling," I say with a suspicious smile.

"Did you cry in the plane bathroom?" she asks.

"Okay, yes, but only once, and there was turbulence." Josie takes one look at my expression and snorts.

"Oh, babe, you're not allowed to combust until after he wins. Then you can cry and faint and throw up all you want; we'll even hold your hair."

"Thanks. That's reassuring."

"Also," Josie adds, linking her arm through mine as we walk toward the elevators, "don't worry about the room situation. We made sure your boy's getting the penthouse suite."

"Oh?"

"Yup," Margot grins. "One king-size bed, a shower big enough to hold a group therapy session, and a view that screams 'championship sex celebration.' You're welcome."

I glance up at Maverick, who's now chatting with a bellhop like they're best friends, and feel that ache in my chest ease just a little. My nerves are still there, tight and coiled under my skin, but suddenly, I don't feel so alone. My girls are here. We're in Abu Dhabi. And ready or not — this is it. I glance over at Maverick just as the clerk hands him our room keys, and he winks. Of course, he planned this. He knew I'd be a wreck stepping off that plane and decided reinforcements were non-negotiable. God, I fucking love him. He strolls over, grins at the girls and slides their keys into their hands before pressing a quick kiss to the top of my head.

"Let's go...warm up the room, baby," he murmurs, that trademark smirk in full effect.

"Girls," I call as we head past, "You'll meet us for dinner?"

"Absolutely," Josie chirps. "And you better make that reservation for 5 people, please."

Maverick comes to an abrupt halt, eyebrow arched.

"Josie... what did you do?"

She just flashes him a grin that's far too pleased with itself. "Oh, nothing you need to worry about."

He stares at her, scandalised. I slip my hand into his as we head for the elevators. Whatever Josie's up to, I'm just grateful he's got my back and that my hot mess express has a flawless Plan B.

FIFTY-EIGHT

MAVERICK

Sage and I step into the suite, and I can't help but wonder why Josie insisted we bump our dinner reservation up by one. Sage makes her way to the balcony, looking like something out of a dream, hair catching the late afternoon light, taking in that insane view. The track snakes right past our windows, and she could literally watch the race from here if she wanted to. But I don't want that. I want her down in the garage, headset on, screaming my name. I want her lips to be the first thing I taste when I win this championship again. I join her, wrapping an arm around her waist, pulling her close. The city hums below us, but right now it's just us.

"Enjoying the view, baby?" I murmur, chin resting on her head. She nods, eyes bright.

"It's incredible. I might just watch the entire race from out here."

"Not a chance," I say with a grin, spinning her to face me. "I need you there when I win. And I need these lips to be the first thing I taste."

I kiss her long, deep, the kind of kiss that makes everything else disappear. Reluctantly, I break away and give her ass a playful squeeze.

"I'm going to shower and get ready for dinner," I announce. "Time to figure out who Josie snuck onto our guest list."

Sage's grin is wicked. "Please don't think about Josie in the shower; do you need me to join you so you can think about something else?" I laugh.

"Trust me, as tempting as that sounds, we'd starve if you did."

Stepping out of the shower, I'm greeted by the sight of Sage in a lilac dress that shimmers against her skin. Her blonde curls cascade down her back, and those purple heels lengthen her legs into something unreal. She's a living masterpiece, one that I want permanent gallery rights to.

I cross the room in two strides, not bothering to hide the way my jaw drops.

"Wow," I breathe, trailing my fingers over the fabric. "This is definitely my favourite colour." I capture her lips in a soft, hungry kiss. I pull on a pair of chinos and a button-down, slide my shoe one, and Sage reaches for more, but I gently catch her hands and guide her toward the door.

"Come on, trouble," I tease. Sage pouts all the way to the elevator.

We arrive at the restaurant to find the girls already settled in, drinks in hand and grins that could part the room. I pull out Sage's chair, settle beside her and let my hand rest on her thigh.

Leaning close, I murmur, "I'm going to eat you like my favourite snack later." She freezes, then smiles like the devil just took a vacation. Yeah, I'm going to be battling a raging boner for the entire dinner.

Sage shoots a look at Josie. "Josie, who's this mystery guest?"

Margot winks because, of course, she's in on whatever's about to drop. Josie clears her throat and grins.

"Well," she says, leaning forward, "You and Margot are going to be spending the weekend getting railed, so I figured it's only fair if I do, too."

I see the moment Sage's brain clicks. "Josie, you sneaky bitch, you didn't—" just as Drew slides into the empty seat across from us.

"Maverick, buddy," he says, knocking my shoulder. "Didn't think I'd miss the championship race, did ya?" I laugh, shaking my head.

"Mate, something tells me you're not here for the race." He winks at me, Margot hoots behind him, and Josie just smirks. The chaos has officially begun, and I wouldn't have it any other way.

I WAKE BEFORE SAGE; the room is still tinged with dawn's soft glow. Carefully, I disentangle her leg from mine and slip out of bed. Today and this entire week is packed: team meetings, interviews, media obligations.

Apex Racing has its sights on its first Constructors' Championship in years, and every second counts.

In the kitchen, I fire up the coffee machine and pour two steaming mugs. Returning to the bedroom, I find Sage stirring, hair tousled and eyelashes heavy with sleep. I hand her a cup and wrap an arm around her shoulders, pulling her into my side.

"I'll be out most of the day," I whisper. "If you want, you can come hang out at the track." She smiles, dipping her head into my chest.

"Thanks, but the girls and I were planning to explore Abu Dhabi. Who knows if I'll be back?" I give her a gentle squeeze.

"Hey now, trouble."

She laughs, then tilts her head so her eyes flash up at me.

"Well… if you really want me there at the track, I can come." I press a kiss to her temple.

"Go enjoy the city with your friends. I'll leave my credit card on the dresser, so I'm expecting to see some serious spending notifications coming through today." Her grin is wicked.

"You sure? If I max it out, how much trouble will I be in?"

I lean in, our lips nearly brushing. "Go ahead, try to max it. I dare you." I nip her playfully on the lip, and she giggles.

"As much as I'd love to stay in bed all day," I murmur, planting a last kiss on her forehead, "I've got to get going, my love."

She watches me with half-lidded eyes as I roll out of bed, her smug smile the best good morning I could ask for.

I toss my credit card on the dresser and head out, the elevator ride down reminding me that no matter how much I adore Sage, there's a day to conquer. Starting with a chat with the team principal, a TV interview and then a sponsorship photo call. I exit the lobby and enter a waiting car; I slide in and pull out my phone. I message Drew to try and find out what's going on with him and Josie.

> Me: Mate, time to tell me what's going on between you and Josie?

Replies immediate.

Drew: I'll tell ya, Mav, she's got me wrapped around her little finger. I think I might be in love

Me: You've what? Slept together 3 times?

I roll my eyes.

Drew: Shows what you know - you're not the only one who can drag a woman halfway around the world.

What the fuck does that mean?

Me: Drew…. What the fuck, mate?

Nothing, no reply. I'll deal with that later. I've arrived at the track now, and I need to meet with Benny in 5 minutes.

Benny's office is buzzing in that strangely silent way, like the calm eye of a hurricane. Screens flash data behind him. Sector deltas, tyre deg windows, wind shift probabilities. The kind of stuff you'd think would make a man unravel. But not Benny. He's in his zone, calm as ever, pointer in hand, walking me through our final shot at this thing.

"The tyres will be tight around lap 42," he says, tapping the screen.

"If Havoc pits early, don't bite, hold the line. DRS opens at T5. If you're chasing, stay patient. You've got the straight- line speed." I nod, absorbing it all. But then he stops and turns toward me fully.

"Bring it home, Maverick. For everyone."

That lands hard. He's never said it like that before, never so personal. I press my tongue to the inside of my cheek, then nod once.

"I will." Because I'm not just racing for points today. Not just for the ninth title. I'm racing for everything this season's meant: the nights on the road, the pit wall glances with Sage in my line of sight, the mornings tangled up with her legs over mine, that mouth on my shoulder whispering you've got this when she thinks I'm asleep. It all means something more this time. As I leave Benny's office and make my way to the sponsor photo call, my phone dings - it's a notification from the bank.

Good, Sage is spending my money, and I couldn't be happier. I fire off a text

> Me: Good to see you're enjoying that card, trouble.

> Trouble: You don't have to ask me twice. Want anything?

I grin

> Me: Surprise me, but make sure it's lace and easy to remove with teeth.

I smile to myself and tuck my phone back in my pocket because today's major partner wants me in their signature race suit, under the hot sun, logo big on my chest, and there is no room to hide a boner. I smirk for the cameras, give them the trademark Maverick lean forward and wink. All while my phone blows up in my pocket - Sage is giving my credit card the workout it deserves - that's my girl.

SAGE

I don't know what I expected from Abu Dhabi, but I wasn't prepared to fall completely head over heels. The city is like a damn luxury dream, sun-drenched buildings, luxury oozing out of every corner, the kind of place that makes you feel like your life should come with a private driver and a couture wardrobe. Honestly? I could live here. Give me air conditioning, an icy margarita, and I'll start looking at real estate.

The girls and I kicked off the day with brunch, and yes, it included alcohol. Then we hit the shops like we were on a mission from God. I'm still adjusting to the whole 'Maverick's black card is your black card' thing, but Josie literally threatened to take the card and spend it for me if I didn't let her enjoy it. So… I did. Maverick doesn't know it yet, but a few of today's purchases are for his eyes only. He'll get the full show if he wins; it's all about incentives, right?

We finally collapse into a long lunch, arms full of shopping bags, feet sore, stomachs rumbling. The second we sit down, I know I'm in trouble. Josie's got that look, that smug, curious look, just waiting to pounce.

"So…" she starts, drawing the word out like she's narrating the beginning of a scandalous story. "Have you told him yet?"

Ah. That. I glance over at Margot. She's practically glowing while grinning at me over the rim of her glass like the cat who's got the cream. Josie already knows the answer — she just wants me to say it out loud. I sigh and give in.

"Yes. I told Maverick I love him." Screams. Literal screams. The server jumps. Josie and Margot are beaming like I just told them they won the lottery.

"Okay, okay, tell us everything," Josie demands, leaning forward. "When? Where? Were there tears? Was there sex? Wait — don't answer that. Actually, do answer that."

I roll my eyes, grinning despite myself. "It was at the wedding. After I had a little… confrontation with Tim."

Margot gasps. "Tim. Tim, nice but dim Tim? Ugh, that man is a walking red flag wrapped in discount cologne."

"Exactly. Anyway, after that mess that Maverick overheard, we walked away and I just… told him."

Margot nods like this all makes perfect sense. "We could tell something shifted between you two at dinner last night," she says softly. "You, especially. You looked… at peace. Like being with him doesn't just make you happy; it makes you whole."

I blink. "That's… weirdly profound for you."

She smirks. "Blame the wine."

Then Josie leans in again, and I know what's coming before she even opens her mouth. "So," she says, eyes sparkling with mischief. "Let me ask you again — the same question I asked on your birthday. If Maverick asked you to marry him tomorrow, would you say yes?" I toy with my glass, pretending to think, even though the answer's already on the tip of my tongue. I look up and smile, honest and soft.

"If he asked tomorrow… probably not." Josie gasps. "But", I continue, "if he asked in a few months, yeah. I would."

Now they're full-on shrieking. Josie's banging her hands on the table like she's at a concert. Margot's nearly tearing up.

"Yes, Sage!" Josie says, grabbing my hand. "This is all we've ever wanted for you. A man who worships the ground you walk on, who waits for you, who would follow you anywhere. That's Maverick. He's so obsessed with you; it's almost disgusting."

I laugh, blushing a little. Not because they're wrong but because they're right. And maybe, for the first time, I'm letting myself believe it too. My phone buzzes on the table. I flip it over - Maverick

Playboy: Drunk yet? I hope Margot hasn't been arrested.

Me: Shopping turned into a long lunch. Sorry about the damage done to your card... oops ;)

Playboy: As long as I get to see you model the damage later, I'll allow it.

Me: Oh, you'll be seeing everything, don't worry. Assuming you win. No trophy = no show.

Playboy: Noted. Providing I don't crash from the distraction. Do you want me to go into the wall, Sage?

Me: I want you to focus, champ. So, you can absolutely ruin me later. Priorities.

Playboy: Fuck. You're evil. Hot. But evil.

Me: I prefer chaotic with amazing boobs. Josie says hi, btw.

Playboy: Tell her to stop corrupting you. And you do have amazing boobs.

Me: Too late. Also, a small thing… I may have mentioned that I told you I loved you. Cue emotional girl screeching. Hope that's cool.

Playboy: Cool? I just got hard in a strategy meeting.

Me: You're welcome. Also, Margot says I look "at peace" with you. Should I be offended? Or planning our wedding?

Playboy: Planning. Offence comes after I finish what I started in the shower.

Me: You better win this weekend. Because I've got a little white number, that's practically illegal. Might need help taking it off.

Playboy: You're going to kill me. I hope they put "Died doing what he loved" on my grave.

Me: It'll just say: "Death by thighs." With a tiny margarita glass emoji.

I'm grinning like a total idiot when I put my phone down. That stupid, smug man. I swear he's going to kill me with those texts one day, death by flirting. Or dick. Either works. Josie narrows her eyes at me from across the table like a hawk circling its prey.

"Oh, my god," she says, slamming her margarita down. "That's your 'Maverick just said something filthy' face."

Margot leans in over the table, both elbows planted and eyes wide. "You're flushed. Texting flushed. What did he say?"

I try to school my expression, but my lips betray me and twitch upward, anyway. "Nothing."

Josie gasps. "Nothing? Lies. LIES, Sage."

"You're not slick," Margot says, reaching for my phone like a thief. "Is it a dick pic? Oh my God, please say it's a dick pic."

I snatch the phone away before she can reach it. "It was not a dick pic! He's in a strategy meeting."

"As if that would stop him," Josie mutters under her breath, sipping dramatically through her straw.

I shrug, coy. "Let's just say I might have promised him a private runway show if he wins this weekend." They both scream again. I shrink into my chair and grab my margarita for cover.

"Sage!" Margot cries, fanning herself with the menu. "You can't just drop that and expect us not to combust!" Josie reaches across and clinks her glass to mine.

"To you and your Olympic-level seduction game. Honestly, I'm so proud."

"To Maverick," Margot adds with a dramatic sigh. "The man does not know the chaos he is in for."

"Oh," I say, biting back a smirk as my phone buzzes again. "I think he does. And he's very into it."

I tilt my head, fluff my hair, and wait until Josie and Margot are deep in another margarita-fuelled debate about whether Maverick's trainer is hot or just 'objectively symmetrical.' The sunlight's hitting just right — golden and glowing, and my dress has just enough plunge to make things interesting. I lift my phone, bite my lip, and snap the photo. A little smile, a little cleavage, and a whole lot of 'I know exactly what this will do to you.'

> Me: For motivation. Win the race, win the rest of the dress.

Send. Less than thirty seconds later, I see the typing dots appear, then vanish, then appear again.

> Playboy: Are you trying to make me cum in pants? I'm already picturing that dress on the floor.

> Me: Be a good boy, and you'll get to see it up close. And maybe what's under it.

Josie leans over, completely ignoring boundaries as usual. "Did you just send him a thirst trap mid-lunch?" I slide my phone under my thigh and grin.

"Maybe."

Margot raises a brow. "Girl. His blood pressure is going to spike harder than his lap times."

Josie perks up, suddenly inspired in the way that means someone's about to get in trouble. "You know what we should do?"

"Oh no," I say immediately.

"Yes," Margot replies at the same time.

Josie's already rifling through her bag for a pen. "A post- race surprise. Something to absolutely blow his mind."

Margot sips her drink. "You mean besides Sage's boobs?"

Josie rolls her eyes. "Yes, like… actual chaos. Decorations. Maybe we show up to the paddock in custom T-shirts with his face on them. Full WAG energy."

"Big 'I love my fast big dick energy boyfriend' energy," Margot nods solemnly. "Tacky but perfect."

I blink. "Can we not get banned from the track?"

Josie ignores me. "Or… we book out the hotel bar. Turn it into a private victory party. Just us, his family and the team. We get him on a table, shirtless, and we do shots off his abs."

Margot claps. "Yes! And Sage can lick the lime from his, uh…. crouch."

"You two are unhinged," I mutter, but I'm already texting the team's PR manager to see if the hotel bar is bookable. Because let's be honest… It's race week. If Maverick wins, we will all be celebrating just in slightly different ways. And I already bought the lingerie.

"Alright," I say as I gather my bags, "Let's go, ladies. Maverick's parents are arriving soon, and I want to hide all of this shopping before they arrive."

FIFTY-NINE

MAVERICK

My day's done. Practice prep sorted, debrief reviewed, questions answered, well mostly. Now I'm back in the hotel, stretched out on the lounge with one eye on the track notes and the other on my phone, waiting for Sage to text back. She's still out with Josie and Margot, off living her best life somewhere in the malls of Abu Dhabi, probably two dozen margaritas deep and charming half the sales staff into giving her discounts she doesn't need. I smile to myself, thinking about that runway show she promised me later. I swear, that woman has no idea the chokehold she has me in.

There's a knock at the door. Definitely not Sage, she has a key unless she's lost it, which is a kind of thing Sage would do. I stand, a bit confused, and glance through the peephole. Mum and Dad. I booked them a room in the same hotel but made sure it was a few floors away, mostly for sound-proofing reasons. Sage can be… enthusiastic. And loud. I open the door and before I can get a word out, Mum's arms are around me.

"Maverick," she says, her voice warm and tight. "It's so good to see you, darling."

"Hey, Mum," I say, hugging her back. "You too."

Dad claps me on the back with one of those steady, grounding hands. "Hey, champ. You ready for the weekend?"

"As ready as I'll ever be." Then it hits me, the weight of this moment.

My parents gave up so much to get me here— weekends, holidays, sleep, security, all for this dream that started in a beat-up go-kart on a rainy track. Having them here now, for this part of my career, when everything is on the line, when a record is hopefully broken… It means more than I can say. Mum's already surveying the suite like she's ready to take inventory.

"Where's that beautiful Sage of yours?"

"Out with the girls," I say with a smile.

"Probably drunk and dragging three poor hotel staff behind her, carrying shopping bags." Mum laughs, her entire face lighting up.

"I've missed her."

Mum's reaction hits somewhere deep. My chest warms and I lean down to press a kiss to the top of her head as she floats around the room doing classic Mum things, checking the mini fridge, fluffing pillows, asking if I've been eating properly like I'm not a grown man on a race team's diet plan.

Dad and I step out onto the balcony, watching the sunset burn over the Abu Dhabi skyline.

"So," he says, nursing a water bottle like it's a whiskey, "what are your plans for the break?"

"Not sure yet," I reply, stretching out in the chair. "But I want to take Sage away. Somewhere quiet. Just us."

He nods. "You're serious about her."

It's not a question, but I answer it anyway. "Yeah, Dad. I am." I pause, trying to find the right words. "She's… more than just someone I'm dating. She's the first person who's ever made me feel like I'm more than just a driver. More than the guy on the podium or the headlines in the media. She makes me feel like me, just… Maverick. Not the brand. Just a man. And for the first time, I want to think about life after F1." He watches me for a beat, nodding slowly.

"I can see the shift in you," he says. "You're lighter. Happier. Not just going through the motions on race day anymore, you seem to be enjoying it all again."

"I am," I say simply. "Truly."

He claps my shoulder again, solid and sure. "Then you hang onto that, son. That kind of thing doesn't come around often." I nod, glancing at my phone one more time. Still no text from Sage. But when she walks through that door tonight? I'm going to kiss her and tell her everything I just told my dad.

"Playboy, you here?" Sage's voice rings out from the balcony, all bright and bold and completely unaware that my very British, very present parents are seated in the living room behind me. I wince. Shit. I practically vault off the lounge, through the balcony doors and make a beeline for the front door, throwing it open just as she barrels in, bags on both arms like she's won some kind of luxury shopping triathlon. I scoop them out of her hands in one move and kiss her quickly. It's half a greeting, half a silent plea to dial the flirt down by about twenty per cent. Too late.

"Sage!" my mum calls from the lounge. Sage freezes for half a beat, then lets out a little squeaky giggle. Her cheeks flush as she leans into me and whispers,

"I didn't know they were here; if I did, I wouldn't have come in so... loudly." No kidding. But she squares her shoulders and steps into the living room like she owns the place. That's my girl.

"May," she says sweetly, walking over and wrapping my mum in a warm hug. "So nice to see you again. Sorry, I was hoping to be home before you both got here."

My mum smiles, not missing a beat. "That's okay, sweet girl. Did you enjoy your day?"

"Yeah, I sure did," Sage replies. "This place is beautiful."

She turns to my dad. "Hi, Mr Carter, how are you?" Dad waves her off.

"None of that, Mr Carter crap. It's Ron. And you look like you've done some damage to Maverick's bank account, that's a girl."

Sage laughs, cheeks still flushed but totally relaxed now. "I tried my best."

She looks back at me, her expression softening. "I'm just going to put these bags away and freshen up for dinner. Be right back." And then she heads toward the bedroom, hips swaying, legs bare under that sundress that's tempting me to cancel dinner with my parents and keep Sage in bed all night long. I trail after her like a damn puppy, still carrying the bags, because of course I do.

"She's got you wrapped around her little finger," I hear my mum say behind me. I don't even deny it because she's not wrong.

As soon as the bedroom door clicks shut behind us, Sage turns, a smirk already forming on her lips.

"You going to tell your mum that 'Playboy' was just a... situational nickname?" She teases, stepping closer and plucking a shopping bag from my hand.

"Absolutely not," I mutter, dropping the rest of the bags by the dresser. "I'm going to pretend I didn't hear it and pray she does the same."

Sage hums as she toes off her sandals. "You could've warned me they were here."

"You could've sent a text before yelling it like we're in a goddamn porno."

She laughs—God, that sound. It softens me instantly. She's standing there barefoot, glowing from the sun and radiating that dangerous blend of sexy and sweet that makes me forget my name.

"Come here," I murmur, grabbing her wrist and pulling her in. Her hands slide up my chest, nails dragging lightly.

"You going to kiss me like a gentleman with his parents in the next room?"

"Nope," I say, before I take her mouth in a hot, messy kiss. All tongue and teasing and way too intense for the three- minute buffer we probably have before my mum calls for us.

She moans against me, fingers sliding into my hair. "You smell incredible, good enough to eat."

"Is that your way of saying I should fuck you before dinner?"

She laughs against my jaw. "It's my way of saying you want to, but you won't."

I groan. "You're a menace."

"You love it." She slips away, unzipping her dress with one graceful tug and disappearing into the ensuite.

"Gunna freshen up. Splash some cold water on your face, too, before your mum gets a good look at your situation." I glance down at the obvious hard-on straining my shorts and sigh.

"This is actual torture."

From the bathroom, she sings, "Welcome to my world, Playboy."

By the time we're all seated at the outdoor table under the warm golden lights, Sage is the picture of elegance, in a fresh dress another lilac one, that's full length and respectable v cut down the front and tie up bows on the shoulders, it gleams against her glowing skin and her hair is in a messy bun that's somehow both casual and sexy. My mum is already pouring wine, chatting with her like they've been best friends for years. Dad's asking about her job plans and trying to rope her into some investment scheme I'm pretty sure he made up this morning.

I watch her handle it all with grace and that signature sass, never missing a beat.

"She's good for you," Mum says softly, leaning toward me.

I nod. "She's everything."

"Don't screw it up, then."

"Trying not to."

Sage catches my eye from across the table and raises her glass. I raise mine, giving her a wink. She blushes slightly, but there's that fire in her gaze again. The one that says, Later, you're mine, and I can't fucking wait.

We're halfway through dinner, and my dad's on his second glass of red, so naturally, he's telling the story of how I once drove a golf cart into a fountain during a sponsor event when I was fifteen. "Fully submerged," he declares, gesturing dramatically with his fork. "The water was up to the steering wheel! And your man here he gets out like it's a Bond movie, dripping wet, and just says, 'It was a flawed corner entry.'"

Sage is losing it beside me, hand over her mouth to stifle her laugh.

"Oh my God, that's iconic."

"No, no, no," Mum cuts in, pointing her knife at me like it's a court-room trial.

"What's iconic is that he still tried to flirt with the sponsor's daughter afterwards, while soaking wet."

"Ambition," I say, shrugging. "You've always said I was determined."

"Delusional, more like," Dad mutters.

Sage leans over and whispers, "So… were you successful? With the sponsor's daughter?"

I grin. "She gave me her number. Texted me once to say I owed her a new pair of heels."

"Wow. Smooth, Playboy," she teases.

My mum raises a brow at that. "Alright, you two. Am I finally allowed to ask about the nickname, or do I need another glass of wine first?" Sage chokes on her water. I shoot her a do not look, but she's already grinning like the devil in lip gloss.

"It's… contextual."

"Uh-huh," Mum says, clearly loving every second of this.

"Do I even want to know?" my dad asks, cutting into his steak like he's reconsidering every life choice.

"Nope," I blurt. "You absolutely do not."

"I bet it's from one of those racy fan forums," Mum muses. "You know the ones. They had a whole thread dedicated to his arms last year."

"Mum," I groan. "Stop."

"I liked that thread," Sage adds, and I nearly fall out of my chair.

Mum clinks her glass against Sage's. "I knew I liked you."

"Traitors. All of you," I mutter, reaching for the wine.

After dessert, some fancy chocolate tart, Sage probably pretended not to love while stealing my second slice. My dad and I end up on the terrace, watching the lights of Abu Dhabi twinkle against the sky. Mum and Sage are curled up on the lounge inside, whispering and giggling like old friends.

"She's good for you," Dad says eventually.

"I know."

"And you're different with her. Calmer."

I nod. "She makes things quiet in my head. Even when it's loud."

He claps a hand on my shoulder. "Don't fuck it up."

"Jesus," I say, shaking my head. "Do you and Mum share a script or something?"

"Pretty much."

I glance back through the glass. Sage's eyes meet mine, all soft and knowing, full of that fire that pulled me in from the very beginning. I'm not sure how I got lucky enough to have her here… but I'll do whatever it takes to keep her. Even if it means surviving more stories about golf carts and sponsors' daughters.

SIXTY

SAGE

It's qualifying day, and I'm a bundle of nervous energy with nowhere to put it. Maverick left for the track hours ago— calm as ever—while I've been pacing the suite like a panicked cat in a thunderstorm. So naturally, I called in backup. There's a knock at the door, and I practically sprint to it, hoping it's not one of those overly chipper hotel staff. It's not, it's my girls. Margot and Josie stand there like visions, arms full of salvation: breakfast and coffee. My kind of pit crew.

"A latte for the lady," Margot says, holding it out with a dramatic flourish.

"She lives," I mutter, taking it like it's holy. One sip in, and I can already feel my blood pressure stabilising.

Josie chuckles. "Kind of poetic that this whole thing started with a latte, huh?" I roll my eyes, but she's not wrong.

"Don't remind me." We plop down on the lounge, inhaling food and caffeine like it's our last meal. For me, it sort of feels like my stomach is twisting with nerves. Maverick needs P4 or better today to set up the championship tomorrow. No pressure, right?

Once all the food and caffeine have been inhaled, we move to the bedroom, and now the chaos begins. I yank my suitcase onto the bed like it insulted my family.

"I want sexy, but not stripper-next-door. You know? Classy track, girl-friend, not who let her in the paddock."

"Then why did you pack five crop tops and zero bras?" Josie asks, deadpan.

"Because I'm a Libra."

"Say less."

I rifle through options, rejecting them all like a diva at a fitting. Finally, I hold up a slick white shirt and a black pleated leather skirt that hits mid-thigh.

"Too much?"

Margot eyes it, then nods. "It's hot. What shoes?"

"Heels feel try-hard. I was thinking the white Air Forces."

"YES," Josie says immediately. "Sporty Spice realness."

I get dressed while they dig through my lipsticks like they're raiding Sephora. I throw on a touch of makeup just enough to look like I tried but not like I'm trying to steal a spotlight, and I leave my hair down in soft waves. One final mirror check and… damn. I don't look like someone having a quiet panic about race strategy. I look like I belong. Am I ready? I have no idea. But I feel like myself, and today, that feels like enough.

By the time we reach the paddock, my nerves are practically doing doughnuts in my stomach. The car drops us off, and Josie is already buzzing, snapping pics of everything and everyone like she's on a red carpet. Margot's in her zone too, chic sunglasses, an iced coffee in hand, cool as ever and me? I'm trying not to throw up on my shoes. The paddock is already chaos, a hive of energy, team gear everywhere, cameras flashing, fans pressed against barricades with signs and flags. The championship atmosphere has its own pulse. It's loud. It's fast. It's real.

Maverick's car sits at the far end of the garage, glinting under the lights like it knows it's about to be crowned king. I spot Benny first, already gesturing animatedly to someone with a laptop. He sees me and throws me a wink.

"Your man is in the sim trailer," he calls over the noise. "Might want to go distract him, he's a bit heated."

Josie smirks. "You heard the man."

I find Maverick inside, helmet off, suit half unzipped, and his eyes focused like hell on a screen. He's tapping through data with his race engineer, his jaw tight, eyes locked in. Laser- focused doesn't even begin to cover it. But then he sees me. And just like that, everything softens. His whole face shifts. His stern and calculating one second, lit up like the sunrise the next. He stands immediately and pulls me in by the waist, lips brushing my cheek before anyone can pretend not to notice.

"Hey, baby," he murmurs, low and close. "You look…"

"Hot?" I offer.

"Criminally hot. I might need to get you kicked out before qualifying starts."

"You'd miss me too much."

He leans in like he might kiss me properly, right there, consequences be damned, but then Benny pops his head in. "Two minutes to briefing!" Maverick groans and rests his forehead against mine for a second.

"Stay and watch from the garage?" he asks softly.

"Always." He pulls back and runs his thumb down my cheek like he doesn't want to let go. And then he's gone, all business again, race suit zipped all the way up and helmet in hand. I stand there for a beat, catching my breath. Josie comes up beside me.

"Okay, not to be dramatic, but I think I just ovulated."

Margot snorts. "Sage, you might actually be dating the hottest man on Earth."

"Might?" I deadpan, but my chest is warm. Not just from lust—but from pride. Mavericks on the brink of something huge. And I get to be here. With him. For this. Let's fucking go, Playboy.

I've watched qualifying before. I've stood in this exact garage, headset over my ears, heart in my throat. But today? Today, it's like I can feel the track under my skin. The noise is constant—engines screaming, engineers barking instructions, tyres screeching during pit exits—but under all of it, there's this unbearable buzz. Awaiting. A breath caught in the world's lungs, suspended until someone either flies or falls.

Maverick's already through Q1 and Q2 clean. Fast. Controlled. That signature, laser-sharp confidence pulsing through every lap. But now we're in Q3, and everything depends on the next 10 minutes.

He only needs P4 in the race tomorrow to secure the championship.

Top four. That's it. So, he needs a good starting position, but the grid is brutal today, the weather's changing, the track temp is a bitch, and two rival cars have suddenly pulled surprise upgrades. Everyone's jostling for a final-lap miracle. My hands are clammy on the edge of the garage workbench as I watch the monitor. Maverick's out for his final run, green sectors in the first two. Not purple, but solid. Good. Then Benny's voice cuts through the headset, low and commanding. "Push through the exit. Don't lift." I don't breathe. His car takes the last corner, engine screaming like it's in pain, like it knows it has to give everything right now.

And then— P3. The garage erupts. Mechanics fist-pump the air, Benny lets out a rare whoop, and someone slaps the wall so hard a wrench falls off a shelf. But all I can do is stand there, blinking at the screen.

P3. He did it. He set himself up nicely for the race tomorrow. I rip the headset off and race toward the pit wall. Maverick's already pulling into the pit lane, helmet still on, visor down, but I know his smile is blinding under there. I watch the team swarm the car. Someone slaps the top of it like it's a goddamn war horse. The adrenaline in the air is suffocating in the best way. He climbs out, and even before the cameras get to him, his eyes find me. Through the chaos, through the noise, his straight to me. And he lifts two fingers in a tiny, subtle salute. Just for me. My throat tightens. He doesn't need to shout. Doesn't need to say anything. That look says it all. One more race. One more night. And the championship is his.

Josie squeals behind me, practically jumping on Margot. "He fucking did it!"

"Almost there," I whisper, still locked into him. "Bring it home, Playboy."

THE HOTEL ROOM IS DIM, just the glow of the city lights outside creeping through the curtains. I'm lying on the bed, one leg bent, still in that leather skirt, the white shirt now unbuttoned halfway down my chest. Waiting. He doesn't knock. He never does. The door opens softly, and then he's there. Maverick. Hair slightly messy, hoodie loose over his race tee, still smelling like the racetrack and adrenaline and victory. He closes the door behind him, turns to me and just looks for a beat.

Then that smirk. "You were watching me like a sniper in the garage today," he says, voice low, almost teasing.

"Thought I was going to combust under the pressure." I lift an eyebrow, letting my smile tug lazily at the corners of my mouth.

"You love the pressure. You get off on it."

He kicks off his shoes, tosses the hoodie, and walks toward the bed.

"You're not wrong; it's also not the only thing that gets me off." His hands find the edge of the mattress as he leans over me. I reach up, fingers skimming his jaw, tracing the faint shadow of stubble there.

"P3. You did it."

"I told you I would." His voice is rough now. Honest. I pull him down to me, just enough for our foreheads to touch.

"One more race," I whisper. He nods.

"Then I'll take you anywhere you want to go."

We kiss slowly, deeply and deliberately. Not rushed. Not desperate. Just… us. His hands slide under the hem of my shirt, palms spreading over my bare waist like he's claiming it, like it's his anchor. My fingers find the hem of his tee and lift. Clothes disappear in seconds. We move like we've done this a hundred times—because at this point, we have, but this time it feels like we're memorising each other. Like we both know, tomorrow will be chaos, so tonight… Tonight is sacred.

He settles between my thighs, hard and heavy against me, but he doesn't rush. His lips find the hollow of my neck, the curve of my breast and the underside of my jaw.

"I love you," he murmurs into my skin. I tangle my fingers in his hair.

"I love you more." He pauses. "Impossible, but I love hearing you say it."

Then he slides into me slowly. Deeply. Like it's not just sex, like it's reassurance, devotion, everything we can't say when the entire world's watching. I moan into his shoulder. He groans into my throat. And we stay like that. Moving together. No games. Just us. He and I. By the time we finish, I'm curled against his chest, our legs tangled, sweat cooling between our bodies. He presses a kiss to my temple, then whispers, "Tomorrow, baby. I'll bring it home."

SIXTY-ONE

MAVERICK

It's race day, my heart's already going, and I haven't even stepped onto the grid. I'm staring at my reflection in the bathroom mirror, toothbrush in hand, jaw tight, eyes sharper than they've been all season. This is it. One race. One shot to finish what I started years ago, a ninth championship. History. The hotel suite is quiet, too quiet, but I know Sage is here. I can feel her presence; it's like gravity.

"Playboy," I hear her voice float in from the bedroom. "You're going to shatter that mirror if you keep scowling at it like that."

I smirk, spitting the toothpaste and rinsing my mouth out. "Just going over my race strategy." She appears in the doorway, barefoot, wrapped in one of my team's hoodies that's way too big on her, which only makes it hotter. Hair tousled, coffee in one hand, her other tucked into the pocket of the hoodie like she's been living this life forever.

"You're going to win," she says simply, like it's already a fact. "So, maybe relax that jaw before it locks up?" I walk toward her, my hands going to her hips.

"What if I told you I'm more nervous about seeing you in that hoodie than I am about the race?"

Sage leans up and kisses me slowly. Exactly what I need.

"You've got this," she whispers, her breath brushing my cheek. "And either way, I'm yours. Title or no title." Fuck, I love her.

The paddock is buzzing when I arrive. Media, sponsors, and engineers are all moving around each other like bees in a hive. The air's thick, hot, humid and electric. The last race of the season, energy always hits differently. The pressure sits heavy, but I let it sharpen me, not shake me. I see Benny at the garage entrance, headset already on, clipboard in hand.

"Let's go to war," he says with a slap on my back. I nod, slipping into the garage like it's a cave. Then across the crowd, I spot her, Sage. She's in the back, behind the ropes, standing between Josie and Margot, sunglasses on, calm but tense. Her hand lifts subtly, just enough for me to catch it. A silent signal. I nod once. That's all I need.

Grid. Lights. Engine on. Helmet down, visor snapped. The roar of the crowd fades. Everything tunnels, and it's just me, the machine and the championship. Nine laps in, it's been smooth. I'm running P2. The car's balanced, tyres holding, but the guys behind me are hungry. Ricci's voice comes through the radio, calm but clipped. "Hold position. He is too far to start closing in. You've got clean air."

Lap twenty-two, DRS opens, pressure behind. I defend, take the inside, brake late. Aggressive. Calculated. Ruthless. My thoughts flicker to her. Just a second. Her hands on me this morning. Her words in my ear. You've got this.

Final laps. My heart is pounding. Sweat down my spine. We're clear. P2 is mine. The flag waves. I cross the line. It's done. I fucking did it. I scream into the radio, voice hoarse.

"That's it, boys! We did it! Number fucking nine!" My team explodes around me. Cheers, horns, radios going wild. But all I want is her. As soon as I'm out of the car and through the media chaos, I'm scanning. Past the cameras, the fireworks, the noise and then I see her, just past the garage barrier. Our eyes lock. She breaks into that smile, the one that ruins me every time. I push through the chaos, and I pull her into me, lifting her clean off the ground, lips crashing into hers. Everyone's watching, everyone's shouting, and I don't give a single shit about any of it because she's in my arms.

She pulls back just enough to say it: "I told you, you had it." I grin; forehead pressed to hers.

"Nine looks good on me, doesn't it?"

The podium is chaos; the champagne hits before I'm even fully up the stairs. I get sprayed in the face by one of the other drivers, don't even know who, it doesn't matter. I laugh, chest heaving, soaking it all in while taking the second step of the podium. Nine. Nine world championships. The crowd is wild. Fireworks explode overhead, gold confetti raining down, and the national anthem plays as I raise the trophy over my head. I look down at the sea of people, and right at the front of it, there she is. Sage, smiling proudly with my family and her girls and Drew, of course - he raises a beer in my direction and nods. Benny stands next to them, surrounded by the team. This is the team's first constructors' championship and years, so they are all glowing. Sage's eyes are glossy but steady, proud. For a second, I forget there's a crowd watching; I forget there's a trophy in my hand because all I can focus on is her.

Everything I did to get here. Every fight. Every crash. Every lonely fucking night. All of it is worth it, because she's here. I toss the champagne over my head. My fingers are sticky, my arms tired, but my heart's still racing. Cameras flash in every direction. I hear my name chanted like a battle cry. Maverick. Maverick. Maverick. Damn right.

They finally move us out of the crowd into the back corridors of the paddock, past the media and congratulatory hugs. I'm sweaty, champagne-drenched, and buzzing. Benny claps me on the back again and says, "I'll give you five."

I push open the door to my driver's room. And there she is already waiting, sitting on the bench like she's been holding her breath the entire race. When our eyes meet, she stands. I shut the door behind me and cross the room in two long strides. I don't say a word. I just grab her and pull her into the tightest embrace I've ever given anyone in my life. She wraps around me like she was made to, like this is the only place she wants to be, and maybe it is.

Her hands thread into my hair, still damp with sweat and champagne.

"I'm so fucking proud of you," she whispers against my neck.

"I couldn't have done it without you," I breathe, voice rasped from shouting and adrenaline. "You kept me steady." She pulls back slightly to look at me, her fingers brushing along my jaw.

"You were never steady, Maverick. You were fire. I just kept the world from burning down around you." I laugh, but it's raw. My heart's cracked wide open. I press my forehead to hers, hands gripping her waist, like I'll fall without her.

"I love you," I say. No hesitation. No noise between the words in a way I've never said before. Her eyes go wide for a beat, and then she smiles, that slow kind that climbs up one corner of her mouth, soft and sexy and filled with everything we've been building.

"I love you too, Playboy," she murmurs, just before she kisses me, and it's not wild or frantic. It's slow. Deep. Like she's memorising the shape of my mouth. Like she's been waiting for this exact moment to sink into me. She pulls away just an inch.

"Now, get changed before your balls stick to those race pants." I laugh, the weight of the entire season falling off me. Yeah. This is it. This is everything.

SAGE

The hotel bar is already a blur of alcohol and noise by the time we arrive. The team is in fine form tonight. Maverick's still wearing his race suit, half unzipped, his fireproof under shirt clinging to his abs and a whisky in one hand. He's glowing, and it's not just that sweaty, post-race fiery glow; he's actually glowing. Like adrenaline and shock and pride all wrapped in a six-foot-something smug, victorious race car driver. He spots me across the room instantly.

"Trouble," he mouths as he makes his way over.

I grin. "Victory looks good on you."

He grabs my waist like he owns it and presses a quick, breathless kiss to my mouth and then another, hungrier one when he realises I'm wearing the dress from the selfie I sent him earlier this week. It's shorter now, or maybe I just wore it tighter. And the look in his eyes says he's not going to last long in this bar. Josie's already at the bar, lining up tequila shots.

"Team celebratory chaos, round one!" she announces.

Maverick leans close to my ear. "How long do we have to stay before I can rip that dress off?"

I hum. "Long enough for you to thank your mechanics, your race engineer, and maybe the bartender. After that, I'm not responsible for what happens."

He mutters something that sounds like "worth it" and taps out a few quick thank-you hugs and fist bumps. Josie and Margot are dancing already, dragging Drew onto the floor. May — yes, his mother — is sipping champagne like a queen in the corner, completely unfazed by the chaos, and his dad is downing whiskeys with Benny like there is no tomorrow.

After about an hour of loud celebration and three tequila shots too many, Maverick grabs my hand and tugs me out of the bar.

"Say goodnight," he murmurs in my ear, his tone dark and thick with promise.

"Why?" I ask innocently.

"Because if we don't leave now, I will fuck you in that corner booth in right front of the team."

"Oh no," I fake gasp, clinging to him. "Don't threaten me with a good time."

We make it two steps into the hotel room before he's got me pinned against the wall, tongue already in my mouth, hands roaming like he's been waiting for this all-race weekend.

"I thought about you all day," he growls, nipping at my jaw, hands sliding up under the hem of the dress.

"Every lap. Every damn straight."

"You won," I whisper, pulling his shirt up and over his head.

"Time for your reward." He tosses me on the bed with a growl, and I'm laughing until he drops between my thighs like a man starved, His mouth finding the sensitive spot between my legs. My back arched, my hands gripping the sheets as waves of pleasure wash over me. I'm lost in the sensation, my body on fire, my mind consumed by the intensity of the moment. I suck in a sharp breath as he toys with me, pinching and rolling my nipples between my fingers as I feel him grinning against my cunt, savouring the way your body responds to him without resistance. My thighs tremble, wetness slicking around his mouth. Maverick laps at my cunt with insatiable hunger. It's delicious the way his tongue glides through my folds, swirling around my clit while he lets out soft grunts that only push me closer to the edge. One more slow, long lick is all it takes. I'm twitching, screaming his name, absolutely soaking his face. My hands are clawing at his hair, and I ride out my orgasm.

Maverick pulls himself up, face hovering over mine, his skin flushed and glistening, dripping with me, satisfaction written all over him. That cocky smile, God help me, it lights a fire low in my belly.

"Baby," he murmurs, breath hot against my lips.

"I didn't know you could do that." The way he's looking at me. Like I'm the whole damn universe. I don't get a chance to reply. His mouth crashes into mine, all rough edges and heat, his kiss stealing the air from my lungs. It's wild. Messy. Hungry. His hands slide down to grip my ass, fingers digging in like he owns every inch of me, and let's be honest, right now, he does. He shifts me easily, spreading me wide as he settles between my thighs again.

"Mav…" I breathe, already squirming as he drags himself through my folds. Slow. Torturous. His teasing is deliberate, smug even, like he's savouring every second of my unravelling.

"Tell me how much you want it," he growls, hovering right at my entrance. I look up at him, flushed and desperate.

"So bad it hurts."

He grins. "Then I'll make it hurt so good." And when he finally pushes back in deep, steady, possessive, I forget my name.

He sinks into me slow and deep, like he's got all the time in the world —and he wants me to feel every inch of him moving. My back arches.

"Maverick…"

"Yeah, baby?" he says, breath ragged near my ear, hips grinding into mine at a rhythm that's both maddening and divine.

"You feel that? How perfect you are around me?"

His voice is low, cocky and way too damn effective. He's not just moving; he's moving like he's claiming me. Every roll of his hips sends sparks straight through me. My fingers dig into his back, dragging across the sweat-slick skin, desperate for more, always more.

"You drive me insane," I pant, lips brushing his jaw. "You make me completely unhinged."

"Good," he mutters, dragging his mouth down my neck. "I want you wrecked, Sage"

He shifts, hooking one of my legs over his shoulder. The new angle has me gasping, my nails raking down his spine as he thrusts harder, deeper. I'm on the edge again, and he knows it. His thumb circles low on my stomach, he slowly brings his hand up around my neck and applies just enough pressure to tip me over.

"Is this okay, baby?" he growls. I just nod, it's all I can muster before I come undone beneath him, eyes shut, body shuddering, screaming his name like it's the only word I can speak. He follows with a low primal groan, hips stuttering as he lets go, his body pressed flush to mine. We collapse into a tangled mess, limbs heavy, skin warm, breath short. He presses a soft kiss to my shoulder and then one to the centre of my chest.

"You, okay?" he murmurs. I nod, dazed and grinning.

"Better than okay." He brushes the hair from my face and smirks.

"Good. Because I'm not done with you yet."

He is still rock hard and wet with me when he grabs my thighs and spreads me wide open again. My back arches off the mattress, breath caught in my throat as his mouth crashes back to my nipple, tongue hot and greedy, tugging at the piercing like he wants to claim it. I whimper, head thrown back. Round two it is then.

The sunlight filtering through the sheer hotel curtains is rude this morning. Like obnoxiously rude, it's golden and shiny while my entire body feels like it got hit by a Formula 1 car. Which, to be fair, is what happens when your F1 driver boyfriend wins a world championship and then treats you like a victory lap for six straight hours. My thighs ache. My abs ache. I'm 87% sure I pulled something in my left toe. So fucking worth it.

I roll over and groan into Maverick's chest. "I think you broke me." He hums, smug and sleepy.

"You're welcome."

"You say that like I should thank you because I can't feel my legs." He stretches, arms going above his head, muscles flexing in that way that makes me seriously consider throwing out my plans for the day and just crawling back on top of him.

"You did thank me," he says, eyes still closed. "Several times and very loudly."

"Oh God," I mumble, covering my face. "The poor people in the hallway."

"Please. You should be proud," He peeks one eye open. "You sounded so fucking hot screaming my name like you were possessed by a sex demon." I groan again, but I'm laughing now.

"You love the sound of your own name."

He rolls on top of me without warning, pinning me with that post-win/post sex smugness and a very hard morning situation pressing against my hip.

"I do, but not as much as I love the sound of you screaming it while you come."

"Maverick," I mock-moan in a ridiculous porn voice. "Oh God, don't stop, you absolute beast of a man, take me right here on the trophy shelf—" He cuts me off with a kiss, one hand sliding under the covers to palm my ass.

"You're such a menace."

"And you love it."

He grins. "I really do."

I poke his chest. He kisses my forehead and sits up, hair a mess, looking like a Greek god who just got out of a very successful orgy.

"You want coffee or more orgasms first?"

"Coffee. And then maybe… an orgasm in the shower?"

"Deal," he says, already out of bed and gloriously naked.

He pauses at the mirror, flexing like an idiot. "Y'know, I think I'm still glowing."

I throw a pillow at him. "That's my glow, you thief."

He just laughs, dodging it easily, and heads toward the bathroom. "One latte coming right up, ohhh, and I'll start the playlist. And get the trophy, you might want to sit on it this time."

"Oh my god, Maverick."

"What? You did say I could have anything I wanted if I won."

"…Damn it. I did."

"Are you two decent?!" Josie's voice echoes through the apartment, way too loud and way too chipper for this time of the morning. Maverick doesn't even flinch. I, however, nearly rocket off the bed.

"Don't answer that," Drew calls, footsteps growing louder. "But if you've destroyed another hotel mattress, Carter, I'm not covering for you with management again." I shoot a look Maverick's way, and he just giggles

"Damn it, Drew" he yells.

"Define decent," I yell back, scrambling for the sheet while Maverick just stretches like a cat, totally unbothered.

They round the corner like it's their room. Josie is holding a tray of iced coffees and a brown paper bag of something that smells suspiciously like fresh croissants. She stops in her tracks when she sees us.

"Well," she says, eyes raking across the state of us, the sheet is wrapped half-assed around me, Maverick shirtless and smug as we stand in the kitchen, the very obvious evidence of a night well spent. "Someone's glowing this morning."

Drew's already shaking his head. "You guys are a hazard." Maverick just lifts his head.

"You brought coffee?" Josie tosses one his way.

"You're welcome, horn dog." Yeah, he caught it without spillage, impressive.

"Wait, are those almond croissants?" I ask suddenly, now very awake.

"Obviously," she says, handing me one and plopping down on the armchair, making herself at home. "I figured you'd need to refuel after the soundproofing failed us last night." I groan, burying my face in my hands.

"We are never staying in the same hotel again, at least not on the same level, anyway."

Maverick just chuckles, leaning over to steal a bite of my croissant. "They love us."

"Sure," Josie smirks. "I love waking up to what sounded like a very dramatic murder. Or very aggressive sex. Possibly both."

Drew leans casually on the wall. "So, when's the wedding?" I throw a pillow at him. He dodges it like the rugby player he is. "I'll take that as a 'soon.'"

By the time we throw clothes on and make it downstairs, Josie has already charmed the concierge into moving our brunch reservation to the terrace overlooking the marina. It's disgustingly scenic, sunlight sparkling off the water, luxury yachts bobbing like they're part of a commercial, and a soft breeze that almost makes me forget we were literally mid- round-two when she burst into the room this morning. Maverick's hand is on the small of my back as we walk into the restaurant, his thumb brushing my skin in slow circles. The smirk he gives me when I glance at him tells me he hasn't forgotten either.

"Behave," I whisper.

"I am," he replies, lips at my ear. "You're the one not wearing panties." I elbow him.

"You told me not to."

"I'm a man of vision,"

Josie's already halfway through her first mimosa when we arrive. "Took you long enough. I ordered for everyone."

"You mean you ordered six different things so you could eat half of each?" I ask, sliding into the seat next to her.

She lifts her glass in salute. "Correct."

Drew's seated across from us, sunglasses on and nursing what is definitely not his first Bloody Mary.

"You guys look... energetic," he mutters, eyeing Maverick. "Which is rude, considering some of us are running on two hours of sleep."

Maverick raises an eyebrow. "Should've picked a room a few floors down. "

"I didn't expect someone trying to break the headboard three doors down."

I grab a croissant and toss it onto his plate. "Eat something sweet, you'll feel better."

Margot arrives last, slipping into the seat beside Drew, oversized sunglasses hiding most of her face. "If anyone speaks above a whisper, I swear to God I will cry."

"Rough night?" I grin.

"Someone thought shots were a good idea," she glares at Josie.

"Tequila, Josie." Josie shrugs, unapologetic.

"Tequila is always a good idea. You just need better stamina."

The server arrives with three plates of eggs Benedict, a mountain of fries, and a suspicious number of pastries.

"This is... excessive," Maverick says, looking at the spread.

"Darling," Josie says, sipping her second mimosa like a seasoned pro. "This is brunch. Excessive is the whole point."

As Drew wraps his arm around the back of her chair, I notice that his thumb gently brushes her shoulder. Maverick slides his hand under the table and immediately to the inside of my thigh, his fingers creeping closer and closer to my bare pussy, I shoot him a warning glance, and he just raises his brows, innocently, like he didn't practically ruin me up against the window an hour ago.

I lean in close, lips brushing his ear.

"You keep that up, and you'll be eating your brunch off my stomach later." His fork stills mid-air. Across the table,

Drew groans. "You two are disgusting." Margot grins under her shades.

"And weirdly inspirational." Josie lifts her glass again.

"To the disaster crew. May we brunch harder than our emotional damage." And just like that, we toast to sunlight, croissants, chaos and all.

SIXTY-TWO

MAVERICK

Brunch is done, and the season is over. We've said our final goodbyes to Josie and Margot, oh and Drew. I'm not convinced that Josie and Sage didn't cry behind oversized sunglasses and call it 'sweat.' My parents are waiting in the car downstairs, bags already loaded, punctual as ever. Sage and I? Still upstairs.

Correction: I'm zipping up the last suitcase while Sage sits on it in my hoodie and a pair of bike shorts, she swore would not make the flight. We've already packed once, got distracted twice by sex, of course, and now we're officially ten minutes late. Again.

"Baby, I swear to God, if my parents miss their flight because you can't find where you put your sneakers, they'll have to fly with us—"

"I packed the sneakers twenty minutes ago," she fires back, grinning as she rolls off the bag. "You're the one who stopped to eat me out on the carpet."

"Don't blame me for having good taste," I mutter, dragging the suitcase upright.

"Flattery won't get you out of May Carter's death glare." That shuts me up.

We finally make it out the door, down the elevator and into the waiting car where my parents are—unsurprisingly— seated, calm and absolutely judging us. Dad raises a brow. Mum gives us the look.

"You're late," she says, sipping from her travel mug like she's not watching me squirm.

"Elevator traffic," Sage says, " she's all charm and no shame. I climb in beside her, hand resting on her thigh.

"We made it, didn't we?" The driver pulls away, and Sage leans into me, her head resting on my shoulder like she's already half-asleep. It's been a long few days—hell, a long few months—but for the first time in a while, everything feels quiet. No grid, no media. Just her warmth beside me and the soft hum of the road under the tyres.

We'll be in Monaco for a few days, just enough time to swap suitcases, recharge, and maybe have a few rounds in the shower with the good water pressure. And then I'm taking her away. Just us. No team schedules. No sponsorship appearances, nothing but the two of us.

The season's over. The trophy's at home. The fire is still burning, though; the only difference is, I'm not chasing anything now. She's it. She's all of it. I glance down as she yawns against my shoulder, mouth parted, eyes fluttering closed.

Three months. That's what I've got before I start my last Formula One season. Three months to make her forget the rulebook entirely. Three months to ruin her for anyone else. Three months to show her exactly what forever might look like—one day at a time. Three months to ask her for that forever. And fuck if I'm not already counting the hours.

WE LAND in Nice just before sunset, the sky glowing peach and gold, and there's something about flying into this city that always hits differently. Maybe it's the curves of the coast, maybe it's the way Monaco always feels a little too glamorous for real life or maybe it's the woman walking beside me in a hoodie and sunglasses, dragging her suitcase like she owns the damn walkway. Because Sage in Monaco? That's danger in heels. Even when she's in sneakers.

We bypass the main crowd and head straight into a waiting car, and Sage immediately kicks off her shoes and tucks her feet beneath her on the seat like we're in an Uber headed home after a night out, not pulling into one of the richest zip codes on earth. She turns to me, sunglasses slid low on her nose. "So, what's the plan, Playboy?"

"Unpack. Shower. Get you naked. Maybe not in that order."

She smirks, head tilted back and lets out a low laugh that does things to my brain.

"You missed this place, didn't you?" I

grin. "I missed you in it."

We arrive at my place, well, our place now, maybe, if I have anything to say about it, and the moment I unlock the door and step inside, it's like exhaling for the first time in weeks. The space is still, warm with late afternoon light, the windows overlooking the marina glowing like a goddamn postcard. Sage wanders in ahead of me, dropping her bag with a thud and stretching like a cat. Her shirt rides up just enough to tease me. I drop my duffel by the door and watch her walk into the open living room like she's reclaiming it.

"You're staring," she calls over her shoulder.

"Hard not to," I reply, already stepping toward her. "You've got that Monaco glow." She spins to face me, backlit by the light.

"That's just travel ick and overpriced skincare."

"Whatever it is, it's working." I reach for her waist, pulling

her in until there's nothing but fabric and heat between us. "Your place feels different after some time away," she murmurs.

"Because it's not just mine anymore," I say. "Not really." Her eyes flick up to meet mine; there's something unreadable in them. But then she grins, breaking the tension.

"If this is your way of seducing me into a shower…" I shrug, hands already sliding under the hem of her hoodie.

"Is it working?"

"Depends," she says, lips brushing mine. "Does the shower come with a very naked, very bossy race car driver?"

I kiss her, deep and slow. "Always."

The water's still running in the en suite when I step out of the bedroom, towel slung low around my hips, hair damp and messy from Sage's fingers pulling through it. My skin's still humming, but not from the shower. From her. She's still in there, humming off-key to whatever's playing from her phone. I think it's Dolly Parton. Or maybe Beyoncé. Either way, she's off-key and smug about it. I can hear her moving around—probably stealing my shampoo again.

I wander into the kitchen, feet bare against the cool tiles and pull open the fridge. There's nothing but a bottle of champagne, three condiments, and a single sad lemon. We've been gone too long.

She yells something unintelligible from the bathroom. A second later, her voice rings out clearer.

"Why do you own three types of exfoliators but no milk?" I grin, popping the cork on the champagne like it's a normal Tuesday. "Priorities, baby."

"You're a menace."

She walks into the kitchen in nothing but one of my shirts and a towel twisted around her head. Her legs are still damp, bare, her skin flushed pink from the heat. And that shirt? It should be illegal how good it looks hanging off her, sleeves swallowed by her hands, hem grazing the tops of her thighs.

I hand her a glass. "To being home."

She clinks it gently. "To hot water and zero press outside the front door."

We lean against the counter together, sipping slowly, her shoulder brushing mine. There's no rush to fill the silence— just the sound of the city outside, soft and distant, and her presence wrapped around me like a second skin.

"This feels weird," she says after a minute.

"Weird, good or weird bad?"

Her eyes flick up, teasing. "Weird like… domestic. You and I, in a kitchen, half-naked and tipsy on a Tuesday."

I lean in close, brushing my lips to her jaw. "Would it feel better if I bent you over the counter?"

She chokes on her champagne. "You're terrible."

"You love it."

She narrows her eyes like she wants to deny it—but she doesn't.

Instead, she takes another sip, then reaches out and steals the bottle from where I left it on the counter.

She tops off my glass, then hers, and says, "Fine. Domestication isn't the worst thing."

"You're getting soft on me."

She shrugs. "You did say the season was over."

"I didn't say I'd stopped racing," I murmur, tilting her chin toward me.

She smirks. "That a threat, Playboy?"

"Promise." And then I lean in and kiss her again—slow, unhurried, full of heat but anchored in something quieter. Something steadier. She sighs against my mouth like the world just stopped spinning. And maybe it did. For now, this is everything.

"Also," I say as I break the kiss, "I've got a surprise for you. We leave in three days."

SIXTY-THREE

SAGE

The thing about Maverick Carter is that he doesn't do anything half-assed. Not a race. Not a kiss. And certainly not a surprise. So, when he told me to pack a bag and 'wear something I can rip off you without being arrested', I should've known I was in for it. Now I'm barefoot, blinking under the golden sun, standing on a private dock in the middle of nowhere, surrounded by turquoise water so clear it looks fake. The air smells like salt and sunscreen; the only sounds are waves and the soft hum of a boat engine retreating in the distance, and Maverick?

He's smirking like the smug bastard he is.

"Welcome to your island, trouble," he says, pulling off his sunglasses and sliding his hand into mine.

"My island?" I arch a brow. "You bought this?"

He shrugs. "Leased. Borrowed. Bribed a guy. Semantics."

I let out a breathy laugh, turning in a slow circle to take it all in—the overwater bungalow at the end of the dock, the hammocks swaying between palm trees, the open-air bar with two coconuts already sweating on the counter like they knew we were coming.

"Just us?" I ask, heart hammering.

"Just us," he confirms.

I bite my lip. "So basically, no pants for four days." He grins. "Four days, baby? Try two weeks."

I whip my head toward him, eyes wide. "Two weeks?"

"Season's over. I've got nowhere else I'd rather be." And maybe it's the sun, or the ocean breeze, or that he's shirtless in swim trunks and I can see the curve of his tattoo under his collarbone—but I melt. Right there on the dock. Heart, brain, ovaries. All of it.

"You planning on feeding me at all, or just fucking me into a coma?" I ask mostly to keep my voice steady.

He leans in, lips brushing my ear. "Both. Obviously."

I'm about to give him some sassy reply, but then he lifts me—like it's nothing—and tosses me over his shoulder, bridal-style, as I squeal-laugh and beat my fists against his bare back.

"Maverick!"

"Can't waste daylight," he says, striding toward the bungalow. "Or that tiny little bikini you packed."

"I didn't pack a bikini—"

"You did. I put it in your bag." He glances down at me with a wicked smile. "And I plan on removing it with my teeth."

Okay, maybe I'll let him have this one. Maybe.

The bungalow is ridiculous. Glass floors with coral beneath us, floor-to-ceiling windows that slide open to the ocean, a bed big enough to host an orgy, though Maverick has made it clear it's a party of two. He sets me down gently, like I'm made of something precious, and for a second, I just stare at him. Wind-blown hair, sun-kissed skin, mischief written in every inch of him.

"I should be mad you packed my bag without asking," I say, crossing my arms even though my whole body's buzzing from how he carried me in here like he already owns me. He steps closer, one hand brushing my jaw, the other skimming down to rest just above my ass.

"You'll forgive me when you see what else I packed."

"Yeah?" I tip my chin up.

"What else did you sneak in?" He kisses me slowly and full of heat and whispers,

"Me." And then he drops to his knees.

"Wait—Mav—"

He's already tugging my sundress up, sliding it off in one smooth motion. I'm standing there in the tiniest set of lingerie I own, a barely there lilac lace that leaves exactly nothing to the imagination.

"Holy fuck," he mutters, like he's seeing me for the first time. "This might be my best work yet."

He palms the backs of my thighs and presses his lips to the inside of my knee, trailing soft kisses upward until I can barely breathe.

"You going to let me worship you, like it's your birthday, Trouble?"

"It's not my birthday."

He grins against my skin. "Doesn't need to be."

He presses his mouth against me through the lace, his tongue tracing the damp fabric, slow and teasing.

"Maverick," I breathe, my fingers threading through his hair, hips already tilting toward his mouth. He hums like he has all the time in the world.

"Mmm, taste that. That's mine."

"I swear to God if you don't—" He moves the lace aside with one lazy swipe and licks into me, deep and filthy, until my knees nearly give out.

"Oh, my god."

"No gods here, baby. Just me." He keeps at it, lips and tongue and hands gripping me like he's starving and I'm the only thing on the menu. When I come, it's with a cry that echoes off the vaulted ceilings, and I swear I hear him groan like he's getting off on just the sound. He stands slowly, licking his lips and wiping his mouth like he just had dessert.

"That was round one. Are you good to walk or should I carry you to the bed?" I'm panting, barely standing, but I don't flinch.

"I'll crawl if I have to." He lifts me again anyway, lays me down on the cool white sheets, and covers my body with his, cock hard and heavy against my thigh.

"Now," he whispers, voice low and full of promise, "let's see how many times I can make you beg before the sun sets." Spoiler: it's a lot.

I barely register the cool press of the glass doors as my back hits them. Maverick's mouth is already on my throat, tongue hot, teeth dragging along my pulse like he's starving for it. For me.

"Your trouble, you know that?" he growls, hands roaming, possessive, greedy, like I'm already his and he's just reminding my body who it belongs to. I gasp when he lifts me effortlessly, like I weigh nothing. My legs wrap around his waist on instinct, and I feel him hard, thick, rubbing right where I want him. My breath catches.

"Was this your plan?" I manage as he walks us toward the massive bed. "A secret island escape so you can keep me too ruined to walk?" He grins against my skin.

"Exactly." He drops me onto the bed and peels off my lingerie slowly, teasing, dragging the wet fabric of my panties down my thighs, eyes locked on mine the entire time. My nipples tighten under his stare, chest rising and falling as he leans down and kisses the inside of my knee. And then higher. And higher.

"Maverick," I moan, hips lifting as his mouth finds its target, wicked and slow and all tongue. My hands knot in the sheets, back arching off the bed as he devours my cunt like it's his last meal. When he finally pulls back, lips slick with my release, pupils blown wide, I'm a shaking mess.

"You taste like sin," he says hoarsely, crawling up my body, letting his cock drag against my thigh.

"I need to be inside you. Now." And he is. One slow, punishing thrust. Stretching, filling, claiming. The sound I make isn't even human.

"Eyes on me," he whispers, hand sliding to my jaw.

"I want you to watch how pretty you look falling apart on my cock." I do. I watch. I feel every inch of him, every filthy word, every deep stroke that hits just right. And when I come, it's loud, legs trembling, hands clawing down his back, but he doesn't stop; he just flips me over, grips my hips, and keeps going. Driving me straight into oblivion all over again. Hours blur. The sheets are twisted. My voice is hoarse from screaming his name. And Maverick Carter is still worshipping me like I'm a goddess. By the time we collapse, soaked in sweat and something far messier, he's grinning like the smug bastard he is.

"You good, trouble?" he murmurs against my shoulder. I can't even answer. So, he does it for me.

"Yeah," he smirks, lips brushing my ear. "You're very good."

I don't know how long we've been in bed. The sun's dipped lower, casting golden light across the sheets, and Maverick is still wrapped around me like he's trying to brand me with every inch of himself. My skin's sticky with sweat and sex, my body aching in the best possible way. He rolls me onto my back, eyes heavy with want. Lazy, confident, and utterly ravenous.

"You should be asleep," I whisper, dragging a finger down his chest.

"I should be buried inside you again," he murmurs, voice low and rough. And then he's kissing me like he's starving. Mouth hot and possessive. Hands tracing the curve of my hip, my ribs, the underside of my breast with reverence that feels almost holy— like he's rediscovering something he'll never get enough of.

"I want all of you," he breathes against my collarbone. "Messy, greedy, loud—you, in every damn form."

I moan when his mouth finds that one spot beneath my ear, the one he now treats like a secret only he gets to touch. His hand drifts lower, slow and unhurried, and I'm already arching into him—needy, impatient, feral for more.

"I could spend the next three months right here," he growls, sliding against me with maddening precision. "Getting drunk on your body. Losing track of the days. Reminding you exactly who you belong to."

"You make a lot of promises, Carter."

"And I plan on keeping every single one of them."

When he finally pushes inside, it's slow and deep—like he's got nowhere to be but here, drowning in me. And I swear time stops. Everything outside the bungalow disappears. It's just him. Me. Our breaths tangled between kisses. The wet slap of skin against skin. That inaudible sound he makes every time I clench around him. His name—Maverick— on my lips like a prayer and a curse.

We lose ourselves again. And again. And again. Until I'm too spent to move and he's pressed against my back, lips brushing the dip of my shoulder blade, whispering something like mine. And I believe him. Because at this moment, on this island, in this bed, I am his.

SIXTY-FOUR

MAVERICK

As much as it physically pains me, we finally peel ourselves out of bed.

Two days. That's how long we've been here, holed up in this beach-front bungalow like a couple of sexed-up fugitives. The only evidence of our existence? A parade of room service trays, at least one very startled housekeeping staffer, and that we've managed to christen nearly every damn surface in this place. Twice. I've got absolutely zero complaints. Sage's skin still glows from the last round, flushed and marked. She's wearing nothing but one of my t-shirts that barely skims the top of her thighs. I think that's becoming her uniform. She stretches, arms over her head, like she's trying to kill me all over again. I lean back against the counter, sipping my coffee and watching her move.

"You know, if this trip was just an excuse to hold you hostage in bed, I'd consider it a raging success."

She smirks over her shoulder. "And yet you're the one dragging me out of it."

Touché.

"I have to," I groan, placing my mug down as I walk over and wrap my arms around her from behind. "I've got a surprise planned. Plus, if we don't step outside soon, they're going to assume we died of dehydration and send a search party."

Her eyes narrow, sceptical and amused. "What kind of surprise?"

"The good kind," I whisper in her ear. "The kind that involves you in a bikini, a private boat, and absolutely no one else." She turns in my arms and blinks up at me, that slow smile tugging at her lips—the one that always does things to my chest I can't quite explain.

"Fine," she sighs, mock exasperated. "But I'm not promising to jump you on said boat."

"Oh no," I grin, dragging a hand down the back of her thigh, "I'm counting on it." She rolls her eyes, but I catch the way her cheeks flush when I slap her ass as she turns to walk toward the bathroom.

And yeah, I'm half-hard again just watching her walk away and disappear behind the door. I finish my coffee, grab my phone, and check that everything's ready. The boat's waiting at the dock. The champagne's chilled. The sunset's timed just right. I didn't plan this trip to be this romantic, but somehow, with Sage, it feels right. Even when we're covered in sweat and sand, swearing like sailors, she feels like something softer. Something real.

The sun is low, golden and slow, casting everything in that perfect end-of-day haze. The kind of light that makes the ocean look like it's glowing. The kind that makes Sage look like she belongs in a goddamn painting.

She's barefoot, legs out, stretched across the padded lounge at the bow of the boat like she owns it—like she owns everything. And in that red bikini? Yeah, she fucking does. I lean against the railing, beer in hand, sunglasses pushed up onto my head just so I don't miss a single goddamn second of this. The wind's playing with her hair, and she's laughing at something I can't even hear anymore because all I can focus on is how fucking lucky I am.

She catches me staring, of course, she does, and raises a brow. "See something you like, Playboy?"

"Like? No," I say, walking over and dropping down beside her. "Obsessed with, yes."

She smirks, but I see the heat in her eyes, the way her fingers toy with the tie on her bikini bottom.

"Are you planning on doing something about it?"

I slide my hand onto her bare thigh, fingers tracing the tan line. "You know I am."

We're anchored just far enough out to be alone. No crew, no interruptions. Just the sound of water lapping against the hull and the way her breath hitches when I drag my lips down her neck.

"I don't think you understand the kind of problem you've created," I murmur, fingers brushing over her stomach, slipping under the hem of her bikini bottoms. She gasps, low, soft, teasing.

"Poor thing. Should I make it up to you?"

"Too late for apologies, trouble." I grin, pulling the string on her bottoms loose with one slow tug. "Now you're mine to play with," She laughs, breathless and wicked, and the sound alone is enough to make me want to ruin her right here under the sunset.

So, I do. I lay her down on the cushions, the salt air tangling with her skin, and kiss my way down her body like she's a secret only I get to keep. She arches into me, her hands in my hair, moaning my name like a prayer that's about to go unanswered if I don't get inside her soon. And when I finally do—when she wraps around me and the world blurs—I swear I forget what gravity feels like. It's just us. Just this moment. Just her. And I never want it to end.

She's wrapped in one of the boat towels, cheeks flushed, lips kiss swollen, and hair a wreck—and I swear she's never looked more gorgeous. We're both lying back on the cushions now, tangled in each other and still catching our breath, the ocean rocking beneath us like it's in on the secret. I'm sticky with salt and sweat, chest rising and falling while she giggles into my neck like she didn't just scream my name loud enough to scare off any fish within a ten-kilometre radius.

"Okay," she pants, still breathless, "I get it now." I glance at her sideways. "Get what?"

"Why people say, 'sex on a boat' is a thing"

I grin, pulling the towel tighter around her. "I'm pretty sure we just started a category."

She slaps my chest with a playful groan. "You're disgusting."

"Disgustingly in love with you," I tease. Her eyes narrow, amused. "Cheesy."

"Maybe," I smirk, "but it got you naked in under three minutes."

She laughs again, that full-body kind of laugh that shakes her shoulders and makes me want to kiss every inch of her just to hear it again. We sit there for a few more minutes, her head resting against my shoulder, the breeze cooling our flushed skin.

I glance at my watch and groan. "Alright, as much as I'd love to stay out here and have a round three or four, I've lost count—we've got a dinner reservation back on land."

Sage mock-pouts. "What if I show up in just this towel?"

"Then I'm cancelling the reservation and eating dessert right here," I growl, nipping at her jaw.

"Behave."

"Never."

She kisses me, soft and slow this time, before rolling off my chest and wobbling to her feet. "Fine. Feed me before I faint."

I stand, pulling on my shorts and throwing her one of my shirts to wear. She slides it over her head, and it nearly swallows her whole. Sexy little menace. "I'm never getting that shirt back, right?"

"Correct," she grins, popping the 't.'

We dock just as the sun is kissing the horizon, painting the sky in streaks of pink and gold. I help her off the boat like a gentleman—despite the not-so-gentle things I've done to her in the last hour—and we walk up the dock toward the beachside restaurant I booked earlier in the week.

People glance at us as we pass, but I barely notice. She's beside me, fingers tangled in mine, wearing salt on her skin and a glow that's all mine. Dinners next. Then maybe a walk under the stars. And after that? I plan on making a mess of her all over again. Just with a nicer view this time. She's barefoot in the sand, wearing my shirt like a dress and smiling like she owns the whole damn world.

We're led to a table tucked under a canopy of fairy lights, just far enough from the other guests that it feels like we're the only ones on this stretch of island. Candles flicker on the table, and the ocean hums just beyond. She looks around, suspicious. "You're being way too calm for a man who made me walk twenty minutes up a beach in nothing but his shirt," I smirk, pulling out her chair. She plops down, sand still stuck to her calves, and I sit across from her. I order champagne. She arches her brow.

"What are we celebrating?"

I shrug, casual. "Being here. Surviving boat sex and your terrible taste in tropical cocktails."

She grins, and that's when I know. I could do this forever.

Dinner comes in courses—something with grilled fish and too many garnishes I can't pronounce, and I can barely taste. She talks about her childhood summers by the beach, about the first time she snuck a bottle of tequila out of her parents cabinet with her high school friends, girls I've never heard her speak about - I want to push further on that, but I don't because I can see the pain behind her eyes of friendships lost and about how she used to think being in love would feel like giving up on herself, her independence, how grief makes it hard to love.

"But it doesn't," she says, gaze steady on mine. "With you, it doesn't feel like giving up anything." She pauses. "With you, I'm learning that grief and love, sadness and happiness can live side by side," I swallow. Hard. Because I've been waiting for that moment. The ring's burning a hole in my pocket.

She reaches for her drink again, and I catch her hand midair. "Baby," I say, suddenly feeling like I might throw up. "I've spent my whole life chasing wins. Lap times. Glory. All of it." She smiles, but her brow furrows slightly.

"Mav…"

"But you… You're the one win I never saw coming. The only one that matters." I stand, walking around the table, dropping to one knee in the goddamn sand like a walking cliché. "You're the only finish line I care about."

She gasps, both hands flying to her mouth. I pull out the ring box custom, of course, just like the woman in front of me and flip it open.

"Sage Davidson, your chaos and light, your tequila and fire. And I love you more than I ever thought I could love anything. So, marry me. Be my next big risk." Her eyes shine. She stares for a beat too long, probably just to make me sweat.

SIXTY-FIVE

SAGE

FUCK.

He just proposed. Like, on-one-knee, sand-between-our- toes, sparkly ring-proposed. Fuck. Fuck. Fuckity fuck. I mean, I knew it was coming. Deep down I've felt it. The way he's been looking at me lately like he already knows the future. Like his absolutely certain I'm it for him. But I didn't think it would be now. Not this soon. Not here, on this goddamn magical- ass island, after we've spent two straight days in a blur of sex, sunscreen, and orgasms. I thought we had more time. I thought I had more time.

My brain is screaming — run! My heart is confused and spinning. And Maverick? He's just… waiting. Calm. Steady. Eyes locked on mine with a softness that almost makes me crumble right there in the sand. Do I love him? Yes. Shit, yes. But am I ready for forever? Marriage? Vows? Joint tax returns? I don't know. And now the silence has stretched way too long. I need to say something, do something, because he's still looking at me like I'm his whole world, and I can't breathe.

"I… um…" My voice cracks.

Shit. "Fuck."

Smooth, Sage. Real smooth. I stand abruptly, shoving the chair back as it topples into the sand with a soft thud. I barely hear it over the thundering in my chest. And then I do what I do best. I run. Not far—just up the beach, feet sinking into the sand with every frantic step, air burning in my lungs. Toward the bungalow, toward safety, toward anything but the massive, overwhelming truth of what just happened.

What am I doing? Why am I running from the man I love? He's never given me a reason to doubt him. Never made me feel small or unsafe or anything other than chosen. And yet… Here I am. Running like the old me, like the me who promised herself she'd never get close enough to be broken again. But this is Maverick, and he's never been anything but disgustingly perfect. So why does forever still terrify the shit out of me?

I slam the door to the bungalow behind me and immediately regret it. It's too quiet here now. It feels like the silence is judging me. I collapse onto the floor at the edge of the bed, my knees pulled tight to my chest like that might hold the pieces of me together. My heart is still racing, blood pumping so fast it feels like my whole body is vibrating. What the actual fuck am I doing?

I just ran from Maverick. From the man who loves me like it's a religion. Who has never once flinched at my messy life. Who has never tried to fix me, who just held the parts I was willing to hand over and waited, patiently, for more. I rest my forehead on my knees and try to breathe. My chest is tight. My brain won't shut up.

I can't do this.

I want to do this.

I don't deserve this.

God, I want to say yes. I do. Not because it's romantic or perfect or because he made a grand gesture under fairy lights, but because he's Maverick. And he's not promising some Hallmark version of forever. He's promising me. Us. The chaos and the grief and the growth. The fights and the makeup sex and the mornings where I'm too in my head to be soft. He wants all of me. And the scariest part? I think I want that too. Even if it means breaking every single rule I ever wrote for myself.

The door creaks. Goddamn it, he found me. I should've known he would. He always sees straight through me, even when I'm actively trying to disappear.

He doesn't speak right away. Just walks in slowly, like he knows one wrong move might send me running again. I lift my head, and there he is, kneeling in front of me. Those eyes, sharp and soft all at once, locked on mine like I'm not curled on the floor in full emotional meltdown mode, like I'm still worthy of that ring in his pocket. And then he says the one thing I didn't even realise I needed to hear.

"I'm not here to pressure you," he says quietly. "I just needed you to know what I want. What I'm choosing."

My lip trembles.

"I'm scared," I whisper, voice cracking on the truth.

He nods. "So am I."

That surprises me. "You don't look scared."

"I'm terrified. But not of you saying no. I'm scared you'll keep running from the things you actually want because someone, somewhere, once told you you didn't deserve them."

That's the thing about Maverick. He never raises his voice, but he always hits the mark.

"I'm not asking you to say yes tonight," he says, reaching out slowly — just enough to take my hand. "I just need you to stop running long enough to consider that maybe… This isn't a disaster waiting to happen. Maybe it's the one thing that was always meant to." I stare at him.

This stupidly beautiful, infuriating man with salt in his hair and sand on his knees and a future in his hands.

I exhale. Finally, Like I've been holding my breath since the moment I fell for him.

"I didn't run because I don't want you," I say. "I ran because I do. And that scares the living hell out of me."

He smiles, just a little. "So, stay scared. Stay messy. Just… stay."

I let that settle in my chest. And maybe I'm not ready to say yes. But I'm ready to stop running. So, I lean forward, press my forehead to his, and whisper, "I'm still here." And somehow, that's enough. For now.

"I've got time. I'm not going anywhere." He says, and it shatters me. Right there. Right in front of him.

I break open — loud, messy, ugly crying. All the stuff I've kept locked behind sarcasm and sex and sharp little quips pours out of me in choking sobs. He doesn't flinch. He just gathers me in his arms like I weigh nothing, like he's been waiting to hold this broken version of me all along. His hand strokes the back of my head, and he whispers things into my hair I don't even hear, but somehow, they still stitch something back together inside me. I don't say yes. Not yet. But I bury my face into his chest and whisper something else instead.

"Are you sure you're going to stay?" It's a question and a plea.

His grip tightens, like he'd planned to, anyway. "I'm right here, baby."

And for the first time in a long damn time, I believe it because his energy is filling the room like gravity. Like a tether I can't cut.

The sunlight is too bright for how emotionally wrecked I feel. It filters through the curtains, warming the sheets tangled around my legs, and I blink slowly, trying to piece together exactly where we landed. Not physically, we're still in the island bungalow. But emotionally? That's a whole other storm.

I shift slightly and feel the weight of his arm draped over my waist, heavy and grounding. Maverick is still asleep, hair a mess, lips slightly parted, one leg hooked over mine like his afraid I'll run if he lets go. And I get it. Because last night... I did. Ran away from facing my future. I didn't say yes. I didn't say no either. I said nothing. I just ran like my demons were chasing me, and somehow—somehow—he still stayed. I stare at the ceiling, heart tight and raw in my chest, and wonder how the hell I'm supposed to be enough for a man like this.

"Stop thinking so loud," he mumbles beside me, voice rough and sleep-wrecked. "You're making the bed vibrate." I laugh.

Just a breath. "Sorry."

His arm tightens around me, tugging me closer. "Don't be. Just... talk to me, Sage."

I pause. Then roll over slowly to face him. "I panicked," I admit. "You scared the shit out of me."

"I noticed," he says, eyes soft but amused. "The whole 'fuck' moment kind of gave it away."

"Shut up." I hide my face on his shoulder. "I'm mortified."

"Don't be. It was very you. Honest. It's a little chaotic. Kind of hot."

I snort. "You're such a weirdo."

He presses a kiss to my forehead. "I meant it, Trouble. I'm not going anywhere if you're not ready. We do this on your terms. Our time. I'm not keeping score."

My chest tightens again—only this time, it's not fear. It's something gentler. Like hope.

"I just…" I pull back enough to look him in the eye. "I'm scared of ruining something that finally feels good. Fantastic."

"You won't," he says. No hesitation. "Even if you try. I'll be right here. Reminding you. Fighting for you." I'm quiet for a moment.

"I don't have an answer yet," I whisper. He nods. "I don't need one. Not today."

"But I want to find one," I add. "I want to be brave enough for this. For you."

He cups my cheek and kisses me. Not rushed or frantic. Just soft. Like his saying okay, I'll wait with no need to speak it out loud.

When he pulls back, he grins. "So… breakfast? Or sex?" I laugh and thump his chest.

"Jesus, Maverick."

"What?" He shrugs. "Both cure emotional hangovers. I'm just being practical." I roll on top of him, straddling his hips and pinning his arms to the bed with a slow, teasing smile.

"Then let's be very practical," I whisper. "But I get to ride. You scared me, too." His smile turns downright filthy.

"Deal, baby. Wreck me however you want."

And just like that, we're okay. Still messy. Still figuring it out. But okay.

After getting absolutely and thoroughly railed by Maverick—like, legs-still-shaking, seeing-stars kind of railed— I'm sitting upright in bed with the sheets bunched around my waist and my hair in a state that could be mistaken for post- storm debris. My thighs are still quivering. My brain? Not far behind.

Meanwhile, he's in the kitchen like a menace, shirtless and smug, making us what his calling 'breakfast' even though it's pushing 2 pm. The smell of coffee is divine, but honestly, I need something stronger. Like tequila. Because while my body is blissfully wrecked, my heart is still a goddamn battlefield. I still can't believe I said no to his proposal.

Well, technically, I didn't say no. I ran. Which is arguably worse? Honestly, what the hell is wrong with me? I love him. I know I do. I can see it—our life together, loud and chaotic and sun-drenched. So why didn't I just say yes? Why did my first instinct have to be to run? Maybe because the last time I loved someone that much, she was ripped from me without warning. Maybe because grief still has its claws in me, whispering that everything good is temporary. That people leave. That forever is a lie we tell ourselves to feel safe. And Maverick Carter? He's a risk. A beautiful, terrifying risk. Because he loves me loudly, fully. With no exit plan. God, I hate that my first instinct was to bolt.

"Sage, you're spiralling," I mutter to myself. "You're sexy, smart, and spiralling. Great combo."

I flop back dramatically against the pillows, staring at the ceiling like it's got answers. I need a drink.

"Mavvvvvvv," I call, stretching the syllables like sugar on my tongue.

"Yes, baby?" he answers from the kitchen, far too chipper for someone who just folded me in half less than an hour ago.

"Can you make me a margarita?"

He laughs, and I swear I can hear the eye roll. "You want tequila and coffee?"

"Yes, please. I need both. Emotionally and spiritually."

"You got it, Trouble," he says, still amused. "Strong, salty, and slightly chaotic—just like you."

I smirk. Because I'm going to need that margarita for what I'm about to do. Because I'm done running, permanently.

Maverick strolls back into the bedroom like he owns the damn resort—shirtless, barefoot, one hand holding my margarita, the other my coffee, and that smug little look on his face that says, 'We're absolutely making poor decisions today, and I'm thrilled about it.' Honestly, Iconic behaviour. He hands me the coffee first, like the gentleman he sometimes pretends to be, setting the margarita down on the bedside table like it's dessert. Then he drops down beside me with his own coffee, clearly pleased with himself.

The second I take that first sip, I swear I feel my soul return to my body. I groan—like, full-body, eyes-closed, might've been a little pornographic if we're being honest—and Maverick watches me like I just offered to blow him in gratitude.

"Jesus," he mutters. "You could ruin me with coffee alone."

"You say that like I haven't already ruined you," I reply, cocky as hell.

Touché, race boy.

I place the mug down, grab the margarita, and take a long sip. The tequila hits my bloodstream like liquid bravery, and I feel the warmth coil in my chest. My fingers tighten around the glass.

Okay. Okay.

I glance over the rim at him. "Okay."

His brow arches. "Okay?"

"That's all I get? Okay?" He leans in with that crooked grin. "Need me to put my dick in the margarita to upgrade the rating?"

I snort—because of course he says that—but nerves fizz in my stomach. My heart's doing cartwheels— but my mouth is dry despite the tequila. I set the margarita down with a little too much care.

Then: "Okay, I'll marry you." Maverick goes completely still. Like, frozen. Blinking. Processing. Then he takes my hands, and suddenly he's pulling me up— standing me on the bed, his eyes never leaving mine.

"What'd you just say?" His voice is low, rough with something that feels suspiciously like hope.

I smile, slow and surely and start planting kisses down his chest.

"I said yes." Another kiss, just above his heart. "I'll marry you. If the offer still stands, that is. "

His hands fist closer to the hem of my oversized t-shirt. "Say it again."

I look up, locking into those ridiculous ocean eyes. "Yes, Maverick Carter. I'll marry you." The grin that breaks over his face could probably power the island. And I know right then, in that stupid bed with tequila on my tongue and his heartbeat under my lips—this is it. This is the start of the rest of my messy, chaotic universe, asking for a beautiful life.

And I wouldn't change a damn thing.

MAVERICK

I walk back into the bedroom, shirtless, smug, and carrying two drinks like a man with a plan—which I am. Margarita in one hand. Coffee in the other. And a face that says, 'we're absolutely making poor decisions today, and I'm thrilled about it.'

Sage's sitting in bed, legs tangled in the sheets, hair wild, face glowing from too much sun and too many orgasms, and I swear—she's the most dangerous thing I've ever looked at.

I hand her the coffee first, like a peace offering. Or maybe foreplay. Let's be honest, it's always both with her.

She takes a sip and moans. Loud. Low. Needy. Jesus. I nearly dropped my damn mug.

"You could ruin me with coffee alone," I say, watching her with the same intensity I use before launching off the start line.

She doesn't even flinch, just shoots me a smirk over the rim of the cup. "You say that like I haven't already ruined you."

She has. Fully. No question.

She swaps the coffee for the margarita, and I watch her lips wrap around the rim, sip, swallow. My girl knows how to make tequila look like an aphrodisiac.

Then she says it.

Just casually, like she's ordering another drink. "Okay."

I pause. "Okay?"

She nods, eyes locked on mine, nervous smile playing at her mouth.

"Do I need to put my dick in the margarita again to upgrade the rating?" I tease, trying to keep it light—because holy hell, what is this moment?

But then she sets the drink down with purpose and looks me dead in the eye. "Okay, I'll marry you."

My brain short-circuits.

I stare at her, completely frozen. Did she just…?

No. No way. But then she says it again, softer this time, with those kisses trailing down my chest like she's branding the moment into my skin.

"I said yes," she whispers. "I'll marry you." And now I'm the one who can't breathe.

I grab her hands, haul her up off the bed and onto her feet—on the fucking mattress, because she deserves to stand on mountains when she says something like that. My heart's in my throat and pounding out a rhythm that feels dangerously close to forever.

"What'd you say?" I ask because I need to hear it again. I need it burned into memory.

She meets my eyes, glowing and sure now. "Yes, Maverick Carter. I'll marry you."

The oxygen rushes back into my lungs so fast I nearly laugh. Instead, I kiss her like I've just won the world again. But this time, the prize isn't a trophy—it's her.

And it's not just a win. It's everything.

She said yes.

She said yes. And everything inside me fucking erupts. Not just relief. Not just adrenaline. Something deeper. Wilder. Like every part of me finally has permission to be hers. Because now she's mine—really mine.

So, what do I do?

I growl, grip the back of her thighs, and toss her back on the bed.

She squeals—half laugh, half gasp—as I crawl over her like a man possessed, because that's what I am now. Possessed by this woman. Owned by her, "yes." Addicted to the way she looks up at me like I'm her entire world when I know she's mine.

"I'm going to ruin you," I whisper, pinning her wrists above her head with one hand. My other hand trails down her side, tracing her ribs, her hip, until I reach that spot between her thighs that's already soaked for me.

"Again?" she breathes, teasing. "I don't think there's any part of me you haven't ruined."

I drop my head and bite the edge of her jaw. "Then I'll start from the top."

SIXTY-SIX

MAVERICK

Sage and I finally peeled ourselves out of bed—mostly because the champagne ran out and our stomachs started growling louder than she did last time I made her come. Room service is spread across the table like we're royalty with no responsibilities. Late lunch? Early dinner? Who cares? Time doesn't exist when you've spent two straight days fucking like rabbits and drinking like retirees on holiday. She's sitting across from me in one of my t-shirts, legs bare, hair a wild halo around her face, cheeks flushed from booze and post-sex glow. God help me. We're halfway through another bottle of champagne when she lifts her glass and grins, slurring just slightly.

"So… we could go back to bed for round… what, nine?" she teases, licking her bottom lip. "Or we could go out, dance a little, get even more delightfully silly."

I raise an eyebrow. "You wanna dance, trouble?"

She nods enthusiastically, practically bouncing in her seat. "I feel like a boogie." She says boogie like it's 1975 and she's on Soul Train.

Yep—definitely drunk.

I lean back in my chair, eyes glued to her as she saunters away toward the bedroom, hips swaying, legs on display. She throws a look over her shoulder and giggles.

"Let me put something a little more appropriate on."

My eyes drop to the way my t-shirt skims her thighs. Barely. "I don't mind your heading out in nothing but that shirt," I call after her with a grin.

She laughs, all sass and sunshine. "Yeah, you will—once other people start looking at what's yours." I pause at that. Because she's right. The idea of someone else even thinking they could touch her. That they might see those legs, that smirk, that damn sparkle in her eyes and think she's up for grabs?

Yeah. That would test every ounce of my self-control. "Good point," I mutter, draining the last of my glass as I

hear her rifling through her bag. "Guess I'd better stay close tonight." Not to keep her from anything. Just to remind everyone exactly who she belongs to.

Sage steps out of the bathroom, and everything in me short-circuits. Strapless black dress. Painted-on perfection. Hugs every single curve like it was custom-made to ruin my night in the best possible way. Her skin's still golden from days in the sun, glowing like she's got her own damn lighting rig. Her hair's pulled up into a high ponytail, baring that perfect neck, those soft curves of her chest, and all I can think is—easy access. My jaw? On the damn floor. She always knocks me sideways. Doesn't matter if she's in heels or hoodies—she's it. But this? This is criminal.

"You are... fuck, baby. You are unbelievable," I say, still staring like a lovesick idiot. "You ready to go dance your life away?"

She just smirks, all glinting eyes and power in heels. "Let's go," she says—and grabs my hand, dragging me straight out the door.

The bar is packed. Loud. Hot. Music blasting through cheap speakers that weren't built for dancing, but we're making it work. Somehow, in fifteen minutes, we've managed to get even drunker, and honestly? It's been a blast. She's spinning around, laughing into her cocktail glass, and I can't stop grinning.

"Let's play a game," Sage slurs, setting down her drink with a thud.

"Baby, there are only two of us," I chuckle, raising an eyebrow. "So, what exactly did you have in mind?"

"Truth or dare," she says, like it's obvious.

I narrow my eyes. "Trouble... what have you got up your sleeve?"

She just grins, wicked and glowing. "You go first."

"Alright," I say, playing along. "Truth or dare?"

"Truth!" she almost shouts.

I smirk, leaning in. "Okay. Did you Google me when you found out who I was? And is that why you call me Playboy?"

Sage takes a long, slow sip of her drink, eyes dancing. "Yes, I did," she says, totally unapologetic. "And yes, that's why. 'Maverick Carter: Women in Every Country.' I nearly booked myself in for an STD test just reading the headlines."

She fake-gags for dramatic effect, and I laugh, shaking my head.

"You little shit. I'll get you back for that."

"Your turn," she sings, resting her chin on her hand and looking at me over the rim of her glass. "Truth or dare?"

"Dare," I say without thinking.

Her grin gets bigger. Dangerous. The kind of grin that usually means I'm about to do something illegal, ridiculous— or both.

"I dare you…" she says, dragging it out for effect, "to marry me. Tonight."

The music fades in my ears. Did she just—

"You serious?" I ask, my voice catching. "We're wasted, Sage."

"I'm sure," she says, suddenly clear-eyed, suddenly serious. "Everyone will be expecting the whole big white wedding thing. The media. The whole circus. But I want this. Just us. Something that's only ours. No one even has to know."

She's completely calm. Like she just dared me to order shots, not tie my life to hers forever. And fuck me, I've never loved her more. I pause. For dramatic effect, really. Because there's not a single part of me that's hesitating.

"Hell yes, baby," I say, grinning as I take her hand. "Let's go find someone to marry us."

She squeals, grabbing her purse like it's a bouquet and nearly trips on her heels as I pull her off the stool and into the night.

This is wild.

This is insane.

This is so us

Thankfully, Hawaii has the same rules as Vegas, and we can get married on the same day.

SAGE

One minute we're drunk off cocktails and post-sex giddiness, the next we're charging through the streets like a couple of love-drunk lunatics with one goal: marriage.

"Wait," I pant between giggles, as we nearly collide with a decorative palm. "Are we really doing this? Like—actually doing this?"

He stops, turns, cups my face like he's never been surer of anything in his life.

"We're doing this." And God help me, I melt. Right there. He could've dropped to one knee again, and I'd have sobbed in a puddle of tequila tears.

Thankfully, Hawaii is just as down for chaos as we are. Same-day marriages? No problem. No cooling-off period, no lectures about commitment or long-term planning—just a signature, a smile, and someone vaguely official with a floral shirt and a certificate.

We find a cute little beachside chapel that looks more like a surf shack dressed in fairy lights. The officiant is wearing thongs and a flower crown. I'm barefoot, heels discarded a while ago and blissed out. Maverick's shirt is halfway buttoned because of the make-out session halfway down the beach, and he keeps looking at me like I'm the only thing in the world he can see.

I think I black out somewhere between "do you take" and "I do," because the next thing I know, we're kissing, hard, and someone's clapping, and the officiant is saying something about how we're now husband and wife, and I'm just... I'm married. To him. To Maverick freaking Carter.

He lifts me straight off the ground, spinning me in a circle as my dress flies up and I scream-laugh into his neck, my fingers clutching the back of his hair like I might float away if I don't hold on tight enough.

"What now, Mrs Carter?" he murmurs into my ear. I grin, breathless and a little drunk on him.

"Now?" I whisper. "Now you take me back to that bungalow and show me exactly what a husband's capable of."

His eyes darken. "Oh, I plan to, trouble."

And just like that, I grab his hand again, and we run into the night like two idiots in love, hearts racing, legally bound, and so very ready to make some extremely inappropriate holiday… oh, guess it's our honeymoon now, memories.

The moment the door clicks shut behind us, Maverick pins me against it. His mouth is on mine before I can catch my breath, all heat and hunger and promise. His hands are everywhere—tugging, teasing, claiming. One hand fists in my hair; the other slides up my thigh, under the thin hem of my dress.

"We really just got married," I pant between kisses, trying to sound composed but failing epically as he drags his tongue along the shell of my ear.

"You saying you regret it, wife?" he murmurs, voice dark and cocky and hot enough to make me forget my name.

"Not even a little," I whisper, grabbing his face and kissing him hard. "Now stop talking and fuck me like you mean it."

His eyes flash. "Oh, I mean it."

In one smooth move, he lifts me—hands under my thighs—, and I wrap my legs around his waist like we've done this a thousand times. Like it's instinct. He carries me through the villa like I weigh nothing, our mouths never parting as we knock into walls and furniture, too frantic to care. He drops me onto the bed and peels his shirt off like a man on a mission. My dress is next—yanked over my head and tossed aside—leaving me in nothing but lace panties and a wedding band that's barely had time to warm against my skin. He pauses for a second—just one. His eyes rake down my body like it's the first time he's seeing me. Like he's starving and I'm the only thing on the menu.

"You look like a fucking dream," he growls, sliding his palms up my legs and hooking his fingers into the waistband of my panties. "And I plan on rewarding you for breaking all of your rules, Mrs Carter."

He drags the lace down my legs with maddening slowness, kissing his way up my thighs until I'm squirming beneath him, already soaked, already aching. And when his mouth finally finds me? Holy. Shit. My hips arch off the bed as he licks, sucks, and groans like I'm his favourite fucking dessert. I thread my fingers through his hair, tugging, grinding shamelessly into his face as he eats me, like his got nowhere else to be for the rest of the goddamn year. I come hard, hips shaking, back arching, his name a strangled moan on my lips. But he doesn't stop.

"Oh my God, Maverick—"

"I'm just getting started," he says, voice rough, kissing his way up my stomach. "I haven't even been inside you yet." And then he is—slamming into me with a force that has me gasping, clutching, clawing at his shoulders. He fills me so perfectly it's almost too much. Almost. We move like wildfire—fast and chaotic and raw. His mouth on my neck, my nails down his back, legs locked around his waist like I'm never letting go. He thrusts harder, deeper, hitting that spot that has me unravelling all over again.

"Say it," he grits out, hand sliding between us to circle my clit.

"I'm yours," I cry out, already close again. "Only yours."

He groans as it wrecks him—as the words burn into his skin.

"Forever Trouble."

And we fall apart together—loud, messy, tangled in sweat and love and way too much tequila.

When it's over, we're both breathless, limbs tangled, the sheets a disaster. Maverick brushes a damp curl off my forehead and smirks. "So… how does it feel being a married woman?"

I laugh, dizzy and wrecked and so damn full of him. "Honestly?" I grin. "If this is married life, I should've said yes sooner."

"Good," he says, leaning in for another kiss, "because I plan on fucking my wife in every room of this villa before sunrise."

I bite my lip and raise a brow. "Even the outdoor shower?"

"Oh, especially the outdoor shower." Husband of the year.

OUR HAWAIIAN HOLIDAY is officially over, and we're heading back to the icy grip of a European winter… as husband and wife.

Yeah. Wife. Shit.

Maverick called me "wife" at least once every hour for the last three days his claimed it's his new favourite word—and honestly? I kind of love it. Mostly because I haven't spiralled yet. Yet. Marriage doesn't feel as terrifying as my brain has made it out to be for the last six years. Though granted, it's only been three days. Still, it feels... easy. Like slipping into something that already fits.

On the flight home, we agreed to tell people slowly. No dramatic announcements. No Instagram posts with cheesy captions and ring close-ups. Just the people we love, face-to- face.

First up: Maverick's family at the annual Carter New Year's party next week—apparently, a mandatory event with fancy champagne, absurd dress codes, and enough Carter family stories to fill a novel. Then, mine. We'll tell my family when we fly to Australia for the Grand Prix in March. One milestone at a time.

But the wedding? The actual wedding? That's just for us. Our little sun-drenched, tequila-fuelled secret. Maverick unlocks the apartment door and drops our bags with a dramatic sigh of relief, then turns to look at me with that familiar mischief lighting up his face.

"What are you doing?" I ask, narrowing my eyes as he steps closer. He grins, bends, and suddenly scoops me up into his arms like I weigh noth-ing. I let out a surprised yelp as he holds me horizontal against his chest.

"Carrying my wife over the threshold," he says proudly.

I giggle against his chest, wrapping my arms around his neck. "You're ridiculous."

"You married me. Who's the real fool here?"

He carries me straight into the bedroom and deposits me on the bed like a royal offering.

"Welcome home, Mrs Carter," he murmurs with a smug smile.

I grab him by the shirt and pull him down into a kiss, slow and soft... until my stomach interrupts with a loud, tragic rumble.

Maverick pulls back, laughing. "Hungry, baby?"

"Starving."

"Alright, let's order something and veg out. Let our livers recover."

"Too late," I mutter, reaching for his phone. "She's already halfway to her grave."

We order Thai food—some of the best I've had in my life— and park ourselves on the lounge in pyjamas, wrapped in blankets and half a bottle of wine deep. I'm pretty sure I moaned louder at this coconut rice than I did during our beach quickie yesterday. No regrets.

I reach for the last peanut skewer when Maverick pulls me closer to his side, his body suddenly still, his voice low.

"This season's going to be my last," he mumbles. I freeze. Skewer mid-air.

"I'm sorry—what?"

"I'm going to retire," he repeats, his gaze steady but soft. "I'll tell the team at pre-season testing. This'll be my final year in Formula 1."

I stare at him, words fumbling somewhere behind my lips. Retire? I always thought he'd be racing forever. That the circuits would age with him.

"Why?" It slips out before I can filter it. "I mean—why now?"

"Because I'm ready." He shrugs. "I've done it. I've got the championship, the money, the noise. And now… I've got you. Everything else feels less important. I want the next chapter, Sage. I want to support you— whatever you do next. Maybe, eventually," he adds with a grin, "I'll be a stay-at-home dad."

That one hits me straight in the chest. I lean in and kiss him, slow and soft and full of unspoken things. He could keep racing for ten more years, or he could walk away tomorrow. I'd still be beside him. Always.

"Sounds good," I whisper against his lips. "You sexy little retiree."

He groans. "Please don't make me horny while I'm full of pad Thai."

"Too late," I grin. "You married a menace, remember?"

"Yeah," he says, eyes warm. "And I'd do it again in a heartbeat."

And just like that, I feel it again—that impossible, grounding certainty. This? This is everything.

SIXTY-SEVEN

MAVERICK

The Carter New Year's party is a tradition. A loud, glittery, over-catered, over-dressed, champagne-drenched tradition. Every January since I can remember, Mum's thrown this party like it's a royal event. Dad plays host with a glass of whiskey, Mum floats around in sequins and red lipstick, and the house smells like candles that cost more than most people's monthly rent. And tonight? It's a little different. Because tonight, I've got a wife on my arm and a secret burning a hole in my pocket.

Sage looks like sin in silk—navy blue, backless, with that little smirk on her lips like she knows exactly what kind of chaos she causes just by existing. She slips her hand into mine as we climb the stairs of my parents' house, her heels clicking against the marble.

"You ready for this?" I murmur, leaning down. She exhales through her nose.

"Not even a little."

"Same," I grin.

"Perfectly matched."

The second we step inside, it's the usual assault—music, laughter, someone already too drunk yelling my name. Eden waves from across the room, dragging Lachlan and the kids toward the snack table. Drew's here, too, God help us, already at the bar, looking like a sad puppy. We're home. Sort of. Sage squeezes my hand and glances up at me, nerves flickering behind her confidence. It's not the party that's making her anxious—it's what we're about to say. My parents don't know we're engaged. They don't know we ran off and got married in Hawaii after three days of champagne and beach sex and one very questionable officiant named Gary.

And while Sage might act tough, she wants this moment to go right. So, do I. I spot Mum first, holding court near the fireplace. She sees me and lights up like a chandelier, making a beeline toward us. "There's my boy," she says, kissing both my cheeks. Then she turns to Sage, eyes sparkling. "And my favourite girl." Sage melts a little. She always does around my mum.

"Alright," I say, rubbing the back of my neck, already feeling the weight of what's coming. "Mum, can you grab Dad, Eden, and Lachlan? Meet us in the office in five? We've got… something to tell you."

Mum tilts her head, that knowing look in her eyes like she's two steps ahead of me. Of course she is. She's my mum.

A few minutes later, Dad strolls into the office with Eden and Lachlan on his heels, all of them with drinks in hand. Dad leans on the doorframe like he's already dissecting whether this is good news or bad. Eden, on the other hand, is practically vibrating with curiosity, Lachlan quietly amused beside her.

I glance at Sage. She nods steadily, even though I can feel her pulse racing through the hand I'm holding.

"We're engaged," I say, my arm tightening around her waist. The words feel right solid. "Happened in Hawaii. It was… kind of perfect." There's a long beat of silence.

Then Mum squeals. Hands to her mouth, tears welling up, her voice catching as she rushes forward to grab Sage's face like she's holding something rare and precious.

"I knew it! I just knew! Oh my god, finally, a wedding!" Dad shakes his head, but he's smiling, that soft pride in his eyes I don't see often.

"About time you found the one," he mutters, pulling me into a hug and clapping me on the back so hard it almost knocks the air out of me.

Eden and Lachlan are grinning like they've been betting on this moment for months. Eden lets out a triumphant, "Yes, baby brother! I'm so proud of you!" before dragging both Sage and me into a hug.

Lachlan keeps it cool, offering Sage a genuine smile and me a firm handshake-turned-hug. "Congratulations, guys," he says, and it's the kind of quiet sincerity that sticks.

I look over at Sage, and she's glowing, cheeks flushed, eyes bright. This, right here, feels better than any podium I've ever stood on. Because this is the part that matters. This right here is the way she fits into my world like she's always belonged here. And yeah… I haven't told them we're already married. Not yet, and I probably won't. Because that is just for us, Sage Carter and me, and I just want to live in that moment with my Wife.

By the time the party dies down, I'm half-drunk on champagne and the way Sage looked tonight, like she's meant to be standing next to me, with my last name on her lips and my ring on her finger. We slip upstairs to my old bedroom—Sage giggling at the football posters and faded trophies like they're some sort of time capsule. I shut the door with my foot, drop the half- empty glass of wine on the dresser, and pull her into me like I've been waiting all night. The second the door clicks shut, I've got Sage pinned against it, her back hits the door softly as my mouth claims hers, slow but insistent. She tastes like vanilla cake and wine, and I can't get enough. my hands on her thighs, fingers digging into that silk dress like I might rip it just for the excuse to see her bare in front of me. Her laugh is low, wicked.

"Maverick…" she whispers, her voice teasing, knowing exactly what it does to me.

"Yeah, baby?" I murmur against her jaw, trailing kisses down her neck. "You know what you do to me?"

She smirks, hooking her leg around my waist. "Show me." God, she's going to be the death of me.

I scoop her up, tossing her onto the bed. I drag the zipper of her dress down slowly, watching it slide off her shoulders to reveal lace I'm already obsessed with.

"You wore this just to kill me, didn't you?" My voice is rough, my thumb tracing the curve of her breast through the thin fabric.

"Maybe," she says, tilting her head, eyes dark. "You're mine now. Gotta keep you on your toes."

"Baby," I groan, lowering myself to kiss along her stomach, "Maverick…" she teases, but it's not a protest—it's a challenge.

"Do you know what you do to me?" I growl against her neck, teeth scraping the soft skin there. Her breath catches. "I'm supposed to be celebrating with my family downstairs, but all I can think about is you. My wife." She moans at that word. God, I'll never tire of calling her that. My wife.

I hoist her higher, her legs wrapping around my waist. My lips crash into hers, and it's all tongue and teeth, like we're both drunk on each other. I kiss her like she's oxygen, like I'll drown if I stop. Her hands thread into my hair, tugging hard enough to make me groan into her mouth. The sound makes her grin, makes her grind down on me, the friction unbearable through my jeans.

"Bed. Now," she breathes, voice wrecked.

I don't need to be told twice. I carry her across the room, dumping her onto the bed with a bounce that makes her giggle, all messy hair and flushed cheeks. She's the most beautiful thing I've ever seen.

"Take it off," I tell her, nodding to the dress. My voice comes out lower, rougher than I mean it to.

She bites her lip, eyes sparkling with mischief. "Make me." I drag a hand slowly, deliberately up her thigh, until I reach the edge of her panties, teasing her just enough to make her

whimper. "Careful, Trouble," I murmur. "You know I'll win."

Her answer is a sly smirk, and then she lifts her hips, letting me peel the dress up and over her head. Her body arches as I trail kisses down her chest, slow and deliberate, tasting the salt of her skin.

"God, Mav…" she gasps, her fingers curling into my hair.

I look up at her, smirking.

"Say my name like that again."

My hands roam everywhere over the curve of her waist, gripping her hips, dragging her closer to me like I can't get enough. I can't. I'll never get enough of her. She tries to flip me, but I pin her wrists above her head, my breath hot against her ear.

"Not tonight, baby. Tonight, you're mine."

The sound she makes when I rub the head of my cock against her flaps is raw and desperate, nearly undoes me. I press her legs wider, feeling her tremble.

"Please," she whispers, and it's the sweetest, filthiest thing I've ever heard.

I'm teasing her, making her squirm, kissing her so hard it feels like we're burning up from the inside out. Every moan, every twist of her body under me, drives me higher, makes me want to give her everything. I push in, deep, fast and unforgiving. Sage screams. I'm grunting. And my thrusting gets harder. Brutal. Sage shatters first, loud, breathless, back arched. I follow, the world going white as I bury my face against her neck, both of us trembling, sweat slicked and tangled together.

We're sprawled out across the bed, chests heaving. I'm tracing lazy circles on her stomach with my fingertip when she laughs, that throaty, blissed-out laugh I swear I could live on.

"Why are you laughing?" I murmur, kissing her shoulder.

"Because", she says, grinning up at the ceiling, "if this is what being married to you is like… I'm in deep trouble." I chuckle, rolling on top of her again just enough to make her squeal.

"Oh, Trouble, you have no idea how much trouble you're in."

I grab a towel and clean Sage up as best I can, even though a part of me loves the idea of leaving her exactly how I made her—wrecked, marked, mine. By the time we're dressed and heading back downstairs, I'm still riding that post-orgasm high, my body thrumming like I just crossed a finish line. Everyone keeps stopping us on the way—questions, congratulations, chatter—but I barely register any of it. My focus is on Sage, on the way her cheeks are still flushed, and her lips are kiss-swollen, and the fact that my cum is probably still dripping down her thighs while she stands here, smiling like a goddess in my parents' lounge room. That thought alone is enough to have my cock twitching, heat pooling low in my stomach again. I grip her hand tighter, leaning in so only she can hear me.

"Knowing that you're standing there, with me dripping down your legs, it's doing things to me, Trouble," I murmur against her ear. "I could take you upstairs again right now and make a mess of you all over again."

Her sharp inhale, the way she glances at me through her lashes with that sinful little smirk, tells me she knows exactly what she's doing to me.

SIXTY-EIGHT

SAGE

Maverick's parents seriously know how to throw a party. Holy hell. Everyone is either drunk or on their way there, the music is vibrating through the walls, and the food. Unreal. I've eaten my body weight in canapés, and I have zero regrets. I was nervous walking in here—still am, if I'm honest. I haven't spent a lot of time with the Carter clan, and technically… I'm now their daughter-in-law. Yeah, that part still freaks me out a little. I thought telling them about the engagement would be a minefield— that they'd think it was too fast, or that I wasn't "enough" for their golden boy. But no. They were ecstatic. They love me. And that tiny fact alone made my chest go warm and stupid.

Now? Now I'm only panicking about what my family will think. Maybe I don't even have to tell them. Maybe I can let the media find out first—rip the band-aid off. Except my Nan would absolutely murder me for that. Right. I guess I'll tell them the old-fashioned way. For now, Maverick and I are playing the polite couple game, mingling with guests. He's done all the handshakes and introductions, but my brain is still running on a loop of holy- shit-we-just-had-sex-in-his-childhood-bedroom. Not exactly a recipe for remembering anyone's name. Especially when all I can think about is how I'm probably leaking down my thighs in the middle of his parents' lounge room. Perfect. Classy.

I'm in the middle of nodding politely to someone when I feel Maverick's hand tighten around mine. A warning? No. A reminder. That hand says, you're mine. Then he leans in close, lips brushing my ear, voice low enough to shatter me.

"You have no idea what you do to me, Trouble," he murmurs, heat dripping from every word. "I could take you upstairs again right now and make a mess of you all over again."

The dripping turns to a gush. I swallow hard, knees slightly weak, praying no one notices the blush creeping across my chest. When can we leave? Would it be horribly rude if we just snuck out right now? God, I should've packed a spare pair of underwear in my bag. Rookie mistake.

Maverick doesn't stop after that one filthy whisper. Oh no, the devil doubles down. We're talking to some older couple—family friends of his parents—and he looks every bit the charming, polished golden boy they think he is. Except his hand is on my ass. Not my waist. Not the small of my back. My ass. And every few seconds, his thumb dips lower, tracing lazy, infuriating circles that are driving me insane.

I try to discreetly swat him away, but he just smirks like I'm a petulant child.

"You're going to behave," I hiss under my breath as we walk toward the bar.

"Define behave," he whispers back, leaning down so his lips brush the shell of my ear. "Because all I can think about right now is what it'd feel like to bend you over this bar, rip that little dress off, and—"

"Stop it," I snap, but it comes out more breathless than authoritative.

The bartender hands me a glass of champagne, and I down half of it like water. I need something to cool me down because Maverick Carter is making me feral. Every time someone stops to congratulate Maverick on the season, his hand finds a new place to tease me—a slow drag along the back of my thigh, a subtle squeeze of my hip. At one point, while his parents are literally three feet away, he leans in and murmurs, "You're still dripping for me, aren't you? I can feel it on my hand."

I nearly choke on my drink.

"Would you stop?" I grit through a too-bright smile, nodding politely at whoever's talking to us.

"You don't want me to stop," he says smoothly, as if he knows. "I'm giving it five minutes before you drag me out of here, Trouble."

The worst part? He's right.

By the time the clock ticks past midnight, my patience and self-control are gone. He's leaning casually against the wall, talking to some friends of his dad's, when I slide up beside him and grab his hand.

"Say your goodbyes," I whisper, low and sharp. "We're leaving."

He turns, that wicked grin already spreading across his face. "Two minutes? I gave you five minutes, baby."

"Shut up and move," I shoot back, tugging him toward the door like a woman possessed.

We make it as far as the front gate before he spins me around and pins me against the wall, his mouth crashing onto mine. I moan into him, my fingers tangling in his shirt like I might rip it open right here.

"Car," I breathe. "Now."

We don't even make it halfway down the driveway before I'm climbing into Maverick's lap, straddling him in the backseat like I own him. The driver hasn't even had time to ask where we're going; he's probably too terrified to look in the rearview mirror because I'm already grabbing fistfuls of Maverick's shirt and kissing him like I'll die if I stop.

"Trouble," he growls, hands instantly finding my ass, squeezing like he's been waiting all night to get his hands on me again. "You're making a mess; you're going to wreck the interior of this car."

"Good," I pant, dragging his bottom lip between my teeth before pulling back just enough to look at him. "You've been teasing me for hours. I'm done waiting."

I reach for his belt, my fingers clumsy but determined, and he hisses when I brush against him. "Fuck, Sage."

"Yeah, that's the idea," I whisper, smirking as I unbuckle him and free his cock, already hard and heavy in my hand. The sight alone makes me ache.

"You're not—" He's cut off when I lift my dress and sink onto him in one slow, relentless slide. Taking every inch of him.

"Maverick," I moan, my head tipping back as my body stretches around him. He's thick, long, perfect and hitting every nerve in me. I can feel his grin against my neck as I move.

"Fuck, baby. You're so wet," he groans, his hands gripping my hips, guiding me faster. The car rocks with every motion, and I don't even care if the driver hears.

"Is this what you need? Hm? My cock filling you up?"

"Yes," I gasp, nails digging into his shoulders. "Harder."

He obeys, thrusting up into me so hard I see stars, his voice a low growl in my ear.

"I should make you pay for this all night. Make you scream my name until the driver knows exactly who you belong to."

"Then do it," I challenge, meeting his thrusts with reckless abandon.

The sounds of skin slapping, my breathy moans, and his curses fill the car. Every time he hits that spot inside me, I feel my control unravelling.

"Mav... I'm—"

"Come on, Trouble," he urges, one hand sliding between us to rub me exactly where I need it. "Soak me. Let the driver know just how good I make you feel."

It's too much. I break with a sharp cry, my entire body trembling as I come around him, clenching so tight he swears and pounds into me harder, chasing his own release.

"Fuck, Sage—" His voice is guttural as he spills into me, holding me down on him like he never wants to let me go.

I collapse against his chest, both of us panting, sweaty, a total mess. He laughs, breathless.

"We're definitely banned from this car service after this." I grin into his neck. "Worth it."

MAVERICK

By the time the car stops outside the gates, Sage's lipstick is smeared across my jaw, her dress is wrinkled to hell, and I'm pretty sure the driver is seconds away from quitting his job. I give him a generous tip, mostly guilt money and scoop Sage out of the car before she can even think about straightening herself up.

"Maverick!" she squeals, laughing as I hook an arm under her knees and carry her bridal-style through the gate "Put me down before someone sees my ass!"

"Too late," I smirk, not slowing down for a second. "If they haven't seen it yet, they've seriously missed out."

Her jaw drops. "You're impossible."

"Yeah," I grin, hitting the door handle with my elbow, "but I'm your impossible, Trouble."

She shakes her head, cheeks flushed, hair all messy from our backseat chaos. God, she looks edible like this. Barely put together, still dripping with me, still mine. The second we're inside, I don't even bother with the lights. I carry her straight into the bathroom, kick the door closed, and pin her against the cool tile.

"Shower. Now. You're not walking around with my cum running down those perfect legs for a second longer."

Her grin is pure sin. "You just want an excuse to get me naked again."

"Damn right." I flick on the water, stripping her dress over her head as the steam fills the room. My hands can't stop touching her—every curve, every inch of warm, soft skin. The water hasn't even fully heated before I have her pressed against the wall, her back arching, her breath hot against my lips.

"Maverick," she moans as I drop to my knees, my mouth trailing down her stomach.

"We just—"

"Exactly," I growl, kissing her inner thigh. "And I'm not done tasting you." I drag my tongue through her folds, slow and deliberate, and she lets out a sound that's half gasp, half desperate plea. My fingers grip her thighs, holding her wide open as I work her, sucking and teasing like I've got all the time in the world.

"God, you're going to kill me," she pants, her hands fisting in my hair.

I glance up at her, smirking at her. "Nah, baby. I'm going to ruin you first."

Her moans echo off the tile, mixing with the sound of water cascading over us. She tastes like salt and sweetness, like something I could drown in and never come up for air. I suck her clit into my mouth, slow at first, then harder, teasing with my tongue until she's trembling so hard I have to pin her hips against the wall.

"God, Maverick… don't stop. Don't—"

"Wouldn't dream of it, Trouble," I growl against her, the vibration making her gasp.

Her thighs start to quiver, and I know she's close. I slide two fingers inside her, curling them just right, and her head hits the wall with a soft thunk. She's soaking me, my face, my hand, everything—and it's the filthiest, hottest thing ever.

"Come on, baby," I coax, tongue relentlessly. "Give it to me. Let me feel you fall apart." She does. She shatters.

Her legs clamp around my shoulders, her cry echoing in the steam-filled shower, and I swear I could come just from watching her lose it like that.

When she finally stops shaking, I stand, my mouth wet with her, and kiss her deep, making sure she tastes herself on my tongue.

But I'm not done.

I spin her around, pressing her chest to the slick tiles, and drag my cock along her ass, teasing her entrance. She moans, arching back.

"Maverick…"

"You feel that?" I murmur in her ear, sliding just the tip inside. "That's all yours, Trouble. Every inch."

She gasps as I push into her, slow but deep, burying myself until I'm all the way inside. My hands grip her hips as I set a pace that's filthy—hard, relentless, water splashing everywhere.

"Oh my God," she cries out, bracing herself against the wall as I slam into her.

I reach around, fingers finding her clit again, and the combination makes her wild. She's panting, moaning, begging for more, and I give her everything—every ounce of me.

"Who do you belong to?" I growl, my breath hot against her neck.

"You," she gasps, barely able to speak. "Fuck, Maverick, you—"

"Say it again." I slam into her harder.

"You! All you!" she screams as she comes again, clenching so tight around me I almost lose it.

I groan, pulling out just long enough to spin her around and lift her, slamming back inside as I kiss her like I'm starving. Two more thrusts and I'm done, spilling into her with a guttural moan, holding her so tight she might bruise.

We collapse on the shower floor, water pouring over us, both of us breathless and grinning like idiots.

"Okay," Sage pants, brushing her wet hair out of her face. "You officially win. I can't feel my legs."

"Good," I smirk, kissing her nose. "Means I did my job right."

She laughs, giving my chest a lazy smack. "You're impossible, Carter."

"And you're my wife now, which means you're stuck with me."

She smirks, grabbing my jaw and pulling me into another kiss. "Yeah… I think I can live with that."

I KNOW I can't put it off forever. I've got to announce my retirement at some point. The only person I've told is Sage, and that's only because I couldn't keep something this big from her. Everyone else? My team, my manager, the sponsors… yeah, they're in for a surprise.

The "right" way would be to set up a formal call with Annabel, my manager, give her the whole heartfelt spiel, and let her prepare the team for what's coming. Instead, I stare at my phone, thumb hovering, and just… rip the band-aid off.

> Me: Hey Bel, sorry to do this over text, but I know you're enjoying your time off. Just wanted to let you know this is going to be my last season in Formula 1. Okay, see ya soon, bye.

I stare at it for three seconds, grimace, then type again.

> Me: Oh, also… Sage and I are engaged. On the DL. Okay, love ya, bye.

I hit send before I can overthink it. There. Done. Easy. Maybe too easy.

I lean back, exhale, and mutter, "She's going to kill me for that text."

It's easier this way. Less chance of her arguing with me, less chance of me backing out of saying the words that still feel surreal even in my head. I glance over at Sage, who's lounging on the lounge scrolling through something on her phone, her legs tucked under her, wearing one of my hoodies and looking like the best reason to walk away from all of it. Yeah. This feels right.

The second I toss my phone onto the lounge, it lights up like a goddamn Christmas tree.

Bel: Excuse me? Bel: EXCUSE ME?!

Bel: You're RETIRING and ENGAGED, and you text me like it's a grocery list?!

Bel: Maverick Carter, you absolute coward.

Bel: CALL. ME. NOW.

I run a hand over my face, groaning. "She's gonna kill me."

Sage, sprawled out on the couch in one of my t-shirts, raises a brow and sips her coffee like this is better than any reality TV show.

"Oh, I don't know, Mav. I think she might just murder you, resurrect you, and murder you again for that text."

"Babe, I can't call her right now. She'll start yelling, and I'm not mentally prepared for yelling before noon."

Sage laughs, tossing her phone aside. "You literally face death every race weekend, but a pissed-off manager? Too scary?"

"Bel is scarier than death," I mutter.

"Coward," Sage singsongs, leaning back against the lounge cushions with a smirk that could ruin me.

I narrow my eyes and climb over the back of the couch, pinning her under me in one smooth move. "Oh, yeah? You think I'm a coward?"

She grins up at me, all sass and challenge. "Mhm. Big, bad Maverick Carter can take Eau Rouge flat out but can't face one angry woman on the phone."

"Trouble," I growl, leaning close enough that my breath hits her lips, "I'll show you, coward."

"Not sure that's how that works," she teases, but her legs are already wrapping around my waist. My phone buzzes again, probably Bel screaming in all caps, but right now? I don't care.

SIXTY-NINE

SAGE

Group Chat - Chaos Coven

Josie: Bitch, are you alive?

Margot: Yeah, we haven't had eyes on you in DAYS. Are you buried under a pile of Maverick's abs?

Me: Alive. Barely. Send help. Or snacks. Or a new spine.

Josie...Oh my God. You're still on the sex-bender, aren't you?

Margot: She's absolutely on the sex-bender. Look at her, texting all vague and mysterious like she hasn't seen pants in 72 hours.

Me: First of all, rude. Second of all, accurate. Third... send electrolytes? My legs don't work.

Josie: SCREAMING. Girl, how is it possible that Maverick Carter looks like a sweet golden retriever on TV but is apparently rail-you-until-you-forget-your-own- name energy in bed?

Me: …Confirmed. Also, I may or may not be engaged. Margot: EXCUSE ME WHAT.

Josie: I'M SORRY. WHAT THE FUCK DID YOU JUST SAY?

Me: Ok but like… it's chill. I was drunk. In Hawaii. There were margaritas.

Margot: DRUNK. HAWAII. ENGAGED. I'm going to need more details, ma'am.

Josie: WHEN are you coming home? Because we are not letting you just drop "btw I got engaged" into a group chat like it's a meme.

Me: Uh… maybe never? I live here now. In this bed.

Send my mail here.

Margot: I swear if we have to drag your ass back from Monaco, we're bringing tequila and a bullhorn.

Josie: And a sign that says "FREE THE WIFE" because clearly, you're being held hostage by orgasms.

Me: That's not wrong. But don't save me.

Josie's face fills the screen the second I accept the FaceTime call, her hair piled in a messy bun, oversized sunglasses perched on top of her head even though she's clearly indoors. Margot leans in from the side, waving like a lunatic.

"THERE SHE IS!" Josie shrieks, practically deafening me. "Mrs. Carter."

"Stop," I groan, already rolling my eyes. "No one calls me that yet."

"Yeah, well, you're marrying the world's hottest playboy, so…" Margot smirks. "It's our duty as best friends to remind you that you officially ruined every woman's chance on the planet. Including ours."

"I did not!" I protest.

"You did," Josie says, dead serious, pointing at the screen like she's accusing me of a felony.

"Anyway, where are you? Still in Hawaii? Are you drunk?

Are you pregnant? Did he tie you to the bed again?"

"JOSIE!" I hiss, glancing over my shoulder in case

Maverick hears. "Oh, my god."

Margot's eyes widen with faux innocence. "Wait. Again? So, it's true then?!"

I cover my face with my hand. "You guys are the worst. I'm fine. I'm alive. No, not pregnant. And no, we're not still in Hawaii—"

Before I can finish, Maverick strolls past behind me. Shirtless.

I swear the girls' jaws drop simultaneously.

"HELLO, ARMS," Josie yells. "SAGE. YOU DID NOT WARN US THAT WE'D BE BLESSED BY THE HOLY SIX-PACK."

Maverick turns, grinning like he just heard the best compliment ever. "Hi, ladies," he says, leaning into the camera without a shred of shame. "Don't mind me. Just your favourite soon- to -be - husband."

"OUR favourite soon -to -be -husband?" Margot practically swoons. "Wow. So confident. We love a man who knows his place in the friend group hierarchy."

"Mav, put a shirt on!"

"What? No." He kisses the top of my head and smirks at the screen. "I mean, why would I when they're clearly enjoying the view?"

Josie fans herself dramatically. "Sage, blink twice if you need help surviving all that man."

"Pretty sure I'm thriving, thanks," I shoot back, trying to push him out of the frame, but he just wraps an arm around my shoulders and refuses to budge.

Margot cackles. "So, when are you coming home? You've been MIA for weeks. We're worried we'll forget what you look like—unless Maverick plans on posting more thirst traps, in which case, we're fine."

Maverick smirks. "I'll think about it."

"Maverick!" I swat his chest, and the girls laugh like they've just witnessed a rom-com in real life.

Josie leans closer to her camera. "Seriously though, when are you back?"

I groan. "Soon. I promise. And I'm bringing tequila, because I'll need it to survive this level of interrogation in person."

Josie cheers, Margot blows me a kiss, and then, because Maverick can't help himself, he says, "Don't worry, I'll make sure she's properly relaxed before she sees you."

The girls both scream, and I hang up before they can get another word in.

Maverick and I stayed in tonight. As much as I've loved getting swept up in London's nightlife these past few days, it's our last night together for the next two weeks, and I want him all to myself. Tomorrow, he's flying to Bahrain for pre-season testing—where he'll publicly announce his retirement. I'm proud of him, but I'd be lying if I said I wasn't anxious to see how the world reacts. His fans… they worship him. Some might be expecting this, but others? They're going to lose their minds.

While he's out there, doing his thing, I'm heading back to Melbourne to spend time with my girls and break the news to my family that I'm getting married. Married. Just thinking about how that conversation is going to go makes my stomach twist. I've got a 24-hour flight to figure out how to tell them without sounding like I've lost my mind.

Tonight, though, Maverick's made sure I'm not thinking about any of that. He's cooked dinner—a ridiculously good pesto chicken pasta—and we're working our way through an impressive amount of wine while Morgan Evans hums through the speakers. Then I notice it. That look in his eyes. The one that says he's planning something. Before I can ask, he pushes his chair back and stands, moving around the table.

"Dance with me," he says, voice low but commanding as he takes my hand and pulls me to my feet. Roll my eyes, but it's useless when his hand is already sliding around my waist, warm and sure.

"We don't even have a dance floor," I protest weakly, gesturing to the tiny gap between the table and the sofa.

Maverick just smirks, tugging me closer until my body is flush against his. "Don't need one. Got you."

God, this man.

The wine is warm in my veins, but he's hotter. His hand moves up my back, the other guiding mine to his chest. He's still in that black Henley that clings to him like sin, and I can feel every slow, steady beat of his heart. Morgan Evans is crooning about love and home in the background, and suddenly, our Monaco apartment feels like the only place in the world that matters.

"You're such a sap," I tease, but my voice is softer than I want it to be. He catches it, of course, he does.

"Only for you, Trouble," he murmurs, leaning down just enough that his breath brushes my cheek.

We sway together, his hips moving lazily against mine, his hand sliding lower on my back until he's practically cupping my ass. My pulse spikes. He feels it because his lips curve into that dangerous grin—the one that promises I'm not making it out of this dance with my clothes on.

"You're not even trying to be subtle," I whisper.

"Subtle?" he repeats, leaning closer so his lips graze the edge of my jaw. "Baby, it's our last night. I'm not trying to be anything but greedy."

I feel my resolve break in an instant. I'm done pretending I don't want him like I'm starving for him—because I am. His mouth finds mine, slow and deep, like the song demands, but there's heat simmering under it, that edge of hunger that only he can pull out of me.

His hands are on my hips now, guiding me to sway against him, and holy fuck, he's hard. Through the thin fabric of his jeans, I can feel just how worked up that slow dance is making him.

"You're not playing fair," I murmur between kisses, nipping his lower lip just to hear him groan.

He grins, dark and wicked. "Who said I was playing at all?" The slow dancing doesn't last. It never does with us.

One minute, I'm swaying in his arms, pretending we're some soft, romantic couple who actually finish a song before ripping each other's clothes off. Next, my back hits the dining table, and Maverick is kissing me like he's got two weeks of separation to make up for already.

WE PULL up to the airport, and I'm already feeling that stupid knot in my chest. Maverick offered me the jet — of course, he did — but the idea of taking something that massive just for me felt... excessive. And lonely. First class is fine. If I'm going to be stuck in a flying tin can for 24 hours, I'm damn well going to be comfortable. Plus, my husband can afford it.

Husband. God, that word still makes my stomach flip.

Maverick steps out first, all smooth confidence, and rounds the car like he's on some slow-motion runway. He opens my door, hand outstretched, and helps me out like I'm something delicate and precious. We don't say anything at first. We don't have to. The weight of it is there — the ache of two weeks apart, which suddenly feels like forever when you've spent every waking moment tangled up in each other.

"You're sure you don't want to come to Bahrain with me?" he asks finally, his voice low, almost pleading.

God, I want to.

"I do. I really, really do. But I need to go home. It's been too long."

"Ugh." He drags a hand through his hair, clearly unhappy but trying not to push. "You're right. I'm already counting down the hours, though."

I slip my wedding band off — the cheap little thing we bought the morning after our drunken Hawaiian wedding — and drop it into his open palm. "Keep this safe for me? Best if it stays with you, so my family doesn't see it. I can't trust myself not to get drunk and blurt it out."

He stares at the ring for a second before nodding. "Of course, baby. But I'm putting it right back on your finger the second I see you, because you're mine."

That earns him a grin — and a kiss. A deep, slow, memorise-the-shape-of-you kind of kiss. "I've gotta go, babe," I murmur against his lips.

"I love you," he says, kissing me again.

"I love you more." Another kiss, longer this time, because letting go feels impossible.

I pull back — but he tugs me right back in, kissing me like he's trying to brand me with his mouth. I'm breathless when I finally break free. "Mav. I really have to go, but just so you know, the next time I see you, I'm sitting on your face"

"Ugh, trouble. Fine," he grumbles, but there's a wicked glint in his eye

"Just know I'm watching your ass as you walk away." I laugh, shaking my head as I grab my bag, but I can feel his gaze on me every step toward the terminal. And hell, I kind of love it.

There was a time when I thought attention equalled love. The more eyes on me, the more I felt wanted. The more bodies I collected, the less space I had to feel hollow. I used men like shots of tequila—quick, hot, numbing, and always leaving me worse the next morning. A blurred memory instead of a warm one. I wore my loneliness like red lipstick— loud, smudged and begging someone to kiss it off. And they always did. None of them meant anything. That was the point: no strings, no risk, no getting left behind. I told myself I was free, untouchable, unbothered. But if I'm honest? I was just... tired. Of pretending I didn't care. Of laughing too loudly, so no one noticed how empty it all felt. Of leaving before anyone had the chance to leave me first. And then came Maverick Carter. Cocky, arrogant, larger-than-life. The man I should've run from, because his type was dangerous for me—the type who didn't need to try to make me fall.

Except... he didn't just want my body. He wanted the messy, broken parts too. The ones I'd hidden under tequila shots and one-night stands. He looked at me like I was worth more than just a distraction. Like maybe I wasn't just something to survive the night with, and that terrified the hell out of me. Because settling down? Choosing one person? That was a commitment to being seen. To be known. To let someone close enough to watch me fall apart and trust they wouldn't leave when I did. But slowly, he made space for me. In his bed. In his chaos. In his heart. And I started wanting to stay. Not because I was scared to be alone, but because with him... I wasn't lonely anymore. It hit me like a crash—sudden, violent, loud: I don't want fast exits anymore. I don't want nights I can't remember. I don't want temporary. I want him. The arguments. The laughter. The mornings tangled up in sheets and limbs. The messy, complicated, imper- fect forever. The forever kind of love, the kind of love I broke all of my rules for.

SAGE DAVIDSON'S Post-Rulebook Manifesto

(for one exception only—Maverick Fucking Carter)

1. Get out before sunrise.

→ Nope. I want to wake up wrapped around him like a koala.

2. No sleepovers?

→ We basically live in each other's skin. Deal with it.

3. Kiss anything but the mouth.

→ His mouth is my religion now.

4. No men in my house.

→ He has a toothbrush here. And a drawer. And half my closet.

5. No plans in advance.

→ Booked flights, booked dinners, booked solid—with him.

6. No cuddling.

→ I will fight someone if they try to remove me from his chest.

7. No bareback.

→ We're exclusive. And slightly unhinged. So yeah, skin to skin.

8. No names, no numbers.

→ I've got his emergency contact info. I am the emergency
contact.

9. No pillow talk.

→ We literally solved all our childhood trauma during
round four.

I didn't just break every single rule for him – I torched them. And I'd
do it again in heels, with tequila in my hand. And now I write new ones—
with him, in every city, one messy, chaotic, perfect day at a time.

SEVENTY

MAVERICK

"WHAT THE ACTUAL FUCK?" I roar, pacing my hotel suite like I'm hunting for down force in the carpet. "She can't be serious with this shit. There is no way that kid is mine."

Bel (Annabel—my manager, crisis wrangler, and professional fire-stomper) doesn't even flinch. She's perched on the arm of the sofa with her laptop open, the PR team clustered around like we're launching missiles instead of statements. My lawyer's on video, frozen mid-blink thanks to hotel Wi Fi.

"Maverick," Bel says in that calm tone she uses when I'm two seconds from lighting myself on fire. "You need to breathe. We're going to sort it."

Two weeks of pre-season testing in Bahrain without Sage have already been hell. We've been FaceTiming to sleep every night. The car feels good. The team feels sharp. I've been in fine form. Everything was perfect—until this morning, when a U.S. tabloid dropped a story claiming I fathered a baby last year on a stay in America on a sponsorship, two months before I met Sage

Nope. The only person I've ever gone bare with is Sage. Yeah, I had a Playboy phase. Yeah, I wasn't a saint. But I was careful. Always. And the kid in the photos? Cute but not mine. And Sage isn't answering her phone.

"Maverick." My lawyer's voice crackles through the laptop.

"The woman has agreed to a DNA test. She's adamant the child is yours."

A hit of relief—finally something verifiable. "Good. Do it."

"She wants compensation, though." Of course she does.

"How much?" I snap.

"Five hundred thousand."

I stop pacing. "Pay it. Whatever. Get it done." I'm past the point of caring about the number. "Clear this mess. The only thing I care about right now is talking to my—" I choke it off too late. "—my wife."

The room pivots. Bel's brows lift. PR blinks. No one says a word—but the air changes. We never told them. Not yet. I stab redial. Again. Again. Nothing. Straight to voicemail. My pulse is a jackhammer. She knows me better than this. She knows I'd never hide something like this. If she's not answering, she's either panicking… or— Don't go there. I shove out onto the balcony for air just as my phone rings in my hand.

Josie. Thank fuck.

"Josie, listen—before you tear me apart, please just tell me where Sage is. Are you with her? Is she safe?" I don't bother with hello. I put it on speaker. I don't care who hears.

Silence. Too long. My stomach drops "Please, Jo. I need to know she's okay."

"Maverick." Her voice is sharp, threaded with something I don't like. "I should rip you a new one for your slutty Playboy past and for not warning that beautiful girl about some surprise love child—"

"The kid isn't mine," I growl.

"I. Don't. Care." She fires each word like a bullet. "That is the least important thing right now."

White noise rushes in my ears.

"Josie—Sage. Is she there? Can I talk to her?"

A beat. Then softer.

"Mav… there was an accident." Everything in me stops. "They won't tell us anything because we're not 'family.' They keep saying husband only. And apparently? That's you." Her tone cracks into a shout. "You need to get here. Now."

The line goes dead. I turn, already moving.

"Bel—get me on the next flight. Private if we have it, commercial if we don't. Dubai to Melbourne. Move." She's on her feet before I finish, barking orders. I grab my passport, duffel bag and anything within reach. Retirement. DNA. Headlines. All of it can burn. I'm going to my wife.

Author's Note

Ahhhhh my debut novel. This is crazy. THANK YOU, THANK YOU, THANK YOU to those who read it. It means everything to me. I fell in love with reading again while I was breast feeding my youngest baby and then decided to try and write a romance. I wrote this book while I was toilet training a 3-year-old and 20-month-old - I don't recommend it. It's likely the reason I didn't know how to end the book, so I wrote 3 chapters of nothing but smut… hahaha

To all of those who supported me on this crazy journey, I appreciate you all more than I can every show. Especially my husband who supported the late nights and the forgotten chores so I could get this book done. Writing this book was therapeutic in a way, getting my real- life grief down on paper, made me feel free. To my Instagram community - you ladies know who are, the ones that read each chapter as I wrote, raw and unedited. Thank you. To the beta readers, thank you for taking the chance on reading this smut, your feedback was invaluable, and I appreciate you all.

To Rose, you absolute icon! You read this book, entirely - front to back before the beta process began and then demanded book two… I'm so grateful for you, especially when I know you prefer dark romances. Sarah, beautiful Sarah, we met at a time in our lives when we were trying to complete a different goal and you supported me then and now you've supported me through this. I'm forever grateful for you. You're the best person I know.

To my real-life Josie and Margot - you know who you are. I love you, both of you. Thank you for letting me use your likeness and our friendship in this book. You ladies are so much fun, and I can't wait to write your stories, one day soon. THANK YOU to every single person who supported me on this journey, I had so much fun, and I hope that I can continue to write the flight or fight series. Stacey xx

About the Author

Stacey O'Leary has combined her love of Formula One and books to write a laugh-out-loud romantic comedy packed with messy heroines, swoony heroes, and the kind of chaos that makes you feel right at home. She's the author of *The Hot Mess Express*, a rom-com that proves love is never as simple as it looks—especially when life goes completely off the rails.

When she's not untangling fictional disasters, Stacey can be found over-caffeinating, wrangling her kids like a pro (or at least like someone who deserves a medal), and pretending she's on top of her laundry pile. She firmly believes sarcasm counts as a love language and that happy endings are non-negotiable.

The next book in the series, *Off The Rails* promises more laughter, swoons, and just enough chaos to keep things interesting.

Find Stacey online @staceyolearyauthor where she overshares about writing, books, and life as a certified hot mess.